THE WILDE CARD

ASHLEY R. KING

CITY OWL
PRESS

THE WILDE CARD
Aces of Hearts, Book 2

CITY OWL PRESS
www.cityowlpress.com

Cover Design by MiblArt. All stock photos licensed appropriately.

Edited by Charissa Weaks.

For information on subsidiary rights, please contact the publisher at info@cityowlpress.com.

Print Edition ISBN: 978-1-64898-058-9

Digital Edition ISBN: 978-1-64898-057-2

Printed in the United States of America

Praise for Ashley R. King

"King debuts with a delightful, character-driven rom-com, *Painting the Lines* about two underdogs working toward redemption... an expert at balancing chemistry and tension to create a couple readers will root for. Fans of slow-burn romance will be swept away."
— *Publisher's Weekly*

"*Forever After* is SUCH a fun read-the perfect blend of paranormal and contemporary romance with a side of mystery. The unique premise of a vampire reality show hooked me instantly, and the descriptions and details from the confessional booth to the coffin beds kept me absorbed in the fantastical world that Ms. King created."
– *Kat Turner, author of Hex, Love, and Rock and Roll*

"*Painting the Lines* is a fast-paced, chemistry-filled, feel good sports romance! Who knew tennis could be so sexy? Game. Set. Match. You'll fall for Amalie and Julian in straight sets, guaranteed."
— *USA Today Bestselling Author Natasha Boyd*

"Lovely characters, smart dialogues and a great romance! Both characters were lovable, and I couldn't get enough of them!"
— *Read More Sleep Less*

"The characters in *The Wilde Card* are so sweet and their connection is so so genuine. I cried and I laughed, and I laughed until I cried. My heart is so connected to this story, and I'm honestly blown away."
— *Colby Bettley, author of Christmas at the Grotto*

"I really cannot wait to see what Ashley comes up with next! There was absolutely no hesitation in deciding to rate this book five stars, it's truly well deserved!"– *Naomi, This Ginger Loves Books Blog*

"I love Autumn. I love Oliver. I love the whole concept of this book. I loved it all so much I got a paperback so I can read it all over again. If you want to read a paranormal romance with memorable characters, a clever premise, and a compelling mystery, you *need* to read *Forever After!*"
– *Gabrielle Ash, author of The Family Cross and For the Murder*

For Mom and Dad. I miss you both every day but am so thankful for your love and encouragement. Thank you for teaching me to go after my dreams. I love you.

Chapter One

SIMONE

THE LAST THING SIMONE WARNER EXPECTED WHEN SHE WALKED INTO THE Victoria ballroom at the Fairmont Chateau in Lake Louise was to have the wildest night of her life.

She stepped into the crowded room—replete with a rented disco light spinning over a parquet dance floor, a free bar, and thumping music—and read the sign near the main doors. *Welcome to The Tennis Ball, hosted by Alex Wilde.*

Simone rolled her eyes, hard, and glared down at Amalie, the beloved little sister who'd convinced her that a vacation out of the country was exactly what she needed. Amalie hadn't been wrong. So far, the trip to Canada had been a relaxing break from Simone's busy life as Tallulah's worn-out mom and Warner Hotels' hanging-by-a-thread CEO. But attending this party? That had taken a lot more convincing on Amalie's part. Yet somehow, as always, Simone gave in.

"The Tennis Ball?" She couldn't help but laugh, shouting over the music. "Really?"

Who knew Alex Wilde had a thing for puns?

Simone glanced around the ballroom. Was he even here?

Though she'd watched Wilde's tennis game devolve over the last few years, she had to admit that she found his whole persona intriguing. He was passionate, gorgeous, and didn't seem to care what anyone thought of him. Still. Being that they were at one of Alberta's most elegant resorts, she'd expected more from the French-Canadian tennis star than a college-style kegger, though she wasn't sure why. Wilde was a legendary lothario and not even thirty yet. She supposed a kegger with fangirls bouncing around everywhere fit him perfectly.

"Don't start." Amalie strained her voice over the music. "It's the perfect place for you to mingle and get your single on." Donned in a stunning black cocktail dress, she made an elegant, sweeping gesture toward the gyrating masses of tennis players, agents, coaches, and one too many admirers.

If Simone glared at her sister any harder, laser beams were going to shoot out of her eye sockets. She and Damien divorced a year ago, after one hell of a public scandal. With his cheating exposed, and what felt like the whole world scrutinizing their lives, Simone withdrew. It wasn't easy going from the working mom and wife life to single mom. Being a party of one had yet to become her new skin.

And dating? That was totally out of the question. At this point, even walking across a dance floor in a ballroom packed with hot tennis players made her want to melt into the wall.

She shrugged. "I'm not really feeling it. I think I'll stick with you for now."

The truth? She'd been there less than five minutes and already wanted to leave.

Simone clutched her bag under her arm, turned on her stiletto heel, and took one step toward the exit.

"Oh no you don't!" Amalie dragged Simone away from the door. "No one knows who you are here, and they don't give a damn about what Damien did. Besides, you haven't had a fun night out in forever. Just promise me this *one* night. Pretty please?"

Simone was defenseless when it came to her little sister.

"Fine," she groaned. "But I'm not dancing."

Amalie beamed, thoroughly pleased with her methods of persuasion, and looked out over the party. She motioned to the far side of the ballroom where her husband, Julian Smoke, and his former coach and business partner, Paul Mercado, stood chatting up some guy who looked vaguely familiar.

Amalie wiggled her brows. "Now *he's* cute. Let's see if his personality matches his pretty face." She grabbed Simone's wrist and hauled her across the crowded space, just missing Paul as an older gentleman whisked him away.

Amalie was determined to help Simone get out of her funk, and that meant letting loose and being open to whatever the universe brought Simone's way—including men. But Simone hadn't come to Canada to husband-shop or even *fling*-shop. Romance equaled complications, as did sex, and she wasn't up for any of that in her life. After her divorce she'd tried to be as low-key as possible, for her and for her daughter.

"Bastien, this is my wife, Amalie, and my sister-in-law, Simone," Julian said as they arrived, slipping an arm around Amalie's waist. He seemed tense, a rarity for him. "Ladies, Bastien Demers is a top ten player from Canada with his sights on his first US Open title."

Simone realized why he looked familiar—he was Alex Wilde's stepbrother. She'd seen him on television once or twice.

Julian and Paul were well known for their dream run at the US Open six years ago. Julian, a Cinderella story, won the Open even though he was an underdog. Now he owned the Oliver Smoke Tennis Center, named after his dad, back in Atlanta. He had a big meeting with someone at the chateau, which happened to be the current location of the US Open series kickoff party *and* this after-party, but everything was all very hush-hush. Was Bastien the focus of all the secrecy? Amalie had been tight-lipped on the subject as well, which had Simone doubly intrigued given that Julian and Paul had been hounded with offers over the last few years to coach players, including some of the biggest names in the sport. Still, the two always turned them down flat, so Simone knew without a doubt that the meeting didn't have anything to do with coaching. Maybe some sort of sponsorship? Whatever it was, they were afraid to jinx it.

"Pleasure to meet you both." Bastien seemed chill when he shook Amalie's hand, but when he took Simone's, his demeanor shifted like the wind. His fingers danced over her bare ring finger, and his mouth ticked up into a smirk.

Sure, she supposed Bastien could be deemed attractive, if one liked overly clean-cut—and *young*—preppy types, but that sleazy leer that suddenly took over his face, complete with narrowed eyes and puckered lips, made Simone want to roll her eyes. Again.

Bastien's gaze dropped to her chest. Granted, her cleavage was on display to the world thanks to Amalie's insistence on this particularly low-cut dress. Simone loved the emerald green satin, but she did *not* like being ogled. No one had seen this much of her body since...

Damn. It had been a really long time.

Bastien bent to kiss Simone's hand, but before he could bring his mouth to her skin, she jerked away from his grasp. He could've been as gorgeous as Alex Wilde himself and that look still would've made her want to run the other way.

His eyes roved over her, from head to toe, and not in a welcome, seductive way. "Simone, you're quite stunning, aren't you?" He was still talking to her boobs.

Julian elbowed Bastien, giving him a dangerous scowl, his voice menacing even over the music. "Easy, man."

Simone shot her brother-in-law a grateful look but would fight this battle herself. "Bastien," she almost purred as she sidled closer, "tell me how you feel about women nearing forty with an eight-year-old child? You look like the paternal type."

When he paled, her lips tilted in a wicked smirk.

"Um, a kid?" he croaked. "And forty? That's amazing." He glanced away and lifted his beer, aiming the bottle at a cluster of men who hadn't acknowledged him in the least. "Tom!" he cried. "My man!"

And just like that, he disappeared.

Amalie nudged Simone in the side. "Do you pull that trick on all the hot guys who come on to you?"

"It usually works on the younger ones. Besides, he wasn't my type." Simone looked at Julian. "No more introductions tonight. Please." She eyed the exits again, wishing she was in her room reading a book.

Julian held up his hands. "Hey, I had no idea Bastien would be such a douche when he approached us to ask about coaching. Trust me. I learned what kind of guy he was quick. You don't have to worry about any more introductions from me."

Suddenly, Paul returned with an older man at his side. "Julian! Amalie! I want you to meet someone!"

Amalie pointed at Simone. "Don't leave. It's still early."

The moment Amalie turned her back, Simone took her chance. She grabbed a glass of champagne off a nearby tray and slinked toward the exit that led to the balcony. She wouldn't leave the party completely. She'd promised her little sister, and she never broke promises to Amalie. But fresh air and less noise and fewer people?

Yes, please. Now maybe she could hear herself think. What better spot to do a little introspection about one's life than somewhere beautiful like this?

She stepped onto the chateau's miraculously empty terrace. The light from the party spilled outside, and string bulbs hung above like twinkling stars. She released a sigh that made her entire body deflate before lifting the drink she'd pilfered to her lips, clutching her purse in her other hand. She was so glad to be alone. Coming to this party had obviously been a mistake.

Simone strolled toward the stone-cobbled edge overlooking Lake Louise, admiring the way the moon reflected on the water. Along the way, her heel caught on a nick in the concrete, causing her to stumble and spill some of the champagne on her dress.

"Shit!" She wiped frantically at the fabric. It was no use. It looked like she'd wet herself.

Just wonderful.

"Pardon, but I think if I go any longer without speaking, I'll scare you," a deep, rumbly, velvet voice spoke up—a voice with a strong French lilt.

She turned and squinted into the darkness but couldn't make anything out aside from a long silhouette leaning against the side of the chateau.

"Fleeing the masses?" the lovely voice asked.

Simone straightened, that voice sending a trail of soft chills along her arms. "Yeah, you could say that." She studied her hidden companion, hoping for a better look. "Not really my scene."

"Mine either."

Finally. Someone who agreed with her.

She grinned at the shadow. "It's really awful in there, right? I mean, The Tennis Ball? Come on." She rolled her eyes playfully before taking another sip from her glass. She might be wearing most of the alcohol, but she was determined to at least drink the last drop.

A husky laugh, decadent and warm, emanated from the darkness before a man stepped into the light. "I don't think the host is much of a party planner."

Simone choked on the champagne, spitting it out…

…and onto the very expensive-looking shoes of Alex Wilde, aka "The Wilde Card."

Of course, she'd just insulted him *and* spit on his shoes. It was on par for her night.

Simone looked up at him, and her mouth went dry. Holy hell, he was close. She could even smell the woodsy scent of his cologne. To be honest, she felt a little overwhelmed, because this man was *a lot* to behold.

He tilted his head, such a subtle movement, savage beauty sharpening the planes of his face. It should be illegal to look like that.

He scrubbed a hand over a neatly kept beard that was a shade darker than his shoulder-length, sandy blond hair. Simone might've had a slight beard fetish, which made this moment even more awkward. And those eyes. Were they brown? Or black as the night itself? She couldn't tell in the light, but she felt absorbed by his gaze, felt its heat caress her skin. But unlike with Bastien, the moment wasn't uncomfortable. It made her…*hot*. Was her heart beating faster?

She drew in a deep breath to steady herself. She was not interested in men right now. Nope. None of them.

Not even Alex Wilde.

Alex studied her a moment longer, and then a slow, heart-stopping grin unfurled across his face. He glanced down at his feet. "It's all right, *chérie*. I didn't like these shoes anyway." He shifted, and the golden glow from the string bulbs accented the rich, tawny color of his skin.

Simone cleared her throat, even though it still burned from coughing. Her cheeks threatened to do the same, and she fought the urge to squirm, to do anything aside from standing there blushing like a schoolgirl.

Unable to stifle said urge, she brought her clutch under her arm and toyed with its clasps. "Oh, ah, no. I actually like your shoes. Very...shiny."

Brilliant words there, Simone. She turned, placed her champagne flute on one of the tables, and let out a huge but very silent exhale, trying to get herself together.

Feeling slightly better, she twisted back around and shot him a nervous smile.

Alex held out a hand, his handsome face still illuminated with mischief. "I'm Alex Wilde, and I swear, I had nothing to do with that train wreck inside. The party planner is the one to blame for that."

Simone hesitated but finally took his hand, trying to ignore how good his skin felt when his long fingers folded around hers. "It's so nice to meet you. Sorry about what I said. About the party. It's really great, I'm just...a little too old for this kind of thing."

After a long beat, their hands fell apart. Alex slipped his fists in his pockets, the corners of his mouth quirking. "You? You can't be a day over twenty-five."

She shot him a smirk, knowing full well he was flattering her. "I'm many days over twenty-five, actually. Enough that *that*—" She pointed at the party. "—gives me a headache."

He laughed, the skin around his eyes crinkling. "Age is just a number. Hasn't anyone told you?"

Simone's voice was bone-dry when she volleyed back. "Says the twenty-nine-year-old tennis star."

Oh geez. She wanted to yank those words back inside her mouth.

His eyebrows shot up. "You know how old I am?"

Saving her from further embarrassment, Simone's phone buzzed. Normally, she wouldn't scan her messages in front of someone, but with Tallulah being at camp, she wanted to make sure it wasn't her.

"Sorry, I need to look at this." She pulled her phone from her clutch.

Alex nodded, and then her eyes were on the screen.

Not Lula. It was a text from her father. *Again.*

Simone clenched her jaw, as she shoved her cell back into her clutch. Her father hadn't noticed that Simone had been less enthused lately with her work as Warner Hotels' CEO. Everyone still looked at her with pity, asking how she was handling Damien's indiscretions rather than asking about the latest business deal she just closed. Besides, the CEO life wasn't exactly something she'd chosen for herself. She wanted out but hadn't figured out how to handle disappointing her father in such a massive way.

"Is everything okay?" Alex asked.

Simone lifted her head and shoulders, realizing she probably looked as adrift as she felt. "Yes, thank you. It's nothing that won't eventually work itself out."

"Want to talk about it? I've been told I'm an excellent listener." He propped against the wall and crossed his legs, his slim black pants hugging muscular thighs.

She scanned him from head to toe, her focus quickly traveling back to his face. She didn't doubt that he was an excellent listener—*among other things*. Things she really didn't need to be concerned with.

She fought the urge to smack her forehead. "In all honesty, I came outside because it was stifling in there, and I wanted to have a moment to process some things going on in my life, but now I find myself not wanting to think about any of it at all."

He folded his arms over his gray dress shirt, black tattoos dancing along his forearms. "I can absolutely distract you if needed. But before I can do that, I think I should know the name of who I'm distracting, *non*?" He angled his upper body toward her, his eyes glinting, a small smile playing on his full lips. Warmth radiated from him, the smoky scent of his vetiver and amber cologne mixed with musk tickling the air between them.

Being distracted by the enigma otherwise known as The Wilde Card was the absolute last thing Simone had expected out of this night.

"I'm Simone." It was funny. Just moments ago, all she wanted was to leave this party, and now she wasn't sure if anything could drag her away, which surprised her to no end.

Alex dipped his head. "*Enchanté*, Simone." Her name rolled off his tongue, drenched in an accent that made her toes curl.

She gripped her clutch, grounding herself. Her confidence had wavered the past year—something about a husband of ten years cheating on you will do that. Throw in the fact that she was only three years away from forty? Yeah, it had been rough. Turning forty wasn't precisely the issue, but for someone whose life had always been planned to the letter, she was approaching the milestone less sure of herself than she'd like.

"Now that we've properly met, may I ask why you're not inside? This is your party, after all, and you're out here lurking instead of mingling."

Yikes, did she really just say that?

Alex laughed, a sweet, honeyed sound that reminded her of the summer nights of her youth, filled with lightning bugs, stolen kisses, and broken curfews.

He kicked off the wall, looking completely roguish as he fully faced her. "*Lurking*? That makes me sound like some kind of stalker, *non*? Besides, aren't you the one who knew my age?" He shrugged playfully. "I'd rather like to think I was brooding."

She couldn't contain the surprised laughter that burst from her lips, happy to gloss over the part where her brain had saved tiny little factoids about this man.

"*Brooding*? Is that what you'd call it?"

Alex shifted his shoulders, still smiling. "Why not? Maybe I grew tired of talking about tennis and wanted some air." His voice was lighthearted, but she sensed a tightness stretching out his words.

Simone knew he'd been struggling with his game lately, but she didn't know why, exactly. He had a killer serve, but there was still something...*off*.

He spoke again, looking out toward the lake. "Or maybe I'm avoiding someone."

Of course. "Ah. An ex?"

"*Non*. I don't have exes. It would be my stepbrother, Bastien."

Simone put away that first part for later but scrunched her nose at the mention of the guy who'd ogled her. "Oh, yes. I met him earlier. He's..." Well, really what was there to say? He was horrid.

"Trust me, I know." Alex rubbed his bearded chin and leveled her with his stare. "Simone, may I ask you something? Why did you come to this party?"

That was a loaded question, yet suddenly, she found herself more comfortable with Alex Wilde than she had any right to be. Besides, it wasn't as if she'd ever see him again after this *tête-à-tête*.

"My sister made me." Her lips formed a small smile at that. "But also, I came out of curiosity I suppose."

His captivating eyes sparkled. "What do you mean?"

"It's hard to explain," she confessed, "but I feel like I've done everything I'm supposed to do, and yet I still ended up in the wrong place. Now I wish I would've taken a few chances along the way, maybe even made a few bad choices." She lifted a shoulder. "I thought this party could get me out of a rut."

A breeze blew in off the lake, ruffling her hair. Alex reached out and tucked a flyaway strand behind her ear, his fingers dancing over her skin so delicately, yet electricity sparked between them. It wasn't hard to see how Mr. Wilde attained his playboy status.

He was bewitching.

With a quick sweep beneath her chin, he drew back to catch her eye. "Perhaps we can help each other, if only for a night. What do you think about that?" His hand fell back to his side, but he was still close enough that she felt fully enveloped by him.

Her body swayed toward his, of its own volition, a coquettish answer on her tongue. "I think you have my attention."

But was that all that came out? No, of course not. She also *yawned*—the kind that made her eyes water and her mouth stretch wide enough to pop her jaw. She shielded Alex from most of that, but still. Without question, she felt a thousand years old.

"Sorry." The apology was part yawn. Could she possibly get any sexier? Yeesh.

He chuckled, not bothered in the least. "Listen, if bad choices are what you're looking for, I can spend the rest of the night sharing my terrible advice. Trust me, I have plenty, with experience too. And then you can make all kinds of poor choices."

She arched her brow and bit back a grin. "And what do you get out of it?"

"Maybe you'll rub off on me, and I'll never make another bad choice." He tilted his head. "Maybe it will help get my awful tennis under control."

Simone liked that idea...*a lot*. Suddenly, she wanted to get messy and make mistakes.

Alex continued before she could reply. "As a matter of fact, I can be your first bad choice." His words were pitched low, and he punctuated them with the sexiest wink she'd ever witnessed. Good God, this man had skill.

Emboldened, she brazenly held his stare when she spoke. "And what exactly do you suggest?"

"Tennis. Do you play?"

The confidence in Simone's shoulders faded a little. "Hold on, is that your move?"

Maybe she'd misread him. Maybe she was *that* old, old enough that she couldn't even recognize flirting anymore.

But then the corners of his mouth curved, and his voice was nothing more than a dark melody. "I have other moves, *chérie*, but you might not be ready for those yet."

She smirked, somehow bolstered by the innuendo. "You're not the only one with moves. I used to play, and I was really good."

Alex lifted his chin, a challenge glittering in his eyes. "Show me."

Show him?

"There's a court on the grounds," he continued. "Just waiting for us."

"Wait." She blinked, her breath coming out in a rush. "You want to play with me? Now? Tonight?" God, that sounded way more sexual than she intended. "I mean, tennis. Play *against* me. In tennis."

He laughed, clearly catching her faux pas, but then he moved closer, his voice a little quieter, a little more serious. "Yes," he said. "I want to play with you. Very much."

She could barely breathe. She was definitely skirting her comfort zone here, but something told her she'd regret it if she walked away now. She shouldn't be so intrigued by Alex Wilde. Her ex had a thing for the ladies too—any and all of them. But it seemed that, for tonight at least, tennis-playing men with sandy blond hair, fuck-me eyes, and a slightly wicked reputation were Simone's catnip, despite the fact that she'd been staunchly against any sort of romantic entanglements approximately ten minutes ago.

Funny how things change.

"Sure," she finally said. "I'll just go up to my room to change my clothes. Meet you down there in half an hour?"

Alex dipped his chin, and when she turned to walk away, a light touch grazed her hand. It was the barest whisper, a few fingertips, and then it was gone.

"See you soon, Simone."

She offered a small wave, her entire body vibrating. After all, she had a feeling Alex Wilde might be the best bad decision she'd ever make.

Chapter Two

ALEX

THE TENNIS COURT LIGHTS FLICKERED AND BUZZED AS ALEX FLIPPED THE switch, the night air holding its usual chill. The court was state-of-the-art pristine green. Fairmont Chateau spared no expense.

Alex had visited the chateau a few times as a child with his parents. It was home to one of the few happy memories from his childhood—of the time *before*. Before his mom died. Before his dad remarried and sent Alex to the Archambeau Tennis Academy in France. Before his dad died, leaving Alex's stepmother and stepbrother *everything* and Alex with nothing, in a foreign country at sixteen.

But that was in the past, even if it always crept up on him, like Bastien showing up, uninvited, to his party. He did things like that, constant needling, and Alex didn't feel like dealing with it. Thankfully, he'd found the perfect distraction.

Simone.

That name fit her perfectly—sexy, sophisticated, and so far out of his league. Earlier, when she'd stepped into the pool of light on the balcony, something in him sputtered to life. He'd been spellbound. It was ridiculous to feel so drawn to a woman from a mere glance, and yet the need to be near her had been—and still was—overwhelming.

Despite that, she wouldn't be more than a one-night stand. He didn't do relationships. *Ever*. That had been his rule for as long as he could remember. As a matter of fact, he'd never had a serious relationship, and it suited him just fine. Hookups were much more manageable without the emotional effort.

Movement at the corner of his eye drew his attention. Simone made her way down the pathway to the courts, that lithe figure taunting. Anticipation pulsed through his veins, his mouth curving into a genuine smile, the kind that he usually saved and parceled out.

"Hey!" She stepped onto the court and strolled to his bench.

He couldn't resist staring as she approached, admiring the way those black leggings clung to long, shapely legs along with a gray sports top that hugged every single curve. *Calice*. Needing to do something other than stare, Alex grabbed two rackets from his bag and closed the short distance between him and Simone.

"*Mon Dieu, tu es belle*," he said, because she *was* beautiful, and a woman like that should be told often.

Playing up the charm, he pressed a kiss to her cheek. He took his time, brushing his lips against her soft skin, trying not to think about how soft she was elsewhere. He let his breath skitter over her lips, his mouth close enough to kiss her, but he moved to the other cheek, kissing her there instead.

When he pulled back, Simone bit her lip and met his gaze, her eyes wide. The air between them hummed, alive and exhilarating.

What in the hell was that? *He* was supposed to be flirting with *her*, soaking in the way she trembled beneath his touch. But instead, he was just as affected.

He tightened his grip on the rackets, inhaling deeply to clear his addled head. It didn't help that her perfume now clung to his senses, a clean lavender and sugar scent reminding him of summer nights on the beaches in the south of France.

Simone blinked a few times before touching an earring. She did that a lot, especially when trying to pretend she wasn't flustered.

Merde. He shouldn't be noticing these kinds of things.

"Ah, my French is a little rusty." She squinted. "I'm not sure what you said...but I caught *belle*. Maybe you called me Belle from *Beauty and the Beast*? Which is fine because she's my favorite."

Alex laughed and pretended to twirl a fake mustache playfully. *"Oui, that was it. Would you like to see my library?"* His brows jumped suggestively.

She snickered. "Is *library* code for something else?"

So many filthy responses filtered through his mind, but instead he shrugged. "I actually said that you're beautiful."

Simone's response was a tiny gasp. "Oh. Well, you don't have to compliment me, sweet talker. I'm already here," she joked, but her shaky voice belied nerves.

"Yes, but what if I wish to take you somewhere else? After our game?"

More like his suite on the fourth floor.

His attention snagged on her lips, wondering what her mouth would feel like, taste like. What would other parts of her body taste like? More than anything, he wanted to know.

"Then you better be as good at tennis as you claim," she shot back, her eyes twinkling with mischief.

"And what if I'm not? Are you trying to make a bet with me? Because I'm quite competitive, in case you didn't already know that."

She cocked her hip. "Maybe I'm competitive too. And maybe you're underestimating me." She held out her hand. "So yes. Let's make a bet. If you win, you can take me anywhere you'd like after this. If I win, I decide what we do next."

Alex narrowed his gaze, shaking Simone's hand. He swiped his thumb over her pulse point, gently holding her a little closer than necessary.

When he let go, he managed to form a playful answer. "Making a bet on whether you can beat a professional tennis player at his own game. Living dangerously, I see."

She crossed her arms, pushing her breasts up higher. Was she aware that each of these tiny movements slayed him?

"Perhaps. See, the thing is, you know very little about me, but I promise you're about to learn how good I am on the court."

He ran a finger across his bottom lip. "I always like a challenge, *ma chérie.* Shall we begin?"

"Let's do it."

He extended both rackets like a peace offering. Simone danced her lovely fingers over the strings of the neon blue one before she plucked it from his grasp and tucked her hair behind her ears. His hand twitched at the movement, itching to reach out and do the same. He'd done it earlier while on the balcony, but it happened too quickly. Still, her hair had been smooth against his fingertips, and even now, it shined like black silk beneath the tennis court lights. How would it feel fisted in his hands?

Desperate to pull his attention away from all the things he wanted to do *to* and *with* this woman, he said, "Do you need something to tie your hair? I might have a band in my bag."

She absently patted her head. "Oh, that would be great actually. Thank you. I didn't pack any since I sort of decided on this trip last-minute."

As he grabbed a hairband and handed it over to Simone, he opened his mouth, wanting to ask where home was for her, but figured it was best left for another time.

Wait. There wouldn't *be* another time. Tonight was all they had.

He pushed wayward thoughts aside, ignoring the adorable way she put her hair in a ponytail and gestured to the court. "Any preference as to which side?"

She pointed at the baseline behind her, walking backward toward it, a smirk playing across her pouty mouth. "I'll take this one. And hey, Wilde? Don't be too rough. Take it easy on me." She winked.

The things those words did to Alex. Suddenly, all he could think about was rough sex. With her.

Alex bowed in concession and flashed a wicked grin. "I'll give it to you any way you want, Simone."

He swore she brightened at that. *Maudit.*

Shaking his head, he headed to the opposite end. When was the last time he'd tried this hard for sex?

Never.

Something inside him kept whispering that Simone was different though, but he disregarded that little voice and turned around, spreading his arms wide. "Don't worry. I'll take it easy on you…at first. You might need a minute to get used to me," he quipped. "I can be a lot to handle."

She scoffed. "You'd be surprised at how much I can handle." Her hips swayed from side to side as she waited for him to hit the ball.

Seeing her bent over like that, coupled with her words, was nearly too much. Alex imagined taking her from that angle.

Why had he even bothered with tennis? Why didn't he ask her straight to his room?

The answer was obvious, and he hated it. Alex wanted more time with her, even though that was something he never entertained. Her honesty and humor were refreshing—it wasn't often a gorgeous woman spit on his shoes and told him how awful his parties were. Clearly, he wasn't himself tonight.

Alex laid up one of the slowest serves he'd ever hit during the entirety of his career, feeling like he'd aged twenty years just watching the ball fly over the net. Simone wasted no time. Her racket connected with a satisfying thud as she smashed the ball back across the court and right past him.

He wasn't sure when he'd developed a liking to being dominated— things usually worked the other way around—but that move and the sound that left Simone's body sent a jolt of desire through him. He wanted to hear her make that sound for him.

Arching both brows, he turned from where the ball landed. "I see you have a few tricks up your sleeve."

Simone lifted a shoulder, completely nonchalant. "Like I said, I'm *really* good."

Alex scratched his beard, that strange stirring in his chest swelling with each moment, a sort of excitement he hadn't felt in so long. "I see that. You've got quite a bit of power in you."

"I just thought of my ex-husband, which seemed to do the trick."

Alex balanced the ball on his racket while focusing on her. "Ex-husband?"

What kind of dick would let someone like her go?

"Yeah. Long story. Now are you going to serve again or just stand there all day?" Simone's throaty laugh broke through the night as she strutted back to the baseline, twirling her racket.

After playing a set, Alex won, to no one's surprise. But sweat trickled down his brow, Simone surprising him with her skill. She was good— really good—yet there was no way she could beat him, and she'd known that when she made the bet. She'd known that he would get the chance to name their fate, at least for the rest of the night.

And she'd wanted it.

He didn't celebrate too much—sportsmanship and such—but he couldn't stop the smile that spread across his face when he met Simone on her side of the net. She looked tired yet exhilarated. He knew that feeling— the look suited her.

"Okay." She dragged the back of her hand across her forehead. "Consider me impressed."

"Did you think you wouldn't be?"

She appeared to mull over her next words. Finally, she looked up at him and said, "I guess I hoped I wouldn't be. Yet I am."

He gravitated a little closer and whispered, "You haven't seen anything yet. There are so many more things I could show you. *Impress* you with."

A blush bloomed across her already flushed skin. "I bet you say that to all the ladies."

"I think you'd be surprised to learn that I don't."

Curiosity and eagerness—and maybe even a little fear—flickered in the ice-blue depths of Simone's eyes. "Fair enough."

He gestured toward the bench where his bag lay. "Let me grab my things, and then we can continue with our night."

She followed alongside him, even if reluctantly at first. He knew exactly what was going through her mind: *Should I? Or shouldn't I?* But by the time they reached the bench, everything about her held a different air, as though she'd found courage and made her decision in the short walk across the court.

"So where are we off to next?" she asked.

"I have a few ideas, but seeing as how I pride myself on being a gentleman in the streets, maybe I should let you have this one. Your call. Whatever you want."

She froze, the expression on her face one of momentary confusion, like he'd asked her a million-dollar question and she didn't know the answer.

He stilled too, studying her. He had a sneaking suspicion that the idea of "whatever you want" wasn't a thing Simone was used to. What a shame.

She shrugged and let her hair down. "I concede. You won fair and square. I'd kind of like to see what you have in mind."

Music from the party drifted across the court, something slow and jazzy, instantly sparking an idea. If Simone was going to let him pick, he knew exactly what to do. Lady Destiny herself smiled upon them.

He set their rackets on the bench and moved closer, the toes of his shoes meeting hers as he reached for one of her midnight tresses, running it through his fingers. Like silk, just as he thought.

When he spoke, his voice was gentle. "I want to dance with you."

Simone jerked her head back. "*That's* what you're spending your win on?"

He couldn't think of anything better. Of course, he hoped that the sexual tension simmering between them would come to a boil once he got her in his arms.

Alex's chest brushed against her arm as he leaned in. "*Oui*, more than anything. So will you dance with me, *chérie*?"

Alex offered his hand, and she eyed it as if it were a snake. That wasn't the reaction he was going for.

He dropped his arm. "Did I do something wrong?"

Simone took a deep breath and let it out in a *whoosh*. "No, sorry. I just feel a little like Molly Ringwald right now, and you're my Jake Ryan. At least for the moment." She faltered. "But I bet you've never watched *Sixteen Candles*, have you? Oh my God, you weren't even alive in the '80s." She covered her face with her hands.

Stifling a laugh, he gently pulled her hands from her face. "And what does that have to do with anything?"

"I'm almost forty, and you're *you*." She gestured around him.

She was cute when flustered.

He couldn't contain a chuckle any longer. "So? I told you earlier tonight that age is just a number. And it's just a dance, *non*?" He paused and extended his hand again.

She laced her shaking fingers with his. "You know," she said, "I'm not the best dancer."

"I don't care." He grinned. "I'm just using dancing as an excuse to finally touch you."

Simone relaxed against him.

He brought his lips to her ear. "Do you mind if I hold you close?"

When he looked down at her, her eyelids were heavy, her breathing faster than before. She liked this game, and that sent a thrill through him.

"Not at all."

He pulled her against his body, reveling in her softness. His nose grazed her cheek, and her breath hitched. He smiled against her skin, pressing a featherlight kiss at her temples, so weightless that he was sure Simone would question if it even happened at all. He tightened his grip on her waist as they swayed to the music.

Simone surprised him by drawing even closer, her chest brushing against his with each ragged inhale, her chin resting on his shoulder. The song played on, weaving its spell as they danced beneath the fluorescent lights.

Alex twirled Simone around before drawing her near once more. She caught herself against his chest, curving her hands around the muscles there.

She laughed, the sound painting starlight between them. "This is kind of magical."

Alex couldn't help but laugh as well, especially at seeing the wonderment on her face. "It is, isn't it? It's probably because you dance as well as you play tennis." His voice was rough as he moved his hand to her cheek, caressing her skin. When she rested against him, he nearly fell apart right there.

"As do you. This is lovely," she whispered.

Before he could reply, the song ended, but they remained wrapped up in each other. Alex drew back enough to see Simone's face. His heart pounded, and when he slid his fingertips down her arm and over her wrist to take her hand, he could feel her pulse racing as well.

"I...I don't want to let go," he said.

She looked up at him, meeting his stare head-on. "Then don't."

Now was his chance. Time to make his move or stay on this court all night, and while he'd take anything he could get when it came to Simone, tennis court dancing was the least of his desires right now.

"I want to take you back to my room."

A breath shuddered out of her, and her hesitation from earlier returned, a war of indecision playing across her face.

"You're in control of what happens tonight," he assured her. "Just like with the game. Whatever you choose, whatever you want, I will follow. I just don't want to say goodbye yet." He dipped down, speaking his next words so that she could feel them against her lips. "Will you come?"

Her eyes sparkled, her gaze darting to his mouth and back again, a fire stoked within. "Yes."

ALEX'S PALMS WERE SWEATING BY THE TIME THEY REACHED HIS SUITE. HE brushed his shoulder against Simone's back as he scanned his key card, her nearness irresistible as he opened the door.

He moved inside so he could hold the door open for her. "Please, come in."

Simone slipped past him and he followed, dropping the tennis bag at the door. He hadn't zipped his bag all the way, and his worn copy of *The Outsiders* came tumbling out. Simone zeroed in on it right away.

"You carry books in your tennis bag?" She bent to pick it up, running her delicate fingers over the cover.

Alex hesitated for a split second. "Well, let's just say my tennis game isn't at its best, so I have a lot of free time. And I love to read—prose, poetry, you name it. I cut my teeth on E. E. Cummings."

"Somehow, *that* doesn't surprise me."

He gave her a half-smile before turning on some jazz. He went to the bar while Simone flipped through the book, the inside just as worn as the outside, and not from neglect but from years of using it as a lifeline.

"Would you like a drink?" he asked, pouring himself three fingers of scotch.

Looking up from his note-covered margins, she said, "Wine, please. Any kind."

Simone seemed more comfortable than he'd expected, but he still noticed a little uncertainty and rigidness in the set of her shoulders. More than anything, he wanted her to feel at home.

He grabbed their drinks and went to her. Closing the book, she accepted the wine and eyed him appreciatively, then handed the book over. She moved further inside the room, her gaze roaming over every corner of the suite. There was a large sitting room with a stone fireplace, the fire already burning thanks to a quick text to the staff. The windows were floor to ceiling, showcasing the beauty of Lake Louise.

His bedroom could be seen from where Simone stood, the edge of a bed barely peeking out. He took a long swig of scotch and let the burn soak through him, thinking about the kind of heat he hoped the night before him held.

Simone crossed to the windows, looking out over the lake as she sipped her wine. "I just can't get over it. You're nothing like I thought." She faced him, her words pulling him toward her. "I don't understand why the press makes you out to be someone else," she continued. "They've given you all these personas, and I can't quite figure out which is real or if they're *all* real and you're piecing them together." Simone canted her head, bringing her hand to her chin as if in thought.

Alex wasn't shocked. People never knew what to expect from him, and he liked that, liked the wild card factor of it all, to keep people guessing. That kept them from getting comfortable. That kept his vulnerabilities safe.

That kept his heart safe.

Those thoughts spurred him forward. Setting his drink aside, he went to Simone, her body backlit by the starry night behind her, the moon glittering off the lake. No more talk. No more hesitation. No more waiting. It was time.

He took her glass and placed it on the table beside them, then trailed a fingertip from her temple to her cheekbone, down the length of her jaw. Her pupils darkened with desire.

Desire. Lust. Sex. *This* was what he was built for.

"I suppose I should ask..." He bent his head so that his lips were at her ear. "Which Alex Wilde persona do you want right now? Do you want bad boy Alex, smart Alex, funny Alex, philanthropist Alex? The list goes on, Simone. What do *you* want?"

He backed away just enough to notice her skin flushing, her chest rising and falling quickly. Catching a glimpse of her hardened nipples through the thin material of her shirt, he fought back a groan, but couldn't resist cupping her face before he gently pushed her against the glass.

She touched his hand. "Just be yourself, Alex."

He tensed. When had anyone asked for that version of him?

Unable to help it, his hand trembled against Simone's smooth skin. "For you? For tonight? Of course."

He'd wanted to pace himself with Simone, but with the halo of stars around her, her body so pliant, he knew he couldn't hold back any longer.

He pressed his thumb just beneath her bottom lip. "Simone, can I kiss you?"

She slid her hands up his arms and tightened her grip around his biceps. "I've been waiting for you to ask me that all night." She rose on her toes, and he realized that she looked him in the eyes. Simone was tall and willowy, and that whiskey and honey voice made the back of his neck heat.

Alex gripped her waist and brought her fully against him. He was already hard, and he rocked against her core, eliciting the sexiest whimper.

Her body melted into his as his mouth hovered at the curve of her neck, the scruff of his beard moving over her pulse. Then he kissed her there, reveling in the sigh that tumbled from her lips, becoming drunk off the way her head fell back against the window, offering more of herself to him. One hand held her neck, his thumb pressing lightly into her collarbone as he trailed kisses along her exposed skin.

A moan escaped her just as she tightened her hands on Alex's shoulders, her nails digging into the fabric of his shirt.

His lips moved to hers, and finally he kissed her. Softly at first, coaxing, exploring, but then Simone ground against him, causing him to groan into her sexy little mouth.

He pulled away. "You already know that I'm not subtle, so pardon if it offends, but I want to fuck you."

Simone's eyes went hazy, and of all things, she giggled.

That was certainly new for him, but it made him smile.

He held her chin, tilting her head back, voice playful. "You're laughing? I tell you I want to fuck you, and you're laughing?"

She giggled again. "I'm sorry, no. It's just that...when I left my room earlier this evening, this is the *last* thing I imagined happening tonight. I mean, I'm glad it is. This is all just new to me. Not sex. I've had sex, obviously. Just not with someone I've just met."

He slid his hands through her hair. "It's only one night if that makes you feel better."

Relief flickered across her face. She didn't want more than one night, and that bothered him. But why should he care?

She held his face in her hands, her expression ardent as she spoke. "I think I can handle that."

"*Dieu merci*," was his simple yet revealing response. He was desperate at this point.

She drew him down for another kiss. Her mouth was seven kinds of temptation. *Criss*, the things he wanted to do to that mouth.

Simone slipped her hands over his shoulders and dragged her nails down his back, making him ache with desire. Her touch felt more intimate than his usual hookups. He wanted her to touch him *everywhere*.

"I need you, Alex." She fisted his shirt, her words tracing pathways across his lips.

"You're sure, Simone? You really want this?" He tightened his hold around her body. "You might never even see me again."

When she looked at him, her wide eyes sucked him in even further. It took a moment, but finally she answered. "Yes. I want you. Not forever. Just for now."

He knew she meant to ease him, but her words stung. He'd always been so easy for people to throw away. Still, she was in his arms and arching against him with want.

He would not disappoint.

Chapter Three

SIMONE

Simone liked soft and sweet, had thrived on it most of her life, but that was not what her heart yearned for tonight. Tonight she wanted rough and wild. Unknown. She wanted unbridled passion.

Alex, being the experienced lover she was sure he was, picked up on her cue, deepening the kiss. He pressed her against the window, his tongue delving deeper into her mouth. She tasted the scotch on him, knew he could taste her wine.

Alcohol and wanting.

This. This was what Simone craved. Nothing else existed outside this kiss, outside of *them*.

One hand cradled the back of her head as Alex groaned, the sound sending a hot shiver dancing across her body. His other hand slipped up, up, up her shirt, his thumb brushing along the band of her sports bra, leaving fire in its wake. She cursed the barrier, wanting to feel him inch his way higher, to feel the roughness of his hand on her breast.

His mouth returned to her neck, his teeth gently biting into flesh. She sighed and squirmed against his length. She couldn't wait any longer.

Was she really about to have sex with Alex Wilde? Her body screamed HELL YES, YOU ARE, but her mind, that evil bitch, desperately tried to convince her otherwise. That's how she operated though—overthinking every move, constantly weighing it out.

Simone had always imagined that when and if she ever did have a fling, it would have to be under the right circumstances, like the moon had to be full, and Jupiter had to be visible to the naked eye, and a wolf had to howl in the east, and the lights had to be off, and she had to have time to groom everything down below.

This was so spontaneous. Not prepared for. Not expected.

It was perfect.

Amalie's words came floating back to her. Her sister had taken her hands once and ever so seriously said, "Guys who play tennis are really good at sex. Like, they hit the right spot every time like it's their job. Find yourself a tennis man. Trust me on this."

It had seemed so silly at the time. Yet now, the idea of sex with a tennis player—a younger one at that—sounded heavenly, her body burning even hotter with the prospect. Damien never knew how to hit the right spot and had no interest in figuring it out.

She bet Alex could hit the right spot every single time, especially if his mere touch threatened to unravel her.

His hand drifted away from her breast, settling on the bare skin of her waist, his touch a brand, a reminder. "Tell me how far you want to go tonight," he rasped.

Rubbing her thighs together, almost desperate for relief, a very inconvenient realization smacked her in the face. She wasn't twenty-five anymore, and she wasn't some sort of sex goddess.

She was just Simone.

An unhappy CEO.

A disgruntled divorcée.

A mom.

Would Alex be disappointed?

Somehow she found her voice. "I don't know. I mean, I *know*, I'm just not sure you're going to get what you might be expecting."

Alex shook his head, expression earnest as he tucked her hair behind her ear. "I'm not expecting anything other than what you want to give. I hold no expectations of you, Simone."

When was the last time someone had *no* expectations of her? When they simply allowed her to be herself? It was freeing yet terrifying at the same time.

She brought a hand over his, flattening it against her cheek. "Are you sure? Because listen. Only one man has seen me naked since I had my daughter, and I don't normally do this, and I don't know *how* to do this, and what if I do it wrong? Do I stink from playing tennis? Do I need a shower first?" She fought the urge to lift her arm and sniff her armpit right there. Surely that would've been the death knell to this night.

"You have a daughter?" He smiled, the edges of it sweet.

She sucked in a breath, realizing what she'd said. Alex Wilde now not only knew that she was almost forty but that she had a kid as well, and yet he didn't seem the least bit fazed by the news.

Alex kissed her hairline, his mouth skating over her jaw, lingering, hovering over her lips. "You are beautiful. I don't care about anything but being inside you. I will make you forget about everything but me tonight. But..." A wicked grin made her entire world tilt. "If it will make you feel better, I'll shower with you so we can both get clean before getting dirty again."

Oh. Well then.

Feeling brave, she smirked. "Where's the shower?"

WARM WATER SLUICED OVER HER SKIN, SENDING A CHILL THROUGH HER BODY. She faced Alex as he followed, stepping into the shower too. The space suddenly felt tiny, and it was all she could do to keep her eyes on his face.

The corner of Alex's lips kicked up. "You can look, *ma chérie*. I *want* you to look. To see what you do to me."

His words undid her, and her gaze dropped, lower and lower, until she let out a small gasp. Alex chuckled, the sound smooth and deep and impossibly sexy.

The man had every right to be confident—Simone wasn't sure how he was going to fit.

Hell, it would definitely knock away the cobwebs, that was for sure. And at least he'd handled the condom situation without her having to ask.

Simone brought her hands to his shoulders, taking her time as she ran her fingers across his tattoos, making a silent promise to explore each one later. She tugged him closer, his cock hard and slick against her stomach. Alex let out a deep groan, and she shivered. His desire for her was evident, and the thrill it sent through her veins made her heart pound like a drum against her ribs.

She lifted her eyes. His dark stare spoke of every dirty thing he wanted to do to her, and Simone lost herself in his gaze as he shifted, sliding between her legs.

Simone moaned, maneuvering so that she could feel him where she needed pressure the most—ready for him to be inside of her already. She reveled in the hot feel of his skin on hers, as if a fire blazed within his very bones.

A feral sound rumbled from Alex's throat as he palmed her breasts with large, calloused hands, moving his hips so achingly slow against hers. His fingers circled her pearled nipples before he bent low and sucked one into his mouth, gently biting with his teeth, only to soothe the small hurt with his lips.

Simone let her head fall back against the shower wall as something completely incoherent fell from her lips. This man was worshipping her, his roaming hands reverent as he tasted her skin, his lips branding her with every kiss.

She slid her hands down, searching out his length, eager for him to fill her—she needed him *now*.

Alex nipped at her skin as he pumped into her grip. "I get the feeling that you want it rough, *oui*? You want me to take control? Hmm?" He moved to her other breast.

"Yes," she gasped, her senses overloaded. "Yes to all of it."

Alex brought his mouth from her breasts to her ear. "*Je veux te sentir.*"

She had no idea what he said, but she hoped he uttered filthy French things all night.

He pulled back, raw hunger darkening his eyes, his fingers digging into her backside. "Do you know what those words mean, Simone?" His cock prodded at her, teasing, but one hand moved between them, rubbing the bundle of nerves at the apex of her thighs. She shuddered at the contact, a spike of pleasure shooting into her core.

"No. What does it mean?" Her breath hitched as a finger drifted over her entrance. God, he enjoyed teasing her.

He looked down, watching as he slipped his finger inside her, water beading across his sooty lashes. "It means I want to feel you. I want to feel you clench on my hand, my tongue, my dick."

Her heart slammed against her rib cage, her nails digging sharply into his muscled shoulder. Oh, this was going to be a wild ride indeed.

"Are you ready to come for me, *chérie*?" He pressed a wet kiss to her mouth.

A whimper left her lips, and she nodded, though she wasn't sure if she was ready at all. But then he lifted her, forcing her to wrap her legs around his waist, his cock nudging against her entrance. Simone gasped as he thrust up, filling her so completely that she wasn't sure where he ended and she began.

"You feel amazing, Simone." Alex bowed his head, stilling inside of her, seeming to savor the sensation of her wrapped around his length. He pulled back slowly, only to drive back into her heat, his chest rumbling with a moan of pleasure.

She let out a choked cry, her nails likely piercing skin. It was all too much—too much *feeling*. "Please," she whispered, not sure what she was begging for. "Please, Alex."

At the sound of his name, his eyes locked on hers. "Say that again."

She opened her mouth, but nothing came out except a strangled gasp as he pushed deeper, hitting a spot no man had ever reached. He did it again and again, like he knew exactly what he was doing to her—because he did. He had to. The way he moved his hips concentrated the press of him *right there,* making an orgasm coil tight inside her.

Her eyes shuttered closed as pleasure rose and rose, the edge of bliss so close.

"Say my name, *chérie*," Alex demanded, suddenly stilling.

Simone opened her eyes, clutching him tightly, willing to do anything for him to move again.

"Alex, please." Her voice came out barely above a whisper, a desperate plea.

One corner of his mouth lifted into a devilish smirk, and then those lips were on hers, devouring her air and stealing her thoughts.

There was only Alex. Only this moment.

"Beautiful," he murmured against her mouth, and then he started thrusting into her again, just like before, until the ache she felt so deep within no longer belonged only to her. Alex's desire rushed through him like a pulse as his movements quickened.

Simone was helpless to do anything but hold on as he pushed them closer and closer to release. He moved like a man possessed, his groans of ecstasy the most delectable sounds she'd ever heard. She swallowed them with her mouth and arched her hips, meeting his every thrust.

When Alex whispered her name like a prayer, she fell.

And God, did she fall *hard*.

Simone might've screamed, might've called out his name, but one moment she was teetering on the edge of sheer bliss, and the next the air left her lungs, the tension in her core unleashing. When she clenched around him, Alex moaned, thrusting harder, his grip on her body tightening.

She could feel him swelling inside of her, his length impossibly hard.

"I'm coming," he said against her ear, and when he found his release, it was her name he called out. Her name that he repeated over and over again.

Simone had never loved her name more than at that moment.

Chapter Four

ALEX

Sunlight warmed Alex's back as he stretched in the sheets, his naked skin gliding against the smooth fabric. Slowly, he turned over, reaching out a hand, wondering if Simone was up for one more round before he had to go to his business meeting. He patted the space beside him, only to be met with emptiness.

Alex hissed, sitting up straight, blinking several times before fully waking up. He swept a searching glance across the room, looking for remnants of the night before. He and Simone had sex not just once, *non.* They had sex enough times that he lost count after four, and that didn't include the shower. *Merde,* he was getting hard again just thinking about the wet slide of her body.

Running a hand through his hair, he slid out of bed, knowing that she was gone and not just to grab breakfast and return. Gone were her clothes that he'd stripped off so slowly, savoring each time she'd sucked in a gasp whenever his hands touched a new sliver of skin. Gone were the wine glasses they'd drank from around midnight, and parts of the room that had been disheveled were neatly put back together. All traces of her were erased as if she were nothing more than a ghost.

Alex looked at the clock and sighed, knowing he had to get downstairs, but his mind was all over the place. How could he concentrate and process a business proposal when all he could think about was the raven-haired beauty who disappeared without so much as a goodbye or a note?

This was new.

He shoved his legs into his boxers and went through the motions of getting ready, even if he was on autopilot. A woman had never taken off without morning sex, or at least an *au revoir*. And *non*, he'd never done it either, which wasn't to say someone was bad for doing it. It was simply going to take some getting used to.

Usually, when a woman left his bed, they didn't part on awkward terms. Things were easy, carefree like he'd designed them to be, to hide the cracks in the façade.

But Simone. She'd seen right through those cracks. The one time he felt that flicker in his chest, that he wanted something more profound, a connection—and she vanished.

He knew the sex wasn't awful. He more than made good on his promise to worship every inch of Simone's stunning body, and she appeared to enjoy it. Was it his bedside manner then?

Criss. Along with his tennis game, had he lost his pickup game? His best friend, Rhys, would no doubt laugh and call him a wanker.

As he stuffed his wallet into his back pocket, he sighed. He couldn't help but wonder what Simone would be like first thing in the morning. Did she like breakfast? If he were to surprise her in bed with coffee, what would she drink? What was a typical day for her? How old was her daughter? Where was she from?

"*Chu dans marde*," he muttered, finally headed down to breakfast.

Indeed, he was screwed. No one had ever gotten under Alex's skin, and he didn't even know Simone's last name. It wasn't like she left behind a glass slipper that he could use for clues. But maybe it was better that things turned out this way. He didn't need to change what had worked for him all these years, and at least he had one hell of a memory.

Alex's mind switched to tennis as he made his way to the hotel restaurant. He seemed to balance on a dangerous *what if* in every aspect of his life right then. The thought of the business meeting had him strung tight. He'd run his hands through his hair so many times that he probably looked like he had when he woke up that morning—like a man who'd tumbled a long-legged beauty all night.

He hadn't had a coach since the first two years he went pro at eighteen. There was a reason he stayed away from any entourage or team. He didn't want to be told how to play. He craved the freedom to explore his game. Rhys was a pro tennis player as well and had done the same. Except Rhys explored and then found himself and decided to hire a coach to help give him an edge.

But when Alex was eighteen, his stepbrother, Bastien, won Junior Wimbledon and the Junior US Open, like Federer. Despite being an asshole, Bastien Demers was a star before he'd even hit the tour, which Alex hated to admit caused a snag in his mental game. His stepmother, Claudette, spent most of Alex's inheritance on making sure that Bastien beat him at a sport he originally had zero interest in—the switch had been because of Alex's father.

But Alex was determined to show his demons that he could rise above them, that he was better than they thought. Even if it meant finally hiring a coach.

Tension crept along his neck as he entered the chateau's dining room. The Fairmont Bar & Restaurant was huge, with a row of simple golden chandeliers hanging from the ceiling. Dark green chairs were nestled around square tables, each one set with a burning candle as the centerpiece.

The room hummed with activity, waitstaff buzzing around with silver platters and trays, large families and groups headed to their seats, and diners who'd just finished up and were trying to squeeze past it all.

Alex scanned the sea of faces, looking for Julian Smoke and Paul Mercado. Everyone in the tennis world knew their names and spoke about them with a sort of reverence like they would Agassi or Sampras or Williams. Smoke and Mercado were legends for the miracle run they pulled off six years ago at the US Open. Julian, a washed-up tennis player, made it to the final and won the whole thing, inspiring pretty much everyone in the world. He'd certainly inspired Alex.

The two men sat at a table tucked away near the windows, with Lake Louise and the picturesque Rocky Mountains behind them. Paul was older, probably in his sixties, with a salt-and-pepper beard and mustache. He wore a white RF hat, his hearty guffaw traveling across the room. Julian ran a hand through his dark brown hair, mussing it as he laughed at whatever his former coach said.

Alex stood taller and made his way to their table. It was time for him to don his business persona and play the part of the infamous Alex Wilde who wanted to win at any cost. That personality might've been the one he hated the most, because it reminded him of Bastien and Claudette.

"*Bonjour*. Welcome to Canada," Alex said, approaching his possibly soon-to-be coaches.

Coaches. Such a foreign concept.

Alex took a chance reaching out to them, knowing that they'd turned down coaching opportunities for several players who were better than him. Yet deep down he knew that he'd be able to connect with them, that they might understand his style better than any other coaches out there. And that's what it would take to get him where he wanted to be. It would take a coach.

Or two.

Julian and Paul straightened as he reached them. Paul was the first to speak. "Bon-jore." At least that's what his accent made it sound like.

Julian tried not to snicker and instead gestured to an empty chair. "Thanks. Why don't you have a seat, Alex? It's nice to finally meet you." He extended a hand, which Alex shook, Paul following suit.

"Nice to meet you, son." The older man took a bite of his pancakes, nonchalant about the entire ordeal.

Alex felt the complete opposite as he dropped into a chair between the two men. He folded his shaky hands in his lap, his leg already bouncing beneath the table. "*Non*, I'm the one who has the honor. You won me over with the US Open, and I like how you run things at your center." Moreover, he liked Julian's "I don't give a shit what you think" attitude and wished he could be more like that when it came to tennis.

"Well, I gotta say, we don't travel to a whole other country to meet with potential trainees often." Paul put his fork down, wiping his hands on his serviette, shooting Julian a look before swinging his gaze back around to Alex. "Actually, we've never done it, have we, J? We've never even entertained the idea of coaching a pro, which says a lot about what we think of you, kid. You've got what it takes." He sized Alex up, his bushy eyebrows doing some sort of dance.

Merde. It'd been quite some time since anyone thought Alex's tennis game was up to par. He directed his attention to the older man. "You coached Julian, so at least you have one pro under your belt."

Paul deadpanned, "Again, I've never coached a pro."

Julian side-eyed Paul. "Really? I *did* win the US Open."

"You played *one* tournament, and you think you're a pro."

Julian lifted his middle finger and placed it to the side of his temple, shooting Paul the bird before continuing, "*Anyway*, we were pretty sure we wouldn't get into coaching pros until much later, since the clients at the center keep us busy. But your email struck me, and I knew we had to at least meet you." Julian slung his arm across the back of the chair nearest him, his green eyes alight with curiosity.

"*Alors.*" Alex bit the inside of his cheek.

"*Alors*? Who's that?" Paul asked as he looked around the restaurant. Julian looked confused as well, and Alex suppressed a laugh.

"I'm sorry, I meant the word *so*," he emphasized. "I'm still surprised you responded," Alex said with a chuckle. His knee continued bouncing, albeit a little slower now.

Julian's cheeks dimpled. "I reached out because you've got something special about you, and you've got enough reason to be pissed off when you get on the court."

Alex's forehead wrinkled, and even Paul looked intrigued by Julian's direction of conversation. "What do you mean by that?"

Julian shrugged. "I've read up on your history. I know who your stepbrother is. I met him last night, and he was a douche—"

"You can say that again," Paul mumbled around a mouthful of food.

Julian went on, undeterred. "So knowing the kind of guy Bastien is and then seeing him rising up the ranks, I figure you gotta be really pissed off and ready to change up your game. Maybe even your life. That's where real winning is done. I mean, your stepbrother is a little prick who's gonna spin out pretty soon if he doesn't get his act together. Future legend or not."

Paul jumped in. "You may be The Wilde Card, kid, but Bastien's not charming in the way he comes off when he loses his cool."

"Are you calling me charming, Paul?" Alex asked jokingly, pretending to be smug about it.

The older man angled forward on his elbows. "So far, you're a lot more charming than this guy." He hooked a thumb toward Julian. "I mean, you act like I coached a real pro." Julian huffed and rolled his eyes. Paul ignored his sidekick and continued. "Bastien is a bastard. Let's just call him that from now on. Bastien the Bastard." He tapped the table with his knuckles. "With that said, we'd be happy to train you, kid."

Alex took a deep breath, crossing his arms over his body before he spoke. "*Alors—*"

Paul clapped. "So." He poked Julian with his elbow. "*Alors* means so. See, I'm learning. I'll be speaking French to seduce Charlotte in no time."

Julian groaned. "Dear God, make it stop." He plugged his fingers in his ears and looked to Alex, expression pleading. When he spoke again, his voice was a little louder. "Please don't teach this man *any* French. For my sake *and* my mother's."

Alex laughed. These two were fun to watch, and he knew there would never be a dull moment with them around. But more importantly, he could tell they cared for each other despite the ribbing. It made him miss Rhys, who was all the way in England.

"*Oui.* No French lessons," he agreed.

Julian pulled his fingers from his ears, carefully watching Paul, who raised his hands in surrender. "Alex, please continue."

Alex twisted the edge of the serviette in front of him before pushing it away, his voice cool and calm. "All right. If we move forward with this, what's the earliest that you could be in Calgary?"

Julian and Paul froze and began having some sort of telepathic conversation. From the looks of it, it wasn't a positive one.

Alex scooted his chair a little closer. "What is it? Did I misread the situation?" Had he misheard them when they said they'd coach him?

"*Well,*" Julian stretched the word into three syllables, his Georgia accent strong. It almost reminded Alex of Simone.

Simone. He fisted his hands and pushed images of her away. *Calice,* not now.

"That's the thing we needed to discuss," Julian continued. "First, you should know that I won't be around much for a while because my wife, Amalie, is a writer, and she's got a book tour, and it's kind of our thing that

I go with her. When I come back, I'll pick up and help train, but until then it would just be Paul working with you."

"And Paul can't come to Canada to train," Paul added, picking up his glass of orange juice. "It's too damn cold. And besides, I can't leave my girl down in Atlanta."

Julian pushed his plate forward, a sour expression twisting his face at the mention of his mom. "We wouldn't be able to come to Canada. With me gone, Paul needs to be in Atlanta to run the center—"

"*And* to be with Charlotte."

Julian waved his hand. "Yeah, yeah, to be with my mom. God help me, my breakfast is about to come up." He did look a little green. "And, as Paul mentioned, it says a lot that you're the first guy we've been interested in working with, so I hope you'd consider coming down to Atlanta to train."

Alex winced. "Georgia is way too hot for me," he said, altering Paul's words about Canada. "But I'm willing to do whatever it takes to get my game back, so Atlanta it is."

Julian and Paul erupted into cheers, several patrons turning to gawk at them. Each man took turns shaking Alex's hand.

"Welcome to Team Smoke," Julian said, a proud smile stretching across his face.

Paul puffed his barrel chest and adjusted his hat. "I think you mean Team Mercado."

Alex snickered. "Whatever it is, I'm thrilled to be a part of it."

And he meant it.

Chapter Five

SIMONE

Simone sat at the desk in her suite in a daze. She looked out at Lake Louise, at the stunning mountains, and sighed.

Wow. That one word was the best way to describe everything that happened between her and Alex Wilde last night. She wasn't one to blush. That was always her sister. But oh, the things she did and said the night before.

The heat from her face moved throughout her body, pooling low in her stomach. She still couldn't believe she'd done something so outside her norm. If anything, that cemented that she was ready to shake up her life.

She opened her laptop, watching it start up, and thought about the fact that she'd left Alex without waking him. Dropping her eyes to her computer, she caught a wince in the black reflection of the screen before it booted to the home page. Simone had no idea what else to do, or how awkward it would've been if he woke before she disappeared, because she did some wild stuff…*and liked it*, but still. That didn't mean she was ready to chat about it over breakfast with a man she barely knew.

Her thighs squeezed together as she recalled the way Alex mapped every inch of her body with his hands and mouth, his deep, husky accent muttering *magnifique* along every dip and curve.

She squirmed in the chair, achy from having *so much sex* for the first time in forever. Maybe playing tennis before that hadn't been the best idea, because her muscles screamed in protest from that too. Hell, it was worth it.

She bit her lip to suppress a smile. A very *sated* smile.

But now she needed to avoid Alex around the hotel. There was no way she could run into him again or she'd die from embarrassment. He'd seen and heard things from her no one else ever had, and while it wasn't romantically intimate, it was still intimate enough to be weird about since she didn't know Alex very well. Add in the fact, "Hey, you fucked me in nearly every way I've ever fantasized about in one night, and then I left you hanging the next morning. Thanks," and that tripled the awkwardness.

Pulling up the video chat icon, she cringed. Either way, it was for the best that she left like she did—less messy. Alex Wilde was not a man she'd start a relationship with. He lived in Canada, for crying out loud, and he was so much younger than her. So as long as she laid low at the chateau, she was good. Alex had been exactly what she needed, for one night—a wild card to help her solidify her life plans. Plans that had taken a back seat for far too long.

Besides, he led a life that was high profile, in the spotlight. If she'd learned anything with her divorce, it was that there was safety in retreating, in keeping things out of the public eye. She'd agreed to pay Damien off with alimony for that very reason. She couldn't stomach parading Lula through a messy divorce hearing when the cheating scandal was bad enough.

She clicked to join the video chat. Her father, Andrew Warner, was already waiting, which made her stomach knot. She itched to tug at her ears, which she did when she was nervous, but instead sat on her hands. Her pulse thumped in her throat, but she had to do this, even if it disappointed her father. She wanted to be more like Amalie, who went after her dreams regardless of the outcome. That girl clawed her way through the fire, and now she was happy doing what she loved.

Simone craved that more than anything—even if she had no idea what she wanted to do after stepping down as CEO of Warner Hotels.

"Hey, Sim." Her father waved at the screen. His glasses slid down the bridge of his nose, and with the frames balanced there, it made him look older for the first time in his life. Andrew Warner had come a long way in the emotional department, but his vanity was still unmatched. She waved back, sparing her video screen a glance to double, triple check that she looked put together, although her insides were a jumbled mess.

"Hey, Dad. How are things going down there?" She pasted on a smile, because that's what she did best. For thirty-seven years, she simply grinned and bore everyone else's expectations, even if it tore her apart inside. What used to matter was the approval of others above all else, and it still did to some extent. But Damien's cheating had been the wake-up call she needed.

Of course, no one wants to catch their husband with someone else, but she realized for the first time that this was not *her* life. That she was not herself. And more than anything, she wanted to find that woman. To be someone who could show her daughter that life was about finding true happiness. And that search needed to begin today.

Her father shuffled papers around on his desk and picked up a pen, clicking it a billion times as Simone's eye twitched. Usually, she'd tell him to give it a rest, but she had to play it cool.

"Things are good," he said. "Business is good. You've done a phenomenal job with the new hotels, honey. I don't think I'd feel comfortable leaving the company in anyone else's hands but yours. You were born for this." Pride lit up his face.

Ouch.

Simone stifled a sigh and held her back straighter when all she wanted to do was slump. She shoved the guilt way down when it threatened to claw its way up her throat. *Born for this*. More like *trained* for this.

"Well, that's kind of you to say..." The words trailed off as her mind flicked to a memory that was distant, yet always seemed fresh, like a wound that refused to heal.

She remembered when her mother left when Simone was in high school. Katharine Warner ran off with her yoga instructor after saying that Andrew suffocated her by not allowing her to be who she really was. That day still stung for a lot of reasons, but her mother's parting words had really been the icing on the crappy cake. The last thing Katharine said before she left was that she was disappointed in Simone, disappointed in the fact that she tried so desperately to please her father, to do as he asked, to agree to being the hotel heiress instead of forging her own path.

After that day, almost as if to spit in Katharine's face, Simone worked twice as hard to be the best CEO she could ever be, even if it killed her inside, because she would rather be stable like her father, than like her mother—the woman who walked out on her kids without ever seeing them again.

Sure, Katharine sent cards and gifts sporadically, but the fact was that Amalie and Simone hadn't seen their mother since she left. They didn't know what she was up to, nor did they care. All Simone wanted was to be the antithesis of her, and that meant putting Tallulah first and her job a very close second. In doing so, it created a habit that when her father asked her to jump, she never hesitated to ask how high.

Andrew wagged his finger at the camera as he watched his own video. Bless his poor narcissistic heart. "No, it's something I mean, Simone. You really were born for this job. You of all people know that I don't say things simply to say them."

Simone's smile was still bright but brittle, wavering and cracking beneath the surface. "I know that, Dad."

Andrew moved closer to the camera, his glasses falling even further off their perch before he slid them up unceremoniously. "What is it? Did something happen up there?" His nose was the only thing she saw for a minute before he backed away. Apparently, her brave face wasn't fooling him at all.

"Oh, well, you could say that." She laughed awkwardly, trying not to think of Alex.

"You're flushed, and you never get flushed. Are you sick? Is that why you called this meeting? Do I need to come and get you?" He moved to stand, but Simone shook her head.

"No, no, I'm not sick." Whew, could this get any more uncomfortable? She swallowed and fanned herself. "It's just hot in the room is all. I called this meeting because..." Andrew sat on the edge of his chair, his laser focus on her. "Because I want to step down as CEO of Warner Hotels."

Best to pull off the bandage fast, right?

She squinted at the screen, grinding her teeth together as she waited for the inevitable fallout. Oh, she was going to be sick.

Her stomach rumbled, and she couldn't be sure if it was from hunger, hanger (which could sometimes be a real problem for her), or the fact that she'd just secured the upheaval of her life, of all she'd ever known.

For a second, she thought the video feed had frozen, but it hadn't. No, of course not. She could see the slight twitch of her father's salt-and-pepper eyebrow. His mouth was set in a grim line, but he hadn't moved an inch. He sat there looking at the screen, unflinching.

She refused to give in first. She knew her father's tactics well enough and had even found herself mimicking them (unfortunately) on several occasions. So she stared right back at him, showing him she meant business.

After another minute of the Warner showdown, her father blinked and smoothed his tie over his shirt. He did some kind of cough-laugh before skewering her with a glare. "I'm sorry, I thought you said you wanted to step down as the CEO of Warner Hotels?"

Simone fought the urge to press her fingers into her eyes. "What you thought is correct. And there is no want. I *am*. Effective immediately." She made sure to bite off each word, her voice stern.

Andrew pinched the bridge of his nose. "Simone, you know that's not possible. I don't know what that mountain air has done to you—"

"It's not the mountain air, Dad. It's *me*. It's always been me. I'm grateful for this life and always will be, and I'd love to continue my charity work through the hotel, since those causes are dear to me, but I'm not happy."

"Is it because of Damien?"

She squinted. "A little? Our divorce woke me up, and now I need to forge my own path, find what makes *me* happy. Being a CEO does not. I dread going to work every single day. Honestly..." she paused. "I had more fun when I was in charge of marketing and public relations. But being at the top? It's lonely and doesn't challenge me anymore, doesn't feel like *me* anymore. I want something new. I want adventure. I want to start over." She let out a proud huff as she finished her impassioned speech.

Andrew pulled his glasses off, slung them onto the desk, and then covered his face with his hands. "This is not good, Simone. You're almost forty. Isn't it too late to start over?"

Man, life sure was making an effort to remind her of that milestone lately.

She jerked back. "It's never too late to find who you are. To do what your soul desires." She weighed her next words cautiously. "Surely you learned your lesson with everything that happened with Amalie. If not, know that you're going to want to choose how you respond here very carefully."

He'd threatened to disown and disinherit her little sister if she continued trying to make it as a writer. What did Amalie do? Basically, she gave him the middle finger and kept on plugging, tough as it may have been. Simone was ready to do the same if he pushed too hard in the wrong direction.

Andrew studied her in silence and then averted his attention to the stack of papers before him. The breath he let out was long-suffering. "Well, I was getting tired of playing golf every day anyway. You can only get so good and not be Tiger Woods. I suppose I can come back until I find a replacement...or until you decide to return. I could probably hold things off for about a year." He still looked a little grim. "I don't want to lose you, so if this is what it takes to make you happy..." Another pause. "Then so be it. I'm not pleased, and I disapprove, but I won't stand in your way. And you'll always have a place here in some capacity if things don't work out."

Simone's hands trembled as she tamped down the delighted squeal building in her throat. "Things are going to work out. I know it."

Although, it was nice to know she still had Warner Hotels to fall back on. Who knew what she'd do after this, or if it'd even work? At least she had a safety net.

They talked for a few more minutes before ending their call, and well, screw it, Simone yelped and did a little chair dance, pushing back from her desk.

She'd done it. Holy shit, she'd done it. She just threw off the chains of her old life and already felt like a new woman. Now *that* deserved a delicious carb-filled breakfast.

The only thing was that she didn't want to run into Alex.

Her stomach growled again, sounding like a monster from the deep. She needed sustenance, especially after all the physical activities she'd just put her body through. If someone had told her that at thirty-seven years old, she'd be getting ready to slink through a hotel, avoiding a gorgeous one-night stand she'd completely ghosted, she would've called them ridiculous. Her? Simone Warner? One-night stand? *Right.* Yet, here she was, picking through her wardrobe for all black clothing.

Life had definitely thrown her one hell of a curveball, and the thing was...she kind of liked it.

Chapter Six

SIMONE

SIMONE SNUCK AROUND EACH CORNER OF THE HOTEL, HIDING IN THE SHADOWS like a thief. Anytime a man approached with even remotely the same hair color or style as Alex, she pulled on her oversized black sunglasses and darted behind the nearest fern or column.

The scent of breakfast wafting from the restaurant made her mouth water at the idea of loading up on carbs. Damien caused her carb ban to begin, always asking if she wanted to work out after having a breadstick or two. Sadly, she'd kept the ban in place even after she cut him out.

She rushed into the restaurant, about to take a table near the kitchen when her little sister yelled out, "Sim! Over here!"

Simone froze, her hackles up, and scanned the crowd, making sure a familiar sexy tennis player wasn't among the guests before turning toward Amalie. There she was, her fiery red curls bouncing around her face as she waved from their seat in the corner, one of the best seats in the house. Julian and Paul sat with her, making conversation while she ate.

Pulling her sunglasses over her face again, wishing she'd thought to rock an Audrey Hepburn style scarf, Simone headed to their table.

"Last night must've been wild if you're wearing sunglasses right now. Did you hit the mini-bar in your room?" Amalie asked as Simone slid into the chair next to her.

Simone blanched even though her sister had no idea how right she was. *Wilde* indeed, in all the ways.

"Something like that," she muttered, skimming the menu a waitress handed her.

Paul and Julian said hello and then went back into work mode, discussing tennis strategy.

Amalie waved them off. "The business meeting went well, but I'm not allowed to say anything about it because they're still worried about a jinx."

Simone nodded, having forgotten all about the reason they'd come to Canada in the first place. She wanted to ask questions, assuming they snagged some sort of sponsorship or maybe even worked out some kind of expansion of the center. Either way, she knew she'd learn soon enough, and she'd rather not be the jinx. She came from a sports-minded family— well, *father*—who believed in such things.

"But that's not what I want to talk about." Amalie bumped Simone's shoulder playfully. "Where did you disappear to last night? I hope you didn't spend all of your time in your room and at least explored the grounds a little."

"I explored something all right."

Amalie inched closer, her voice dropping to a whisper. "Excuse me, big sis?" She blinked rapidly, staring at Simone with her brows raised to her hairline.

Simone lifted a shoulder. "Let's just say...there was a guy. And leave it at that for now."

"What?! Oh my holy hell! Simone! Who?!" Amalie's face lit up, and she all but flailed in her chair.

"Shhh! Calm down." Simone grabbed her sister's hands and shot an exaggerated wide-eyed look at Paul and Julian, who were blessedly still deep in conversation, regardless of Amalie's outburst. The last thing Simone needed was those two ribbing her about a fling.

Amalie's mouth opened and closed several times. "Fine, but I'll need to know every detail *soon* because the suspense will kill me."

Simone pushed her sunglasses into her hair. "I need food before we get into all that."

The smell of syrup was divine, and Simone was starving, but thankfully she didn't have to wait long before the waitress returned. She ordered brioche French toast and bacon, earning a strange look from Amalie.

"You do realize French toast is bread, right? Meaning it's a carb. Meaning..." Amalie's voice trailed off as she scrutinized her sister. She tossed her napkin onto the table. "All right. Who are you, and what have you done with Simone?"

"Oh, you haven't seen anything yet." Simone sat up straight and tapped the table, going into boardroom mode. Paul and Julian stopped talking, sliding their glances toward her.

"Now that I have your attention, I have news. I've already called Dad, and it's important that you know too."

The rush Simone felt when she closed her laptop this morning was the feeling she reached for deep inside her heart, the feeling she clung to as she prepared to march ahead with her journey toward self-discovery.

Paul, Julian, and Amalie leaned forward, expressions of concern etched on their faces.

"I've decided to step down as CEO of Warner Hotels."

Amalie choked on the sip of water she'd just taken. Julian patted her on the back, eyes wide. But Paul? Paul just beamed, almost as if he was proud.

"Say what now?" Amalie's voice was hoarse. "Do you mean temporarily or...?"

Simone shook her head, the smile unfurling across her lips genuine and broad. "Permanently. Or at least I hope permanently. We'll see. I know it's a shock—"

"Holy shitballs, yes, it's a shock, Sim. You *are* Warner Hotels. Being CEO is what you've worked for your entire life, and I thought...I thought you loved it." Amalie narrowed her gaze, her forehead wrinkling, and Simone felt like maybe, just maybe, her sister was truly seeing her for the first time.

The fact was, Simone had never loved it. After Damien's fiasco, running the family business became even more of a prison for her. The "How are you holding up?" and "Did you have any idea?" comments had grown stale.

She gestured with her hands, although she couldn't wipe the exhilaration from her face. "What can I say? I'm thirty-seven years old and have never done a single thing for myself, and it's time that changed. My decisions have always been based on the greater good of the hotel or Damien or for Tallulah, who I'm thankful for and will continue to consider, of course. But I've done things for them that came at the expense of losing a piece of myself. Each day chipped away a larger piece, and I'm just... done." She sighed because what came next was a hard truth. "After everything last year, I took a long look at my life and realized *so* much. Apart from being a CEO for my family's hotel, I don't know who the hell I am. Who am I, if not Damien's wife, now ex-wife, or Andrew Warner's daughter, or Tallulah's mother, Amalie's sister, or Julian Smoke's sister-in-law? I've got to do my own thing."

Sure, it was terrifying because who knew what awaited her? Her mind flashed to Alex Wilde, to his stunning, perfect *everything*—and that absolutely criminal V that led from his hips straight to his...

Whew. She had to stop thinking about that, *about him*. Period.

That image flitted away when Amalie spoke. "I'm proud of you. I know this can't be easy, but it'll be worth it. And I'm proud of Dad for being okay with it. He's come a long way."

Amalie's expression softened when she met her husband's stare. Of course, his eyes were already glued to her, much like always when they were in a room together. Simone could almost picture what they were thinking. No, not *that*—but that Andrew Warner had become a softie in the last few years, all because of Julian.

"Good for you, Simone. I think this is a good move," Paul spoke up as his eyes crinkled.

"Hell yeah. If I know anything about you, it's that no matter what you do, you kick ass at it. You do you, big sis." Julian offered his fist to bump. Simone laughed and bumped it without hesitation.

Amalie sat back. "So will Dad be taking over or...?"

"He said he'd hold my spot until I decided to come back or until they find a replacement, but honestly, I don't even want to think about that. I just want to focus on the future."

Amalie reached a hand forward, wrapping Simone's in her grasp. "I'm proud of you, Simone, truly. This is a big deal, and I know if anyone can do it, it's you."

Simone squeezed her sister's hand. Now it was time to go home and start over. Begin again. To take her first steps into a new life.

SIMONE SIGHED AS SHE BOARDED THE PLANE BACK TO ATLANTA, SHOULDERING her carry-on between the crowded seats before stowing her luggage and sliding into the window seat. The last day of the trip went smoothly, and she'd gotten entirely too good at sneaking around the chateau.

Still, that didn't mean she wouldn't hump her poor vibrator to death once she got home, and all of the scenarios in her head would star Alex and an incredibly endowed part of his anatomy. She got hot just thinking about it.

Oh, she was going to miss Canada, a place that would forever be special to her on so many levels.

A secretive smile played on her lips as she stared out the window. Whoever this woman was that she was becoming, she liked her.

Paul shuffled down the aisle and lifted his suitcase into the overhead bin before taking a seat next to her. She'd always liked Paul Mercado. He was blunt, and she respected that. How liberating it must be to say exactly what you feel.

"This ended up being a nice little trip, didn't it?" Paul mused as he started digging through the back of the seat, leafing through the safety pamphlet and catalogs.

Simone nodded and searched her purse for hand sanitizer. Just watching Paul touch those magazines that a thousand other people had handled made her skin crawl.

After wiping down her hands, she lifted her head. "It really did. From what it sounds like, things worked out well for you guys too, even though Amalie is tight-lipped." She rolled her eyes to exaggerate the point.

Paul chuckled. "I think we're past being able to jinx it now. We finalized things this morning, so we're good to go." He paused. "I can tell you the news if you want?"

Simone stilled. "Of course I want to know. Did you get the sponsorship?"

He pursed his lips. "Sponsorship?"

"Yeah, I just assumed…" Her words trailed off as she gestured.

Paul shook his head. "No, we came here because this player is interested in working with us."

"And you two accepted?" That was the last thing she expected to hear.

"We did. There's something unique about this kid, a drive I haven't seen since Julian. Kind of hung up on the mental aspect of the game, I think, and we might be able to help him break through that barrier."

"A kid, huh?" She'd seen a lot of young tennis players on the courts each morning and evening, so it could've been any one of them.

"Yep. A good one, I think. We'll see. But he's coming down to Atlanta to train with us for the remainder of the year, so he must be serious."

"Wow." That was some intense commitment. Simone wondered where the kid lived or if he needed help finding a tutor since he'd be missing school once August rolled around in a few weeks. She was about to ask when Paul began speaking.

"Simone, I know we don't talk often, but I gotta tell ya, I think it's wonderful what you did. That had to take a lot of guts."

She picked at her travel cardigan. "I don't know about all that, but thank you. It means more than you know, because I have no idea what I'm doing."

Paul took off his hat and messed with the fuzz on his head before situating it again. "Isn't that the best part? The not knowing?"

Simone blew out a breath, letting her head fall back on the headrest. The high she'd felt sputtered for a moment, doubt vining through her thoughts. "I don't think so. Not for someone like me who's always had every little part of her life planned out. Earn valedictorian, Simone. Go to UGA, Simone. Study business, Simone. Turn down a tennis scholarship, Simone—"

"I thought I heard Amalie mention that once," Paul interjected as the pilot came over the speaker, directing everyone's attention to the safety video on the screens in front of them.

"Yeah. I wanted that scholarship more than anything. It was my dad's fault in the first place that I ended up loving the game like I did." She released a quiet laugh, remembering how it felt to fall in love with the sport. "Tennis always felt like an ex, like the one that got away. Something about it just made me feel free—the wind in my hair when I'd rush to make a shot, or the adrenaline that coursed through my body when I'd hit a winner." Chills dotted her arms. "It's been years since I played competitively." She looked over at Paul. "You know, my daughter doesn't even believe me when I tell her I used to play." She couldn't contain her smile at the thought of Tallulah and her sassy self.

"Simone?" Paul's voice was serious, a tone she rarely heard from the man.

She turned so she could see him better. "Yes?"

"You know, since you're currently unemployed, have you ever thought about coming to help at the tennis center? I'm short-staffed with Julian leaving for Amalie's book tour soon, and I think you'd like the work. It'd give you a chance to get back into the game and allow you time to figure out your next move in life. You could even help me train the new kid. I call that a win-win."

Simone couldn't ignore the excited tremor that ran through her at the prospect. She could see herself out there, teaching others how to play. She'd love it, and she might even see if Lula had an interest in tennis. Although she doubted it, what with that child's obsession with soccer.

"You're serious?"

This could be good. This was something she'd always thought would be fun, ever since she was a kid. Her father had laughed when she said she wanted to be a tennis player, and then when she said she wanted to be a coach, he'd laughed even harder. So she kept her head down and did her thing, knowing CEO was her endgame. But now…

The plane started down the runway, and Paul leaned back in his seat, a mischievous light flickering in his brown eyes. "I'm serious. What do you say, Simone? Wanna help me coach?"

A surge of happiness bloomed in her chest at the idea of getting back on the court again. Thinking about it made her feel lighter than she had in years. "I would love to, but does it matter if I don't know the first thing about coaching?"

"You know tennis."

Simone canted her head. "If you think that's enough…"

"You'd be surprised. But hey, think about it—no rush to make a decision, especially right now. I want you to do what makes you happy. Just let me know in a few days." Paul patted the armrest between them in punctuation and then started flipping through the Sky Mall catalog as the plane soared through the sky.

"I can do that. And Paul?"

"Hmm?" He glanced up from the magazine.

"Thank you."

"Of course. And for what it's worth, I think you'd make one hell of a coach." And then his attention was back to the catalog.

Simone's lips curved as she dug her headphones from her purse with shaky fingers. This put her one step closer to figuring out her life, and the feeling was staggering.

She'd be able to be around the game again, have a goal to focus on, and she'd have more time with Lula. During the summer her daughter was off to soccer camp—she was an outgoing girl and loved to travel, something she got from her mother for sure. When school started back, Damien would be happy to keep her whenever needed—they traded off every other week—as long as it didn't interfere with his social life.

The more Simone thought about the offer, slipping the headphones onto her ears, the more confident she was that she was going to do it.

After all, it sounded like the perfect plan.

Chapter Seven

SIMONE

Simone walked into the Oliver Smoke Tennis Center feeling like she was all that and a bag of chips…if that's even what the kids still said these days. She'd just finished listening to Nina Simone's "Feeling Good" and was amped. Nina's last name was her namesake, so of course, as soon as Simone was old enough to buy her own cassette tapes, she bought Nina's first. But that song became her power mantra, the one that made her feel like she could tackle anything that came her way.

She tightened her ponytail. A week had passed since she started working at the tennis center, and when the day was through, she could honestly say she was happy. She loved being out on the court again, helping the kids.

She'd also received great news from her family lawyer regarding her alimony to Damien. Her lawyer noted that nothing in their five-year alimony agreement stated that she had to maintain a certain salary. Who would have ever thought she would leave that life? Still, Julian's check from the center was pennies compared to her CEO pay. She knew Damien would lose it when he found out, but right now she still had the hotel as a backup, should she need it. Oh, how she prayed she wouldn't.

As it was, Damien only thought she was coaching as a passion project type thing—he had no idea she'd stepped down, nor did Tallulah, who would be home from camp in a few weeks. Simone did tell Lula she was working at the tennis center, and even with soccer as her first love, she *did* express interest in checking out the center and maybe giving tennis a try. Of course, that made Simone's heart squeeze with joy. She looked forward to having another way to spend time together when her daughter came back in early August, the week before school started.

It'd taken a while, but she'd finally told her sister the identity of her mystery man back in Lake Louise, swearing Amalie to secrecy. Amalie had gone dead silent for a long time, then babbled on and on about how cute he looked on television, and then changed the subject. Which was very unlike her. Simone shrugged it off as Amalie being worried about her book tour.

Arlo, Simone's best friend, thought the entire situation brilliant, promising they'd have drinks as soon as she returned to the States. Even though she was in Scotland for a big PR assignment, they hadn't missed a beat. Well, that and Arlo couldn't stop sending Simone texts about how hot Alex was and asking where she could find a tennis player of her own. Simone tried not to think about all that, needing to focus on the task at hand.

Today she was scheduled to meet the kid she'd agreed to help Paul train. Dizzy with anticipation, she turned down one of the immaculate hallways that led to each of the coach's offices. Julian wouldn't be in until later, since he and Amalie had several errands to run before leaving on the book tour.

She hovered at Paul's doorway for a moment, watching as he sat hunched over a notebook, scribbling furiously. Pictures of him with other tennis greats lined the wall at his back, ending with one of Paul with Julian, Julian's mother, Charlotte, and Amalie at the US Open after Julian's win. Paul was a handful, but she couldn't help but admire the man.

"Morning," she called out, stepping inside his office.

"Hey, there. You ready to get your coaching hat on?" He gestured to his own tried-and-true Federer cap, then pulled out a pack of gum from his desk drawer and shoved two pieces in his mouth.

Pride swelled through Simone at having decided to take this step, even if it was a little nerve-wracking. What if the child hated her? "Absolutely, I'm ready. Where's the kid? Are we going to meet his parents first?"

Paul raised one white eyebrow, confusion marring his expression. "Huh?"

She unzipped her backpack, eventually putting it on the desk. "His parents. I figured we'd meet with them to discuss his options for tutoring once school starts. You know that's only a few weeks away. I don't want him to fall behind in his studies while he's here. Not on our watch." She lifted a printout with the names of several highly recommended tutors from her backpack with triumph.

"*Oui*, we wouldn't want him to miss anything at all. Perhaps something such as an *au revoir*?"

A familiar, sultry voice slid over Simone's skin, causing her to press her hand into the wooden surface of the desk.

"Alex?" She twisted around halfway, still propped up, needing to remain grounded.

There he stood, looking as if he'd just walked off a runway, an effortless chic about him. His jeans were ripped and fell over black motorcycle boots. He wore a white V-neck that dipped low, showing off a few of the curves and swirls of the sparrow that she knew was inked on his left pec. His shirt clung to his biceps, revealing tattoos she'd touched, licked, kissed.

On the outside of his forearm, a large, black compass spanned from elbow to wrist. On the other side was a minimalistic *I choose* in typewriter font. She knew that higher up, there would be a sun with its rays peeking over a simple straight-lined ocean. Beneath his shirt, *Stay Gold* had been scrawled across his bicep with a skeletal hand holding a wilting flower. On his rib cage, an inked wave, crashing. She could spend all day cataloging each piece of art on his body again and again. After all, they were branded in her mind.

Alex ran a hand through his sandy blond hair, his muscles flexing with the movement. His beard was a little longer but still neatly trimmed. This man looked like he belonged on the back of a motorcycle instead of on the tennis courts.

"What the hell are you doing here?" she asked, having finally found her voice again.

Alex tilted his head and took a step inside the office. His scent, deeply sensual and warm, enveloped her. She fought against the desire to drag an inhale through her nose, the smell bringing back all sorts of memories. Memories that were probably broadcasted plainly across her face.

"Ah, I'm training with Paul and, from what I hear, *you*."

That one syllable sounded like sex. Or maybe that was just because her mind was there. Geez. Paul was in the room, for crying out loud.

She straightened, acting like she hadn't had the single hottest night of her life with the gorgeous, bearded man standing before her. She turned to Paul, hooking a thumb over her shoulder at Alex. "He's not who we're training. You said it was a kid."

Paul spread his hands in front of him, a sheepish expression etched on his face. "Everyone's a kid to me, Simone. You never asked for details, and I didn't think..." He straightened the papers on his desk, almost as if to have something to do with his hands. "I didn't think it mattered."

"I'm not training him." All those good feelings, those *hear me roar* vibes flowing through her veins, ran cold with her admission.

Because she couldn't. Alex Wilde was a one-night stand who was supposed to stay that way. It was supposed to be a *thank you very much for the fun, but let's never see each other again* kind of situation. But this? This was a brand-new complication she did not need in her already twisted up, scrambled life.

Paul tapped the desk. "If you're that upset, we can get him a tutor. Just seeing he's twenty-nine and all, I wasn't sure..."

Simone huffed, throwing her hands up. "That's not what I meant, Paul."

Her fingers connected with her unzipped backpack, knocking it off the desk and sending its contents scattering across the floor.

"Ah shit," Simone muttered under her breath as she bent down to pick it up.

Heat coursed through her veins, pinking her cheeks—because, really, who wanted to fumble in front of someone who'd seen them naked and who was as handsome as Alex Wilde?

"Here, allow me," Alex offered as he bent down, his voice taking on that sexy gravelly pitch.

Allow me.

That's why they were currently in this mess. Because she *did* allow him.

Hell, she *allowed* him more than a few times, and she currently fantasized about several more.

"No, I got this," she finally managed, although it was too late.

Alex knelt beside her, picking up all the papers and random crap from her backpack with the steadiest of hands while hers trembled.

His nearness wrapped her up in a heady trance. It didn't help that she could smell the mint of his gum mixed with his cologne. All that was missing was a taste of scotch on her tongue and...*nope.*

A throaty chuckle from Alex broke the tense silence stretching between them.

"Is this funny to you?" Simone hissed, snatching a tube of her lipstick off the floor, all the while her mind kept repeating on an endless loop: *Don't look at him. Don't look at him. Don't look at him.*

So what did she do? She looked at him.

Alex's brown eyes flared as he studied her face. He pulled his bottom lip between his teeth and dropped his dark gaze to her mouth.

She swallowed. He tracked that too, arching his brow.

That movement broke her from his stare as she fumbled her hands across the carpet, searching for something to shove into her bag. Instead of being met with papers, her hand landed on warm skin.

Alex's hand.

She froze and he leaned closer, his breath skittering across her cheek.

Paul cleared his throat, reminding both Simone and Alex that they weren't the only two people in the room.

Simone quickly gathered her strewn items and stuffed them into her backpack. After one last shared glance, they stood, slowly, and though it wasn't easy, Simone finally averted her gaze from Alex Wilde's annoyingly gorgeous face.

Paul's narrowed eyes darted to Alex and back to her, almost as though he could read the tension stretching between them. "*Alors*—"

Simone frowned. "*Alors?*"

"Yeah, *alors*," Paul said. "Alex taught me. It means *so* in Quebecois."

"Oh dear God," Simone muttered to herself.

"As I was saying," Paul said. "If Alex is too much for you to handle, then..."

A teasing smile tugged one corner of Alex's mouth, and Simone knew precisely why.

He reclined against the wall, crossing his arms over his chest. "*Oui,* Simone. If I'm too much to handle…"

"He is *not* too much to handle." She dug her fingertips into her hips, moving from foot to foot, doing her best to avoid Alex's gleaming stare roving over her like a touch. "I'm perfectly capable of teaching him a thing or two."

Alex's smirk spread into a wide, wicked grin. "Is that so, *chérie*? I can't wait, then."

Chapter Eight

ALEX

CRISS. SIMONE WAS JUST AS ELECTRIC AS THE NIGHT THEY MET, EVEN IF SHE seemed less than thrilled that he was there. Perhaps he should've expected as much.

When Paul called and explained he'd brought on a new member named Simone Warner, Alex didn't waste any time looking her up. He was pleased that the woman was the very same he'd spent the night with at the chateau.

Rhys thought the entire situation hilarious, of course, and kept taunting him that he'd caught feelings for the woman. Alex fought a scoff at that. The only feeling he caught was confusion—confusion that someone had finally captured his attention for longer than a night.

"I look forward to *all* you can teach me, *Coach*." He understood she was Paul's assistant, yet he couldn't resist having a little fun.

Simone shook her head and faced Paul. "Well. When do we start?" Her voice held a slight waver. She cleared her throat before speaking again, tapping her foot forcefully. "I'm assuming today?"

Ah. There was the woman who'd commanded a boardroom. When he'd looked her up online after learning her full name, he'd been a bit surprised to find she'd spent the last six years running one of the largest hotel chains in the States. In the bedroom, she'd been submissive, a woman needing to be taken, to be had, and he had more than obliged. Only once had he glimpsed her dominant side. The thought sent a tingle straight to his groin. He'd loved it. That was the CEO side of her, clearly. A job she'd left for this. For tennis.

Admiration twisted in his chest. It was hard to reinvent oneself, yet here she was doing it.

Paul scratched his beard, the sound deafening in the suddenly quiet room as he surveyed them. "You know what? I think we'll start tomorrow. I can see you two aren't going to be in your best form today, so..." His head snapped up to meet Alex's stare. "Alex, I'll show you around. Also, if you need to work out, you're free to use the gym and any other amenities you're interested in. Our fitness trainer, Romina, is on vacation. But trust me, with this heat, you should probably be thankful."

Alex didn't know what that meant, but just like he wasn't a fan of coaches, fitness trainers weren't at the top of his list either.

"Also, you can hit if you want," Paul added. "I can get you a hitting partner over from Georgia Tech."

Simone made a hissing noise at the mention of Georgia Tech. Alex raised a brow.

"She went to UGA. They're like the Montagues and Capulets," Paul explained.

Alex blinked a few times at the reference.

Before he could say anything, Paul gestured to his face in what was probably meant to be a suave manner. "Yeah, that's right. I'm not just a pretty face. I know things."

Alex laughed, and Simone snorted. When she met Alex's gaze head-on, all traces of humor disappeared.

"Fine, tomorrow it is," she said. "And actually, Paul, I have some errands to run, if that's okay?"

Paul nodded. "Of course. Oh! Before you leave, I need to talk to you both about Julian. He won't be practicing much before he heads out with Amalie or when he gets back from her tour. At least for a bit. He just saw the doc, and it appears he messed up his knee. Nothing serious, but no running around for him for a while."

Alex winced. He knew how painful knee injuries could be. Thankfully, he hadn't had anything like what Julian was most likely dealing with.

Simone's mouth twisted as she digested the news about her brother-in-law. "Thank you for telling us." She paused, looking between Alex and Paul. "If there isn't anything else?"

"Nope. You're free to go. See you later, Simone!"

She snatched her backpack from the desk, turned, and waved to Paul but walked out the door without sparing Alex a backward glance.

"See you tomorrow, Coach," he called out playfully.

Silence answered.

Paul let out a low whistle. "I take it you two have already met."

Alex cringed. "*Oui*, you could say that."

Paul rounded his desk, sitting back against the edge, studying Alex in a way that made him feel measured.

"Look," he said. "I know you got a thing for the ladies. But I hope Simone isn't the reason you came down here."

Alex's posture went rigid. As intrigued as he'd been about Simone working here, she wasn't why he came. At least that's what he kept telling himself.

"I'm here to train," he said. "That's all. To get my mental game back on track."

Simone being involved had felt like a bonus. Besides, it wasn't like he could turn down this opportunity just because his presence would create an awkward situation. He'd assumed she'd known about the arrangement anyway, and yet the offer remained. Obviously, she hadn't known, but that wasn't his fault.

"Perfect. Because Simone is a wonderful girl," Paul said. "You hurt her, you'll answer to me. Remember that."

Alex's reputation followed him everywhere it seemed, even to Atlanta, Georgia.

"I wouldn't dream of hurting her."

"Good talk then," Paul said, though his expression held a bit of restraint now, a little worry. The older coach clapped Alex on the shoulder before leaving him standing alone in the office.

Calice. Alex dragged his hand over his beard.

What had he gotten himself into?

Chapter Nine

SIMONE

S IMONE PULLED UP TO A MALIE'S HOUSE, HER FINGERS ACHING FROM GRIPPING the steering wheel. With an aggravated sigh, she stomped up to the porch and banged on the door, forgoing the doorbell. Her little sister would know she was *pissed*.

Red curls bounced into view in the half-circle window at the top of the door. "Oh, holy shitballs," Amalie said from the other side before slowly backing away from the door.

Simone clenched her fists and knocked on the door again. "Seriously? I can hear you. Open the door."

There was a moment of silence before the door swung open to reveal a very guilty-looking Amalie. "Oh, it's you. Hey, sis." Her expression was slightly guarded as she motioned for Simone to come inside.

Simone gave her the stank eye, not relenting until they were in the living room. Amalie fell back onto a creamy-white chair. "So what's up?"

Oh, so she was going to act completely clueless?

Simone loomed over Amalie, hands firmly on her hips, too wired to sit. "You *knew* Alex was the *kid* I was supposed to coach. Seriously, Amalie?" Amalie jumped up, opening her mouth to interrupt, but Simone held out a hand to silence her. "No, let me finish. You let me waste all that time researching all kinds of high school tutors for the fall because I wasn't sure about his age, when you knew? And on top of that, you had to know how weird seeing him for the first time would be! I looked up today and *bam*, there he was, in all of his ridiculous sexiness, at the tennis center." Simone paced and massaged her temples. It was that or strangle her little sister.

"I knew you wouldn't accept Paul's offer if you knew Alex was coming, and well, since you told me he'd already *come*..." Amalie wiggled her brows as if that sad little joke would help lighten the mood.

Simone straightened. "Oh, you think this is funny?"

At that point, Julian walked out from his and Amalie's shared office, papers in hand. He lifted his chin at Simone, and then his gaze darted to Amalie. "So she knows, huh?"

Simone's nostrils flared, and she crossed her arms. "I know, no thanks to *either* of you."

Julian gave her an innocent smile and a shrug before shuffling off into another room. Simone noticed the hitch in his step, the slight grimace from walking on his knee. "We're glad to have you working with us though!" he called.

Simone rolled her eyes, and her lips flattened as she zeroed her attention back on her sister, who was lounging in her chair again.

Amalie gestured toward her. "Well, you seem to be handling it well." Sarcasm dripped from her words, but her demeanor shifted when she dropped her voice low. "Like you handled that dick in Lake Louise."

Simone's lips trembled, wanting to laugh at Amalie's humor, but she couldn't crack, not yet. Instead, she'd hit her sister where it hurt. She made her way into Amalie's kitchen, which she knew as well as her own.

Amalie trailed on her heels. "Whatcha doing?"

Simone pulled the cheese puffs out of the pantry and waved them in front of Amalie's face.

Amalie's nose scrunched. "What the hell? You don't even like cheese puffs."

"I know, but I don't like you either right now, so I'm taking the cheese puffs hostage." She tucked the bag under her arm, feeling victorious.

"Fine, fine." Amalie put her hands on her hips and narrowed her eyes on Simone. "But like I said, if you'd known about Alex, you never would have agreed to work at the center or coach, and I haven't seen you this *alive* in years. It's good for you—well, that or the one-night stand was good for you. I don't know which one, but either way, Alex can check *all* of your boxes, if you catch my meaning." She circled closer, probably strategizing how to snatch those cheese puffs away.

Simone clamped her arm down on them harder, earning a glare from her sister. "Amalie, I realize you're fairly new to the tennis world, but it's not a good look to be having sex with your coach. It happens, but..."

Amalie shrugged. "It was a one-night stand, right? So nothing to worry about then?"

Simone swallowed any response, felt her heart trip over itself. She could lie, but what was the point of that?

Amalie bounced on the balls of her feet, eagerness alight in her face. "*Is* there something to worry about?"

Simone deflated. "I mean, I don't know." She tore open the cheese puff bag, grabbing a handful and shoving them into her mouth. Amalie gasped but said nothing. Simone waited until she'd chewed before speaking. "Oh my gosh, these are—"

"Amazing, wonderful, delicious?" Amalie interrupted.

Simone looked down at the bag and back up to her sister. "All of those things." Junk food wasn't something she ever allowed herself to have, but it seemed like forbidden things were growing on her.

Cheese puffs temporarily forgotten, Amalie put a hand on Simone's shoulder, expression earnest. "Look, you're at the first real turning point of your story."

"I swear if you're talking novel stuff to me..."

"I'm just sayin'. You came back from Lake Louise a changed woman. I could see it. That night with Alex was your inciting incident, a catalyst for change. You've never stood with your back so straight, your shoulders so loose. Now he's here, you have a choice to make. Move forward or retreat. And I really hope you move forward. This is where you're supposed to be, Simone. Yeah, it's gonna be awkward and hard—" She had the audacity to wink. "—but see where it takes you. You might find that coaching is your next act."

Her next act. Simone liked the sound of that. It was much better than not having your life together.

She brushed her bangs from her eyes. "But what about Alex?"

"What about him?"

Simone's voice came out as barely a whisper, causing Amalie to press in even further. "He knows what I look like naked. And I know where *all* of his sexy tattoos are." She widened her eyes meaningfully.

Amalie let out a low whistle. "Oh damn, I forgot he has tattoos." She stepped back on her heels and shouted, "Hey Julian!"

"What?" he called out from somewhere in the house.

"We should get tattoos!"

A muffled chuckle was his response, but Simone could only shake her head. "*Anyway*, you're not helping. Bless your heart, you're trying, but you're struggling because you keep getting sidetracked by the fact that Alex and I had sex."

"And? He's a nice guy, despite his media reputation. I can't help but cheer for him. I get sidetracked by *that* because I was there to see how Damien made you feel. Alex is—"

Simone sounded dreamy as she interrupted her sister. "Different. He's sexy and sophisticated, and if I'm totally honest, I just want to pull that hair and ride that—"

Amalie's eyes went round, and she held up a hand between them. "Whoa. Down, girl."

Just then, Julian came into the kitchen, hands over his ears. "I'm not listening anymore because I made the mistake of not covering my ears sooner, and now they're bleeding from all of that, and I just wanted a snack." He pulled a granola bar out of the pantry as fast as he could and hightailed it out of there without looking Simone in the eye. She couldn't contain her laughter, Amalie joining in.

When they finally settled down, Amalie shot her a conspiratorial look. "So you're going to do it? Ride him? I mean, coach him?"

Simone almost blanched at her sister's slipup, wanting to tell her she'd thought of nothing else since that night in Lake Louise, but instead, she blew out a heavy sigh. "Yeah. I suppose I am. I'm not letting anyone stand in the way of my dreams again."

Chapter Ten

ALEX

ALEX DROPPED HIS KEYS ONTO THE IMMACULATE TABLE OF HIS RENTAL HOME, one Amalie located for him in Ansley Park. Thankfully, he'd unpacked before heading to the tennis center, because he was exhausted from hitting with the kid from Georgia Tech, having taken Paul up on his offer.

He paused at the window for a moment, admiring the skyscrapers, and yet the neighborhood was completely residential and filled with exquisite homes. Amalie may have also dropped a hint that Simone lived nearby, which intrigued him.

He plopped onto the comfy, dark sofa, focusing on how it felt to be on the court today and how it felt to be *here*. In Atlanta. Finally. He couldn't believe he was actually training with Julian Smoke *and* Paul Mercado. Paul could work miracles, and Alex needed all the help he could get if he ever planned to beat Bastien.

That thought had him pulling up Julian's US Open final on his phone. Watching would give him a sense of how Paul would train him, since Julian would be out of the picture for the first part of their time together.

His phone buzzed. Rhys.

"Hello?"

"Alexander!" Rhys's English accent filtered through the phone. "How are you settling in? Did you make any new friends at school today?"

His face twisted into a cringe. "I didn't, but I did see Simone. I wouldn't exactly call her a friend."

Rhys let out a low whistle. "And how did she react? I have to know how this played out."

Alex grinned at Rhys's interest in the unfolding drama. He stood and moved to the window, tapping the windowsill. "I suppose you could say she wasn't super pleased, but she agreed to help coach me. At least, I think she did. She could vanish tomorrow for all I know."

Rhys let out a long *hmm*. "So tell me, is she why you're really there?"

Damn. First Paul, now Rhys. Did everyone think he was so into sex that he'd travel across a continent to get it? He sighed. Simone wasn't why he came here, though seeing her was definitely an added bonus.

He scrubbed a hand down his face. "*Non*. I didn't even know her when I reached out to Paul and Julian." Truth.

"Well then," Rhys said. "It's fate if you ask me, because that's one hell of a coincidence. A good one too."

Alex pinched the bridge of his nose. "I'm not sure if that's true. She's giving me very strong vibes that she wants nothing to do with me in that way. It's strictly business—"

"And how are you planning on dealing with that? This is the only woman who's ever snagged your attention for longer than a night. I'm fascinated."

"*Oui*, you and me both."

"I mean, why this woman?" Rhys asked. "Of all the women you've been with, why is Simone the one you can't get out of your head?"

That was a great question, and one that Alex felt he couldn't properly articulate an answer to, but he figured all he could do was try. "The night we first met, there was something so open and honest about her. It's still like that because she lays everything out there, and it doesn't feel like there are games with her. No front. What you see is what you get, and what you get is an incredible woman. She's funny and smart. She was a CEO, you know."

"Well, she's way out of your league then."

Alex chuckled. "Without a doubt."

"Then go for it. Go for her."

"You just said she was out of my league."

"Yeah, but when have you ever not gone after what you want? Besides, how are you going to survive the next few months if you don't give it a shot? Unless you want to give a dating app a try."

Alex let those words sink in. The problem was that he wanted Simone, not someone he met on an app or in a bar or anywhere else for that matter. It really was that simple, if he'd just pull his head out of his ass.

"Fine. Then I'll put the ball in her court. I'll be the man she met back in Canada." The man who swept her off her feet. The man who didn't hold back.

"Hold on a minute—since you're going to do that, I think you know that you have to play it cool with her."

"*Alors*, how exactly do I do that?"

"From what it sounds like, your usual game only applies to Simone when she's not in her normal environment. You can't just go up to her and start talking about how much you want to have sex with her. I don't think Simone will respond to that now, especially since you work together. You have to use that French part of your brain and finesse her. Be suave. Not crass."

Alex scoffed. "I can be suave, wanker."

Rhys was indignant. "That's my line."

They both laughed, but Rhys went quiet for a minute, and Alex looked out over the Atlanta skyline, darkness descending upon the city, the skyscrapers lighting up.

"Have you heard any tennis news?" Rhys asked.

Alex frowned, wondering what tennis news Rhys was talking about. The truth was that he'd stopped caring what lies the media told about him. It irritated him, sure, because people developed preconceived notions about him—like Paul and Simone—before Alex even had the chance to show who he really is.

"The media can go fuck themselves," he said. "You know how I feel about that." Irritation rising, he said, "Listen, I should get going. I need to find dinner."

"Fine. But Alex?" He paused. "You'll get the magic back. It'll happen."

When they hung up, Alex found himself standing at the window for quite some time, hoping his friend was right.

If he lost the spark that fueled him, Alex wasn't sure he'd ever recover.

And that frightened him more than anything.

THE NEXT MORNING, ALEX'S SHIRT CLUNG TO HIS SKIN, STUCK THERE AS A result of Georgia's oppressive summer heat. *Mon Dieu*, he'd only walked from his rental motorcycle in the parking lot to the Oliver Smoke Tennis Center entrance, and he already needed a second shower. The humidity was worse than yesterday, the air thick enough to choke on. But he had to endure for the sake of his game...and his interest in Simone.

He paused at the clubhouse door, hesitating. Alex hadn't had a coach since he was eighteen, so of course, he felt a little apprehensive. He fired his first and only coach, Anton Blanchet, after two years of working together. Since then, Alex had floated in a sea of uncertainty, not sure what to do to help his game, just that he would not be coached by someone who threatened to stifle his creativity and freedom on the court. He and Anton had an explosive disagreement over a few things, and then the man—who Alex had perhaps slowly begun to respect—spat at him that it was evident he didn't share Bastien's DNA. It was over then. Alex called him an asshole and shot him the bird before storming off the court, never talking to him again.

The memory still stung but was quickly forgotten as soon as Alex opened the door to the tennis center. He'd no sooner stepped inside when parents and kids bombarded him. The kids ran all over the place but came to a standstill when a loud whistle pierced the lobby.

At the mouth of a large hallway that led to the courts stood Simone, donning a sleek pair of black bike shorts, clinging perfectly to her ass. She also wore a white fitted tank that revealed a single inch of cleavage. Seeing her always felt like a jolt in the chest. He had to stop walking to keep from stumbling.

Merde, this was about to be next-level torture.

He let out a ragged exhale and hitched his tennis bag higher, trying to get himself together. Children were running around everywhere, and the last thing he needed to think about was his assistant coach's body.

At least talking with Rhys helped Alex develop a plan, although he wasn't sure how well it would work. He wasn't the caring boyfriend type.

What had Simone called him that first night? Sweet talker? That was more apt. He could sugarcoat anything, but could he do it for longer than a single night? He was about to find out.

"I need for all parents to say their goodbyes, and then the kids need to head to the courts. Thank you," Simone called out, her voice firm but kind and authoritative. And just like that, order was restored.

Paul sidled up to Alex with an impish grin on his face. "Hey, son. Ready to get to it?"

Alex gestured to the kids, who were now shuffling toward the courts. "You're going to leave Simone with fifty children?"

"Nah, that's why I brought you in."

Alex froze, fingers tightening on his bag. "Pardon?" Sweat started to bead at his temple. Babies were adorable, but older kids freaked him out a little, with their knowing eyes and endless questions. Other than that? He didn't know much when it came to children, but he supposed he could learn. "How is this going to help me become a better tennis player?"

Paul snickered. "I have my methods. Besides, we need to finish up kids' camp today."

Alex looked toward the exit. This had been a mistake, hadn't it? Simone or not.

He rubbed the back of his neck. "I might need more of an answer than that, Paul." What balanced on the tip of his tongue was, *How would this help him beat his stepbrother?*

Disappointment sank in his stomach like a lead weight. Any possibility of having a decent training day went up in smoke.

Paul shrugged. "Teaching the game helps keep your mind sharp, helps you see things you wouldn't normally see as a player. I learned more about the game from teaching and coaching than I ever did when I played."

Now that was more like it, and it actually made sense. If the end result would help his game, how could he walk away? "I can get behind that, I suppose."

Simone waltzed over, looking no-nonsense, her beachy scent threatening to scramble Alex's brain. Her gaze dropped to the motorcycle helmet dangling from his hand and then back to Paul.

"Good morning." That honey-and-whiskey voice drifted over him, but it felt stiffer than usual, formal. So she planned to play it reserved and polite. He could deal with that, for now. After practice though? It was game on.

His lips quirked. *"Bonjour."*

Simone motioned to the windows where they could see the kids on the courts. "Paul said you love kids. That's why you agreed to work the camp today as your first practice?"

Alex's mouth worked around a response, anything other than standing there with his face contorted like a fish out of water. *Criss.* He looked at Paul, who was now full-on guffawing. The older man said nothing—he just laughed as he made his way down the hall toward the courts.

Simone's expression went slack. "What in the world? That's what he said. Do you not?" She shifted, and he noticed her shoulders were almost up to her chin, strung tight.

"Ah, *non.*" He shook his head. *"Ché pas.* I mean, I don't know." *They sometimes terrify me,* he thought, but he couldn't say that to Simone, who had a daughter at home. "I just thought I was training today."

Simone straightened, sticking out her breasts, which he couldn't help but glance at before looking back at her face. He ran a hand over his hair, swallowing down the desire that made his mouth water.

She merely lifted a dark eyebrow. "Guess you need to change clothes. Can't exactly play in jeans in this heat." Her eyes dipped to his legs and scanned up his body slowly, before darting away as if she'd forgotten herself. She pressed her lips together, lips he'd enjoyed kissing, and hoped to kiss again, *soon.*

"Oui, although I'd much rather you undress me with your eyes like you just did."

She scoffed, though a tinge of pink washed across her cheeks. Alex liked that color on her far too much.

"I didn't just undress you with my eyes," she said. "Though I'm sure you'd like to believe I did."

Alex knew she wished to come across as unaffected, but her voice held too much of a quiver to sound convincing.

Cocking his head, he dared a step closer, enjoying how she squirmed beneath his gaze. She was *far* from unaffected. "Oh, *chérie,* your mouth lies so sweetly, but your eyes? They tell me everything I need to know."

Her lips parted, and the pink on her cheeks spread down her neck and chest. Images of Simone lying beneath him, flushed and writhing, rose in his mind.

"Alex, we should practice—" She shifted on her feet, her throat visibly bobbing. He took another step. "You need to change. *Now*," she enunciated, lifting her chin.

With regret, Alex watched as her sweet blush dissipated, though its memory was still fresh. He wanted to tease her until it painted her skin once again.

Unable to resist messing with her, he brushed her body as he sidled past. She spun around just as he glanced over his shoulder.

"I can't wait to see you on the court," he said, the challenge in his voice clear.

They still hadn't addressed their night together, and while he understood it could never happen again, he still wanted more.

Simone cocked a hip. "Oh, I look forward to it, but I'd hurry if I were you," she said, pointing outside the window to where Paul had the children entranced in some tale. The man crouched low, arms flying through the air. "We can't leave Paul with the kids for too long. Julian said he'll corrupt them." She crossed her arms over her chest, a small, teasing smile playing on her face.

Before Alex thought better of it, he shot back, "And you think I'm any better?"

Simone's cocky smile vanished. "I sure hope so."

Chapter Eleven

ALEX

Sweat dripped from Alex's hair onto the court. That's how hot it was on the asphalt, yet Simone and Paul were running around laughing. Of course, they'd complained about the heat, but they were in much better spirits than he was.

His eyes snagged on Simone as she walked one of the kids through an overhead shot. He'd been sneaking glances at her all afternoon in between teaching different shots, unable to help himself. "Why do you keep staring at that lady?" one of the kids—Ted—asked, just after he'd wiped a booger on his pants. Alex fought a shudder.

Simone shot a curious glance over her shoulder but said nothing.

"*Petit merdeux.*" Alex wanted to use one of his more colorful swears, but instead toned it down given his audience. He dropped his voice to a whisper. "Can you maybe not say that so loud?" *Little shit.*

The boy smiled, showing a missing tooth. Typical for his age, Alex guessed. He was probably six or seven, but that wasn't what bothered him. It was the fact that the kid had one of those evil grins—the kind that meant they'd zeroed in on their target's weakness and were about to obliterate them. *Calice.*

"You like Simone!" the kid crowed. "Alex likes Simoooooone!"

At Ted's outburst, everyone in the whole camp turned to look, most of the kids breaking out into laughter. The younger ones at least hid their giggles behind their hands. The middle school ones didn't.

Simone's eyes glittered as she met Alex's stare and raised her brow, a tinkling laugh falling from her lips. Even though Alex wanted to make Ted run a few extra sprints, he was strangely grateful. It was like Ted let a little pressure out of the situation by saying the thing Alex hadn't been able to...yet. Kids.

Fortunately, Paul walked over and saved him. "Camp's over, kids. Let's go wait in the clubhouse."

Alex sagged with relief. "*Merci.*"

Paul snickered, herding everyone, including Alex and Simone, inside the building. "I didn't do it for you. I just don't want to be late for dinner."

"*Maudit.*"

Paul pointed a stubby finger at him jokingly. "Hey now, don't be cussing at me."

"Not cursing *at* you. Now, *around* you? That's a different story. I'll try to be on my best behavior while I'm here, but my friend, Rhys, says I'd die if I couldn't swear."

"Rhys Westwick?" Paul asked.

"*Oui.*" Alex wiped the sweat from his forehead with the back of his hand.

"Now he's a solid player. We'll have to see about getting him over here. I can give his coach a call and see. Is that something you'd be interested in?"

Alex noticed Simone listening, her face a mask of quiet concentration as they all came to a stop.

"I'd love that," he replied. And he meant it. Playing against Rhys usually helped Alex get on track for a little while, but they hadn't seen one another since Alex made the trip to England last year for the holidays.

Paul clapped Alex on the shoulder, and that was the end of their conversation for the moment. The three of them got caught up in making sure each child was picked up. When the last kid left, Alex grabbed a quick shower, changing back into his motorcycle clothes. He gathered his things, including his helmet, just as Paul walked up to him, waving a green piece of paper, Simone on his heels.

"So, like we talked about, Simone has agreed to help coach you for the time being. Julian's leaving soon, so she'll step in to cover the gap." Paul adjusted his hat. "I know we already established this, but I want to make sure it's all right. With both of you."

For a moment, Simone met Alex's stare, and something silent passed between them. The idea of her coaching him was more than all right for Alex, but he was still a little surprised that she'd agreed to such an arrangement.

He knew people might scoff at the idea of being coached by someone who hasn't been around the sport as often as coaches on the tour, but he didn't want normal. He didn't want a coach from the circuit—he wanted a fresh perspective. Because really, what did he have to lose? Things were already pretty rough regarding his game.

Everything in his body vibrated with the rightness of being coached by Paul and Julian alongside Simone, and as someone who tried to always trust his gut, he went with it.

"Fine with me," Simone said, though he could tell that she still seemed unsure about the situation.

Ultimately, Alex knew why she stayed. He understood that beneath it all, they each had their own clear-cut goals. Simone hadn't left her CEO job just to give up on this new endeavor because of Alex. And well, he didn't leave Canada just to walk away from his end goal of destroying Bastien on the courts.

"*Oui*," Alex replied. "Of course."

Simone focused on the green paper in Paul's hands. Alex didn't miss the way her forehead crumpled as she skimmed the information, the way the corners of her mouth ticked up ever so slightly. She looked perplexed but also like she might burst into a bout of laughter at any moment.

"Good, good. Now. Different coaches have different techniques, as you know," Paul said. "Mine won't be the same as Anton's."

Criss. Alex hadn't heard that name spoken aloud in so long. He motioned for Paul to continue, desperate to leave that ghost in the past.

"I want to try something new with you. I'm gonna give you a survey to fill out so I can get to know you better, get an idea of the approach I want to take. I didn't do it with Julian, but thank God, everything worked out the way it did."

Simone snorted at that. Alex knew the proper thing to do was not to stare, but when had he ever been proper? He couldn't resist and looked over at her. *Merde.*

It was a mistake, especially with how her eyes sparkled in the late afternoon sun streaming through the clubhouse windows. He bit down on a smile before realizing that Paul had stopped talking. When Alex looked up, his coach stared at him like he'd grown a horn out of his forehead.

Paul harrumphed. "So anyway, fill this out and get it back to me."

Alex took the paper and read the top line out loud. "*Oliver Smoke Tennis Center Children's Day Camp Questionnaire?*"

Simone smothered a grin with her hand, faking a cough when Alex cut her a glare.

"Yeah, and what of it?" Paul placed his hands on his hips.

Alex frowned even though he was about to say there was no problem, but then he read the first few questions. "What's my favorite ice cream?" He looked up and met a serious-faced Paul, while silent laughter caused Simone to shake. "What's my favorite animal?"

"And?" came Paul's grumbly response.

"Ah, how...how does this help with tennis?" Alex was half ready to hand it back to his coach.

"I've got my methods. Remember, that's why you picked Julian and me to coach you, out of all the other coaches in the world."

Alex ran a hand through his damp hair. "*Oui*, but you gave me a kid's sheet, Paul."

"So what if I did? Maybe I'll give you an ice cream party if you can get out there and act like you know how to play. Maybe that's why I need to know your favorite ice cream flavor."

"And the animals are because, if it's feasible, we'll bring in a petting zoo if you start doing a better job on your returns." Simone's voice quaked with barely restrained laughter. It was the first joke she'd made toward him since he'd arrived.

Paul lit up. "See? See, she gets it!"

Alex fought a smile. This was entirely ridiculous, but Paul knew what he was doing, even if his methods were a bit juvenile. "What if I said a tiger?" he offered. "What would you do then?"

Paul didn't miss a beat. "Well, we'd take you to a zoo. Now return that questionnaire tomorrow when we meet for our first *official* practice." He checked his watch. "Oh, I need to get going if I want to meet Julian and Amalie at the restaurant."

Simone hoisted her tennis bag onto her shoulder. "I'm running home to clean up, and then I'll be there."

Alex took a half-step back as the conversation shifted to one of more familial chat, something he certainly wasn't used to and didn't belong in.

"How's Lula liking camp?" Paul asked as he walked them to the parking lot, locking up the center as they went. "You said yesterday she comes home in a few weeks?"

Alex followed along because what else was he supposed to do?

"Yeah, and she's having a blast," Simone replied. "She's basically a teenager now, or at least that's what I hear in her voice. She's big and grown and doesn't need me."

"How old is she?" Alex couldn't stop himself from asking.

Simone glanced at him over her shoulder. "Eight. I didn't want to let her go off to camp for an entire month, but she can be a convincing little thing. She usually gets what she wants."

"That's a Warner for ya!" Paul laughed.

"Sounds like she's got spunk."

Simone stopped and faced Alex, and he stopped too. Her eyes sparkled when she spoke. "She's a bit like her grandfather."

Paul began walking backward, waving, as he called out, "With the mention of Andrew Warner, I'm out. I'll catch both of you later."

"Your daughter sounds wonderful," Alex said once Paul was gone. "I'd love to meet her sometime."

Calice. He needed to just stop talking. After this day, he couldn't say he cared if he ever met another eight-year-old.

Simone played with the straps of her bag while she studied him, opening and closing her mouth once, as if she were unsure of how to respond. After a moment, her fingers left her bag and instead went to one of her earrings, messing with it enough to make her ear red.

"Oh, okay, sure. Well, get some rest." Her gaze swung to his rental bike and back to the black helmet in his hand. "And be careful. People ignore bikers."

"I will. *Merci.*"

Alex didn't budge. This was his chance. His chance to talk about that night and how he hoped for another shot with her in some capacity.

He scratched his beard and met Simone's gaze head-on, offering her a crooked smile. "This situation, it's awkward, *non*? Working with the person you spent such a wonderful night—"

Simone held up a hand, stopping him. "I was there. I got it. I know, ah, I know what we did." Was she sweating? Suddenly, she looked as if she'd run a mile, and Alex couldn't help but be drawn to her.

"As do I. I think about it all the time, and I'm not one to deny myself pleasures in life, Simone. Are you?"

Chapter Twelve

SIMONE

SIMONE NEARLY CHOKED ON HER RESPONSE WITH THE WAY THE WORD *PLEASURES* rolled off Alex's tongue, wicked and filled with anticipation.

Now was the time to deal with the elephant on the court. She cleared her throat. "Well, I think there are *some* things I should deny myself, but that's not even the point here."

"Isn't it, though?"

"Alex, I'm your assistant coach now, and I think we can get past what happened between us. You know, move on like the mature adults we are." She lowered her voice. "It was just sex. Just one random night. There's no reason why we can't work together without any weird feelings. No awkwardness. No tension. Right?"

The corner of his mouth lifted, but then it fell. He studied her, those eyes glistening under the evening sky as he stepped closer. "*Oui*. No tension, *chérie*."

Relief washed over her, but then Alex leaned in and she could feel his body heat, sense his mouth just near her cheek. She realized that his demeanor had changed entirely, and when she looked up into his eyes, she saw the Alex who'd made her lose herself, the Alex who'd been so overwhelming that she'd cried out his name.

"I think we both know it wasn't just a random night." His voice felt husky and smooth as velvet against her skin. "Earlier, when I said I think about our time together? It's true. I think about it all the time, Simone. And I think you do too." He pulled back and met her eyes.

Simone swallowed down the breathless sigh inching its way up her throat. This man was going to be the end of her. She took another step back, placing much-needed distance between them. "Look, that kind of thing has to stop."

Because she had to resist him—there was no future for them. Not even one that consisted of casual sex like Amalie suggested. Simone had a job to do and a daughter who didn't need another man complicating her mother's life. It would only work to distract her from real life and the also very real responsibility of raising a child—mostly alone.

His expression turned innocent, and he held his hands out like he had no idea what she was talking about. "What kind of thing?"

She did a wild dance with her pointer finger, aiming it directly at all of him. "*That*. That sexy teasing thing you just did. Even the little suggestive stares you think no one sees. It all has to stop if any of this is going to work."

"Oh, so you think I'm sexy, huh?" His smile widened with a wicked tilt on one side. "If that's the case, you might miss my teasing and staring."

Simone's mouth opened and closed as he shot her a wink and turned on a heel toward his motorcycle. He paused, turning around. "But I'll stop. Because that's what you want, yes?"

No. The word popped into her mind instantaneously. She didn't want him to stop. She just didn't know how to let any of this continue.

"Yes." She forced the response out even if it was a lie.

He nodded once, firmly. "Alright then. Consider it done. No more teasing. No more staring. Just know that if you decide you rather like my attention, I'm here and wanting."

Then he strode off, climbing onto his bike.

Simone walked to her car, willing her pulse to slow. Alex Wilde wanted her.

God, she was in so much trouble.

SIMONE SUNK INTO THE CHAIR BEHIND THE DESK IN HER SHINY NEW OFFICE AT the Oliver Smoke Tennis Center and released a sigh that made her curl into herself. Ugh. She hadn't been able to sleep last night because she kept replaying her conversation with Alex. And when he'd mentioned wanting to meet Lula...well, Simone's heart went soft.

Then there was the issue of their one-night stand, shining like giant flashing arrows every time they looked at each other. Their conversation hadn't really cleared the air. As a matter of fact, it did the opposite, making her hot, unsettled. None of this was just going to go away. Alex had been *inside* her. Multiple times and multiple ways. That was one hell of a coach/player relationship.

Her phone rang, thankfully jolting her from her thoughts. Fumbling with her cell, she saw Arlo's name flash across the screen along with a silly picture of the two of them with Tallulah in the center, everyone sticking out their tongues. Simone expected a video chat with her daughter shortly, but she was glad to hear from her bestie. She looked at the clock on the wall—a cute one with tennis balls as the numbers and rackets as the hands. It was one in the afternoon in Scotland.

"Don't you have some work to do?" Simone hurried across the room and quietly closed her door for more privacy. This was about to be a very interesting chat that Paul did not need to overhear.

"I do, but I'm so excited I had to call— I just booked my return flight!" The sound of an empty can hitting the desk punctuated Arlo's comment. Arlo had been downing energy drinks while adjusting to the new time zone. Apparently, that hadn't changed.

Simone fought back a squeal. "When? I'll pick you up from the airport."

"September 14th. You know I need to get back and keep an eye on you. No telling what kind of trouble you'll get into around that sexy-talking tennis player."

Simone slid back into her chair and kept her voice down. "Whew, you have no idea. Alex is...a lot. And yet..." She let out a long breath, feeling a confession rising. "We kind of talked about that night."

Silence came from the other end of the line, followed by the popping of another drink tab. "Ha. I can't see how discussing the ol' pump and dump helped matters."

Simone could just imagine Arlo pushing up her tortoiseshell glasses, her blonde hair probably styled in a cute topknot.

"Arlo," Simone hissed, earning a chuckle from her friend. "It's not funny."

Arlo chugged her drink, swallowed, then spoke. "Okay, fine. It's not funny. But I knew this was bound to happen at some point. Although if you ask me, now that things are square, you should totally bang him again."

"Arlo!" Simone slanted back in her chair and let out an exasperated sigh. Yeah, Arlo was definitely the devil on her shoulder in nearly *all* scenarios.

"What? I don't see any rules saying you *can't.*"

"*My* rules say I can't. I can't be distracted by Alex right now. I'm starting my new career and can't get sidetracked by a gorgeous face—"

"And a hot body with a perfect ass and sexy tattoos."

Simone couldn't resist laughing at that, even as she admonished her friend. "Again, Arlo. Seriously?"

"Look, there are no rules saying you can't have sex with him for the fun of it as many times as you both consent. There's also no playbook for one-night stands. He knew it was one night. No strings." She paused. "And I'm pretty sure the issue here is he wants more than a one-and-done. Am I right?"

Simone went very still. If she told Arlo what Alex said last night, Simone would never hear the end of it. So for now, she kept that small bit to herself, close to her chest.

Regardless of how charming Alex was, she knew she had to make sure her relationship with Alex stayed on a platonic path, or this whole coaching thing would never work.

Simone sat up straighter, ready to tell her best friend exactly that when her phone beeped, Lula's adorable face popping onto the screen. "It's Lula Bug. Gotta go, but talk later?"

"Absolutely! Tell her I love her and miss her and that Aunt Arlo will see her soon. Bye!"

Simone clicked over, the phone going to video chat. "Hey, Lula!" She grinned.

"Are you wearing matching athletic gear?" Tallulah asked, her nose scrunched while she moved closer to the screen. Simone marveled at how much older her daughter looked, even though it'd only been a few weeks. "You look so cute, Mom."

She looked down at her outfit with a tight smile. She had *not* bought this outfit with Alex on her mind. Okay, that was a lie. Yet there was nothing wrong with wanting to look her best around a hot guy, right?

"Thanks, honey. How's camp?"

Tallulah's smile was slow and familiar, almost like looking in the mirror. The only DNA she'd inherited from Damien was his hair color, which was a lighter shade of brown, and then some of her facial expressions were his to a tee.

"It's good," Lula said, and a beat passed. "I looked up Alex Wilde on the ancient computer here. I think you'll be able to help him. If anyone can, it'll be you." If Arlo and Amalie were always supportive and cheered her on, then Lula was her official hype girl.

Simone laughed, but inside she was a mess. "Thanks. I hope so. Paul knows what he's doing too, you know."

Tallulah shrugged. "I know, but I just have this feeling is all."

"You sound way too mature right now." Simone's heart expanded. Tallulah hadn't thought her stepping down as Warner Hotels CEO was strange at all. Her exact words had been, "I bet you'll be happier."

"And, I decided that I want to learn tennis when I get home." Lula's face got closer to the screen again, her blue eyes large and round as she pushed her unruly curls away from her face.

"Oh yeah? We can do that."

"Great." She paused, her smile blinding. "And I want to meet Alex Wilde."

Simone blinked rapidly and coughed into her fist, trying to cover up her dismay. "Oh, really? Okay. We can, um, we can try to arrange that too."

This was bad. She couldn't say no, because there was no logical reason to deny Lula the chance to learn tennis tips from a pro athlete. It just seemed like Alex was going to infiltrate every part of her life one way or another, no matter how hard she tried to stop it.

Lula's brows pinched together. "You okay, Mom? You look weird."

"I always look weird," was her immediate response, which totally did not fit the situation and made Lula look even more suspicious.

"No, you don't. This is a special kind of weird. Like the way Sam looks when the cute boy from the south cabins talks to her."

Geez, this kid was too observant for her own good and quite the interrogator.

"Sam is eight," Simone said, wiping away the tiny beads of sweat that had formed on her upper lip. "And boys are bad. For now, anyway."

"Even Alex?" Lula giggled, everything about her glimmering with mischief. "He doesn't seem bad when you talk about him."

"Lula!" Simone mocked a stern look, although she failed to contain her laughter. "Yes, even Alex."

A knock came from Simone's door.

"Hey Lula Bug, call me again as soon as you can, okay? We'll continue this boy discussion later."

Tallulah nodded, followed by another tight-lipped giggle that was too cute for words. "Okay. Love you, Mom."

"I love you too, Bug." Simone blew a few kisses at the screen and hung up. "Come in," she called out, and Paul entered.

"I have my first assignment for you as an assistant coach if you're interested. If not, I can do it myself, but I thought it'd be good for you to learn in case one day you decide to branch out on your own."

"Hit me with it."

Paul barreled forward. "Would you get tapes of Alex's matches from the ATP? I'd like you to review them. It's how I learned to be a coach, and it'll build your confidence on the court with him too. At first, you may feel timid, but by getting comfortable with your player's style, you'll feel like you know what you're talking about during practice."

She tried not to think about watching hours' worth of Alex videos featuring his hot and sweaty muscles while attempting to scribble down anything of note. "ATP, Alex's matches, review, and notes. Got it. Anything else?"

Paul shoveled two pieces of gum into his mouth. "Nope, that should be it for now." He chewed slowly. "You ready for our first official practice?"

Her stomach twisted—more unknown territory. The kid's camp had been fun, and lessons with them the week before had been a trip. But this was different. Alex's career was on the line. No pressure or anything.

"As ready as I'll ever be."

"You'll be fine. I think you're a natural. I'll grab the water, and then I'll head out." He gestured to the doorway.

She gave him a thumbs up, immediately feeling ridiculous for doing that. Grabbing her notepad and sunglasses from the couch tucked away in the corner of the office, she decided she might as well head out to the court.

At the end of the hallway, she spotted Alex on the phone. Being the mature woman she was, of course, she dipped into an alcove, wondering what the hell she should do. She wasn't quite ready to face him yet, at least not without Paul as a buffer.

"Let's just say that old habits die hard," Alex spoke into his cell, his back to her. "I didn't exactly do things your way...and I may have told her I thought about our night all the time."

She snorted but quickly brought her hands over her mouth. Alex did a half-turn at the sound, and she jerked back into her hiding spot, practically holding her breath.

Alex huffed a chuckle into the phone. "Subtlety is not my strong suit, but I'll give it a shot. Look, I need to get to the court. I'll try to do as you mentioned. *Salut.*"

Simone pressed against the wall even harder, squeezing her eyes shut as if that would help her disappear. Footsteps moved *toward* her instead of away.

Then there was another set.

"Simone? What are you doing hiding out here?" Paul asked.

Simone opened one eye, squinting at him and...*Alex.* Alex who had the world's sexiest smirk curled across his lips. Because of course he did.

Alex tilted his head, his words tinged with laughter. "It seems like the perfect place to eavesdrop, wouldn't you agree?"

Paul looked between them, confused. "I don't know about that. I've found it's best to eavesdrop over there." He pointed further down the hall. She wanted to ask just who exactly Paul had snooped on, but she was currently in the process of dying of mortification.

She blurted out the first thing that came to mind. "I actually came to talk to you about the tournaments."

Alex watched her with a wicked smile and an arched brow. She felt the need to fill the silence, even gesturing that they start walking to get as far away from the scene of the crime as possible. But he didn't budge.

Simone continued. "Not my fault I happened across your very loud conversation." As she so often did in the boardroom, Simone lifted her chin and adopted a mask of calm indifference. It took effort.

Alex leaned in, the scent of him, a woodsy warmth, threatening to scramble her brain. She swallowed, waiting for his next move.

His voice dropped to a whisper that was better suited for the bedroom. "Tournaments, *chérie*? Nice save."

His words might've well been '*I want to fuck you*, because the velvety, between-the-sheets delivery caused her heart to stutter. Paul set the cooler down in the middle of the hallway. "Tournaments, huh? I guess we should talk about that."

They really were about to have a meeting at the scene of her eavesdropping crime, and she couldn't melt into the floor. So many things whirred around her brain—Alex had been talking to someone about *her*. She had to admit she was curious what his attempts at subtlety would be like, especially since he confessed it wasn't his thing. But nope, no. She couldn't. She would remain steadfast—eyes on the prize and all that.

Alex moved his bag so he could cross his arms. "I've signed up for Cincinnati. I have to compete in the qualifying rounds in order to make it into the tournament, but I think I can do that. My goal is the US Open, to beat Bastien."

Yuck. The thought of Bastien made her skin crawl.

Paul shook his head. "Nope. We're not doing that. I think you need to take time off from tournaments and work on getting your head back in the game." He looked over at Simone. "What do you think?"

Easy. This was something she'd been thinking about, preparing for. "I think that's the right call for now. I see no need to rush."

Alex's shoulders snapped up to his ears. When he spoke, he bit off his words between his teeth. "But I have to play Cincinnati. *Non*, I *need* to."

"It's not going to work. I can tell by watching your matches online that you're not ready. I'll cancel your entry to Cincy. Now let's get out there," Paul said, pointing to the doors leading to the court, "and practice to change it. Maybe then you can make the Australian Open your goal instead."

"Fine." Alex gave them both a curt nod, and when he turned to leave, Simone almost felt bad. She'd just watched one of his dreams get crushed right before her eyes, and all she could think to herself was, *Welcome to coaching.*

Chapter Thirteen

SIMONE

AFTER TWO AND A HALF WEEKS OF PRACTICES, SIMONE HAD DONNED A NEW determination regarding Alex. She could totally handle this. Handle Alex. She'd CEO'd an entire company, for crying out loud. This? Not giving in to the temptation known as Alex Wilde? She had it in the bag...or so she hoped.

They didn't call Alex "The Wilde Card" for nothing.

She shifted her attention to Paul's last drill of the day, which was *rough*.

"Hit the running forehands up the line," he called out to a huffing Alex.

Alex was in great shape—she knew all too well, so that wasn't an aspect of training they needed to work on. That was just the nature of the drill. The thing was, Alex kept missing balls even after chasing each of them down like a dog. He just wasn't connecting.

When Paul called an end to practice, Alex shuffled to the bench and bent over, a little winded. Pouring with sweat, he looked at Paul and then Simone. "This isn't working right now. I can't push the ball up the line like I want. It all feels off."

Simone remembered those days from when she played in high school. There were times when she couldn't get into any rhythm. From the looks of it, Alex had just experienced that.

Paul took off his hat and ran a hand across his glistening forehead. It felt like they were standing inside a pressure cooker on that court. "Oh, you got this, kid. Maybe we keep going, and you hang with it?"

Alex looked like he'd rather gouge his eyes out with his fingernails.

"*Non*. We're done for the day." Alex ran a hand over his face, sweat falling from his hair.

His thin, white shirt clung to his body, each hard ridge on clear display beneath it like little bricks.

Simone curled her fingers into a fist as she tried not to think about what it was like to run her hands over his damp body.

Nope. Don't think about that.

Instead, she tapped her chin and tried to think about tennis and strategy. Paul coached Alex like he'd coached Julian, yet there was a contrast between the two men. Julian played aggressively, as did a lot of American players. Canadian and French players were also aggressive but often in a more calculated way.

Alex usually played like he made love, with masterful finesse and moments of sheer, unadulterated power, but from the short time she'd watched him on the court, she could see why he'd sought a coach. He'd lost that. Unlike in the bedroom, Alex didn't take chances on the court, didn't crush the ball each time.

Now Julian? He smashed every single ball because it was natural for him. Alex wasn't as offensive in his play, and Paul saw that as a weakness and was attempting to cull it from his player's playbook. Why else would he be pushing Alex to complete these useless drills?

Simone wanted to speak up, but to say what, exactly? She didn't have an answer right now, and when she *did* offer her two cents, she wanted to be confident in her suggestions. She was onto something though. She'd watched several of Alex's matches online while she waited for the tapes from the ATP. Slowly, she'd begun brainstorming a few drills of her own.

Paul strolled over to his bag. "That's fine by me, but listen, this is just August. We have plenty of time since we've decided not to go after Cincy."

Alex faced Paul, tension snapping taut in every muscle. The decision to forgo that tournament was still a sore spot between the two. "I don't have plenty of time. I'm almost thirty. I'm not Roger Federer or Rafael Nadal. I can almost assure you that I won't be good enough to keep playing until I'm forty. It's now or never."

"I get that, trust me, I do, but you're not ready now. I say we take our time with this. I'll see you both bright and early tomorrow." Paul slung Big Bird over his shoulder and sauntered off, leaving Simone alone with a gorgeous and very angry tennis player.

"*Calice.*" He dragged his fingers through his hair, ripping out the elastic that held it back at the nape of his neck.

"Hey, you okay?" she asked. She should've followed Paul. She wasn't responsible for Alex's emotions, she knew that, but damn if she didn't want to make him feel better.

"*J'ai le feu au cul,*" he bit out. "*Non*, I mean, I'm pissed off. This is not what I had planned. I needed to play Cincinnati, the US Open." He released a long-suffering sigh. "None of this is working like I thought, and I wonder..." He paused. "I wonder if I made a mistake?"

Alex shoved his things into his tennis bag and swung it over his shoulder, making his way toward the clubhouse. Simone's feet, having a mind of their own, had her trailing close behind. Something he'd said struck her, and watching him deflate as he questioned if he'd made a mistake, well, it kind of broke her heart. She could relate to what he was feeling with the whole move from CEO to tennis coach. Was it a mistake? Would she make any sort of difference in Alex's game?

"I feel like you're following me," Alex tried to joke as he looked over his shoulder, slowing his walk. The attempt felt flat compared to the Alex she'd grown accustomed to. The humor didn't quite reach his eyes.

She offered him a small smile, catching up to him as they stepped inside the building. "It's just that...I wanted to talk to you. Anyone can see that today was a struggle, and I *am* your assistant coach."

He raised both brows, stopping right outside the locker room door. "Would you like to wait out here for me then, or...?" He pushed on the door, revealing an empty locker room.

Simone shrugged and entered. Alex dropped his bag on the nearest bench and moved closer to her, though he blessedly kept a respectful distance.

"Talk," he said, cutting a look at Simone that shouldn't have made her stomach clench, but any command coming from that mouth had a way of rattling her. "I'm listening."

Simone steeled her spine, resolved to keep her thoughts on the issue at hand. "Out there," she gestured toward the door, "you wondered if you made a mistake by coming here, and I wanted you to know that I don't think you did. I think..."

Her words died on her tongue when, without warning, Alex grabbed his shirt by the back of the neck and whipped it off in one fluid, sexy motion. Simone's mouth went dry at the sight of his naked flesh, the tattoos, the trail of hair she'd caught sight of earlier.

Every cognitive thought she'd had just flew out the window.

Alex gave her a knowing look like he was reading every filthy memory that just rushed to the forefront of her mind. A gentle ache settled heavy between her thighs. Why was *normal* so ridiculously difficult when it came to being around Alex Wilde?

He tossed his shirt aside, his eyes never leaving hers, and she became hyper-aware that they were *very* alone, the tension between them thick enough to taste.

"What's wrong, Simone?" Alex's stare trailed her body, up and down, and he inhaled.

Oh, she wanted to melt right then. He had to know exactly what was wrong.

She rocked back and forth on her heels and rested her hands on her hips, considering bolting out the door to escape this moment. "Um, nothing. Nothing at all. I was just saying you did a brave thing by coming here. That's all."

Something softened in his stare, his voice matching. "That's nice of you to say. It's almost like... something a friend would say."

"Is that so?"

He stared at her, then shook his head. "I think we can be friends, don't you? Surely we can manage that."

Friends. She didn't know if it was possible to just be friends with a man like Alex Wilde. But she wanted to try.

She held out her hand. "Deal. Friends it is."

He smiled again and cut an eye at her outstretched hand before he took it in his own.

"Not going to mention what happened the last time we made a deal." He swept his thumb over her pulse point, a featherlight touch that ignited a flame in her core.

In an attempt to appear unaffected, she rolled her eyes, and Alex let go, taking a step back.

"Speaking of *friendly* things..." The gleam in his eye said otherwise. "I need to unwind, preferably somewhere with drinks. Any suggestions?" Alex appeared hopeful.

She bit her lip, thinking. "There's a fun place called The Roof downtown. It's on top of Ponce City Market. That's where I go when I need to let off some steam. It has everything—mini-golf, drinks, food."

"Hmm." The way he studied her, it looked like he was brewing up some idea. "Come with me. Our first date. As friends."

"Not a date," she shot back, crossing her arms. "I can be your friend, but first and foremost, I'm your assistant coach, remember? Things have to remain professional."

The corners of his mouth quirked up. "Of course, I understand. So is that a yes?" He looked away, digging a towel out of his bag.

"Yes, but for research only."

A dark, rumbly chuckle tumbled from Alex's lips. "Really?" He moved the towel over his torso and scrubbed the sweat from his hair before peering at her from the corner of his eye. "Research, huh?"

"Absolutely. One-on-one research."

Oh God. Had she actually just said that?

She didn't miss the way Alex's gaze darted up to meet hers, his mouth doing that sexy tilty thing. She needed out of there and fast.

"*Chérie*, with you, I excel at one-on-one research."

Simone arched her brow, although her body grew heated just thinking about that so-called *research*. If she were to speak, she'd probably breathe flames.

Thankfully, Alex saved her from further embarrassing herself.

"I'll meet you there at eight, Simone." He chunked his towel in the locker room hamper, grabbed his bag, and started walking away backward, shirtless and mouthwateringly beautiful, his lips still crooked at the corners. Her heart fluttered against her rib cage like the disloyal bastard it was.

"Make that five o'clock since it's Wednesday night. I have a FaceTime call with Lula at eight," she answered, wondering what the hell she'd just gotten herself into.

Chapter Fourteen

ALEX

ALEX WAITED OFF TO THE SIDE IN FRONT OF A HUGE ELEVATOR AND A NEON sign shouting ROOF in yellow. Next to it stood a sign that read "Come on Up!" that was so essentially Southern—and maybe a bit Canadian too, in the way of hospitality. Skyline Park, found on the roof of the Ponce City Market, intrigued him the moment Simone mentioned it, but not more than getting to spend a little alone time with her outside the confines of the center and a third party in Paul.

He took a cab there, not wanting to take any chances of not being able to find his way. Simone texted that she was doing the same and would be there any minute. Satisfaction rolled through him as he looked around, noticing the vibe starting to change at the place. More children and families were exiting the elevator, quickly replaced with a twenty-one and up crowd.

"Hey!" Simone appeared in front of him, looking like a vision.

She'd styled her short, black hair the same way she had the night they met at his party—straight, no fuss, yet sexy. He tried to be gentlemanly as he scanned her outfit, picking apart tiny details and saving them. Details such as the fact that she wore wide, black dress pants with a grey knotted top showing the slightest hint of her stomach. More than anything, he wanted to brush his knuckles across the smooth skin there, to watch her eyes widen in delight. He bit his lip at the thought and continued his leisurely study.

Her makeup was different from her usual—darker eyes, redder lips. *Alors*, she'd put effort into her look, which meant she liked Alex more than she'd let on. He could work with that. He almost slipped up in the locker room earlier but remembered that he had to do things differently with Simone. Or at least *attempt* to.

The last thing he wanted to do was scare her away, especially seeing how concern had etched her face after a terrible practice.

"You look beautiful, Simone." He wanted to pull her in for a hug, but her shoulders were already rigid and tight.

Criss, it was a miracle she'd even shown up.

She wagged a finger at him. "There will be none of that, Alex. I'm here in purely a need-to-know capacity."

"Need-to-know?"

"As in, I need to know you and your game better. You're my test run in case I decide to make this my long-term goal."

"Is that something you're interested in? There will be no going back to Warner Hotels?"

Simone canted her head, her fingers tightening on the strap of her purse. "So you did your research like I expected you would. I'm impressed." Each word was filled to the seams with a forced sort of brightness that threatened to crumble each syllable. "I don't know. I like knowing the possibility is there, and if it were to disappear, I'd probably freak out. But also, I've enjoyed working at the tennis center, so there's that. My father is keeping my position open for me for at least a year in case I fail spectacularly." Her arms went stiffer than they already were.

"I get the feeling that you don't fail at anything, *chérie*." He wanted to wrap her in his arms and comfort her, but instead he kept talking, hoping it would help ease her mind. "What you're feeling is understandable. You've made a huge life decision, and when it's all you've ever known, it can be terrifying."

He'd also seen the pictures of Damien's cheating scandal, had read the countless articles during his research. It'd proven to him even further that Simone was not one for a flashy, in-your-face approach. Low-key was the way to go, which gave him an idea, so he continued.

"We came here to unwind, so why don't we put aside everything else? Put aside your fears, and I'll put aside mine. And tonight, we don't have to be coach and player. We can be, as we agreed in the locker room, friends who enjoy each other's company." And bodies, but she would've bolted had he said that out loud. "Everything will still be there tomorrow, and I can help you carry any of it if it gets to be too much, *oui*?"

Usually, he ran screaming in the opposite direction of anything remotely close to offering to be an emotional support system, probably because he struggled to deal with his own baggage. But his goals hadn't changed—in both tennis and his assistant coach.

As Simone looked around at the people coming in and out of the elevator—couples laughing, children running—wistfulness painted in broad strokes across her delicate features.

"That sounds so idealist, and although that was the Simone you met in Canada, it's not the real me. I'm more practical—"

"No, you're not. The façade of yourself, sure? But the Simone I know takes chances, and I'm not even telling you that because I'm interested in you. It's the truth." Her lips twisted to the side in that thinking way of hers, and he took the opportunity to point to the roof. "With that said, should we begin our night?"

She eyed the open elevator, then Alex, then the elevator again. "Fine. Tonight we have fun and still work on tennis stuff."

Alex extended his arm to her, and she bit down a smile. Whether she wished to admit it, she appeared to have a thing for him, her shoulders losing some of their rigidness at his words.

And then a thought uncharacteristic of Alex Wilde flashed in his mind. He wanted to make tonight about her, *for* her. It was clear she still had some concerns about her job transition, which he could only imagine. He didn't want to pile onto her problems, but that didn't mean he'd be completely passive either.

They crowded inside the packed elevator, forced closer together than they'd been in entirely too long. Alex maneuvered around the other passengers, using his body as a shield to keep Simone from most of the jostling. "Thank you," Simone mouthed, even as her arm brushed his by accident, the contact jolting him.

The ride up felt longer than it should have—Alex too aware her body grazing his. When another passenger shifted, it forced Simone into his side, and his arm twitched with the need to wrap around her waist and tug her into his protective embrace. Of course, he didn't, and when the doors opened to their floor, he let out an audible sigh of relief.

Glancing down, he noticed she, too, appeared flustered, the tips of her ears washed in red. At least it hadn't just been him dying in there.

They were the last to exit the elevator, and against his better instincts, Alex reached out and placed his hand on the small of her back. She shuddered at the contact, and he tried not to revel in the heat from her body—that teasing sliver of bare skin, thanks to her slightly short shirt.

Alex took in a deep inhale, thankful they were outside. He needed space from her. Being this close, feeling her so near, made him want to drag her back into that elevator and do things he was pretty sure she wouldn't mind but wasn't ready for.

Yet.

Simone twirled out of his hold, the bulb lights and hazy, orange-tinged sky illuminating her like a Grecian goddess. "Welcome to Skyline Park."

Alex couldn't quite take everything in—and there was a lot. It held many vintage amusements like Skee-Ball, Break-A-Plate, and mini-golf, alongside a ride that dropped people straight down. It reminded him of Coney Island a little, at least of what he'd seen in photographs of the historic Brooklyn landmark.

"This is incredible."

Simone already seemed lighter, the views of Atlanta behind her something worthy of a postcard. She seemed pleased that he liked her recommendation, causing lightning to crackle between them. She eyed him carefully, her tongue running across her red lips before her gaze lowered to his mouth.

"I know how much you enjoy a challenge, so I figured this place was perfect for you."

He grinned at her, the memory of their tennis bet rushing back to him. Like on that night, she was slowly starting to relax around him.

"Come on. Show me where to start."

"Well, that's easy. Allow me to dominate you in Putt-Putt."

Alex winked. "*Oui, s'il te plait.*" Simone still looked slightly nervous, so he had to think of something to keep the night from going off the rails.

"But why don't we grab a drink first?" He pointed to a bar called The Sideshow.

She slumped in relief. "God, yes, please. Lead the way."

They waited in line, Simone trying to pay, but Alex beat her to it. Once they grabbed their drinks, they headed to colorful tables off to the side of the walk-up bar and took a seat.

Simone carefully placed her drink on the table, folding her hands in her lap and wasting zero time. "So maybe we should talk about tennis?"

"Whatever you like." He took a sip of his beer to hide his disappointment.

"Well, that *was* the sole purpose of our night out on the town. Tennis coaching stuff."

It sounded as though she was reminding herself of that fact more so than Alex.

"Ah, yes. Tennis business, where you dissect Alex's brain. Definitely not a date."

Her cheeks went red. "Right. Not a date. And I'm not trying to dissect you."

He gave her a sidelong look, not believing that for a moment.

"Okay, okay." She pinched her pointer finger and thumb together. "Maybe just a little? I can't help you or your game if I can't get into your head."

He had to laugh at that. "Oh, you're in my head, *ma chérie*. Believe me."

He couldn't get rid of her if he tried.

Their eyes met, and all the air rushed from his lungs. Gazing into her eyes was akin to the rush he felt on the court, and his pulse soared as he lost himself in her pools of bright blue.

Simone looked away first, breaking the spell. Lifting her drink, she took a hurried sip, her fingers strangling the glass.

"Right." She cleared her throat. "Well, um, maybe tell me why you were so dead set on playing Cincinnati and the US Open so much? I think we should talk about it."

He brushed his thumb across his chin and winced. *Merde*. Simone was one of his coaches, and maybe explaining some of his history would help his game, although the last thing he wanted to do was talk about his horrible excuse of a stepfamily.

As she peered at him through her lashes, something shifted in his chest.

Alex shook his head, not believing that he planned to pour out his childhood damages on a crowded American rooftop, yet he'd pretty much do anything Simone asked when she looked at him like that.

"Bastien's playing the US Open, and all I want to do is beat him. I want to watch his face crumple when he loses to *me*." He released a sigh as he pictured Bastien and his little weasel eyes, his narrow nose. Bastien's mother's nose. "He's very adamant that the press knows we're not related by blood—he is his mother's son in that way. We were never close, even when my dad was alive. I can't remember my mom much—she died when I was five, but dad and I were a team until...we weren't. Once he met Claudette, that was all he cared about. Sent me off to the tennis academy where he wouldn't have to deal with me. He died when I was sixteen, and my stepmother inherited everything. She stopped my funding at Archambeau and everything."

Simone's brows slammed down, everything about her thoroughly incensed. "*Why*? Who does that? If she loved your dad at all, she should've looked out for you."

He rested his head in his hand and turned to look at the gorgeous woman next to him, his knee bumping hers. The contact grounded him.

"I don't think she loved him. I know he loved her more than anything or anyone, including me, and I'm not saying that for sympathy or pity. It's simply a fact. Now she spends everything on Bastien, hell-bent on making him a better tennis player than me. Although at first, he didn't even want to play the sport." He tried to laugh to pretend that none of it truly hurt, that it wasn't the reason he kept everyone at arm's length, with precious few ever breaking the barrier.

"So what happened at the academy? Did you stay or...?"

"Thankfully, Rhys's parents talked to the owner, who agreed to let me remain at the academy until I turned pro at eighteen, free of charge. The only thing I couldn't do was take classes, which was when I started teaching myself, devouring any book on any subject I could get my hands on."

"I hope you know it was their loss."

He swallowed down the rising emotion. He'd heard those same words from the mouths of others countless times, but coming from her, they meant the world.

He shrugged, ready to move on to the next topic. Simone tilted her head, studying him. It was similar to how she looked at him on the court, but it wasn't entirely calculated. *Non.* She gazed at him as if seeing him for the very first time.

"So why tennis? Why do you love it?" she asked, her voice softer, surprisingly hesitant.

Like he'd done in countless interviews in the past, Alex's first response was to brush the question off. But as he sat back, crossing his arms over his chest, he realized that the answer he always gave was a canned answer, one for the public to consume and go about their day.

He always said tennis was his life. Why wouldn't he love it? And while that was true, tennis was more than that, deeper than that.

When he looked up, he wasn't seeing the stunning Atlanta skyline or the rooftop or the exquisite woman next to him. Instead, he was on the court, moving, working, living.

"There's something pure about tennis. It's just you out there with no one else to rely on as you get locked into a battle with your opponent. It's beautiful." The smile that had slowly started to curl across his lips faded. "Although some days, like today, even these past few months, I feel as though the magic has left me." He sat up straighter. "Other days, I could just hit the ball back and forth, rallying, for hours. Not trying to win the point but just enjoying the artistry of the game, the strategy. But I know that won't win matches."

Eagerness danced across Simone's lovely face as she scooted forward. "It can though. Going out and being aggressive isn't the only way to win, you know."

"But if I continue to play like I do, if I'm not locked in a strategy, I can lose quickly. That's the problem with my game—it's not built for hitting winning shots. I like to think, to analyze—"

"Like playing chess."

"Exactly. That's the best analogy. And I came here thinking if I could just find a scrap of that magic, if I could learn to play aggressively like Julian, like Paul, then maybe…"

"I get that, but I think you're going about it all wrong, because you can't play like someone else. Aggressive play isn't you. That's that." She shrugged. "So that leads me to my next question." She paused, shifting uncomfortably in her seat. "As one of your coaches, I'm asking you what *you* want out of this arrangement."

He offered her a crooked grin. "I think you know what I want."

"Yeah, you've made that loud and clear," she said, smiling as she shook her head. "Your persistence? It's something that should be a part of your game. Just be *in* it, immerse yourself. Do it. All those things, you know?"

She set him up for it, and he could not help what came out of his mouth next.

"So are you telling me I shouldn't hold back? Because if that's the case, I can certainly think of a few things I'd like to *immerse* myself in." He'd done so well up until this point too, but he didn't regret a thing.

Simone's eyes narrowed. "Damn it, Alex. Fine. You want to talk about sex? Let's talk about it then, shall we?"

Alex choked on his drink. *Merde.*

When Simone spoke again, her words were a mixture of humor and irritation. "That's right. I said it. When we had sex, you used all of your moves. You were *incredibly* detailed." She dropped her voice, looking around. "In bed, I felt your brute power. I liked it rough, and not one moment during that night did I feel like you were holding yourself back. You used everything in your arsenal to make sure I, that I, ah, won, so to speak."

Simone sat back in her chair, appraising him, and Alex was content not to speak for possibly the first time in his entire life. Thoughts swirled so quickly in his mind he struggled to form any sort of reply. A shiver raced down his spine, warmth effusing his chest. Of course, he recalled that night and how vocal she was when she, ah, *won*. His cock strained against the fabric of his jeans with the recollection.

"In the bedroom, you aren't missing a single thing. You know what you're doing. It's like art. But your tennis game is not. It's almost as if you're timid and even frozen sometimes, like you don't know what to do and you don't trust yourself. I've also watched you back away from a challenge on the court a few times, but not with sex. At least you didn't with me. I could tell you loved the challenge, loved seeing if I would sleep with you. And then you were intent on making sure you were the best sex I'd ever had. You relished that role. Do that with tennis. Immerse yourself in the game like you did with me. Does that make sense?"

He'd been the best sex of her life? *Maudit.*

Alex pressed a fist to his mouth, his brows raised high, then blinked a few times before finally responding. "It does." He rested his elbows on the table, looking her in the eyes as she took a sip of her drink. Simone was entirely too pleased with herself.

"Good. Glad to know that if I ever need to get through to you, sex is the way to do it." She shook her head, biting back a smile.

Alex smirked. "Sex is *always* the way to get through to me."

"Of course it is." Simone rolled her eyes. "While I'm sure you'd like nothing more than to continue this particular…conversation, how about that game of Putt-Putt?"

Alex smiled. Simone was an expert at deflecting. He simply took it as a challenge to break down her walls.

An hour later and Simone had destroyed Alex in mini-golf. He didn't mind, especially when her smile illuminated the rooftop, a spark he'd yet to see flashing in her eyes. He'd never glimpsed a smile so dazzling, and it nearly stopped his heart. He knew their time together was winding down and he hated it. They walked past an assortment of carnival games that drew both of their attention.

"When I was in high school, I used to dream about having a boyfriend who'd take me to the fair. I'd be wrapped up in his jacket, smelling of his cologne, and so ridiculously in love. Did you ever do things like that with someone?" Simone's face contorted, and she held up a hand. "Oh my God. Forget I said that." A nervous giggle tripped off her lips.

This was yet another piece of Simone Warner, and he tucked it away with all the other little details he'd obtained since July. He stopped walking and faced her.

"I like learning these things about you." He stared off into the Atlanta skyline. "But *non*, I never did anything quite so…sweet. I never even had a girlfriend." It was his turn to laugh, although his sounded wistful rather than embarrassed. Would he have turned out differently? It didn't matter now. "Did your boyfriend not take you to the fair?"

Because if you were mine, I would.

Where had that come from? The thought nearly made him lose his footing, but thankfully, Simone hadn't noticed.

Instead she looked at the booths again, a sadness permeating her eyes and bleeding into her voice. "I didn't have time for a boyfriend in high school. I was too busy studying to be the best." She spared her watch a quick glance. "Oh God. I didn't realize how late it was. I really should get home so I can chat with Lula on time. Do you want to split a cab?"

Anything to prolong his time with her.

"I'd love to."

His gaze snagged on something, just over her shoulder, and he had to tamp down the grin that begged to build across his lips. He pretended to pat his jeans. His years of pretending were finally going to pay off.

"I think I lost something."

Simone stilled. "Oh, do you want me to help you look?" She craned her neck, her eyes perusing his ass before she caught herself.

Alex suppressed his smile, all too pleased by her roaming eyes. He could've said something, but instead he tried to preserve whatever truce they'd found.

He waved her off. "No, I'm good. I'll be down in a minute."

She looked uncertain, but he urged her onward, and he remained frozen until he was sure she'd gotten on the elevator. Not wasting time, he headed to the Break-A-Plate booth laden with stuffed animals on a high shelf. He had set his eye on the large, multicolored butterfly.

Five minutes later, he walked off the lift, searching the crowd for Simone. It didn't take long to find her off to the side, near the street, typing on her phone.

A foreign sensation swooped in his stomach, almost like a fluttering.

Mon Dieu, a woman had never made him feel that way before.

He clutched the stuffed animal tighter as he stepped into her line of sight.

"Fancy meeting you here," he joked, suddenly feeling a little nervous.

Simone looked up at him, eyes dropping to the butterfly. A small smile played around the edges of her mouth.

"That's adorable. Where did you get it?"

"From that Break-A-Plate booth." His words came out a little raspier than intended. He cleared his throat, handing the stuffed animal to her, a current stretching between them and nearly tethering them together. Once Simone took the butterfly, he fisted his hands into his pockets and leaned back on his heels. "It's for you."

He'd rendered Simone speechless, one of her hands cradling the stuffed animal against her body, the other pressed to her chest.

"For me?" she finally echoed.

Had she never received something so spur of the moment? Clearly Damien had no idea what kind of woman he had.

Alex nodded in answer to her question and tried to explain his reasoning, hoping he didn't completely terrify her.

"Butterflies represent rebirth and transformation. You're undergoing this right now in your own life, and I thought it would remind you how lovely and strong you are. How proud you should be of everything you've done."

"Alex." His name was barely a whisper as she studied the butterfly, and he swore her eyes were glassy. "I love it. So much. Thank you."

So many other emotions wanted to bubble up, but he settled for nonchalance. At least for right now. "It's nothing."

"It is *not* nothing. Come here." And then she wrapped her arms around his neck.

Alex let his hands hover around her back for a moment, taken by surprise. How funny that all he'd wanted was to get his hands on Simone's body again, and yet now he didn't know what to do. He would've laughed, but instead he held her around her waist, pulling her slightly closer.

She moved so that her words were at his ear, sending a shiver through him. "Thank you. I mean it."

When he drew back, he accidentally nuzzled her cheek with his nose, and the gasp that tumbled from her lips made him want to kiss her on the spot. Her wide eyes were on his, and those red, pouty lips beckoned. What would she do if he were to dip his head just a little lower?

Fuck. She zeroed in on his mouth, her tongue darting out to wet her lips. He leaned in, catching the hitch in her breath. Her hand went for his bicep, lightly grasping it, holding him in place, holding him close to her. He studied her upturned face, wondering if she could see everything he felt right there in his stare. She swayed closer, fingers tightening in response. She'd seen it all and wasn't scared. Maybe this was his chance then?

A horn honked right next to them, startling them apart.

Simone blinked several times as though awakening from a dream.

Stepping out of his embrace, she cleared her throat and said, "Cab's here."

If it had been another minute later, what would have happened? Would she have let him kiss her? He'd been seconds away from grabbing the nape of her neck and yanking her to him, devouring her lips the way he'd been envisioning this entire evening.

Alex tried not to think about it as he piled into the small car with Simone. Besides, they still had some time left.

Might as well make the most of it.

Chapter Fifteen

SIMONE

SIMONE CLUTCHED THE BUTTERFLY IN HER LAP AS THE CAB FLEW THROUGH Atlanta, the city lights streaking across the window in a blur. Damien had never done anything so sweet, had never been so...poetic about it. He sent her flowers on all the right days, but this? This gesture from Alex came straight from the heart, and it weakened Simone's already struggling defenses.

Sitting cramped in the back of a car didn't help matters either—not when she could shift and touch him or inhale his cologne. The left side of her arm smelled like him, and she knew that long after they'd parted, she'd sniff it—sorry, no shame.

The cabdriver spoke up, shattering the silence in the car as he looked at Alex in his rearview mirror. "Hey man, once we get there, do you mind getting out at her stop, since you two know each other and your stop is so close?"

Oh yeah, they'd talked about how Amalie set him up with a rental nearby—the drive would take no time.

The cabbie continued, "I just got a big-money pickup from the airport, and it'd help me out a lot."

"That's not a problem at all." Alex paused, looking over at her. "If that's okay with you?"

"Sure," she answered as she avoided his stare.

Simone ran her hands over the plush butterfly again, a sort of dread taking up residence in her chest, her stomach, her mind—everywhere. While she loved the butterfly and adored the meaning behind it, it just further proved that Alex wanted more than she could give.

They needed to focus on tennis, not the sparks that flew every time she was near him.

A frown tugged at her lips as she studied the stuffed animal and that feeling of dread tightened its iron fist.

Alex gently knocked her knee with his. "You okay?"

She swallowed, hating that she had to be the one to do this, to put that space between them here. "I feel like I can't get my thoughts in order when I'm around you."

His brow furrowed. "What do you mean?"

Simone lifted a shoulder. "I mean, tonight probably wasn't a good idea."

"Why would you say that?"

"You know why, Alex." She paused. "I mean, I love this butterfly and the heart behind it and will treasure it, but tonight just made things even messier for me. I see you, I want you—"

"Ah! So you *do* want me. I knew it." He ran a hand through his hair, his bicep flexing with the movement. "I just don't understand why we cannot live in the moment like we did back in Canada?"

"Well, for one, we're not there. That was a totally different type of situation for me and so is this. We just...we just can't."

Alex stroked his bearded chin, eyes narrowed. "Simone, what are you so afraid of?"

Irritation simmered in her veins, heating up every single part of her body. She should absolutely just let it go, but she couldn't.

She turned so quickly in the back seat of the cab that she hit her knees on the seat. She hissed out a curse, jolting Alex, whose long frame was nothing short than looking like a twisted-up pretzel.

If her knee wasn't throbbing she would've found it comical, watching him watch her with this knowing little look, with his knees almost to his chest. As it was, it just irritated her even more.

She rubbed her poor knee. "I'll have you know that I am not afraid of anything here, Alexander Wilde."

Lies.

Alex scoffed, attempting to move his body, finally angling toward her.

He pinned her to the spot with his glare. "Is that so? Why are you shutting down then? I can see it in your face, in the way your lips are set —" He reached forward, and his thumb traced the outer corners, sending a bolt of lust to her core.

She wanted to scream at her body to get the memo and work in tandem with her brain, because now was so not the time.

Simone shook her head. "You know what? I almost wish I'd never agreed to help Paul. Maybe I should just quit pretending I can coach you."

She clenched her jaw and met the cabbie's horrified stare in the rearview mirror.

"You don't mean that, Simone."

Something cracked in her chest at the tone of his voice. She could lie, tell him she did mean it, one hundred percent, but something held her back. It was probably the fact that their night together, a simple little non-date, had butterflies swarming in her stomach.

If things were different, he could've been the perfect man for her.

She crossed her arms over her chest, leaning back against the seat with a huff.

She spoke to the ceiling but could feel the weight of Alex's stare on her. "I didn't mean it. I lied. I'm a freaking liar. I'm glad I'm doing this. I just wish I knew how to act around you. My emotions are all over the place."

Warm, steady fingers intertwined with hers, causing her to straighten. "For what it's worth, I feel the same way. I've never had a woman get me so twisted up inside. *Mon Dieu*, the things you say and do..." His words trailed off and he shook his head, his lips curving slightly.

She tightened her fingers around his. "I know what you mean."

Alex scooted closer, threading his hand through her hair, his palm cupping her cheek. "If you do, then you'll know that I'm dying to kiss you right now."

The cabbie snorted, rolling his eyes in the mirror, causing Simone and Alex to quietly laugh, but they didn't move.

She angled her body closer. "Then you'll know I'm dying for you to actually do it. Any day now is fine."

The look he gave her warmed her all the way to her core. It reminded her of beach days when she welcomed the sun on her skin.

Alex's mouth hovered over hers as he tucked her hair behind her ear, his fingertips caressing her jaw. He shot her a heart-stopping grin and then his mouth was on hers.

They'd kissed before, but that had been almost feverish. Now they actually knew each other. That made the kiss even sweeter, hotter in her mind.

Her hands mimicked his, one grasping at his hair, fingering the soft strands.

The pressure of Alex's lips was heavenly. Simone pressed her hand against his firm chest, trailing along the curved muscle there. Alex stuttered a gasp into her mouth, deepening the kiss.

"I want you, Simone."

"I want you too, Alex."

The sound of an irritated cough broke them apart, but Alex never let go of Simone's hand, and he didn't look away from her until the car pulled up in front of Simone's house. Alex got out of the car and helped her out.

He watched her with a silent understanding. They both knew exactly what was about to happen.

Trembling, half with nervousness and half with desire, she paid the driver on her phone, and she and Alex made their way to the front door.

"Well, we're here," she announced, dizzy with awareness. The porch light reflected in Alex's brown eyes, glinting almost wickedly. This man was so much trouble. But recently, on her path of self-discovery, she realized she liked trouble—a lot.

"*Oui.*" He scanned her from head to toe and took a step closer, lust bright in his stare.

She audibly swallowed, and by some sheer miracle she was able to speak. "Are you sure?" she asked, her voice only wavering the slightest bit.

"I'm positive."

And then they collided.

Lips crashed, and hands were everywhere. Simone's purse fell to the porch, quickly followed by her keys, and then the butterfly. Her breath came in ragged gulps, and she clung to Alex, their bodies pressed so close that she could feel the hardened ridge of him between them. Her mind went fuzzy, made even more so with the way Alex tugged at her hair. Oh, he remembered how much she liked that.

A million thoughts crowded on the edge of her mind, worries and reminders of consequences—and the fact that he was younger and this was his game.

But she didn't care.

Until Alex broke the kiss.

He bent down to scoop up her keys, handing them to her with a sexy grin. "We should probably go inside before we end up naked on your porch."

Unable to form a coherent response, she nodded and took the keys with shaking hands. She turned to unlock the door, not quite able to get the key in the lock. The heat of Alex's solid, strong body behind her scrambled her brain. His breath trailed across her neck, and she shivered in response, tilting her head to give him access. Understanding what she wanted, he pressed a trail of tantalizing kisses up and down her skin.

Her heart nearly pounded out of her chest as his hand slipped beneath her shirt, those calloused fingers skating upward until he reached her bra. She sucked in a breath, wondering and hoping that he would touch her there. She *needed* him to touch her there.

He lifted the edge of her bra, his fingers instantly finding their target. Simone hissed when he began toying with her nipple.

She tried to unlock the door again, albeit unsuccessfully. Pressing one hand against the surface to ground herself, she clutched Alex's wrist through her shirt as he sucked on her neck, sending one bolt of lust after another shooting to her core.

Then a series of unfortunate events happened. The door—which Simone had been using as her anchor—opened. She fell forward with a squeal, and Alex—being the incredible athlete he was—snagged her around the waist with his free hand and tightened his grip on her boob with the other.

Simone looked up to find her father standing in the doorway, the look on his face dousing her amorous mood like a bucket of cold water.

His eyes went wide, and he mouthed, "Oh," and quickly blocked the door, his voice taking on a higher pitch. "Hey, I forgot my jacket—"

Alex yanked his hands away from Simone like her skin had scalded him, and he stepped back a little. Simone shot him a glance over her shoulder, hoping he could see the apology in her eyes.

"It's too hot for a jacket, Grandpa, and hey, you didn't even bring one," Lula responded.

Lula?!

Simone turned back to the door. Lula wasn't supposed to be home for another week—they'd planned a chat for tonight! Simone knew that with certainty. The rest of her life might be up in the air, but Tallulah would always be one constant.

"Lula Bug?" Simone called out, trying to collect herself.

Lula bounded into view and across the threshold, launching herself at Simone. "Mom!"

Simone barely had time to steady her footing before catching her daughter in her arms. Despite everything, a laugh tumbled out of her as she squeezed Lula in an embrace.

"Tallulah! This is the *best* surprise! Why are you home so soon?"

Simone looked at her dad, and he stepped forward, eyes narrowed. Andrew Warner was like a bloodhound, but hell, he'd already seen what was about to go down between his daughter and the man she'd yet to introduce.

Thankfully, he skipped right over that as he came outside and closed the door behind him, before shoving his hands in his pockets.

"She missed everyone and wanted to come home a little early. She called Damien, since he was the one who was supposed to pick her up. He's busy and contacted me to get her. He thought it would be a sweet surprise for you."

This *was* a wonderful surprise, but Simone's lips still flattened. She knew exactly why Damien had put off seeing Lula, and it had nothing to do with being sweet. He had a woman coming over and needed his daughter out of the way. The only person Damien ever thought about was himself.

Simone spun around, looking at her driveway and then the road. "So, Dad, where did you park? I didn't see your car when we pulled up?"

That would've been a nice warning.

He arched his brow. "Would it have mattered? You *were* rather busy excavating tonsils."

Simone's face flamed. She glanced at Alex with as much of an apologetic expression as she could manage, but he only bit his lip, forcing back a mischievous smile that made her stomach flip.

"Excavating tonsils?" Lula asked, her face scrunched up in confusion. "What's that?"

Simone shot her father a death glare, and he altered course.

"I parked in the other spot in the garage," he said. "I just had the car detailed, and it was supposed to rain. I didn't want to risk messing it up."

"Well *that's* perfectly normal," Simone answered with a sarcastic roll of her eyes and a smile.

Lula stooped down to pick up the butterfly and pointed at Alex, noticing him at last. "So you're Alex?"

"I am." He crouched just enough to shake her hand. "Nice to finally meet you, Tallulah."

She slid her small hand inside his, but she still eyed him carefully, none too shy about putting her wariness on full display. Simone tried not to laugh.

"Alex Wilde?" her father cut in.

Her dad might've appeared almost relaxed when he opened the door, but she could pretty much bet that he might have an issue now. Alex's reputation certainly preceded him. A reputation that had caused Simone to fall right into his bed back in July.

"*Oui*, nice to meet you." Alex straightened and extended a hand, which her father shook.

He raised a brow and gave a somewhat appreciative glance at Alex's firm grip. "Andrew Warner, Simone's father."

Lula swung the butterfly from side to side, staring at Alex, and interrupting anything else Andrew Warner might say. *Thank God.*

"I'm glad I got home from camp early because if you'd touched my cereal...well, let's just say it wouldn't be good. I have a certain method to how I eat it, and if you ate even one of those marshmallows..." She squinted, not moving her hard stare from him.

Alex pretended to be affronted, bringing an exaggerated hand to his chest, eyes wide. Despite what he said during their last day of kid's camp, he handled children well.

"I wouldn't dare dream of eating your cereal."

"Lula, why don't you go to your room and stay there for a minute? And will you put that on the couch?" Simone patted the butterfly in her daughter's arm.

"How about I show Alex which cereals he can and can't eat?" Lula replied. "Cereal is my favorite food, and I could eat it for all three meals." Lula's light brown curls bounced when she motioned for Alex to follow her inside the house.

"I think that would be a grand idea," Andrew said before Simone could utter a reply. He cut his eyes her way.

She knew that look. Dad and daughter needed to have a talk.

"I'm not about to get murdered, am I?" Alex whisper-joked to Simone as he started after Lula.

She laughed, because no matter how awkward this evening had turned out, Alex Wilde was handling it like a pro, all while being absolutely adorable. Even Andrew chuckled.

"No," she replied. "I think you're safe. For now."

Alex nodded, then grinned nervously at Simone. It was the most endearing thing, until she remembered that these two worlds were *not* supposed to collide. And yet she and Alex had nearly crossed that line —*again.*

Once Alex and Lula were occupied inside with cereal choices, Simone and Andrew sat on the porch swing.

Simone sighed. "Go ahead. Let me have it."

"Simone, I'm not going to make comments on your personal life. You've always been someone I've never had to worry about making the right decision—"

"I don't know if that's true. Look at my life. Divorced and almost forty, completely clueless about what I'm doing." She rubbed her temples. "I'm a mess."

Her father patted her back. "Listen, you are not a mess."

She scoffed, leaning back into the wooden porch swing. "Oh, but I am. Who just walks away from a CEO position?"

"Are you enjoying coaching?"

She thought about that for a minute, about how it felt to be on the courts, to be helping someone. Regardless of that feeling, she'd also questioned if she was doing the right thing.

"I am. I'm happy out there, but sometimes I wonder if I should just go back to Warner Hotels. I don't exactly want to, but this is all new to me, and it gets exhausting. *Rewarding,* but exhausting. But if I decide to stay and keep doing what I'm doing, I'll have to tell Damien. I can't keep playing it off as a side gig, and he's going to shit a brick when he finds out about his alimony being lower. Did you know Lula told him I was coaching and had stepped down, but he didn't believe her? Laughed and said, 'Yeah, right.'"

Her father went silent. After a moment, he leaned his elbows onto his knees, clasping his hands together. He stared at the floor for a long minute, then glanced back up at her.

"I'm not surprised by that. He never listens to anyone. And with that said, you should know that Damien doesn't deserve any consideration when it comes to your life. Forget about him. We'll make the alimony work, though he never deserved a dime from you to begin with. But there is something you should know since you mentioned the hotel."

Dread swirled and settled heavily in her stomach. "What is it?"

A pause sent Simone's heart skittering. Her father was not one to beat around the bush.

"Simone, the board is moving forward with voting on someone to take your place. I thought we had at least a year, but it seems we don't. This is your last chance if you want to come back."

She knew her father supported her, knew he loved her, but she could hear the unspoken, *I think you should, I wish you would.*

The news was a punch to the chest, knocking the breath right out of her.

"Any good candidates?" she asked, her voice wobbly. Her eyes burned alongside her throat.

Her father's expression was grim. "Several, hence the board's rush."

All of her decisions now seemed silly, trifling. Gone would be the excellent retirement plan and health benefits and salary, although she'd have money from Warner Hotels stock, and she'd been pretty good with her savings. But that would eventually run out.

Also, being a tennis coach wasn't a steady profession, if that's what she decided to do for the rest of her life. Working at the tennis center itself did provide *some* stability, but she liked the idea of coaching pros or at least up-and-coming tennis players. The problem with that was that she was a nobody. Who would ever want her as their head coach? Especially when the only client she had was a man she'd slept with?

Numbers and data, now *that* she knew and *that* she excelled at. She could command a boardroom even if she loathed it. She could sit in her head-to-toe glass office feeling as untouchable as she had been. But she'd been so miserable. So unhappy. The idea of a safety net had given her more confidence in her decision to deviate from the plan, and now all she wanted to do was freak the hell out because that was gone. She couldn't falter in front of her father though. And not because he was a bad guy. But because he'd want to fix it, and she needed to do this herself without anyone else's opinion.

This needed to be *her* call.

As if reading her mind, he spoke again, his voice somber. "This is your last chance, Simone."

Last chance not to make a mistake you can't take back. Last chance to throw away everything your entire life was built for. *Last chance.*

But when Simone thought about being around the sport she loved the most, making an impact on a player's life, she felt light. Desperately grasping onto that feeling, she lifted her head.

She could almost hear Arlo's playful voice, "Chin up, buttercup."

Her fingers bit into the material of her pants, pinching the skin beneath to keep from moving. Could her father see her eye twitch or hear the catch in her voice?

God, she hoped not.

"I stand by my decision."

A moment passed, and she thought about the tennis player in the kitchen. The tennis player who she wanted to climb like a tree every second of the day despite knowing she couldn't and shouldn't—the very same tennis player she was supposed to help coach. Thank God, they hadn't gone any further tonight.

Her father's shoulders sank, and his head drooped for just a minute before looking at her again. He sat back a little.

"That's not the answer I wanted to hear, but I'll never push you to do things that don't make you happy." He released a long-suffering sigh. "It's clear I may have caused this in the first place by pushing you into it."

Simone smiled. "It's okay, Dad. Maybe…maybe I should go rescue Alex though? Lula seemed pretty intense."

Andrew's stare flicked to the door, where high-pitched giggles and low-rumbled chuckles resonated. "I can take him home if you need."

"That would be great." Simone stood, putting her hand on her father's shoulder and squeezing. "Thank you."

For that, and for everything.

She left Andrew and headed for the kitchen. She wanted to talk to Alex about this. He seemed to understand her earlier at Skyline, and he was the one who helped her finalize this career move in the first place.

Was she upset? Of course, but ultimately, she knew that leaving the CEO life was for the best. It forced her to step forward into a new future, one foot in front of the other.

It would also force her to stop wanting to make out with her tennis player, because she needed to do well at this—there was no backup plan here.

The thing was, she didn't know if she was strong enough to resist.

Chapter Sixteen

ALEX

TALLULAH WAS NOTHING LIKE ALEX EXPECTED. SHE'D OF COURSE TERRIFIED HIM at first when she all but dragged him through the kitchen, but he'd warmed up to her since. Her round, blue eyes were so much like Simone's it was uncanny; her hair a lighter shade and curly, whereas Simone's was jet black and straight. Her personality, though, was unique. She'd grilled Alex tougher than if he were applying for a job, finally nodding to herself before stuffing her mouth full of cereal. He figured he had her seal of approval.

"Lula, I hope you're not making a mess in here," Simone's gentle voice carried through the kitchen. She caught Alex's eye and smiled, although she looked as if she had the weight of the world on her shoulders.

He stood, his instinct to go to her. *Criss.* When had that become his first response?

"Simone?" His voice was a question as he edged closer, not sure how avid he should be about touching her since her daughter was sitting there, chewing in eerie silence, skewering him with a glare that said, *Touch my mom, and I'll cut off your hand.* "Is everything okay?"

She lifted one shoulder. "It will be, but do you mind if we talk first? And then, if you need, my father can take you home?"

He nodded before glancing back at Tallulah. She scrunched her nose and studied her mom as she strode from the room.

Tallulah's eyes moved from the entryway back to Alex. A small smile curled her lips as she whispered, "For what it's worth, she likes you." She punctuated it with a wink before she went back to eating her cereal.

Warmth spread in Alex's chest, and he couldn't keep a grin from forming on his face.

"Thanks," he said, heading to the back patio, presumably to avoid Andrew at this point. It wasn't every day that he had a woman's father catch them during almost-sex.

Things earlier tonight had been really good, so good that Alex felt they'd turned a corner, even with what happened against the door. His heart still thundered because of it.

Because of Simone.

But *that* Simone was gone. *This* Simone was all tight lines and pinched brows—evidence that Andrew had delivered some sort of news that had her twisted up inside.

They sat down on a loveseat on the patio, close enough that their elbows brushed. He ignored the heat that followed, intent on focusing on Simone's needs instead.

"They're voting on a new CEO for Warner Hotels," Simone said in a huff as she deflated. Her hands shook as she ran them up and down her thighs.

Merde, whatever he'd expected, it most certainly wasn't that.

"Oh, Simone," he whispered.

Instinct had him opening his arms. His embrace was the only comfort he could provide. Alex couldn't explain it if he tried, but seeing her look so beaten, so *crushed*, had his chest constricting uncomfortably. He'd do anything to make her smile again.

Simone eyed his silent offer, biting at her bottom lip. They both grasped how big of a moment this was.

Alex was about to drop his arms when Simone eased closer and pressed her cheek against his chest. She wound her arms around his torso slowly, hesitantly, but then she tightened her grip, fisting the back of his shirt.

He sighed, resting his chin on top of her hair. He rubbed her back, and her body relaxed in his hold. Nothing had ever felt as right as this.

"It's not that I ever wanted to go back, you know? But it makes me nervous because now I *need* this coaching job, and I need to learn how to do it well," she said. "I guess I'm scared, which is normal, I get that."

"I want you to listen." He bent his head toward her ear. "You are going to be a fantastic coach, and I mean that."

This was her dream. Her *true* dream. Alex trusted her—she just needed to believe in herself too.

Simone's head bobbed slightly. "Thank you."

"You weren't happy being CEO of Warner Hotels. You're happy on the court. I can see it. Do what makes your heart happy and the rest will follow, *oui*?"

Simone gave a slight shrug. "I suppose. But then there's Damien. I don't want to deal with telling him."

Every muscle in Alex's body tensed at the mention of her ex. "Will he give you trouble?"

"He might. He's not always been the easiest since the divorce, and he relies on that money more than I ever have."

Alex held her closer, rubbing soothing paths across her upper back. He wanted to kiss her temple, that deep desire to comfort her threatening to drown him, but he somehow managed to resist.

Simone made the right decision to step down as CEO, but it had to be challenging to walk away from everything she'd ever known.

"I can go with you then. You shouldn't have to do it alone."

"He would die if he saw you. You're way too handsome, and it would bruise his fragile ego," she laughed.

He was about to tease her about calling him handsome when his phone buzzed in his pocket. Simone jerked back, and just like that the moment shattered.

Alex gritted his teeth as he dug into his pocket, retrieving the cursed device. When he saw the name lighting up his screen, he blinked.

"It's Paul," he announced before answering.

Simone tilted her head up and shot him a confused look.

"Hello?"

"Hey, son. Sorry to catch you so late, but ah, I've got news that can't wait. Remember when you said you'd registered for the Cincy tournament?"

Alex stood, abruptly pulling away from Simone. *"Oui."*

"Well...let's just say you're still on the entry list."

A thousand different emotions circuited through Alex as he jammed his hands through his hair. How could this be?

"What do you mean? How am I still on the list?"

Simone stood, bringing her hands to her mouth, brows raised. She shifted anxiously but didn't speak, watching him carefully. Alex would've put her out of her misery, but he didn't want Paul to know they were together. A voice in the back of his head pointed out that might be a problem, but he could only focus on one issue at a time.

"I forgot to withdraw your name. I must've thrown that sticky note away or something? Either way, this might be a great mistake because now we can see what you can do. But we'll need to cancel practice tomorrow so we can fly out. That gives us Friday to practice before qualifiers on Saturday."

Alex froze, his eyes growing wide. "Fly out tomorrow?"

Paul laughed sheepishly. "Yeah, tomorrow. Get ready because it looks like we're going to Cincinnati."

Chapter Seventeen

SIMONE

"THERE'S STILL TIME TO CHECK IN AT LINDNER, EVEN IF IT'S GONNA TAKE US almost an hour to get there from here," Paul said as he led Simone and Alex to the taxi pickup area outside the CVG airport.

As a former CEO, Simone was used to whirlwind events, but this had been a little different. Thankfully, her father agreed to keep Lula, since Damien couldn't be bothered. Then there was the fact that Paul booked their flights and had done so with everyone sitting separately, so at least she had a little time to herself to process everything.

She hadn't told Alex that they needed to cool things down again, but then again, she really hadn't had time. He walked beside her, dressed in a slim-fit, gray tee that hugged his biceps and, well, everything else too. Dark denim hugged his long legs, and motorcycle boots capped it all off with a bit of edge. His tattoos stood out in a lovely contrast against his tawny skin.

He shot her a wicked grin that did nothing to help matters.

Damn, he looked like sin.

Obviously, it was going to be difficult to keep Alex in the friend zone, especially with how much she wanted him despite the dumpster fire that would erupt if she ever gave in.

When they stepped out into the warm early evening, a line of cabs awaited. Paul and Alex dumped their luggage into the trunk of the first car, and she placed hers on top.

Paul grinned, opening the rear door. "I love taxis. They remind me of New York." He looked lost in thought as he motioned for Simone to slide in first.

Of course, as she did so, her mind flooded with images of her and Alex in the taxi last night. She'd nearly been undone on a twenty-minute ride and, this would be almost an hour. She was still raw and struggling to rebuild her defenses after his sweetness at Skyline Park.

She turned to look out the window and attempted to shrug out of her airport cardigan. There was definitely no need for it now with the stifling heat. As she did, her arm connected with solid muscle and warmth.

"Easy there, Simone," a teasing lilt drifted to her ears.

Whirling around, she was met with Alex's smirking, gorgeous face, and she dropped her hands into her lap, her cardigan half-on, half-off. On Alex's other side, Paul slid in last and shut the door. He leaned forward slightly. "Hey, Alex, listen, I'm gonna need you to push on over."

Alex scooted closer to Simone, so that they were practically molded from shoulder to hip.

Heat scorched a path across Simone's skin as the cab sped off from the curb. Of course, she'd chosen to wear a sleeveless shirt and had only half-stripped out of her cardigan.

He turned toward her, his gaze roaming over her as he tugged his bottom lip between his teeth.

"A little more. Come on, I'm sure she doesn't bite," came Paul's irritated demand.

Alex cocked a brow, and as he moved even closer, he whispered, "But I like it when you bite."

Sweat beaded at Simone's brow, and she dropped her gaze to his mouth. She did *not* need to be thinking about this man like she was. Not when she needed to do the best job possible with this coaching gig. But there was an invisible tether inside of her chest that tugged her toward Alex. She couldn't help but fall into these moments with him...and like it.

When she managed to drag her gaze back to his, he was already watching her, warm, brown eyes glittering in the late afternoon sunlight filtering through the cab.

"Simone, *chérie*, you look a little hot. Is there something I can do? Something to cool you off?"

Damn him.

"You can cool your own self off," she bit back with a smirk.

His dark chuckle filled the scant space in the back seat.

Paul leaned forward so that his face was almost squishing against the headrest of the front seat.

"No wonder you're about to heat to death, Simone. You still got that jacket thing on. Alex..." He gestured toward Simone. "Be a gentleman and help her, will ya?"

Could an alien perhaps abduct her at that moment? Spirit her away somewhere else? While, yes, she and Alex had reached a new dynamic, this was just...this was all testing it, especially with the memory of his warm skin beneath her touch fresh on her mind.

Alex dipped his head toward her half-crumpled cardigan. "May I?"

She lifted her hands slightly in a "Can I really say no?" gesture and managed a grin.

He was already practically on top of her, thanks to Paul. When Alex shifted as far as the lap seat belt would allow, he fully faced her. His breath tickled her neck, goosebumps having a heyday up and down her arms, and he hadn't even touched her yet.

Alex Wilde was just that good, and she was his assistant coach, and she needed that stamped across her forehead. Better yet, *his* forehead.

Simone twisted, feeling like an overgrown child trying to get out of the other arm of the sweater. Alex's fingertips skated along her bare skin, gently scraping as he tugged the cardigan ever so slowly down to her wrist. He stopped there, wrapping his fingers around the thick material of her sweater, his thumb doing that wickedly delicious thing it did, swiping across her pulse point. She sucked in a gasp at the touch, feeling hotter than if she'd layered on *ten* cardigans. Him undressing her in any manner felt symbolic, a hint to their night together in Canada, but also a reminder of how much she *liked* being undressed by him.

Finally, albeit sadly, he tugged the sweater all the way off, and she turned back so that she was no longer facing the window. Alex remained unmoved as the incredibly loud sound of Paul clicking away on his phone filled the space, along with the low volume of the oldies music the cabdriver played in the background.

Alex folded her cardigan with such care that it tugged at her chest, plucking at several heartstrings. He placed it on her lap with a smile, his pinkie lingering along her thigh, and she marveled at this man before her. He could be sexy and sweet at the same time, and she enjoyed it more than she should.

"There. You should be good now, *oui?*"

"Uh-huh," came her ragged reply as she shifted in the seat, her shoulder brushing the smooth fabric of Alex's shirt, the heat of his thigh burning through the material of her jeans.

She couldn't wait to tell Amalie about this sweet, torturous, horny hell.

Her sister would no doubt find it hilarious.

A few more irritating *tap, tap, taps* came from Paul's end of the seat, and Alex turned slightly. "Paul, what are you doing over there? Are you looking up information? Texting?"

"No, I'm not texting. I'm sexting."

The car went silent, Simone and Alex shooting each other horrified looks. Alex, thankfully, was the one to speak up—because seriously, how does one respond to that?

"*Alors*, sexting, Paul?"

"Yeah, why not?"

Alex blinked several times. "If you're *actually* sexting, then there are a million reasons why not."

Paul took his hat off, scratching the fluff beneath it. "I'm telling my wife she's beautiful and sexy. Isn't that what sexting means?"

The cabdriver laughed and then quickly covered it up with a fake cough, but Simone wasn't as covert. She snorted, and Alex chuckled.

"Paul, my poor sweet Paul," she said in between laughter. "That is most definitely *not* sexting. And since we're in the car together, let's just keep the text messages at that."

Paul scrunched his face. "Okay, well then, I'm just texting my wife." It was safe to say the entire cab drew a collective breath...until Paul spoke again. "So, Alex, you seem to have a way with the ladies." He leaned forward catching Simone's eye. "Right, Simone? He's a ladies' man and knows the right things to say."

Simone's hand went to her chest, her voice a little shriller than it should be. "I don't know about that. Why would you ask *me*?"

Alex's stare burned the side of her face, his grin so smug and sexy. "*Oui*, Simone, why would he ask you?"

She turned so that they locked eyes, his stare a caress...and interrupted by that loud tapping again.

"Well, if you don't know, then I can say I have it on good authority from other people, those other people being Julian and Amalie, that Alex is good with the ladies." Paul lifted his phone, his attention sliding to Alex. "So what can I text Charlotte to really impress her? To be all suave?"

That took Alex aback. His mouth dropped open slightly, brows raised as he held out his hands to his side as much as he could in the cramped space. "I don't really know, Paul."

Another tap and then the older coach pocketed his phone, a grin twitching beneath his gray mustache. "Ah, don't worry. I figured it out. I sent her an eggplant emoji."

Simone let out a groan as she covered her face with her hands, and Alex let out a strangled noise of his own.

Paul, however, was completely clueless. "What? Why are you two acting like that over a vegetable emoji?"

"It is *not* just a vegetable emoji," Simone said, adjusting so she could see Paul head-on.

"The hotel has eggplant parm on the room service menu, and that's Charlotte's favorite, so I don't see the problem."

That was the tipping point for Alex, who started to laugh, his body shaking and brushing hers. "There's no problem. None at all. Why don't we talk about something else? Anything else aside from sexting and eggplants," Alex suggested, voice still wavering.

So, thankfully, they spent the rest of the near hour-long ride discussing strategy for the qualifiers. Alex would have to compete in two qualifier matches before moving into the first round of the Western & Southern Open.

Knots twisted in Simone's stomach, tightening at the very thought of Alex returning to the court and her being in his box. She knew Bastien was playing in this and hoped they wouldn't see him during their down time at the tennis center where the event would be held.

When the cab pulled to a stop at the Lindner Family Tennis Center, Simone practically leapt out, taking gulps of air as she did. Of course, her right side smelled just like Alex, woodsy and spicy and...she secretly loved it.

Alex had already made his way to the trunk, pulling out their luggage. But Paul didn't get out of the cab.

Simone hoisted her backpack, narrowing her eyes at him as she moved to the open car door. "You coming or what?"

"Nah. I'm going to leave you guys here. If you two can pick up my badge for me, that would be great. I'm tired and ready to eat and watch TV and talk to my lady."

Cocking her hip, Simone wrinkled her nose, just as Alex came to her side. "Paul..."

Paul gave her a grin, and honestly, it was nothing less than shit-eating, as he slammed the door shut and tapped the seat of the driver. "Go!" he yelled as if he were a character in a car heist film.

The car sped off, leaving Simone and Alex at the center.

Alone.

"Did he...?" Alex pointed toward the fleeing car and then between them.

"Oh yeah, he did. We just got Paul Mercado'ed, I think." She looked at the entrance, at the small, concrete path to the doorway of the clubhouse, and sighed. "Guess we better go ahead and check in. The sooner we do that, the sooner we can get to the hotel."

Just as she started to walk, Alex gently pulled her to a stop with a tug on her wrist. "Simone, wait."

She took a look at his furrowed brows, and her stomach sank. "What's wrong?"

A small smile curled his lips as he gave a little head shake that was way more endearing than it had any right to be. "Nothing is wrong. I haven't had much of a chance to talk to you about what happened last night—"

"Oh, you mean when we almost had sex?"

He grinned. "*Non*. I meant everything that happened with Warner Hotels, but we can discuss the fact that we almost had sex if you'd like, *chérie*."

She groaned and spun on her heel to face away from him, gathering herself. "I walked right into that one. No, I'm good if we don't discuss that." Sobering up, she faced him again, bringing both hands to the straps of her backpack, needing something to do with her fingers. "That's really sweet of you to ask about the hotel thing. I'm...okay, I think? It's something I'll have to get used to, but ultimately, I think it's for the best."

"I agree. We can't move forward if something from our past, from who we once were, holds us back."

Simone nodded and smiled, although it was a little wobbly. "Exactly."

Wrapping an arm around her shoulders, Alex pulled her against his solid body. The move was familiar and comforting yet still sent sparks across her nerve endings.

"To new beginnings, *oui*?" He tugged her even closer, and she swore she felt his lips press ever so slightly atop her hair. "Come, let's go check in."

Doing something she wouldn't normally do, she leaned into him, snaking her arm around his waist, and they walked into the tennis center as a team.

What a strange and welcoming feeling.

"Let's practice first thing in the morning," Alex said as he penciled in his name on the practice court roster.

Simone leaned over his shoulder, noting the messy scrawl of his handwriting. "That's perfect since your first match is at noon."

"Scheduling your practice courts?" came a vaguely familiar voice, one that made Simone's skin crawl.

Alex didn't budge, instead finishing up what he was writing. Simone turned around and did nothing to stop the cringe that twisted up her face.

Bastien Demers looked much like he had when she met him back at the chateau. Everything about him was too in place, too smug, too *everything*

—and not in a good way. He did that creepy little leer thing, scanning her from head to toe, and Simone crossed her arms over her chest in response.

"Can we help you with something?" she snapped, arching a brow beneath the fringe of her bangs.

That got Alex's attention. His entire body stilled before facing his nemesis. Props to him for keeping his face an indifferent mask.

Bastien shot her an ugly grin, then focused all of his attention on his stepbrother. It felt like a wild west showdown.

"I figure we should practice together, Alex. I need a light and easy warm-up, you know, since I don't have to actually qualify for this tournament like some."

Simone curled her hands into fists, biting the inside of her cheek so she wouldn't tell Bastien off right there in front of everyone. It wouldn't exactly be the best first impression in the tennis world as an assistant coach.

One corner of Alex's full lips tilted up into a crooked smirk as he stroked his beard, everything about him feigning boredom. "*Non.* I already have my partner." He canted his head toward Simone.

Bastien rolled his eyes and snorted. "I shouldn't be surprised that you'd turn down the offer, what with you being The Wilde Card and all. Maybe you can make your old man proud some day and actually win a major, huh?"

And with that parting shot ricocheting in the small space around them, Bastien sauntered off.

Alex threw his shoulders back, jaw feathering as he grabbed his badge from the desk. Simone wrapped her fingers through his, feeling the tension stringing his body tight. The calloused pads of his fingers didn't sweep her pulse point this time. Instead, they gripped her as though she were his very lifeline.

Her voice was filled with forced cheer when she spoke, even as she shot daggers into the back of Bastien's back. "Alex, let's get out of here. We have everything we need, and I think you should get some rest before tomorrow."

She needed time to cool off, because she wanted to punch Bastien in the balls.

Alex nodded, although his eyes appeared glazed over. The usual playful glint was absent as they made their way out of the tennis center, grabbing a cab to take them to their nearby hotel.

The cab ride was quiet, and sure, Alex probably wanted time to think, but Simone had some things that needed to be said.

"Alex?"

He turned from looking out the window, giving her a soft smile. "*Oui?*"

Alex had been so gentle with her over the past twenty-four hours, and really, even during their night in Canada, he'd been exceedingly tender. That just made her even more fond of him. But they were here, at a tournament—one with his awful stepbrother. It was her goal as his friend and his assistant coach to be there for him.

Blowing out a breath, she leaned forward, hating the pain in Alex's eyes, in every single line of his body. She wanted to help carry the burden like he did for her the night before.

"You're not like Bastien, Alex."

A hollow chuckle rumbled from his chest, a sarcastic grin on his lips. "*Dieu merci.*"

"My thoughts exactly, because he's an asshole. The thing is, people like that, they get off on hurting you, on slicing little cuts into your skin with their words and actions. With each one, they think they've cut you down to size, to a stump of the person you used to be, and then those words stick with you. You think about them for hours, or hell, even days after the fact, until they've done exactly what they hoped to do—screwed with you for no better reason than they're jealous. That's Bastien's MO here. I'm all about fighting back and not taking people's shit, trust me, I deal with my ex-husband. But what I'm saying here is don't let him take your joy from you." She gestured to him, where he sat almost hunched, hands folded in his lap. "And he's doing that right now. So I say fuck Bastien and you do you."

Alex studied her for a long time, the intensity of his gaze almost enough to make her go up in flames.

"You're right. I'm happy to be back on the court again, and I can't let him ruin that." He bit his lip for a moment, his expression turning thoughtful. "And having you here with me—it's like a dream I don't want to wake up from."

Her heart cracked open, and she smiled at him. "I agree, it's been lovely."

The car pulled to a stop in front of a Warner Hotel—because, well, of course that's where they'd stay.

As they piled out of the car, Simone couldn't help but think this had been *more* than lovely.

It felt almost perfect.

Chapter Eighteen

ALEX

THE NEXT TWO DAYS WERE A WHIRLWIND AS ALEX COMPETED IN THE WESTERN & Southern Open qualifiers. With Simone a constant presence on the sidelines, he managed to win both qualifying matches landing him in the tournament's first round Monday afternoon.

Playing Bastien.

The day he was set to play Bastien, Alex entered the locker room with Simone and Paul. They were the first to arrive, so it was blissfully empty. He knew Bastien would arrive soon—he always did like to make a showy entrance.

Alex's knee bounced, unable to help itself as Paul and Simone sat on either side of him.

"Remember what we talked about. Be aggressive," Paul reminded him.

Alex nodded, putting on his headband. The problem was, he still didn't know how to make aggressive play work for him.

Simone tapped his leg, instantly stilling him. Her touch had a tendency to do that. "It's amazing to be in this tournament, Alex. Take the time to appreciate that fact too. Your goal was to play Bastien, and here you are."

She was right. Alex had dreamed of this for years, playing his stepbrother and demoralizing him on the court as payback for everything

—for stealing time with his father, for stealing what was rightfully his, for pretending to love a sport for the sake of besting Alex.

Simone caught his eye, and for a moment the locker room vanished. It was just her and him, and his breath caught in his chest. The woman had the power to ensnare him with one look, and he wondered if she was just as entranced.

The door to the locker room crashed open.

Simone glanced away, breaking contact and taking Alex's calm with her.

He turned his head just as Bastien walked in, looking as smug as he had when he sauntered into the Tennis Ball, uninvited. Alex stiffened but knew he couldn't show weakness. He stood up, eyeing his stepbrother.

"So, we finally get to meet on the court after all these years," Bastien all but sneered. Behind him, Claudette appeared, having gone so overboard with plastic surgery that she didn't even look like the monster of Alex's childhood anymore. Her eyes flicked over him dismissively and landed on Simone, perking with interest.

Alex crossed his arms over his chest. "It's been a long time coming, *non*?" He wouldn't trash-talk him. Even though Alex's father broke his heart by sending him away so young, he still lived by Jack Demers's rules on the court—and the number one rule was sportsmanship. Jack insisted that Alex would always have the crowd behind him if he did the right things on *and* off the court.

So maybe he'd slacked on the off-court part, but he'd improved lately, largely due to Simone. When he stole a glance at her, he noticed her hands were clenched into fists, those full lips pulled down into a scowl. Her protectiveness of him was evident, and it lessened the crushing weight brought by Bastien's presence.

"I was wondering the other day where I knew you from," Bastien said, moving closer toward Simone. "We met at Alex's party."

Simone's nose wrinkled in disgust. "Yeah, and you tried to hit on me, and I shut it down pretty quickly. I think it's time for you to go to your side of the locker room. There's nothing for you here, so shoo." She flicked her wrist at him as if he were a wild animal to drive away. Unable to help himself, Alex barked a laugh, because Bastien and Claudette were stunned. Even Paul snickered.

Simone's grit never ceased to amaze him.

"You may have her protecting you in here, but she can't out there," his stepbrother scoffed as he pointed toward the hallway that led to the court.

Alex shrugged, having nothing more to say. He knew that Simone had met Bastien, but the idea he'd hit on her made him grind his teeth together. If Bastien had any inkling that Alex was interested in Simone, he'd go after her in earnest, which was probably another reason why Alex just didn't bother with long-term anything. No one had been worth it until now.

"He's a dick," Simone whispered once his stepbrother and stepmother had disappeared.

"Bastien the Bastard," Paul echoed. "Remember that."

Alex rolled his shoulders. "*Alors,* I got this. I'll make sure *he* remembers today." Even as he said it, an unhealthy amount of irritation and anger boiled and simmered beneath the surface. It didn't feel like something he could channel. Instead, it felt like something that *could* and *would* hinder him. He tightened his grip on his racket, trying to draw in deep breaths to calm himself, but before he could feel fully centered, the security team moved in, calling them to the court.

Paul clapped Alex on the shoulder. "You can do this, son. We're just trying this out, remember. No stress."

Simone gave him a lingering hug, her eyes bright. "We're here to cheer you on, okay?"

The way she looked at him, the belief in those dazzling eyes of hers, was astounding. So this is what it felt like to have a team? It was enough to tamper some of the anger. *Some.* Not all.

"*Merci,*" Alex grinned.

They left, and the guards ushered him in front of Bastien, which made his skin crawl. He didn't like the idea of turning his back on the weasel.

"After today, you'll wish you never played tennis," Bastien hissed.

Look forward. Focus on the feel of your racket. Focus on the security guards in front of you. Focus on anything but Bastien.

Focus on winning.

SILENCE BLANKETED THE CROWD. THE MATCH HAD ALREADY MOVED INTO THE second set, and Alex hadn't even won a game yet. It wasn't exactly unheard of, but it wasn't something that had ever happened to him, despite the downward spiral with his game.

He was off-balance and didn't feel comfortable with Paul's plan of playing aggressively.

This proved why Alex didn't want a team, why he didn't like anyone to be in his box aside from Rhys. No one should have to witness this level of embarrassment.

Finally, Bastien hit a winning serve, closing out the match, 6-0, 6-0. The weight of the utter humiliation of his annihilation threatened to push Alex down, but somehow he managed to make himself walk to the net. He never wanted to shake Bastien's hand. Never wanted anything to do with him once he realized what kind of a person he was. But Jack Demers and his whisper of sportsmanship continued to echo throughout Alex's head.

Bastien squeezed Alex's hand in his grip, his nails biting into Alex's skin as he scowled. "Tell me, Alex, is there another sport you could play? Something more your speed? Maybe shuffleboard?"

"There will be none of that," the chair umpire called down.

Alex remained speechless, and when he walked over to his bench, Bastien called out one word—one word just loud enough for him to hear. "Worthless."

Worthless.

Alex's shoulders hitched higher while he packed up his stuff, waving to the fans as he walked off the court. He got booed, as expected—this happened in tennis anytime a player didn't win a game, since the fans considered it poor effort. It looked like sportsmanship didn't matter in this case, like his father thought. The fans were still disappointed, and honestly, so was Alex. He didn't even spare a glance at his box, not wanting to think of how he was supposed to explain his performance. Worse yet, the woman he'd been, what, trying to "woo" witnessed the entire thing. If that wasn't a hard-on killer, he didn't know what was.

Criss. Maybe this was proof that there was no fixing Alex.

Maybe he should just quit.

Chapter Nineteen

SIMONE

SIMONE LOOKED OUT THE WINDOW OF THE PLANE, WATCHING IT DESCEND slowly. Paul shifted beside her. When they booked their return flight last-minute, they hadn't been able to get seats together. She wanted to sit with Alex, wanted to talk with him since he'd helped her after everything with Warner Hotels. But instead she'd given him space, knowing he probably needed time alone. She sat up a little straighter, looking at the top of his sandy blond head a few seats up.

Alex's beat-down played in Simone's mind on a loop. He got completely shredded out there on the court. Most of the flight, she'd watched his game tape on her phone. As she did so, she realized she needed to have a conversation with Paul. She was the assistant coach after all, and things had begun to click.

She blew out a breath, gaining the coach's attention. "Okay, so team meeting time, Paul."

He looked up from the catalog he'd been perusing, slowly closing it. "What's on your mind?"

Simone tapped her fingers against her leg, not quite sure why she was suddenly so anxious. She knew Paul, was comfortable with him, and knew he'd never make fun of her opinions or ideas and would respect her. It was just...in her tape review, she'd been mulling over some of the things Alex had shared with her last week at Skyline Park.

"Well, after today I think we can agree that Alex seems to be struggling with the offensive game plan," she said. "I wondered if maybe you thought it was time to change up the strategy."

Paul's voice dropped, although they weren't in danger of Alex overhearing them. "He's not Julian, but with his size and strength, he could be hitting with more power. I kind of thought about trying to get him to utilize that, which would hopefully lead to him hitting the lines more."

Simone's lips twisted. Now *that* she disagreed with.

"Even though he's a better mover than Julian?" She narrowed her eyes. "Seems like he could use that as a weapon, more so than power."

"Yeah, he moves well, but he needs to be a more offensive player. At least, I think we stick with that route for a while. Maybe try and shift his game toward that direction. It'll take some time, but I'd like to see where it goes, as long as it's something you're okay with?"

She was pretty sure they just saw where it went out there in the match against Bastien, and it wasn't good. Simone's gut told her that Alex would never be one for power, not with his style of play. Movement? Oh yeah, absolutely. But Paul had coached about twenty years longer, and it was safe to say Simone didn't have the best confidence in her coaching skills yet. So what she'd do is continue to watch the tapes and study. She'd continue to analyze Alex on the court during their training. She'd develop her own strategy, because she had a feeling that the time would come for her to step up and speak up.

She just needed a plan.

Simone knew Paul would do whatever she asked, and he wouldn't shut her down—he'd been great to work with. But this was something she needed to attack like she would in the boardroom.

She tapped out another offbeat rhythm on her leg. "Yeah, I'm okay with it. For now."

THE CAB DROPPED EVERYONE OFF AT THE TENNIS CENTER SINCE THAT WAS where they'd met before heading to the airport.

Paul was on the phone with Charlotte but covered the speaker for a minute. "No practice Tuesday or Wednesday. I'll close the tennis center up so we can all get some rest. I won't come in until Thursday. Sound good?"

Simone gave him a thumbs-up as Alex called back, "*Oui.*"

Then he waved, leaving Simone and Alex alone in the dark parking lot.

"Ah, hell," Simone whispered to herself, realizing she needed to get her work laptop out of the tennis center. She'd locked it in her desk drawer since she hadn't wanted to lug it to Cincinnati.

Alex, who had been quiet in the car, turned to look at her. "Everything okay?"

She started digging for her keys so she could unlock the building. "Yeah. I just forgot that I needed to grab something before heading home. You don't need to wait on me though." It was late, around midnight to be exact, and he needed the rest, mentally *and* physically.

"*Non.* I won't leave you alone here." His tone brooked no argument, so she shrugged, throwing her luggage in her car as Alex strapped his backpack to the back of his motorcycle.

He followed her into her office, the sound of his steps echoing down the hall like a shotgun. Tension snapped between them, and she wasn't sure if it was from the adrenaline from his earlier match or excess emotion, but something felt decidedly *different.*

His stare was a caress, lazy and heated as he watched her from the doorway. She fumbled a few times to open her desk drawers, nearly forgetting what she was looking for in the first place. Finally, she found her laptop and held it up. "Got it. We can go."

But Alex didn't budge. Instead, he moved further inside, stalking toward her.

"Simone."

Her name sounded like a desperate prayer, pained and yet still filled with hope.

She rounded her desk, trying to remain calm and pretend as if being this close to him in the moonlit office wasn't a horrible idea.

She curled her fingers into fists as she propped her hands on her hips. "What's going on, Alex?"

He stopped right in front of her. So much heat poured off of him, his jaw feathering, his stare intent and dark. Like he was playing some sort of game—and this time, he'd win.

"I'm tired of fighting this feeling between us. Don't you feel it?" He took another step closer. "Tell me I'm not alone in this."

Her lips parted, the laptop trembling in her hands. Afraid of dropping it, she put the device on a small side table and straightened again, trying to get herself under control.

"But Alex," she stammered, struggling with turning him down because she wanted it too, wanted it more than anything. "You don't mean it, I'm your assistant coach, and well, we have a lot to work on, and I don't want to be a distraction or a balm for your pain. I know today was rough."

Alex ran his fingers along her cheek, pressing his thumb down slightly on her bottom lip. "I mean it. I've meant it since I met you. You would never be a balm, *ma chérie*. You? You're *everything*. Today showed me that. No matter what happens on the court, I'm still going to want you."

Simone fisted her hands in the thin material of his shirt. She was so tired of fighting this too. She liked him *a lot* and wanted him—how many times had their night together starred in her most vivid fantasies?

"The question is, what do *you* want? Do you want this, with me?" Alex asked, echoing words from when they slept together the first time. He'd been the first man to ever care about what *she* wanted.

"I do," Simone whispered.

A blinding smile broke out across Alex's beautiful face, cast in moonlit silver. "I can't even begin to tell you how happy that makes me." He brought both hands to the side of her face, staring into her eyes with so much longing that it nearly took her breath away. That sort of emotion, feeling, for *her*. "I want to kiss you now. Is that all right?"

She nodded. "Yes. Yes, it's absolutely all right."

"*Dieu merci*," he whispered against her lips, before finally kissing her.

Simone's heart shot off a staccato beat as her entire body ignited. The pressure of Alex's lips moving against hers was slow and steady, even as his tongue slipped into her mouth. He gently pushed her against the desk, his hand at her waist, the other on the desk, caging her in. The amber and vetiver of his cologne enveloped her in a heady embrace as his warmth caused her to relax against him.

"I haven't been able to think straight since I met you." Alex drew back, speaking against her lips, his eyes searching before resting his forehead against hers.

"I know the feeling, but I can't help but worry this will blow up in our faces," she murmured.

Alex grabbed her hand, everything about him so open and earnest. "Say the word, Simone. Say it and I'll turn around and walk out that door, and tomorrow we can pretend this never happened."

Her shoulders slumped at the image of him leaving her tonight, at not exploring this territory with him again.

"I don't want that. I want you to stay." Those words floated between them, shattering the rest of her resolve.

This was Alex. She knew him now. He wasn't a sexy, suave stranger with a sweet-talking accent that could melt panties, although he was still more than capable of doing such—case in point at that moment. But she knew Alex would take care of her. She knew she could trust him with this, even if that little voice in the back of her mind told her to grab her laptop and leave.

But where would the fun be in that?

"Tonight it's just you and me, just like it was back at the chateau, okay?"

Alex's eyes flashed as he understood her meaning, his voice husky when he spoke. "*D'accord.*"

"Now where were we the other night?" she teased, looping her arms around his neck.

A gravelly chuckle fell from Alex's lips before he kissed her once. He drew back and grinned at her. "I think I know exactly where."

Then he pulled her in for a kiss that was different than any of their others. The others had been amazing, toe-curling, but this one held another layer beneath it. Not love—no, it was too early for that. But there was a new level of intimacy that pulsed and flickered between them now.

When they broke apart, both panting, a wolfish grin curled Alex's lips. "Can I tell you what I've dreamed of doing?"

He crowded her even closer to the desk until he lifted her onto it, softly pushing her legs apart with his knees. He stepped in between, but not close enough that she could feel what she desperately wanted. Her hands skated over his broad shoulders and landed there, pinching into the fabric like she might fall over any moment.

"Yes, please do," she whispered, afraid anything louder would splinter the moment.

Alex brought his finger down her neck and hooked it in the collar of her shirt, dipping there at her collarbone. His warm breath was on her neck as he spoke, his tongue brushing her sensitive skin. "I've dreamed of taking my time with you. Starting here." He moved to the hem of her shirt, slowly stripping it off.

His eyes flared with lust as he took in her boobs in a plain old beige bra. He acted as though it was the height of lingerie as he brought his mouth to the curve of her breasts, running his tongue along one, then the other.

She tightened her hands in his hair, urging him forward, but he still wouldn't bring his body all the way where she could rock against the obvious erection straining his jeans. Her mouth went dry at the sight.

"Oh," she breathed as he pulled one bra cup down.

He looked up at her, a roguish light glittering in his eyes as he circled one fingertip around her nipple and then pinched it, causing her to gasp and arch. "I want to lick and bite and map out every inch of your gorgeous body." He dipped his head and sucked her nipple into his mouth, bringing it between his teeth as he had with his fingers, one hand digging into her hip.

"That...that works for me," she managed to utter.

He moved to the other nipple, repeating the act, and then he reached behind her to unclasp her bra, allowing it to drop with a light rustle onto the desk. Alex held her breasts in both of his hands, and he brought them together, licking between them, and she imagined *other* things there, especially with the way his heated stare bore into her. It was a living, breathing thing she felt writhing and dancing along her skin.

"God, Alex." She went to reach for his belt loops, but he moved back, his chuckle husky.

"Not yet, *chérie*."

He gripped her waist a little tighter, his mouth trailing down the middle of her skin and over her soft stomach to the top of her yoga pants. He ran a finger along the hem, dropping just beneath where she could feel the fire of his touch.

"After that," he said as he leaned forward, licking her breast with a flat, slow lingering lick once more, "I'd move lower. I'd take off your pants and start with those sexy legs of yours." He breathed into her ear.

The air between them burned hot and smelled of desire and wanting. Simone didn't know how much longer she could last—her underwear was drenched. She squirmed, frantic for some sort of relief, even if it was just the friction of her pants.

"And then what?" she asked breathlessly, eager for more.

Alex cocked a brow. "You'll see soon enough."

He bent before her, untying her tennis shoes, tugging them off with a certain thoughtfulness. Next went her socks. Alex stood and pulled the waistband of her pants, helping her to sit up slightly so he could tug just the material off. The cool desk bit into her skin but was quickly forgotten thanks to the handsome man in front of her.

He went to his knees and placed tender kisses on her ankle, her calf, stopping at her knee. Then his tennis-roughened hands spread her legs wide enough to accommodate him. His eyes were completely black in the moonlight of her office, otherworldly, like a dream.

"*Merde*, you're soaking wet."

"Because you're teasing me," Simone answered as she moved her hands into his hair, waiting with bated breath for his next move. This game he was playing was hot, and even though she felt like she might shatter, she didn't want to mess anything up.

Another husky laugh. "That's you every day, and I'm not just talking about those short shorts of yours..." He bit his lip, gave a slight shake of his head. "But it's more than that with you. You tease me with your smiles and your jokes, *everything* about you."

Her heart was turning to mush as she leaned forward and kissed the top of his head, his hair soft against her lips, before moving back into position, keeping her legs spread apart slightly. "You are something else, Alex Wilde, something else in the best possible way."

He smiled against the skin of her knee, then moved between her legs, kissing her inner thigh, the coarseness of his beard making her shiver with desire. He alternated between kissing and nibbling before disappearing.

Simone whimpered, but then Alex moved his hands so that his thumbs pressed right above where she needed him, and he licked the outline of her underwear, groaning against her body as he did. Electricity flared between them as she tightened her hands in his hair.

He hovered over her underwear-clad clit, and then he put his mouth over it, causing her to move sharply. The warmth of his breath made her even wetter than she already was.

"Alex!" she cried, every part of her being strung tight.

He ran his tongue up and down through her underwear, driving Simone wild.

She was two seconds from stripping them off when Alex thankfully read her mind.

"These are in the way, wouldn't you agree?" He hooked his fingers in the waistband and grinned. "Perhaps we should get rid of them?"

Simone nodded so hard, her hair brushed against her cheeks. "Absolutely we should. As in right this minute."

And then she helped him pull them off. She nearly released a sigh of relief, but the hunger in Alex's eyes had every single part of her on alert again, shivers of pleasure racing down her spine.

Alex's eyes brightened. "*Mon Dieu*, Simone. You're *magnifique*."

The look he gave her was heated yet sweet, as if she were something precious.

With one last kiss pressed to her hip, Alex dipped his head. He danced his tongue around her clit, coming so close, but never quite reaching it. The anticipation had Simone whimpering, squirming, *begging*.

Finally, he licked her, his tongue moving languidly up her seam to the bundle of nerves. He sucked there, and not caring how wanton she appeared, Simone urged him onward, loving the moans he made against her skin, the vibrations of it, the sight of his head between her legs, the utter pleasure he was giving her.

Alex plunged his tongue into her heat, and Simone's back bowed, forcing him to place a hand on her belly to hold her in place. She moaned as he moved in and out of her, the taste of her seeming to drive him wild with need.

Just as she started rocking against his mouth, he drew back, and a whimper rose from her lips because she was *so close*.

"Please," she pleaded.

"Anything for you, *chérie*." Alex moved two fingers inside of her, curling them up, and hitting her G-spot perfectly. His mouth worked her clit, and she held him against her, her nails digging into his skin as she rode his hand.

Alex mapped out her body like she was his favorite destination. His grip on her thighs was gentle, reverent almost, but his wicked tongue was relentless as he drove her closer and closer to release.

"I've been dreaming of this, Simone," he murmured against her flesh. "Come for me."

Alex's command drove her to the edge. She cried out as she fell apart, her head falling forward on his shoulder. She kissed his neck, desperate for the taste of him. When she moved her palm, she felt Alex's heart racing beneath her touch.

"I think it's my turn to say you're the one that's *magnifique*," she spoke against his skin, her voice nearly hoarse.

"*Non*, that honor is all yours."

Alex kissed her hair before drawing back, their eyes meeting. There was definitely something different in his stare, something she was more than sure was mirrored in her own.

She tugged at his shirt as her lips curved, her chest still rising and falling rapidly. "I want to see you, Alex. All of you."

He began undressing as if this was a private show just for her. Slowly, he lifted the edge of his shirt, revealing one slice of tanned, toned skin at a time, then his dusky, hard nipples, until finally the tee was gone. The way his lips kicked up as he slowly moved to the button of his jeans had Simone nearly on her knees, the sound of the zipper deafening in the bubble they'd created together.

It was *always* like this when they were together.

"How are you so beautiful? It almost hurts." Simone sighed as she watched him step out of his jeans, revealing muscular thighs and calves. His cheeks pinked in the most adorable blush at her compliment, but that wasn't where her attention stayed. Oh no. She licked her lips at the sight of his length in his black boxer briefs.

"You see this?" Alex said as he touched himself through the fabric. "This is for you. You get me so hard, Simone." He stepped out of his underwear and then fisted himself, running up and down his length where she wanted her mouth.

She moved from the desk and wrapped her hand around his, caressing the velvety skin through the gaps in their fingertips, loving the way Alex's body shuddered with her touch, her pace. She brought her teeth to his neck, kissing him first before nipping there, earning a throaty groan.

Uncurling her hands from around his cock, she moved to her knees, cutting her eyes up at him. He looked desperate, on the verge of falling apart in the darkness. She hadn't been joking with him earlier—he truly was so beautiful, inside and out.

More than anything she wanted to bring him a modicum of the pleasure he'd just given her. She shot him a grin that she hoped was sort of sexy, before bringing her mouth to him, moving up and down his length, sucking at the tip.

A moan came from Alex as he fisted her hair in his hand. She moved slow, torturously so at first, reveling in the taste of him, the way she made his knees bow, threatening to give out, and then she went faster, pumping him into her mouth.

"Simone," Alex rasped, his voice gravelly. "If you keep doing that..." He placed gentle fingertips beneath her chin and then lifted her, so they were face-to-face.

"It's only fair. You tortured me," Simone said naughtily, licking her lips, tasting the salt of him on her tongue.

"*J'ai envie de toi.* God, I want you," Alex murmured, but then he paled for a moment, hands in his hair. "*Merde.* I don't have a condom. I didn't think..."

Simone pressed a kiss to his lips, taking his hand in hers. "I'm on the pill, Alex. It's okay."

She led them back to the desk. There was a couch that could work, but one of her fantasies had always involved a desk and well, lo and behold.

"*Dieu merci,*" he said as carefully placed her on the desk, stepping between her thighs. His hands were achingly tender as he wrapped her legs around his waist.

His stare burned into her very core, a brand that she'd carry long after this moment was done. "Are you absolutely sure, Simone?"

"Yes." She smiled and then his lips were on hers as he pushed into her, filling her so deep she nearly forgot her own name.

"Simone," he hissed. "You feel better than I remember."

Simone whimpered, unable to form a coherent sentence as she dug her heels into his ass, using that to help her ride him from the angle they were at. His breathing was ragged, sweat forming along his furrowed brow. He was intent on giving her everything, not realizing he already had.

He moved her back so that she was lying on the desk. Stuff tumbled to the floor, but they didn't care. He bent one leg so that her knee rested at his shoulder, and Simone swore she saw stars.

"Oh God, yes, that," she tried to speak, but the new angle had scrambled her brains.

"I've dreamed about seeing you this way, Simone," he rasped. His hooded gaze lingered on her chest, his eyes drinking in her every inch. She felt so exposed, so vulnerable, but with him, with Alex, Simone just felt...*free.*

Alex drove into her body, his thrusts turning relentless. He groaned when she arched her hips to take him deeper, and his hands cupped her breasts, kneading the soft flesh.

She ran a finger down Alex's chest, down his stomach to where they were joined, loving the sight of his muscles working, working for her.

"So good." She pulled him even deeper into her, so deep she let out a gasp that Alex caught with his mouth.

"This is what I've wanted, *chérie.* I've gone entirely too long without your touch," Alex whispered against her, his nose moving along her cheek, his breath smelling of mint and sex.

"Absolutely. We need to do this every day," she managed to get out, moaning when he pulled back and licked one breast, then the other.

"I wanted to touch you. Taste you." He paused, pulling out of her. She whined in protest as he brought his lips to her ear. "But mostly, I wanted to hear the sounds you make when you fall apart. Whether it's my tongue or my cock that's undoing you."

Simone cursed. God, this man.

"I know the perfect position then, so you can get as close as you need," Simone whispered.

Alex picked up on her hint easily. Without hesitation, he lifted Simone off the desk, twisting her around until she was bent over the smooth surface.

They hadn't done this that night, although she'd wanted to and she'd made a promise to herself that if she ever got another chance...

She bit her lip in anticipation as his hands gently gripped her waist, and then his cock slipped between her legs and inside of her. He put one hand on her clit, the other fisted in the back of her hair. He gave it a slight tug, exposing her neck, so he could alternate between biting it and kissing it.

"Simone," Alex moaned behind her, and she moved her ass up higher, using her purchase on the desk to ride his dick faster, harder, loving the sound of their skin meeting in desperation, loving how he was simultaneously rough and gentle with her. And then he pressed down on her bundle of nerves and drove so deep, everything exploded as she cried out.

She still rode him, despite feeling like she was on a different planet, and Alex groaned, pushing into her one more time. And then he came, hard, fast, his mouth on the slope of her shoulder.

"Holy shit," Simone breathed, still seeing stars dance across her vision.

Alex curled over her body, the warmth of his skin burning her from the inside out, but she loved the feel of him there, loved the pulse of him between her legs. He pulled out slowly, and she marveled at how deep he'd been.

He turned her around, his expression tender and still raked through with heat. "You're beautiful in every way, Simone." And then he kissed her slow and sweet, as he cradled her face.

He led them over to her couch against the wall, and he held her, whispering sweet nothings into her ear until she reached back and stroked him, ready for him to take her again. Ready to get her fill of him, because she knew no matter how much she got, it would never be enough.

Chapter Twenty

ALEX

ALEX WOKE TO THE FEEL OF SIMONE'S ASS PRESSING AGAINST HIS COCK.

Blinking his eyes open, taking in Simone's sunlit office, it took him a moment to remember where they'd landed the night before—on a pallet they made from the couch cushions and pillows. He still couldn't believe it'd happened. He'd been defeated, and he realized that it didn't matter if he won or lost on the court, not if he could just have Simone. *Alors*, he'd gone for it, and then Simone, with that way she had, brought him out of his funk...and into her bed, so to speak.

He didn't want to wake her, but he didn't want to waste a moment with her. He leaned onto his elbow so he could push her hair away from her face. "Morning, Simone."

Slowly she woke up, a smile curled on her lips. "Morning."

Her sleepy voice unraveled something inside of his chest. He pressed a gentle kiss to her shoulder and slid his arm around her waist, drawing her closer. "This is what I wanted when I woke up in the hotel room at Lake Louise." He nuzzled her neck, trailing kisses there.

She relaxed against him, curling into his touch. "Now I know what I was missing," she whispered, grazing her nails down his back, tugging him closer.

He let out a low, husky laugh against her skin, just below her ear. "Definitely worth the wait." He shifted his hips, moving his cock against her. He hadn't been this hard in ages.

"Oh, without a doubt."

"I'm glad to hear that," he grinned as he trailed a hand up to her breast, pinching her nipple the way he'd learned she liked.

She gasped, and he pulled her tightly to him.

"Again, *cherie*?" he whispered in her ear.

Reaching for him, she grabbed his ass, urging him closer, grinding against him. "Again."

Just as he turned to do as she asked, his cell rang. He wanted to throw the damned thing across the room, but he knew it might be important.

He groaned before snatching it from the floor and answering it with a gruff "Hello?"

"I've been trying to reach Simone but can't get an answer," Paul said.

Alex glanced down at her, that wicked smile of hers jumbling his thoughts. She kissed the skin just below his navel and kept kissing until…

"*Mon Dieu.*" A shuddering breath escaped him.

This woman. She was going to kill him.

"You cussing at me again?" Paul said with a huff.

"*N-non,*" Alex managed.

"If you say so. I know we talked about closing the center down today and tomorrow, but I thought maybe we should have practice tomorrow at least. What do you think? Ten o'clock?"

Alex fisted the fabric of the couch cushion. "Ten o'clock. I'll be there."

"If you see Simone, let her know. She needs to come, if at all possible."

Alex slid his hand into her dark hair, closed his eyes as she worked her mouth up and down his length.

"Absolutely," he said. Simone Warner was going to come all right.

Eventually, Alex and Simone managed to pull themselves from the pallet, feeling unhurried since Paul had told them he wouldn't be in until tomorrow. They begrudgingly dressed, pulling on their clothes that they'd thrown across the room the night before.

"What do we do now? About...this?" Simone asked, gesturing between them. Uncertainty strained her lovely face, and like a magnet, Alex moved to where she stood against her desk, which was a mess thanks to their previous activities.

He gathered her in his arms, kissing the top of her head. "What do you mean?"

"I'm not good at this, so I...I didn't know what this meant, I suppose? I know I'm your assistant coach, and that's why I didn't want to give in, but at least it's not like I'm your head coach. If that were the case, then this would be a definite no-go. As it stands, Paul's calling the shots, and I wonder...well..." She looked down at her shoes.

Alex drew back slightly so that he could cradle her head in his hands and kiss her like his life depended on it. When he pulled away, Simone's face turned a few shades of pink.

"Simone, I want to be with you, if you'll have me. That's what this means." A smile curved his lips. He couldn't help it when he looked at Simone.

She seemed to drink in his words, her eyes widening with what he knew to be shock. Alex decided long ago that he'd be honest with her, to always tell her exactly what he wanted, and after last night, the confession came easy to him.

"I—" She paused, swallowing hard. Alex held his breath. "I think I like the idea of that."

The air rushed from his lungs.

Simone closed the distance and placed a gentle kiss on his lips, and Alex knew he was done for.

When they broke apart, Alex rested his forehead against Simone's. He didn't want this moment to end.

Just as he was about to open his mouth to say exactly that, Simone's stomach gurgled a loud growl.

She immediately clutched it, bursting into laughter as she dropped her head to his shoulder. When she spoke, her words were muffled by his shirt. "Oh my God. It sounded like a whale call. Sorry."

Alex chuckled as he kissed the back of her head, gently moving so that she'd lift her head and meet his gaze.

He brought his hands to the sides of her face, cradling it. "Then let me feed you. Let's get breakfast. I..." Might as well go all in. "...I want more time with you, if that's okay?"

His honesty was rewarded with a blinding smile, one that lit a spark in his chest. Simone wrapped her arms around his shoulders. "Absolutely. It's like you read my mind."

He had come to enjoy all of the different versions of Simone that he'd gotten to know, but this one, this one where she was looking at him with starry eyes and a sweet grin, was his favorite. He bent down to kiss her again. When he pulled away, he couldn't help but laugh.

"We French-Canadians aren't known for our restraint, you know."

"Oh, I know all right. And I'm so glad." She clutched his shirt, drew him back to her, and kissed him again.

"You're going to make me drag you back to that couch or, better yet, my bedroom," he whispered against her mouth.

A knock at Simone's office door made them both freeze.

"Hey, Simone! Can I come in a sec?" Paul called from the other side.

Alex's heart dropped like a lead weight, especially as he watched a thousand different emotions flit across Simone's face—the last one hurting him the most: regret. She brought her hands to her face.

"Oh my God," she groaned, but Paul must've thought she said to come in because the door swung open, and there he was.

Paul's smile slid off his face as he looked between them, taking in the fact that they wore the same thing they had on the night before. His brows jumped beneath his hat, and he started backing out slowly. "I...ah, I'll give you two a minute."

Simone stepped forward, one hand out. Her voice was too bright, too forced when she spoke. "No, we're...ah, we're good. What is it?"

Alex rubbed the back of his neck, feeling uneasy and unsure about what he needed to do to salvage the situation.

Paul pulled in a deep breath, releasing it loudly as he moved back into the office, closing the door quietly behind him. "This is awkward," he announced.

Silence. Alex stole a glance at Simone, who looked like she wanted to disappear.

Paul moved to sit on the couch, but catching Simone and Alex's cringes, he froze midway and popped back up, sadly getting their meaning.

Alex was pretty sure he heard the man cuss under his breath, and then he moved back to lean against the wall, splotches of red dotting his cheeks.

Paul lifted a hand. "Well, I obviously changed my mind about coming in today. I thought I'd get a jump on the week." He took his hat off and messed with the bill of it before glancing back up at Simone and Alex again. "I think we need to talk about expectations. I know you're both grown adults, and well, when the attraction is there, it's there. I get that. That's how it was with Charlotte."

Simone rubbed her temples as Alex brought a hand over his mouth.

Maudit, this was painful.

"But…" Alex tried to urge the older coach along.

Paul turned to him. "I knew there was a spark between you two. Hell, anyone can plainly see it, but I didn't think you would, ah, act on it. You may not have, but I'm putting two and two together and—"

Simone shifted, crossing her arms as her face reddened to a hue Alex had never seen before. "What are the expectations, Paul?"

"Well. You two can't have any sort of romantic relationship, even though you're the assistant." Paul scrubbed a hand down his face, appearing as equally pained as everyone else in the room. "It looks bad for the center is all. There. I said it. It looks bad and can be viewed as unprofessional. If I were to allow you to continue and it got serious, and it got out, it'd be problematic. Not as problematic if you were the head coach, but it's still not good. I'm sorry."

Alex met Simone's stare, hoping she could see that he didn't regret anything. He never would, not when it came to her. He really liked her. He'd been intrigued when they first met, and now? Now he could say with certainty that he was captivated.

No one spoke, causing the awkwardness in the room to grow stale and suffocating. Paul shot them both a glance. "I'll give you two a minute to, ah, talk things out and then go home and take a break. We'll be back at it tomorrow."

Simone and Alex both nodded and waved wordlessly as Paul slipped from the room.

Calice. Alex wanted to hold Simone as soon as the door shut. He wanted to kiss her forehead, to hold her hand, something to provide comfort, but instead he remained frozen to the spot.

"Simone," he began. "This situation doesn't have to be forever. It's just for now."

Simone gave him a nod, her lips pressed in a tight smile. "Of course. It's not like we planned on me being your coach long-term anyway." She rubbed her lips together. "It's just for now. We can handle that, yeah?"

Alex didn't want to waste any more time when it came to Simone, but he also understood Paul's perspective. It just sucked, even if it was temporary. No one is promised tomorrow, and it wasn't like he could just turn his feelings off.

He blew out a breath and shot her a grin.

"*Oui*. We can handle that. Easily."

September

Chapter Twenty-One

ALEX

S~WEAT POURED FROM~ A~LEX'S SUNBURNED SKIN AS~ P~AUL RAN HIM THROUGH A~ drill. The thing was, he just wasn't feeling the ball. He knew what Paul needed him to do, but *non*, he couldn't do it.

He stopped, his breathing a little heavy, and lifted his shirt to wipe his face. Normally, he would take his shirt off, smirk, or tease Simone, but after Paul catching them three weeks ago...well, Alex was struggling. He didn't know how to act around Simone when all he wanted to do was kiss her again. Now that he knew what she was like in the morning, it had been absolute torture not to experience it again.

Criss. Alex kept reminding himself that maybe it was a good thing, because he'd been ready to go all-in with Simone—and he knew that he still needed to focus on tennis. If anything, his loss to Bastien last month at Cincy echoed that fact. The defeat had crushed his spirit, although not completely. There was a tiny flicker of a flame burning, and it ran on what it always did—his hatred of Bastien. Alex would train, and he would work, and he would get better. He had to. Walking away from tennis with the horrible record he had wasn't an option.

Alex put his hands on his hips, needing to speak his mind. "Paul, I've been here since July, and I don't feel like I'm getting a grasp on my game. I don't know how to do anything differently than what I've been doing." He gestured with his racket. Perhaps this was the real reason why he'd chosen not to have a coach. It would be one more person to disappoint. "I still can't push the ball up the line like you want," he added, winded.

He looked over to where Simone sat on the bench, scribbling notes and watching her phone, very focused. Her eyes lit up as if she had an a-ha moment, and then she came marching over to them, notes in hand. Alex tried not to think about how stunning she was in the matching workout gear that clung to her body.

"Hey, I have an idea, you guys." She turned to Paul. "Do you mind if I step in?"

"By all means, go ahead. I'll watch from the bench," Paul said as he moved to the seat she'd just vacated.

"Thank you, Paul," she said before she swung to Alex, practically vibrating with energy. "Alex, I've just been reviewing your match at Cincinnati—"

He groaned playfully. It was one thing for that match to play on a loop inside his head. It was another for the woman he had a thing for to point it out, given the humiliating beatdown it had been.

Simone began gesturing with her notes, her voice a honeyed drawl. "I know, I know. But hear me out." Putting down her papers, she grabbed a racket, and when she looked up at him, her eyes were wide and intense. "I don't think we need to change as much as we think, which is a good thing." She cleared her throat and shuffled her weight from one foot to the other, fidgeting with her earring. It had been a while since she'd done that, so it was clear she was nervous about whatever she was about to say.

"Go on," he said, encouraging her, wanting her to speak whatever was on her mind.

He'd been around Simone long enough now to know that she wasn't just intelligent and clever, but observant and careful too, a strategist.

She took a breath and lifted her chin. "What I want you to do is to stop thinking. Turn off your mind and just worry about hitting the ball right."

Alex took a drink of water, swallowed, and then turned back to her. "Hitting the ball *right*?"

She nodded, growing more confident with each minute that ticked by. It made something in Alex's chest yawn and unfurl.

"Think about technique as you hit. Focus on doing the right things. That's what I mean by that."

Alex twirled his racket. "*Oui*, I think I can do that."

"Good. I'll feed you one ball after the other, and that's what I want you to focus on. I don't care where the ball goes—if it's in or out, just do the right things."

Alex shook out his arms. "*D'accord*."

They each took their places at the baseline.

Simone started hitting balls, making Alex move around the court for each shot. His grip tightened on his racket with frustration, since he couldn't let go and just hit the ball without worrying about where it went, despite Simone's instructions.

As soon as one basket was emptied, Simone grabbed another.

Bouncing the ball on the court a few times, she said, "Again."

Alex frowned. He knew Simone had her methods, but he wasn't always the most patient. "What?"

Simone continued. "You're still worried about where the ball is going. I told you not to. *Feel* your shot, don't overthink it."

Alex shrugged and resumed his stance. They repeated the drill, and eventually, Alex understood what she meant and began to feel his shots like pieces of a puzzle clicking together.

Paul moved from the bench—he didn't say anything, just walked up to the net and watched until they ran out of tennis balls. Alex noticed a spark in the older coach's eye though, something livelier than what he'd seen lately.

Simone gestured for them to stop playing, a smile tilting her lips. "See? You know what to do. Your game isn't the problem. It's that you don't know how to use it."

Those words struck deep, echoing throughout his body. Simone was right, and Alex had never seen her so sure of herself when it came to coaching. She held her chin high, her shoulders back, her spine straight—and it was an incredible look.

On top of that, he felt a rush that hadn't moved through him regarding the game in a long time.

Progress.

He *finally* felt it after thinking it was gone forever. He could've wept with the realization.

"You're a beautiful player, Alex. Use that back and forth you've felt in life. Use it in your rallies. Don't just try to force something. Let the opponent come to you and then strike."

A grin balanced on Alex's lips, but Paul's gruff voice broke through the moment. "Both of you to the net." His face was unusually serious as he pulled out a pack of gum from his pocket, pushing a few pieces in his mouth.

Alex met Simone's stare, and she shrugged in response. Paul flicked his gaze between them, the scrutiny there nearly enough to make Alex shrink —and Alex Wilde did not shrink under anyone's stare.

"Simone's onto something." Paul tapped his bearded chin. "Simone, tell me, what would be your plan for Alex?"

She didn't hesitate. "Well, Alex is an artist when he plays, so he doesn't need to worry about overpowering opponents because that's not his style. Feeling his shot goes into strategy *and* style, and that's what I've seen on his tape, and that's what I've seen out on the court." She turned to Alex. "I think once you get the feel, which honestly, I believe happened today, then we'd move onto determination. Once you get that, then we'd focus on getting you the confidence to be who you are and play how you want, to play *your* game. It'd be a three-step process."

Without a doubt, that was the type of plan Alex needed.

"I was too focused on making you a defensive player, and in doing that, I didn't see what was staring right back at me. She saw it though." Paul gestured at Simone, who had her arms crossed, fingers at her chin. "She saw it because she's one hell of a coach. A *head* coach."

Simone's eyes widened as she stammered out a surprised, "What?"

Calice. That was a development Alex hadn't expected. He scratched his beard, trying to digest the idea. After that last drill with Simone, he'd felt his first breakthrough in months. The woman who dominated his waking thoughts had what it took to get him to where he needed to be on the court. That would just make things a little more difficult between them.

But it would be worth it.

"You know, Charlotte knows me so well. That woman knows what I'm thinking before I think it." He paused, and Alex recalled how Paul interacted with his wife whenever she visited the center. It was evident they were a great pair. Paul continued, "Good partners are always like that. Partners of all kinds. Spouses. Best friends. Coaches and players. You two have that kind of connection—*obviously*, given what happened after Cincy."

Alex laughed. "*Mon Dieu*, we get it, Paul."

Simone rubbed her forehead while trying to suppress a smile.

The older coach shrugged. "I'm just saying, use that to your advantage. Your relationship has to stay purely platonic for sure now, because the head coach and player being romantically entangled is *not* a good look, but this is the best option for you." He turned to Alex and then to Simone. "And for you."

Alex ran a hand over his head, feeling hot, and it was no longer from the sun. He knew Paul was right, that it would make not only Paul look bad, but Amalie and Julian too. This was their center, and if he wanted to keep working with Simone, it wouldn't be wise to allow his romantic feelings to get in the way.

Still, Alex hated the very thought.

He wanted it *all*.

Simone met his eyes and held his stare, and an entire conversation was exchanged in a single glance.

"*Criss*. Paul's right." He arched a brow. "You're the only one who can do it."

"Of course, I'm right. But…" Paul's gaze went back and forth between them, sensing the enormity of the decision. "You two still need to discuss it among yourselves. Of course, I'll still be an assistant and help Simone in any capacity needed, but it's clear she knows what you need better than I do. Come find me in the AC when you're done."

Paul gave them a nod and strode off, leaving Alex and Simone alone. It was impossible to read her face or get an idea of what she was thinking, aside from the obvious shock still dancing in her eyes.

Simone toyed with the hem of her thin tank top before reaching out to the net, seemingly for balance. When she spoke, her words were shaky.

"You're the tennis player," she said. "It's your call."

"I agree with Paul. I could feel the difference in my game out there on the court. I need you, Simone. My career needs you." *He* also needed her, but he didn't add that. Alex understood this situation was difficult on them both.

Simone tapped her shoe with her racket. "It's not like we could do anything anyway. We can't make the center look bad, you know? I could never do that to Amalie. I love her, and I know how much this place means to her. Obviously, the same goes for Julian." She scrubbed a hand across her face. "Today is not what I imagined. I never thought I'd be a head coach so soon, but Paul has a point, and most importantly, I want to see you succeed."

"You're the only one for the job," Alex said, meaning every word. Still, a lump formed in his throat. He couldn't think about what he was giving up. Not now. That could come later.

Simone brightened a little at that, her demeanor shifting to almost playful, as if his belief in her buoyed her the same way hers did for him.

She arched a brow. "I would be your boss. Would that be a problem? Me telling you what to do?"

Alex took another step closer, his voice dropping. It was impossible not to flirt with her. He wasn't even sure how he'd resist touching her, but he knew a line needed to be drawn. He would do his best not to cross it, but he could already tell this would be more complicated than her simply being his assistant coach.

"I have no problems taking commands from you."

She scoffed, rolling her eyes. "Okay, sweet talker. So I'm actually your head coach? We're doing this?"

Alex extended his hand, his skin tingling when she wrapped her fingers around his. "*Oui.* We're doing this."

Chapter Twenty-Two

SIMONE

SIMONE WALKED INTO HER HOUSE THAT NIGHT AND SANK INTO THE COUCH, still reeling from the latest development of becoming Alex's head coach. She wanted the position, but it meant more one-on-one time with a man who had already snuck between the cracks of her armor. It was in his laugh, his silly jokes, the way he always tried to brighten her day, and every time she looked at the lovely multicolored butterfly sitting on her bed (okay, yes, her bed), she felt like a teenager all over again. And, of course, the sex was explosive, but that last time it had been liberating.

The thing was, she liked Alex. *Like* liked him. But she understood what was required of her—hadn't she always? She'd been on autopilot nearly all her life. What would a few more months be?

Agony.

And yeah, she knew it wasn't as serious as all that, and that it wasn't like she had a lifetime to wait or anything. But damn, she enjoyed being with him, loved how easy it was—and she wasn't one to easily share her vulnerabilities, but he made it effortless.

Blowing out a frazzled breath, she knew exactly what she needed.

She needed her little sister.

Pulling up Amalie's number, she sent a video call through.

Fiery curls bounced across the screen and then Amalie's blue eyes were front and center, crinkled with utter happiness.

"Simone!" Amalie squealed, bouncing around before settling back onto a hotel bed, cross-legged with fuzzy-sock-clad feet. The phone bobbled with her movements, and once she finally stilled, her outfit became clear. She was beautiful in her distressed jeans and a white V-neck topped by a black blazer—her usual book-signing attire.

Seeing her was a balm to Simone's heart, and she couldn't help but grin. "Hey, sis. I was hoping to catch you in between things."

Amalie beamed. "Well, you're in luck. We just came back to the room for a minute before heading out to dinner. The signings here in California have been a blast so far."

"That's amazing! I'm so glad it's going well." She paused. "Um, so I take it Julian's in there?"

"He's heading down to the lobby now," Julian called from off screen. "I learned my lesson last time when I accidentally eavesdropped on y'all."

Simone snickered because she could imagine him walking out of the room with his hands over his ears. Amalie blew a kiss to the side of the screen and then the thump of a door closing came through. She turned back to face the camera.

"Nope, he's not here," Amalie laughed before her eyes widened. "Which means you want to talk about men...most likely a *certain* man. The book tour schedule is a lot calmer now, so we need to chat more. I feel like I missed some *things*, ahem." She winked at the screen. "Fill me in on everything since we last talked and don't leave anything out. Last I heard you were going to Cincy, and I know Alex didn't do so well against Bastien..."

Simone exhaled loudly before leaning back on the couch. Her expression twisted into a grimace. "Yeah, he didn't, and when we got back home...*wemayhavesplepttogether*." The words came out in a rush.

Amalie blinked a few times before she shot off the bed, landing in front of a window, the view of a beachy city behind her, the sun shining brightly across her body. Her face was awash in disbelief at first, ending in a wide grin.

"You guys had sex! Oh my God. I knew it. I just...I knew it. Now Julian has to pay up."

"Pay up?"

Her sister froze, eyes wide as she shook her head, looking completely guilty. "Nothing. Nothing at all."

Simone let out a groan. "You bet that I would sleep with Alex. *Again*." She smacked her forehead.

"But I mean, you did, so…"

Rolling her eyes, Simone couldn't help but smile. She continued, "And that's why I'm calling you—well, part of the reason I'm calling you. I have other juicy news that will tie into this."

Amalie straightened, adjusting her blazer lapels and looking serious. "Hit me with it. I'm ready."

Here goes nothing.

"What I haven't told you is that Paul actually caught us the morning after." A cringe crept across her features. The embarrassment had been next level.

"So you two got it on at the tennis center," Amalie said with a shrug. And then the words actually hit her, and her mouth gaped open. "Oh my God, you two got it on at the tennis center! This just keeps getting better. Wow, sis, look at you being all adventurous. But wait." She held up a hand. "Paul caught you guys, so were y'all naked or…?"

"No, we were clothed, thank goodness, but it still wasn't pleasant."

Amalie let out a low whistle. "That man has a third eye for cockblocking, I tell ya," she muttered.

Oh yeah, there had been another incident, with Julian and Amalie getting interrupted. Poor Paul, really.

Focusing back on the topic at hand, Simone shifted a little on the couch, running a hand over her bangs before messing with an earring.

"But the thing is, when Paul caught us he told us we needed to put the brakes on things, that it didn't exactly look good for the tennis center since I was Alex's assistant coach."

Amalie tapped her chin with her turquoise-painted nails. "Okay, I see where he's coming from with that, because tennis is all about doing things a certain way. But it's not like you're his actual head coach, you know? That's when everything could hit the fan for our center and where reputations could get damaged. But since that's not the case…" She lifted a shoulder to punctuate her point.

Simone's stomach sank, and she couldn't help but laugh, the sound completely devoid of humor. "That's the thing, Amalie. Alex just hired me as his head coach."

Crickets.

Her sister's eyes were saucers, and she stammered a few times before finally formulating a coherent sentence. "H-h-hold on, wait a minute, you're his *head* coach?"

Simone nodded, raising her brows as she rubbed her lips together.

"Oh shit," Amalie hissed, bringing her hand to her forehead.

With a huff, Simone laid her head back on the sofa cushion, speaking to the ceiling. "*Oh shit* is a pretty accurate representation of all of this."

"Okay, so I totally put my foot in my mouth there, but maybe I can figure out a way to work around this, because honestly, if anyone deserves this, it's you—"

Simone sat up and met Amalie's gaze head-on. "Actually, let me go ahead and cut you off right there. Alex and I already talked and agreed to keep things professional despite how much we may not want to. And besides, I wouldn't want to do anything to hurt the center in any way. I refuse to let you be all sacrificial for my happiness, because I know you and I know that's what you'll do. I love you for it, but I can't let you this time."

Amalie sighed. "Okay, so now what?"

"I honestly don't know. I know it's only a few months because it's not a long-term thing, but I worry, you know? Alex is, well, he's Alex." She smiled at that before continuing. "And you know with everything that happened with Damien, my confidence isn't the best. What if Alex loses interest? What if he moves on and that spark is just gone?"

Amalie frowned. "Then it wasn't real to begin with."

"All of that is easy to say and hear, but it's harder to just sit back and chill and believe that."

"I know that, Sim. I do. And if I could castrate Damien right here and now for making you question yourself, for everything he did, then I would, you know that."

Oh, did she ever know that.

And she loved her sister for it.

Amalie sucked in a breath and released it, the sunlight from the windows catching her eyes and making them sparkle. Her lips curved upward. "But let's talk about the other aspect of this latest development. This is going to be *huge*, Simone, in the best way. You're a freaking head coach! You took a chance and here you are, already being the best at it—"

Simone snickered as she held out a hand toward the phone. "Let's not get ahead of ourselves."

"No, I'm totally getting ahead of myself, and I can't wait for the world to see how brilliant you are."

A blush threatened to burn Simone's cheeks as she dipped her head. "Thank you. I'm nervous, excited, *all the things*, but despite all of that, I know I'm where I'm meant to be."

"With a sexy French-Canadian." Amalie wiggled her eyebrows suggestively.

"With my *player*," Simone playfully scolded.

Amalie waved her off with a scoff. "Oh, please. I see how your eyes light up when you talk about him. Maybe there's a way around this whole tennis center thing."

"No, you already said it before you knew what was going on, and I already told you I'm not doing anything about it right now. That's that."

Her sister's lips twisted to the side. "Hmm, for now maybe, but know that I'm here and that I love you, okay? I'm proud of you."

"Right back at you, Amalie. I love you. We'll talk soon, okay?"

"Absolutely. Bye!"

After they hung up, Simone decided to watch tapes of Alex's matches to take more notes on his game. Maybe that would help her not stare at him with her tongue hanging out of the side of her mouth at practice.

Highly doubtful, but hey, why not give it a shot?

FEELING A LITTLE BETTER AFTER HAVING TALKED TO HER SISTER, SIMONE STRODE into the tennis center the next morning with her chin lifted high. Sure, she still needed to get used to the idea of being a pro athlete's head coach, especially when she was totally into him.

Her eyes landed on said subject in the lobby of the clubhouse. He'd already changed out for practice and paced back and forth, running a hand through his hair—his nervous tic, she'd gleaned. She paid entirely too much attention to him, which was how she'd managed to pinpoint things with his game that needed to be improved.

Simone watched those biceps flex as they lifted, and she attempted to stifle a sigh. She didn't do a great job, because when Alex turned, his entire face lit up.

"Simone! I've been waiting for you." He stopped pacing and met her at the door, his cologne tickling her nose.

She loved that scent. It made her stomach dip and spiral—without a doubt, it featured in some of her favorite memories. The things they did a month ago...ha, and then a month before that. No man had ever understood her as well as Alex—in *and* out of the bedroom.

She forced a smile. "What's up?"

"I just wanted to make sure you were still okay with the decision to coach. I know it puts you in the spotlight, somewhere you didn't want to be, and I've wrestled with it all night."

When Simone looked closer, she could see purple-tinged crescents beneath his eyes. He didn't sleep one bit last night.

A fist squeezed her heart tight, and she brought her hand to her chest in an attempt to massage away the hurt. "You were worried about me?"

She couldn't help that her voice came out hoarse. When had anyone put her first?

It had been, well, never.

Alex picked up one of her hands, stooping only slightly to meet her eyes. The grin on his lips was lopsided and almost boyish. "Of course I worry about you. I only want you to be happy, and above all else, I don't want to cause you any pain."

He placed his other hand on top of hers, gently running across her knuckles. They were so lost to each other right then. Forget the fact that Paul was in his office or that she knew she'd see Damien sooner rather than later, since she had the lawyer send over the alimony paperwork yesterday once she signed on to be head coach.

"Alex." Simone wanted to touch his bearded cheek, to smooth the furrow between his brow, but she couldn't. He'd just reminded her why. "That's so sweet of you to worry about me, but I *want* to do this. I know the risks, and it's something I'm willing to do. For you." Oh crap. That was the truth, but she wasn't supposed to say it out loud, so when Alex's pretty brown eyes flared, she had to abort. She cleared her throat. "And for me, of course."

His smile grew wider, knowing. "Of course, *cherie*."

Shivers danced over her body, her automatic reaction to hearing that term of endearment.

The center door snatched open. "Looks like we have more than one thing to talk about," a familiar voice filled with disdain snarled.

Simone dropped Alex's hands, but from that comment and the bitterness in his tone, she knew Damien had already seen them and drawn his own conclusions.

Recognition dawned across Alex's face, his hands flexing at his side.

Simone whirled around to find Damien studying her and Alex with brows raised. He wore what he always wore—his expensive sunglasses (purchased with *her* money) pushed into his thick brown hair, a polo with the collar flipped (this had just happened post-divorce, as Simone put her foot down against that *hard*) and tucked into khakis, and boat loafers.

After taking him in, she couldn't help but roll her eyes. So much disdain coming from the man who had no idea what their wedding vows meant. She knew it wouldn't take him long to show up. Looks like Mr. Big Shot would have to work a little harder to make his own money. She bit back a laugh at that thought.

"I figured I'd see you soon," she said. "Where's Lula?"

"She's at my place with my mom. I wanted to have this discussion without her around." Damien sounded annoyed and put out.

Alex drew closer to her side but said nothing.

Simone rested a hand on his shoulder, his demeanor relaxing slightly.

"I've got this," she whispered so only he could hear. Might as well get this over with. The testosterone was stifling. "Damien, this is Alex Wilde." She gestured between them. "Alex, this is my ex-husband."

They lifted their chins at each other, their glances searching and measuring. Alex turned to Simone, uncertainty in the wrinkle of his forehead, the pout of his lips. He made no attempt to lower his voice when he spoke. "Do you want me to stay?"

Damien snorted and rocked on his heels but said nothing.

Scrunching her nose, Simone cut her ex a look before turning back to

Alex, who was practically making her insides melt with his sweetness. "I'm good. Thank you though. Will you tell Paul I'll be in my office with my *visitor*?" She tried to make sure that one word was soaked in contempt.

Alex nodded, and when he passed Damien, he skewered him with a *don't fucking mess with her* look. "Damien."

"Wilde," he responded, the first words he'd spoken to the man.

Simone waited until he'd disappeared onto the courts and then headed to her office. When she stopped outside of it, Damien walked past her through the doorway, sat down on her sofa, and relaxed. The evil little inner voice in her cackled, because he wouldn't be getting so comfortable on that sofa if he knew what she and Alex did on it. Multiple times. There was a reason she never let anyone sit there, but hey, Damien deserved it— she just had to repress the urge to steeple her fingers like a villain at witnessing it.

Further proving her point, Damien grabbed the newspaper off her desk like he belonged there, but Simone remained standing, arms folded tight over her chest.

"I have a lot on my to-do list today," she said, "so if we could get this over with quickly, I'd appreciate it."

Damien sat the paper aside and looked up at her. "You could have just called me rather than having your lawyer deliver the news." He leaned forward, resting his elbows on his knees. "What in the hell are you doing, Simone? Walking away from your job?" He motioned to the door. "For some young tennis player? When will you come to your senses?"

She jerked her head back. "Angry because your lifestyle is about to change significantly, huh?"

Damien's face grew red. "It's not about the money—"

She held up a hand. "Don't lie to me. It was always about the money. That's why you're here."

He took his sunglasses out of his hair and folded them. "When Lula said you were helping coach Alex, I thought it was a part-time thing after work. I didn't believe her and thought she was making up stories again. And if it was true, what would it matter? It's not like it would've changed anything, because you still worked at the hotel. Now I find out you've *really* stepped down as CEO, *and* you're the *head* coach? On top of that, you're screwing him?"

"Oh, fuck *you*, Damien. You lost the right to care about who I have in my bed a long time ago. I know why you're really upset—you can't stand the fact that I'm finally happy. And you're pissed because you won't be able to impress women anymore with your income, so now you'll have to work on your personality."

"You can't do this, Simone."

She shrugged. "I can, and I have. There's nothing you can do but live with it."

Damien stood up slowly, anger pinching the lines of his face. "You're right. I have no recourse. But I know people in high places too, and we have a daughter who deserves more than a mother who spends her weekends sleeping with men half her age."

"I never said I was sleeping with him, and besides, he's not half my age. He's eight years—"

Damien held up a hand. "It doesn't matter. It's all over your face, Simone. You've fucked him. And you want to again." He shrugged, slow and calculated. "If you want the spotlight, Head Coach, maybe you'll get it."

Simone's blood went cold as he stalked off toward her door. She followed.

"Are you...are you threatening me?"

Damien opened the door but turned back. "You know me better than anybody, Simone. What do you think?"

And then he left, his words hanging thick in the air, threatening to suffocate her with each breath.

Simone pinched the bridge of her nose, trying to keep her emotions in check. She wanted to throttle Damien. To follow him out to his car and rip his silly status symbol sunglasses from his hair and stomp them to pieces. She bought them. She could do whatever she wanted to with her property.

"Simone? Are you okay?" Alex called from her doorway, causing her to straighten and brush her hands on her shorts.

"Oh, I'm fine. Of course. It's an everyday thing when your ex threatens you, isn't it?" She tried to joke, but it floundered.

Alex's lips flattened, gaze flinty. "He *threatened* you?"

"Just...he's upset about not getting more money—"

"Isn't he a financial advisor? Shouldn't he have his own money?"

Simone scoffed. "He would, but he has expensive tastes."

"He sounds like a *trou du cul* to me." He paused, studying her as he rubbed his chin. "Is there anything I can do to help?"

Simone shook her head. "No, I'm good. This is my problem, and I'll take care of it, but thank you."

He reached for her wrist, gently wrapping his hand around it. She allowed his warmth to soak into her skin, to her bones.

Alex's voice was tender when he spoke. "It's not just *your* problem. That's why you have me. I know we have to keep our distance and all, but it doesn't mean I have to like it. It doesn't mean I don't think about you all the time. So let me help you with this. You said we were friends, so let me be one. Do I need to talk to Damien?"

For a split second, she considered it, but the consequences far outweighed the benefits.

She sat down on the corner of her desk. "No, I think that would make matters worse, and I need to maintain some semblance of order for when I pick up Lula tonight, which I am dreading."

"You have to pick her up from his house?"

She nodded, feeling a little sick.

Alex's shoes touched hers as he drew nearer. He was so beautiful it hurt. Simone attempted to wipe her face clean of any expression, especially with Damien's threats lingering in her mind.

When Alex spoke, his voice was low, earnest. "Let me go with you. He won't say anything to you while I'm there because he's a coward."

"But he just threatened me, saying if I wanted the spotlight, I could have it. He knows we...he knows what we did. I didn't confirm or deny it, but he knows. If I just lay low for a little while, it'll blow over."

Alex's head tipped up toward the ceiling, and he let out a loud breath. "*Merde*. This is what I was afraid of." He looked back at her. "You being forced into the public eye for their consumption again."

She moved out of Alex's orbit and sat down at her desk in an exhausted huff. "It'll be fine."

He studied her for a moment, head cocked. "What time do you think you'll be back home?"

She squinted, thinking. "I'm not sure, maybe around six?"

With a nod, Alex tapped her desk with his knuckles. God, those sexy knuckles. "We have tape to review, *oui?*"

"We do, but we can always do that tomorrow."

She didn't want to thrust her player into her ex drama. It didn't matter that they'd seen each other naked more than once. She still had a job to do and could do it on a day when Damien hadn't tried to make her life hell.

"*Non.* We should do it tonight. Let me make your day better. If you won't let me intimidate your ex," he said jokingly, "then let me take care of you. I'll be at your place at six-thirty. Don't worry about dinner. I'll handle that."

Everything in Simone screamed for her to turn him down. To walk away. But he was Alex Wilde. She felt drawn to him since day one, and the idea of him wanting to help her, to make sure she was taken care of, made her heart swell to the point that she worried it might burst.

"Okay..." She drew the two syllables into three, still feeling uncertain despite the fact that she wanted more time with Alex.

This was for tennis anyway. They had to watch tapes. Or so she reasoned with herself. Damien couldn't say anything about it either.

Alex's lips curved. "*D'accord.*"

And then he walked off, and she wondered if she had finally found herself a knight in shining armor like she'd always read about in books—although in this story, the woman planned to rescue herself.

Chapter Twenty-Three

SIMONE

Simone double-checked her reflection, making sure she was the perfect mix of comfy and cute. She didn't want to look like she was trying too hard, but she also wanted to look put together, coach-like, if that was even a thing.

Thankfully, picking up Lula had gone smoothly—mainly because Simone told Damien to send Lula out once she got there. Simone knew better than to send him a text threatening to kick him in the balls if he came near her at this point, although she had to admit it was mighty tempting.

"So Alex is coming here? I wonder which cereal he'd want?" Lula said, tapping her finger against her chin as she hovered by Simone's side.

This girl.

"Lula, I think he's bringing dinner, but you're more than welcome to have cereal. We've got to watch tape for just a little bit afterward." Simone looked down at Lula to find her daughter smiling. "Why are you grinning like that?"

Lula's curls brushed her face as she shook her head. "I've never seen you this happy. That's all." And then she was gone, disappearing into the kitchen and rummaging through the pantry.

Guess she was going for cereal after all.

Simone turned back to the mirror and inspected her appearance once more. Did she really look happy? What was so different about her reflection? She took in her blue eyes, and *maybe* there was more of a glimmer there. Her shoulders were looser, even if she was about to see the object of every one of her sex dreams. There—just at the thought of Alex, her lips twitched and lifted.

Yeah. She was happy.

Things were complicated, but she'd managed to find the good hidden beneath the surface.

A knock from the door caused all that carefree, chill looseness to dissipate instantly. This was watching tape. They were working.

On the offhand chance Lula mentioned this to Damien, her daughter would obviously say they were working. Damien wouldn't do anything, right?

Suddenly, she second-guessed every decision she ever made, especially once she opened the door.

Alex Wilde was sexier than anyone had any business being. His hair was wavy like he'd spent the day at the beach, his leather jacket beneath his arm, his navy-blue V-neck wrapping around his body like *she* wanted to. His jeans clung to his muscled thighs. The fabric had holes in the knees, resting further down over his black motorcycle boots.

And damn, those tattoos never got old.

Not reacting to her gawking at him, Alex lifted a pizza box. "I brought dinner. I figured we could eat and watch the matches."

She shook her head, coming back to earth. "Of course, that sounds perfect." Suddenly remembering her manners, Simone gestured behind her. "Come in, please."

As Alex brushed past her, she couldn't stop herself from taking a deep inhale of his heady cologne.

"Where shall I put it?" he asked, turning around on his booted heel.

She had a pretty good idea but caught herself on that one.

Finally getting her mind out of the gutter, Simone gestured to the living room, pointing at the coffee table in front of the couches. "We can eat in here and I'll get the plates, if you want to go ahead and sit."

Alex shook his head. "*Non*. Let me help. We can do it together."

Together.

What a lovely thought.

He put the pizza on the table and followed her into the kitchen.

"Alex! You brought pizza—my favorite!" Lula squealed when she ran into him.

"Eat all those marshmallows yet?" Alex asked, referring to when he and Tallulah first met.

Lula laughed. "I did. Mom got me a new box yesterday."

"Good. She should always make sure you have plenty," he said with a wink at Simone.

Goodness gracious, her ovaries.

She tried to ignore how cute Alex and Lula were—how she directed him to get the sodas while she got the napkins, leaving Simone to grab the plates.

Once they had everything, they all moved back into the living room. Simone plopped down on the couch, reaching forward to open the pizza box and grab a slice.

Alex sat down next to her, his thigh touching hers. She sucked in a breath at the contact, then played it off as if she were just breathing— because she wasn't lovesick or anything…was she?

She cleared her throat. "Thank you for dinner," she grinned before peering around Alex at Lula, who had already staked her claim on his other side on the couch. "Lula Bug, you're going to watch tape with us? Won't you get bored?"

Alex pulled two pieces of pizza out of the box, placing one on Lula's plate and the other on his.

Lula bit into her pizza, eyes sparkling. "Nope. Alex said I'd be a big help."

Simone chuckled. "Oh, he did, did he?" She looked at Alex accusingly.

He put the plate down on the coffee table, holding his hands up in surrender. "I thought she would be." He turned the tape on. "All right, Lula, I want you to tell me what you think I need to do better."

She scoffed. "I don't even have to watch it to tell you that. Grandpa—"

Oh geez. Simone groaned. Leave it to her dad to have an opinion since he watched the sport religiously. She rolled her eyes as she met Alex's stare.

He bit down on a smile as if that explained everything.

"As I was saying before I was rudely interrupted," Lula grinned

playfully. "Grandpa said you need to stop being such a baby and just hit
the ball. Stop thinking about it." She took another bite of her pizza,
completely unbothered.

Simone was pretty sure her eyes were wider than saucers, or at least
that's what it felt like. She was about to admonish Lula when Alex barked
a laugh—leaning back, laughing and showing off those perfect white teeth,
that sexy column of a throat. The dirty, downright filthy images
bombarded her brain, her body suddenly hot despite the cool temperature
in the house. She held a hand to her cheek, pretending to think, when in
reality she was judging if the flush that wracked her body had reached her
face.

News flash. It had.

"I think your grandpa is right, Lula. Maybe your mom can help me
with that."

Lula held up her empty glass. "Of course she can. I'm grabbing more
juice." And then she disappeared to the kitchen.

"She is such a ballbuster," Simone chuckled.

Alex sat back, resting his head on the couch as he gazed at her, so at
home. The way he looked there sent a pang to her chest.

"I like her honesty."

Lula flew into the room in a hurry, talking quickly as if she just
remembered something, her cup in hand. "So, Mom. What do you think
about teaching me to ice skate? Do you think you could?"

Ugh. Poor Lula had been hounding her about ice skating for weeks
now. Simone cringed as she thought of how to let her daughter down
easily—it was hard when she already had one parent do it so
consistently.

"Ah, well, I'm not the best at ice skating. Rollerblading is more my
speed."

"I love rollerblading," Alex piped up.

"I'm surprised you know what those are, being that they're more for
my generation," Simone quipped with a laugh.

Alex pretended to be indignant. "You act as if I'm so much younger
than you."

Simone bit down on her lip to keep from smiling even wider. Eight
years was a stretch for her. But not like it mattered if they couldn't be

together, a thought that didn't want to stick in her mind for some reason. Hell, she knew the reason.

She wanted the man—*all* of him.

"So that must mean you like ice skating?" Lula hedged. Simone knew where this was going.

Alex nodded. "I love it, actually." He paused, a sweet, thoughtful expression etched into the planes of his face. "*Alors*, Lula, what would you say if I taught you? After all, I can't have an American," he said, hooking a thumb at Simone, "teaching you how to ice skate."

Lula lit up as her head whipped around to Simone. "Can he, Mom? Can Alex teach me? Please? I'll walk the dog for a week."

Simone froze. "We don't have a dog."

"But we will. So please?" Lula even brought her hands beneath her chin, giving Simone the full-on guilt trip expression that worked every single time.

"Fine."

Tallulah did a wild little happy dance and then stood up with her pizza. "On that note, I'm going to my room because, yeah, watching tennis tape is boring." She waved to Alex and headed upstairs.

Simone blew out a breath. "Sorry about that. I've been on Damien to teach her, and he keeps saying he will, but he puts it off. He..." She shook her head. "He's probably Lula's biggest disappointment. He says he'll be there, do this or that, but he's too busy when the time comes. I try to make up for it, but..." She shrugged because, really, what else was there to say?

Alex edged closer so that his shoulder touched hers as he took her hand and squeezed it. "You're doing an amazing job, Simone. Take it from someone who didn't have anyone parenting them most of the time—you're a wonderful mother." His fingertips brushed over her knuckles, back and forth in a seemingly innocent swipe. "It's Damien's loss if he doesn't see what he's missing out on—with you *and* Tallulah. His loss is my gain." One more soft caress of her knuckles, and then Alex released her from his grasp.

Simone's stomach fluttered, her heart in her throat at his words. "That's so sweet of you to say." She wondered what it'd be like to just curl into him and have a lazy night watching television instead of studying tennis tape. She wanted nothing more than to find out, which was how she knew it was time to get the night back on track. She needed to turn this back around to tennis before she did something reckless (again), and she knew exactly how to do it. "So I've been meaning to ask you, what's your big plan, Alex? For tennis?"

Alex tilted his head back, looking at the ceiling as if thinking about it for a minute. When he had his answer, he turned toward her. "Beating Bastien is my only plan right now. I haven't thought past it."

Okay, so that was part of the problem. Simone shifted on the couch so she could see Alex better. "I think you should though. There are bigger things out there besides this rivalry you have with your stepbrother."

He lifted a shoulder, not convinced. "Perhaps. I *would* like to win one or two Grand Slams eventually, something that erases the Wilde Card nickname. Is that answer better?" His lips curved, eyes glittering.

"It is, thank you." Her fingers moved toward him, wanting to touch his hand, but she snatched them back. "But Alex, being a wild card isn't a bad thing. I hope maybe one day you'll see that."

Alex made a humming noise, one that said he didn't exactly believe her. "Maybe I will. But what I hate most about this is the waiting. In order to play any tournaments at the end of this year, I'll have to get a wild card into them. What's even more ridiculous is that I'm desperate to play in any one of them. I want to get out on the court, wild card be damned."

"You will. I know you'll get into a tournament before December."

He gave her a sad little smile and looked at the television.

After a moment of comfortable silence between them, he sat up a little straighter. "What about you? We both know I'm not the type who keeps a long-term coach and kind of already discussed that this is short-term, so after our arrangement is over, what do you want to do?"

That was something she'd been thinking about a lot lately. She understood Alex wasn't forever in more ways than one, and she wanted to be prepared for the day when he decided he wanted to go out on his own or find a new coach.

"I still want to be a head coach, but I might mix it up. I'd love to help teens getting ready to head to the pros. I could help them find steady footing before going into that world, and then I could stay home with Lula and not lose time with her because of travel." She picked at a loose thread on the couch. "I haven't been able to give her the experiences I've wanted due to my job at Warner Hotels. I traveled a lot, and even with me being the CEO, the board wasn't too keen on bringing kids on-site."

"I can see you doing that and being good at it too. I've told you before, and I mean it, you could do anything you wanted." Alex briefly touched her chin and stood, heading over to her bookshelf, a secretive smile dancing across his lips. "*Chérie*, you have a lot of copies of *Sense and Sensibility*."

Simone followed him, her eyes running over all the spines of her beloved books. She gave him her back as she trailed a reverent finger across some of her favorite titles. "I collect them since it's my favorite."

When she turned around, Alex was *right there.*

"I do the same with *The Outsiders*," he said, but his voice was deeper, more of a rumble that she felt within her bones. He dropped his gaze to her mouth, licking his lips. "Simone," he rasped. "It's so hard not to touch you when I'm around you."

He brought a hand above her, pressing it over her head on the shelf, closing her in between the man she was falling for and the stories that had kept her afloat all these years.

"This makes it even more difficult," she whispered, as she settled her hands on his shoulders, skating along his biceps to his skin, hot beneath her touch.

His eyes darkened, flared when they dipped to her chest, taking note of the way her breath came in fast. They were torturing themselves with these stolen moments, but they were each as desperate for them as the other.

After all, nothing between them was guaranteed. So why did she keep envisioning him and her together at the end of this?

Because you like it. You like him.

Alex brought his head down, hovering just inches from her lips as he leaned in, his eyes on hers. "*Criss*, I bet you're sexy as hell when you read. Maybe that should be my new fantasy?"

His lips touched her ear, moving to her neck. She swayed toward his body, nearly dragging him against her, feeling how affected he was by her, by this moment.

"*New* fantasy?" she managed to ask, moving against him, biting back a moan.

"I have many when it comes to you." He gripped her backside, pulling her against him. "But this one would be you, naked on my bed, reading a book."

She let loose a hushed whimper. "And what would you do when you found me there, waiting for you?"

This had become their game. The what-if game, although when they started playing it that night they returned from Cincinnati, it had turned into something real.

Alex's hand moved beneath her shirt, touching her bare skin as he dropped his mouth to her ear, his breath warm on her skin.

"I'd crawl up your body," he murmured, his voice impossibly deep. "And then I'd part your thighs and taste you, slowly, until you're a trembling mess." He nipped at her ear, moving up and down her neck, leaving warm kisses in his wake. "And then I'd remind you that what we share is so much better than fiction." Alex lifted his head, and while she expected him to ravish her, he placed a lingering kiss on her forehead.

The tender act squeezed at her heart.

"Nothing found within the pages of those books could ever compare to how you make me feel," he said as he drew back, his eyes hooded. "I was lucky enough to find what others only read about. I found *you*."

Simone couldn't breathe. His gaze bewitched her, those heartfelt words echoing in her mind like the sweetest of dreams.

"Alex—"

Thumps sounded above them. Lula was making her way downstairs. Oh crap.

They broke apart, pretending to be scanning the books.

"Yep, that book is my favorite," Simone rasped, trying not to think about how ragged her voice sounded, and they hadn't even kissed or done much of anything.

Thankfully, Lula said nothing as she washed her plate in the kitchen and headed back upstairs.

Simone shot Alex a wide-eyed look. "That was close." She pointed to the couch. "We should, ah, probably watch that tape, huh?" She could hear the threadbare agony in her voice.

She sat down on the couch, Alex sitting beside her, his body radiating more heat than before.

He ran a hand through his hair as he blew out a breath. "Simone, I apologize if that was over the line, what I said. Just…seeing you against the bookshelf, I couldn't help myself. You…you seem to be my one weakness." He tried to punctuate it with a smile, but it didn't reach his eyes.

She understood.

Simone waved him off, trying to go for cool and unaffected when she was anything but. "Oh no, it's totally fine. This is all fine."

Fine. How many times could she say that word?

It was so *not* fine, because she wanted him like she needed her next breath. Each time he touched her, she kindled beneath his fingertips, burning from the inside out.

So they sat in utter anguish next to each other, like school kids in a movie theater, watching tape. There were moments when Alex would shift to be closer to her and she would do the same, neither admitting that's what they were doing. But finally, at the end of the night, after he'd left, Simone imagined that the scene against the bookshelf had ended very differently.

Shaking her head, she looked down at her phone. She'd love to talk to Amalie, but it was late and she was probably already asleep, getting plenty of rest before the next tour stop.

If anyone could keep Simone on the straight and narrow it was Amalie…or her best friend, Arlo. At least she only had a week until Arlo came home. Hopefully, Simone could behave until then.

SIMONE MISSED HER BEST FRIEND AND HAD BEEN COUNTING DOWN THE DAYS until September 14th the week after everything kind of sort of blew up with Damien at the tennis center.

On the ride over to the airport to pick up Arlo, all through traffic an idea kept cycling through her mind, one that made her as uneasy as it did happy. As with anything in her life, Simone wanted to be the best, and she was no different when it came to being a head coach. Along with that title came other responsibilities, and one kept sticking in her mind like gum on a shoe—PR.

She *loathed* the press. Hated being in the spotlight.

But she was best friends with a public relations agent, not to mention the best one in the game. It was her coach-bound duty to set aside her fears and worries and make sure Alex had the best of everything, and that included someone with stellar PR skills.

The press had cultivated Alex's image into something he wasn't, and she figured maybe this would be a good fix. And hell, she knew soon enough they'd be digging into her, so why not try to control the narrative a little?

Her mouth went dry, and her hands started to sweat on the steering wheel. She alternated wiping them off on her pants. As much as this stressed her out, she knew it was something she had to do.

Simone pulled her car to the passenger pickup curb at Hartfield, immediately spotting Arlo and her stuffed-to-the-gills travel backpack. Her rootsy blonde hair was pulled away from her makeup-less face, and she wore olive joggers and a black V-neck, looking put together even after an international flight. PR was her job, so Simone expected nothing less.

They waved, Simone doing a little dance in her seat while unlocking the car. Arlo wasted no time throwing her luggage in the back before sliding into the passenger seat.

"Well, hello there, my gorgeous friend," Arlo said by way of greeting, giving Simone a side hug. "How's that man of yours?"

Simone laughed, returning the hug. "Don't beat around the bush there, Arlo. And he's not my man. He's my player."

It felt good to have her best friend back home.

Arlo chuckled, laying her head back against the seat, adjusting her tortoiseshell glasses on the bridge of her nose. "Whatever. You two are into each other. If you weren't his coach, y'all would've already hit it in every room in your house and his." She smirked. "But for real, I'm so happy you've found someone who does that for you, but I do hate the circumstances you're in since you refuse to, you know…go for it."

Simone shrugged, trying not to think of what-ifs when it came to Alex, especially not when she was working up the nerve to face one of her biggest fears for said tennis player.

Arlo continued. "That Damien though. What a piece of work coming up there to the center like he did. And it wasn't just about the money either, honey.

Men never care about their exes until another man comes into the picture. It's like their testosterone turns them into territorial assholes. He's suddenly seen you in a different light, so don't be surprised if he tries to get you back."

Scoffing, she eased the car into the traffic leaving the airport. Even if Damien came pleading on bloody knees, she would never let him back into her life.

Simone shook her head. "Enough about my out-of-control life. Tell me about Scotland. Meet any hot Scots?"

Arlo laughed and rolled her eyes. "You know I don't have time for men." She gestured at Simone and winked. "Look what meeting a hot man has done to you. I'll pass on the one-way ticket to Complication City, thank you very much."

Complication City was one hell of an understatement.

Which led her to her next topic of conversation.

Simone gripped the steering wheel tighter. "Listen, Arlo, I've been thinking, and I'd like to hire you as Alex's PR agent. We need to put a new spin on who he is, who he *really* is—not who the media says he is, and then focus on what he's doing on the court..."

Arlo was strangely quiet, and when Simone turned her head, her best friend was staring at her wide-eyed and open-mouthed.

Arlo sat up straighter. "You know, doing this puts you out there too, right? Because the first thing I would do is release a separate announcement about you becoming his head coach. As much as you want to focus on Alex, we need to also put the spotlight on you a little bit. This is about building your brand too."

Spotlight echoed in her ears, reminding her of Damien's threat. She tried to shake it off, but it wasn't exactly easy. She swallowed, and the words that came out were sandpaper on her tongue. "I know. That's fine. Whatever you think is best."

Arlo tapped the console excitedly. "Oh, this is going to be so much fun! So when do I get to meet Mr. Sexy Accent? You know I love me some accents, especially English ones."

Leave it to Arlo to make Simone laugh when she was about to freak out. "We have practice at the ice rink tonight at five. He's teaching Tallulah how to ice skate."

Out of the corner of Simone's eye, Arlo froze. Melt would be more apt. "I think my ovaries just exploded."

Join the club. Simone grinned, not even ashamed to admit her thoughts. "I know. I think it's safe to admit that mine did a long time ago when it comes to this man."

"Uh-huh...*and* you're putting aside your aversion to all these public things for him...yeah, I'll be at your practice tonight. Who's picking up Lula from school today?"

"Me."

Arlo pulled the car rider pass from the glovebox. She'd clearly done this enough times. "Let me. I've missed her, and we can go for after-school ice cream, and then I can bring her to you at the rink after I've got her all sugared up. Sound good?

"First of all, thanks for bringing my kid back to me all hyped." She smiled. "But also, you've got to be feeling some kind of jet lag," Simone argued.

Arlo wagged a finger at her. "Ah, no. Screw jet lag. I can't wait to meet the infamous Alex Wilde and talk PR."

Simone lifted one hand from the steering wheel in surrender. "Fine. Tonight you meet Alex Wilde, and finally, you'll get to see what all the fuss is about."

Chapter Twenty-Four

ALEX

A COOL BLAST OF AIR WELCOMED ALEX AS HE PULLED OPEN THE DOOR TO THE ice rink. He'd figured the weather in the South would cool down once fall hit, but Simone informed him that in Georgia, fall didn't necessarily equal sweater weather. Their indoor practice was a welcome reprieve, and he couldn't wait to teach Lula how to ice skate. Most of all, he couldn't wait to see Simone. It was their first practice in a week that didn't include Paul.

A head of black hair shone from the rink, and when he got closer, he found Simone wobbling and skating close to the sides. If she let go, she'd probably be pretty decent, especially since she was able to rollerblade. When she saw him, she waved and made her way over.

His stomach tumbled over itself at the sight.

He tried not to think about the night at her house when he had her against the bookshelf, but it was nearly impossible, since from that day it had pretty much dominated his thoughts. And that little fantasy he'd created? The one with her reading a book naked? That hadn't helped matters either.

"What do you have in store for us today?" he asked, setting his bag down and quickly changing into his skates.

The action instantly transported him back to his days at Archambeau when he and Rhys had learned to skate—they'd been bruised and a little bloody, but it'd been fun as hell.

Simone leaned over the lip of the rink wall, watching him as he stood. "Remember when I mentioned a three-step approach last week?"

With ease, he made his way onto the ice, gliding near her. "I do."

"Well, today is step two: determination. I think you've got step one down, the feel of your shots, your game. Now I want you to learn not to give up."

Emotion knotted in his chest. Determination. Surely, he could discover that fire again?

Pointing to the setup at the center of the rink, he grinned. "I've heard of unusual coaching methods, but I'm intrigued by this. I see the goals and the pucks out there and a...wall?"

He studied the contraption for a minute. The wall was a piece of wood on wheels with small, almost puck-sized holes cut out in various locations at the bottom.

There were fastener straps on the back, and he had all kinds of questions about it, but only managed to get out, "Is that for us?"

Simone nodded, looking proud. "It is. We've got the rink to ourselves for the next hour and a half, but I need to give you a heads-up before we get started."

"A heads-up?"

"Yeah, my friend Arlo Phillips works for Hot Shot PR. She's incredible, so I hired her to work with us, well, mainly you. But she wants to make a coaching announcement and some things about me too. She's dropping Lula off shortly so she can meet you." She bit her lip, seeming hesitant. "What do you think? Is it a horrible idea?" She cringed.

Arlo. Simone's best friend. Worry stirred in the pit of Alex's stomach. He was used to talking to a girl's best friend at a club so Rhys could get her number, but this was different. He'd never actually wanted a woman's best friend to like him because it'd never mattered before.

Calice. This mattered. Despite the chill in the building, Alex started to sweat.

But what bothered him more was that she was second-guessing herself. He gently grabbed her wrist, encircling it completely as his thumb brushed over her pulse point.

"No, it's perfect, Simone. I think it's a great idea, but only if you're on board." He shook his head. "I'm not worried about myself when it comes to PR. I'm concerned about the possibility that you might get caught up in public bullshit again—because of me. *Alors*, I'll only agree to this if you're one-hundred percent sure this is what you want."

"I've got to do it. I can't hide forever. Especially if this is what I want to do with my life now. And it's the best for your career. I want to do it for you."

His throat grew thick as Simone's cheeks tinged pink at her words—she was not one to blush often. He held onto her stare, one fingertip brushing down her cheek. She gasped but didn't move. This was wrong, but touching her was like breathing—automatic and couldn't be helped, particularly when she was doing something outside of her comfort zone for him.

Tennis was the furthest thing from his mind right then.

Simone clutched at the front of his jacket, her body swaying toward him—and not because she was unsteady on her skates.

A loud whistle broke through the haze interrupting all of Alex's thoughts of her lush lips and how he'd like to kiss them again.

They jumped—Simone fumbled and Alex took a step back, but they managed to right themselves as they turned.

A blonde woman wearing brown-speckled glasses stood with Lula, both waving while wearing knowing smirks.

Criss.

"That's Arlo," Simone whispered out of the corner of her mouth. She patted Alex's shoulder. "Just know Arlo's been dying to meet you anyway, so you may be subjected to a full-on interrogation."

Alex raised a brow. "Is that so?"

"Yeah, might as well get it over with and get this PR train moving."

Alex nodded, and then they skated over to the entrance to the ice where Lula and Arlo awaited them. Simone hugged Tallulah while careful not to fall over on the skates, and Lula gave Alex a wide smile.

"I'm Arlo," the blonde interjected, wasting no time. Her eyes peered into him almost as if she could look into his soul. He fought back a shudder. *Merde.*

"Alex Wilde. *Enchanté.*"

"Nice to meet you, Alex," Arlo returned.

Simone placed a hand on her best friend's shoulder. "Thank you for picking up Lula and bringing her here."

Arlo waved a hand through the air. "Oh, it was nothing. I love hanging with my girl." She playfully bumped Lula with her hip before hugging her.

"While y'all have your adult talk, I'll be over there on this," Lula said as she lifted her tablet. She didn't wait for anyone to respond before heading over to a bench and immediately getting sucked into her device.

Arlo looked at Alex, then Simone, and continued her spiel. "So I'm assuming Simone told you about hiring me?" She rocked on her feet, clapping her hands together excitedly.

Alex chuckled. "She did, and I'm in. What are your thoughts?"

"You're starting over in a way, so you need a new persona." She paused before gesturing above her head in an arc. "A new brand, if you will. I can help you with that while my beautiful best friend here helps you with your game." She turned to Simone. "And Simone, you know we talked in the car about this, but I'll work on your marketing as well. Listen." Arlo pulled out her phone, tapped a few times, and then held it up to show Alex's neglected Instagram feed. "We start with your social media pages because, bless it, it's sad."

Simone laughed, causing Arlo to tap a few more times and lift the screen back up, this time with Simone's Instagram feed showing. "I love you, but yours is just as pathetic. But that's what I'm here for! We'll get a few interviews set up here and there, probably would be best to have you do them separately because Lord have mercy…" Her voice dropped after a glance at an oblivious Lula. "The sexual tension between you two is thick enough to cut with a knife, and we don't need reporters picking up on that. Although…"

She steepled her fingers and narrowed her eyes on Alex and Simone. "I'd love to see you both do a nude photoshoot together. Like for the *Sports Illustrated* body issue or something? Look at you two standing there, all gorgeous and happy. You look good together." She brought the back of her hand to her forehead dramatically. "Goodness gracious. I'd buy that issue. But yeah, that could be the only time you could do any type of interview together, because you'd be expected to be hot and bothered there."

Maudit, Alex was starting to get hot and bothered right there just thinking about Simone naked, knowing all the dips and swells of her sexy body. He needed to think about broccoli or something. He wanted to turn and look at Simone, to see her reaction, but he didn't need more indecent thoughts swirling through his mind at the absolute worst time.

"That all sounds great, well, the separate interviews and social media, not the, ah, other thing, the *Sports Illustrated* thing. *Obviously*, so yeah, Arlo, if you want to get going so we can start practice, that would be fabulous," Simone stammered and pointed toward the door.

Arlo lifted her hands in the air. "Fine. I'll leave, but only because my genius is not being appreciated, so I bid you adieu. Farewell. Goodbye!" And then with a bow, she left, blowing kisses to a smiling Lula.

Simone turned to Alex, wide-eyed, throwing a hand toward the door. "And that was Arlo Phillips."

Alex dipped his head to her ear, voice pitched low, unable to help himself. "I'm interested in the photoshoot if you are."

Simone playfully hit his chest, but he caught her hand before she could move it. She murmured, "I bet you are." As if sensing the direction of his thoughts—and maybe even her own, because her pupils were so dilated, her eyes were nearly black—Simone shook her head and headed toward the goal and pucks on the ice.

"Okay, Mr. Famous Tennis Player. Come on. I'll show you what we're starting with today."

A few minutes later, Simone dropped a hockey puck and pushed it toward Alex. "So, like I said, today is about determination. This is a mental lesson—and also, who knows, maybe you'll even have fun?"

Alex tapped his hockey stick on the surface. It wasn't likely he'd have fun, because practices rarely were no matter how hot the coach was, but he was eager to see what Simone had concocted. After all, there was a reason he'd chosen her to be his head coach.

"And what would you like me to do?"

Simone gestured to the net behind her. "I want you to shoot the puck in the goal."

Alex fought back the urge to appear scandalized, since hockey had been his second love as a child. "I can do that in my sleep."

His coach shrugged and took a step back, pointing to the disk. "Fine then. Get at it."

Like he thought, he had no trouble hitting the puck straight into the net. Simone dropped another, and he did it again. They did it once more before Simone skated over to the contraption that was an actual wooden wall on wheels. The holes at the bottom would fit the puck, but he had no idea how he'd send them through while skating around. Surely that's not what Simone would expect of him?

As she fastened it to the net, she explained her process. "So as expected, that was easy for you. No obstacles, no problem."

He picked up the hockey stick again, pointing at the wooden monstrosity with it. "What's the purpose of this?"

Simone placed another puck on the ice. "The opening is not always going to be there like you want it. Guys are fast on tour. One thing I noticed during the drill just now is that you stayed in one spot when I fed you the pucks. It was like you were trying to power it through, and remember, we've talked about this. Aggressive play is not for you."

Cincinnati had taught him as much.

Alex batted the disk in front of him back and forth as he listened to Simone. "I figured if I stayed in one spot, I'd have a better angle because I'm not moving."

She shook her head and picked up two more pucks. "But I *want* you to move around. I want you to find your angles and *don't* stop. If you miss, keep moving. Now hit that one and then I'll send more, but know I won't stop sending them. There are no pauses. Meanwhile, find the angle."

Alex felt his forehead wrinkle. "*D'accord.* But with those openings combined with any type of speed, it's impossible."

She crossed her arms, her tone firm. "That's the name of the game here, Wilde. Buck up."

Not waiting for another word, she motioned for him to start. He missed the first shot, and she sent another. He missed that one too, and his blood began to boil. There was no way he was going to be able to do this circus trick.

Alex grunted, frustration mounting, his shoulders tensing up. But he didn't stop. That had been what she wanted, so he tried to keep going, hopeless as it seemed.

Finally, Simone stopped sending him pucks. She gestured to the wall. "This is about breaking through the barrier, doing something that seems impossible," she said. "The people who win don't quit when things get tough. Just because the angle doesn't work doesn't mean you stop. It means you keep taking your shots." She pushed her bangs from her eyes. "Find a way to win when it looks like there isn't one. You can't stop. There's *always* another answer."

Alex straightened, fortifying himself to continue the drill. Simone fed him one disk after another, and finally, finally, *finally*, he managed to get one through an opening in the wall, sending it straight into the net.

He whooped and dropped the stick, skating over to Simone. She squealed, throwing her hands up into the air, and before Alex could think better of it, he swept her up in his arms, spinning her around like an ice skater as he clutched her to his body.

"*Mon Dieu*, Simone, it worked! I can't believe I did it!"

When he looked down at her, her eyes glittering, her entire countenance beaming, he felt something twist and squeeze in his chest, something that should've scared him given his aversion to relationships. But with Simone, it never did.

His heart expanded, Simone taking up more space inside of it each day, especially when she looked at him like that. He gently set her down before taking a small step back on his skates.

Pride filtered through her voice. "And now you've got determination."

They spent the rest of practice doing the same thing, and by the end, Alex managed to get the puck through the openings nearly every time. When their session wrapped, Lula was already waiting for him at the edge of the rink in her skates, grinning.

Alex offered his hand to Lula. "*Mademoiselle*, may I escort you onto the ice?"

Lula curtsied, and Alex realized two things at once.

He was falling for Simone.

Hard.

And her daughter?

He adored her.

"Yes, you may," Lula grinned and put her hand in his. When Alex looked over at Simone, her face softened and was dreamily lit.

Alex Wilde, the once eternal playboy, had finally fallen for someone.

Chapter Twenty-Five

SIMONE

THE NEXT NIGHT, SIMONE AND LULA WERE CURLED UP ON THE COUCH watching a movie.

Lula reached for the remote, pressing pause before looking up at Simone with wide eyes. "Mom, can Alex come over and watch another movie with us?"

Alex was Lula's favorite person at the moment, and Simone couldn't blame her daughter. The way he'd taught her to skate—he'd been patient, funny, effortless. He'd come a long way from being scared of kids at camp.

Simone fell a little harder for the man each day, and she could do nothing about it. How could she not care about him like she did? If she'd gone into a lab and created her perfect man, it would be Alex Wilde.

"Um, not tonight, sweetie. Remember, he and I work together so…" She tried to reason with her daughter, and hell, herself.

Lula rolled her eyes playfully. "*Right.*" She stretched the word into four syllables.

Simone's phone beeped from the coffee table, and Lula unpaused the movie, settling back in at the opposite end of the couch. Simone leaned forward to see a text from Arlo. This was the one she'd been anxiously awaiting all day.

Arlo: Team Simex, yes, I've given y'all a joined name, and it's wonderful, has

been announced to the world. I've attached a snapshot of the press release and have
already reached out to Alex about his interviews with several sports stations.
You'll have one tomorrow at one.

After texting a thank you, Simone pulled in a deep breath to fortify herself as she opened the image. The first step of Arlo's PR game was to put out a press release announcing Simone as Alex's new coach.

Simone pressed a hand to her chest, praying this didn't all blow up in her face. Because lately, it'd felt dangerously close to playing with fire, thanks to her struggle containing her feelings for a certain French-speaking tennis player.

Sure, Damien had threatened her, but that felt like a lifetime ago—when in reality, it was only two weeks ago—but he hadn't made any moves, so maybe he was just bluffing? He'd probably already found someone to take his mind off Simone and her money anyway.

She skimmed the press release image, happy with the wording of everything, but ultimately that wasn't the issue for her. It was how she'd be received. Would people dig up the photo of her running from Damien's parents' yacht, the one where she'd just found out her husband had been having sex with all of Atlanta? And apparently, some high-profile people too—hence the photo, thanks to a suspicious husband's PI.

Unable to help herself, she did what everyone always advised against. She searched the head coach news on the internet. Alex, still being the highly watched and loved player he was, drew attention for a lot of his moves, even if lately he'd been missing from the public eye more than usual. Just as expected, this announcement was a big deal.

Most of the tennis world had the same question: Who is Simone Warner? As she continued to search, her phone trembling thanks to her unsteady hands, she saw people slowly start to connect the dots, putting it together that she was Julian Smoke's sister-in-law and the Warner Hotels heiress.

And now tennis coach.

Then she saw the announcement for her interview with a tennis station, with Alex's happening right after hers. She used to give phone interviews here and there when she was CEO, but back then, she didn't have to pretend that she wasn't falling in love with a client. Thank goodness Arlo already had a plan in place for that.

She sighed, putting her phone down in her lap, eyes back on the TV screen. This was all outside of Simone's comfort zone, but she couldn't grow if she remained in the same place for the rest of her life. This is what she wanted, so she might as well run after it full throttle.

And it wasn't only good for *her*, but it was good for Alex as well. All of this would be completely worth it if it gave Alex the positive exposure he needed to get into one of the tournaments here at the back end of the year.

They hadn't really discussed any in particular, but Alex had agreed with her that they should keep their options open, and of course, there was always a chance that he'd gain wild card entry to a few.

Wild card. What an understatement.

Simone tried to focus on the rest of the movie, but all she could think about was what in the world she'd wear for her first televised interview as a head tennis coach.

SIMONE WALKED INTO HOT SHOT PR'S OFFICE IN THE CASTLEBERRY HILL neighborhood in Atlanta, loving the design of the open loft with the exposed beams and bricks. Arlo had assured her the rest of the agents would be on lunch break at that time, so they'd have complete privacy.

She had been so deep in her thoughts that she nearly smacked right into Alex's big, firm back. He turned around to steady her, his hand on her arms...and left them there, even as she looked up at him, arching a brow.

"Hey, I didn't know you'd be here too," she said before she thought better of it. Since Arlo said they shouldn't do interviews together, Simone had just assumed they would film even their solo interviews separately.

She still couldn't believe that the whole PR thing had been her idea and that the press release regarding her coaching status just went out yesterday. Sometimes it all felt so surreal, she couldn't keep up.

Alex rubbed his hands up Simone's arms, then down, almost as if he'd forgotten himself in the name of trying to steady her.

He shot her a lopsided smile that did all kinds of things to her insides before he spoke. "I go on after you. I thought I'd come early to support you since I know this isn't your thing." He lifted a shoulder, as if it wasn't a big deal when it totally was.

She wanted to plant a big kiss on those full lips of his because that was one of the nicest things anyone had ever done for her. He kept surprising her, this sweet-talking tennis player of hers.

The sound of Arlo's heels clacking preceded her, and Alex dropped his hand from Simone's arm.

"See, that stuff right there…" Arlo pointed to where Alex's hand had just been as she shook her head playfully. "Simone, we'll set you up in my office since it's a virtual interview. Alex, you're welcome to sit in and watch."

Arlo disappeared into her office, leaving them alone for a moment.

Alex turned to Simone. "Would it be okay if I stayed? Or would you feel more comfortable if I sit this one out, *chérie*? I'm here for you in whatever capacity you need."

She was sure he hadn't meant for that to sound dirty, but his eyes glittered once the words were out there, realization dawning upon his face. His expression turned downright roguish.

Simone knew exactly what capacity she needed from him, but she wasn't going to just up and say it out loud.

She shook the stars from her eyes and managed to answer Alex. "I'm fine with you staying. I could use the support."

He took her hand and squeezed it, his lips dipping to her ear but accidentally brushing her neck with his bearded cheek.

Oh God. All she wanted to do was nuzzle into his sexy-ass beard.

She stilled, wondering—and well, that little devil on her shoulder kind of hoped that despite everything, he was about to just go at her neck with his mouth.

Instead, he spoke, low and serious. "I'm always here for you, *d'accord*?"

Simone nodded, his words not doing anything to help her Alex-induced haze. She managed to croak out, "*D'accord*." She was well aware that with her Southern accent, it probably sounded hilarious, but she'd wanted to at least try.

Alex's eyes crinkled as he barked a laugh. "That's my girl!" He tugged her to his side and kissed the top of her head.

His girl.

This is what it'd be like. They'd have their problems, but it'd be so easy to be with him like this.

He let go of her before they entered Arlo's office. Her desk was a cheerful turquoise, her bookshelves matching. A few vintage Italy travel prints were framed on the wall, along with interspersed artwork.

Her best friend pointed to her gray desk chair, a laptop angled toward it, getting the perfect view of one of Arlo's favorite paintings, Klimt's "On Lake Attersee." She even set up a ring light as well. Wow. Things had gotten more advanced from when Simone used to do the sparse interviews here and there.

Arlo pulled the chair out with a bounce in her step—she was amped, entirely in her element. "You'll sit here, and Callie will log on when she's ready. Sound good?"

Simone sat down and pulled herself up closer to the screen. "Perfect."

Alex and Arlo moved to the couch that ran the length of one of the walls.

Before Arlo sat, she gave a little fist pump. "You got this, okay? You're a badass."

"An inspiration to everyone," Alex added.

Shaking her head, Simone waved them off as Callie logged on. They exchanged pleasantries, and then it was go-time.

Callie sat up straight, her long brown hair hanging in loose curls across her blazer. "I'm Callie Morrow, and joining me today is Simone Warner. Welcome, Simone."

Simone mustered a smile, feeling strange talking to a computer screen. Where did she look? At herself or Callie? Or both? Or would it look like she was staring?

She ran sweaty hands over her pants while attempting to steady her breathing. "Thank you, Callie. It's an honor to be here."

When Simone looked over the top of the computer, Arlo shot her a big thumbs up, and Alex winked. Whew, the thing his winks did to her.

She turned back to the screen, glad Callie couldn't see him. Now she understood Arlo's directive.

Callie looked down at her notes and began. "So, Simone, you go from being CEO of a large company to coach of one player. What's that transition been like for you?"

"It hasn't been easy. I've had to learn a lot, which I'm thankful for my mentor, Paul Mercado. And Alex has helped as well. Even though it's been tough, I would do it all over again in a flash because it makes me happy. That's the ultimate reason I decided to do this. I woke up and didn't recognize my life, and that had to change."

Callie nodded. "That's understandable. You mentioned Alex a moment ago. What's the player-coach relationship been like?"

Hot as hell. Good in bed. The shower. But sweet too... There were so many thoughts that dashed through Simone's mind, and she hazarded a peek at Arlo. She made the "get moving" gesture, and Simone shifted in the chair.

"Well, it's been good."

Callie waited a moment, staring into the computer screen. That's all Simone could say without incriminating herself, because there were times when she got nervous and she just blurted out things.

This could not be one of those times.

When the reporter realized she wasn't getting anything else from Simone, she kind of laughed and nodded. "Oh, okay. I'm glad it's been good. I suppose that leads me to my next question. Wilde isn't known for collaborating much. Has it been tough getting him on board with your ideas for his game?"

Simone moved forward slightly. "Honestly? I think I'm spoiled because he's been on board with everything, fully trusting me. And to have someone give you such complete and total trust with their future, it's not a thing of levity."

She couldn't look at Alex after that answer because she was a chicken. She was afraid of what she'd find there.

Callie tapped her pen once. "I'm glad things are going well for you two. Now I have one final question before we conclude our interview with you before returning to speak with Alex." Callie looked at the script on her desk and back at the screen. "With a guy like Alex known for really struggling to stay focused, do you have to stay on top of him a lot?"

A garbled sound came from the other side of the room, and it was hard to tell if it was Alex or Arlo, but Simone caught her expression in the camera—wide-eyed horror. But also, her lips twitched because, well, she kind of wanted to laugh.

"I, ah..." *I want to stay on top of him all day, every day.* "I don't really have to...yeah, coaching is awesome. Thank you so much for your time, Callie!"

And then she cut off the interview.

Alex busted out laughing, and Arlo had her hands at her forehead as she jumped up from the couch. She was on the brink of giggles too. "Simone...well done. That was one hell of a way to end the interview. 'Coaching is awesome.' I freaking love you." Arlo continued to laugh while trying to be supportive.

"I didn't know what to say!" Simone stood and jokingly covered her face.

"It's okay. Alex, it's your turn now. We have to hurry," Arlo directed.

He got situated, logged back on, and repeated the same pleasantries as Simone had.

Callie got right into it with the first question. "Alex, tell us, why Simone Warner? No experience, never been a pro. You had Paul Mercado. Explain that decision."

Simone tried not to stare a hole into Alex's forehead while sitting on the opposite side of the computer with Arlo. Her best friend patted her hand in support.

Alex ran a hand through his hair. "It was the easiest decision I ever made. She knows what she's doing. Simone saw exactly what needed to be tweaked with my game, and we've been seeing a lot of progress with her plan. Paul is an amazing coach, but as far as clicking and having a good relationship where we understand each other and trust each other, it's Simone. She's my rock."

Simone tried not to make any sort of noise, but here Alex went, giving her more reasons to fall in love with him.

Effortless, although she knew the surrounding situation was anything but.

She grinned at him, meeting his eye, and wondered how long they could last dancing around each other like this? They had so much at stake —Lula, the tennis center, their reputations—and she attempted to remember all those things as she tried not to swoon for the rest of Alex's interview.

Easier said than done.

SIX DAYS PASSED, AND SIMONE'S WORLD DIDN'T BURN DOWN WITH THE television interview out in the world. She felt better than she had in ages, and just as practice with Alex wrapped for the day, Paul came ambling toward them, moving faster than usual.

Like a man on a mission.

He rubbed his hands together as he approached. "Hey, question? You guys have been training hard for a few weeks now, and I was curious if you had your eye on any tournaments in particular?"

Simone nibbled at her lip. Of course, there were a few, such as Basil, Vienna, Metz, Belgium, and perhaps Paris. But it was a wait-and-see game.

Bastien had just announced he was playing the Paris Masters, which rankled Alex to no end. Alex needed a wild card, and those could be given out up until the day before a tournament began.

Alex stretched his arms over his head, most likely knowing it highlighted the cuts and dips of his muscles.

He swung his eyes onto Simone. "I do whatever she says. I think whichever one we can get into, *oui*?"

The serious Alex from practice was gone and replaced by this playful version. Simone had learned that each of the pieces were real parts of Alex, but some shone more brightly than others.

It was hard to think about his past, about how awful his stepmother and stepbrother were, how his father made him feel before he died. She felt so fiercely protective of the man before her—she really wanted to kick their asses, which said a lot for her since she'd never kicked anyone's ass.

She crossed her arms and looked at Paul first. "Yep. Whatever we can get."

Paul piped up. "That's a good move there. You've got a good eye as a coach. Made for it even."

He had this mischievous glint in his eye, causing her response to be spoken slowly, filled with suspicion.

"Oh, well, thank you, Paul."

Alex even had a brow raised, picking up on the vibe.

Paul pointed back to the clubhouse. "By the way, you've got a call waiting for you in my office. Might need to get in there real quick."

Simone scrambled. "Maybe start with that, Paul?"

All she heard was his chuckle as she jogged inside. Standing over the phone, she took several breaths. She had no idea who it was or what it was about, but figured it probably had something to do with Arlo's new campaign to get them some publicity, to build up some good press for Alex.

With trembling fingers, she clicked the blinking red button. "Hello? This is Simone Warner speaking."

"*Bonjour*, Simone. This is Gabriel Cadieux, the tournament director for the Moselle Open." She was familiar with that name. She froze, awaiting his next words. "And we'd like to extend a wild card to your player, Alex Wilde. We had a few last-minute spots open up, and we'd be honored if he'd fill one."

Oh shit. Now it made complete sense as to why Paul was all cheery and impish.

She tried to become boardroom Simone, leveling the eagerness in her voice. "Oh? What an honor."

"*Oui*, but unfortunately, we need an answer today."

"*Today?*"

Her emotions were all over the place, happy and apprehensive, scared to death. She knew Alex put on a good face about needing a wild card to get into tournaments right now, since he didn't have many ranking points. She also knew from that night he watched tape at her house that he was tired of being a wild card.

He yearned for more on *and* off the court.

Would this simultaneously crush and elate him?

She mouthed a curse. But if he won this, it would be great for him.

Winning this tournament would help Alex qualify for other events and maybe get his career headed in the right direction for the first time.

"Today, *s'il vous plaît*. You can reach me at—"

"Yes." Simone blurted the words before she could think about it anymore. She pressed her fingers to her lips, shocked that she'd said it out loud.

"*Oui?*"

Simone nodded even though no one was in the room. "*Oui.* Thank you so much for this opportunity. On behalf of Alex, we're very grateful."

"*Bien.* We look forward to it. *Au revoir.*"

"Bye."

Her stomach rolled, and she brought her hands to her forehead and paced for a minute, trying to gather her wits.

This was a huge deal.

She probably should've talked it over with her player, but he'd just said he'd do whatever she suggested.

When she stepped back outside onto the court, Paul stood there huddled with Alex.

"A little warning would've been nice, Paul," she called out, speed walking to them.

Paul held his hands out to his side. "It would take away the fun. The surprise. The shock value. It's one of the many joys you get to experience as a head coach. I didn't want to take that away from you."

"Well, consider me shocked then."

Paul looked slightly sheepish, but Alex appeared concerned, as he should.

"Who was it?"

Everyone always said it was best to rip a bandage right off, so Simone just went with it.

"I accepted your wild card to the Moselle Open." She adopted a super-cheesy cartoon expression and maybe sad little jazz hands. "Surprise."

Paul and Alex both spoke at the same time. Paul with a shocked, "You accepted it?" And Alex with, "*Calice.*"

She grimaced. "Sorry. I got so nervous and blurted it out. They needed to know today, and we were just talking about a goal, and this would be perfect because if you win—"

"You did the right thing. I should play it. This is what we've been waiting for, *non*? Bastien won't be playing there—"

"And remember, you have to get Bastien out of your head. This is for *you*, about *you*. Fuck Bastien, yeah?" Simone surprised herself by saying.

Alex laughed and nodded. "*Oui*, fuck Bastien."

"Bastien the Bastard," Paul added.

"So it looks like it's time to work a little harder and focus more," Simone began. She looked between Paul and Alex. "Y'all ready to get to work?"

After a chorus of yeses, Paul paused. "But we just finished practice. I need something to eat." He looked to Alex for help.

Alex patted his stomach. "Me too. My stomach is talking. Simone, what do you say?"

She grinned, well aware that it curled and snaked almost evilly. "Welcome to two-a-days, boys. Get your lunch and be back in..." She looked at her watch. "Two hours."

The guys scrambled for the clubhouse, leaving Simone on the court with her thoughts.

This was a big deal, and not just for Alex. This was big for Simone too.

What if she was setting herself up for the whole world to see what a horrible coach she was?

Simone had already put her racket away, but she unzipped it and pulled out a new can of balls and dumped them in the ball hopper. After taking her place at the baseline, she hit one shot after another, practicing, thinking, planning for Alex. She had an idea, a trick up her sleeve that she knew could be the way to help all the pieces of her training click into place.

Simone would not fail. She knew what the press would say. That was the whole reason she'd hired Arlo, to go ahead and start spinning things their way, which was already paying off.

But sadly, a female coaching a male player was rarely done. She'd only seen it once in recent days, and it was amazing, obviously, but there would be those small-minded people out there who thought differently.

Now it was time for her and Alex to show the world that they made sense.

God, she hoped she was good enough.

Chapter Twenty-Six

ALEX

ALEX TESTED THE GRIP ON HIS RACKET AS HE, PAUL, AND JULIAN WAITED FOR practice to start. He was thrilled to have Julian back from Amalie's book tour, but he was even more thrilled about practicing for an actual tournament now. It was nearly enough to make him forget that he had to accept a wild card just to get into it.

Getting a wild card into the Moselle Open wasn't unusual, since the tournament often gave such allowances to French or French-Canadian players. It was how they showed love to kindred spirits.

But to provide Alex with one? Usually, the cards were given to younger players, and here he was pushing thirty. Not old by any stretch—but in tennis years, perhaps getting there.

Thank God he was born in Montreal and trained at Archambeau. There weren't many younger players around who could say the same except, of course, his stepbrother, but he was already committed to a different tournament in France.

Apprehension threatened to creep into Alex's mind as he retaped his racket handle.

He was a tennis player, and he wanted, *needed* to play. However, after his demoralizing defeat in Cincinnati last month, he worried about a repeat. He didn't want to let Simone down, to make her feel as though she'd wasted her time on him.

At least no one was angry he'd gotten the wild card. *Non*, everyone was pleased aside from some of the *trou de cul* tennis writers, of which there were only a few.

Practices had been more intense the last two days, ever since Simone got the call from the tournament director. He noticed his coach had been tougher lately, more focused, more intense.

It wasn't hard to see how she'd graduated top of her class and earned her spot as Warner Hotels CEO, nor how she'd been the best at everything she'd ever done. When Simone wanted something, she went all in.

However, Simone's posture had become more strained, and Alex worried if she'd seen the speculation and anger over her getting her first major coaching gig with no lead-up. Most coaches have to work their way up to get a pro like him, terrible player or not. And here she was going to a master's level tournament.

Alex had ignored the chatter because that's what he always did, that's what he'd gotten good at, but Simone hadn't spent as much time as he had in the spotlight.

Stress knitted in his stomach over the woman he knew without a doubt he loved.

Oui.

Loved.

He'd figured as much, but watching her do her interview the other day, all he could think about was how to comfort her, how to make things better, how to be a partner to her—all things he'd never concerned himself with before.

Alors, if everything blew up in their faces regarding the media, he would carry that blame, because Simone put herself out there partially for him.

He shook his head, trying to think of other things like the here and now. He looked over to where Paul and Julian bounced balls on their rackets, having a competition to see who could do it the longest, when a thought struck him. Alex still needed to get things settled regarding the Moselle Open in Metz. Of course, he knew Simone was coming, but he wanted both of his assistant coaches in his box as well.

"Paul, Julian." Alex turned from the bench, putting his racket under his arm.

"What's up, man?" Julian called out as Alex approached. Paul just nodded in that Paul Mercado way of his.

"You know, I've never really had a team in my box before. It's normally not something that I do. If anyone sits in my box, it's Rhys."

Julian pushed his hair back from his face as Paul narrowed his gaze.

"What do you think about..." *Criss*, Alex couldn't believe the words that were about to come out of his mouth. He'd gone from being a self-imposed loner to this in a matter of three months. "I'd like for you to come to Metz with me, to be my team for this tournament, alongside Simone. Of course, I'd love it if you'd bring Amalie and Charlotte. I'm going to ask Arlo too." He huffed a breath, anxiously twisting his racket. "It'd mean a lot."

They stared at him open-mouthed and wide-eyed, Alex's question taking a moment to process.

Paul looked at Julian, then back to Alex. "I've heard about this kind of thing. This is one of those personal growth moments, right? What's changed?"

"*Everything*. Everything's changed," Alex answered truthfully.

Paul gave him a nod, seemingly satisfied with that answer. "If we go with you, that means we'll have to close up shop for a few days, which I think is feasible. I don't have to share a room with this guy, do I?" He hooked a thumb at Julian, who rolled his eyes and groaned. "Because I don't share rooms with anyone but Charlotte."

"You and Charlotte will have your own room, of course," Alex laughed.

Enthusiasm lit up Paul's face, and he rocked back on his heels, looking at Julian. "Your mom will love it! France is the country of romance and all that."

Julian rolled his eyes and faced Alex. "As for Amalie and me, we're in. I'd be happy to help out." He stepped forward, extending a hand. Alex shook it, feeling good about this.

Paul clapped a hand on Alex's shoulder, and he looked over at Julian. "What did I tell you? I knew this kid was special. Knew he was different. I'm proud of you, Alex."

Movement at the clubhouse doors leading onto the court drew their attention. Simone stepped out, and while Paul and Julian went back to chatting, Alex continued to split his glances between the guys and the woman he loved, who was heading their way.

Julian caught him staring and shot him a look he couldn't quite decipher, but didn't say anything.

Simone, however, was all business.

She put her hands on her hips as she addressed him and Julian. "You guys ready to get started?"

He wanted to kiss her then—he loved when she was passionate like that—but he knew he couldn't disappoint her, or himself, by not focusing.

"*Oui*," he answered.

Julian bounced a ball on his racket, sheer joy lighting up his face. "I've been dying to get back out on the courts, so I'm beyond ready."

Simone pointed to his leg. "Julian, I'm guessing since you agreed to practice with us today, the knee's better?"

"It's much better. I've been able to run every morning."

She nodded. "Well, let's get started. Julian and Alex, I want you both to hit in your normal styles, okay?"

They both gave her a thumbs up before heading to opposite sides of the court, Julian serving first. Julian always had the reputation of being a hotshot on the court, a fan of blasting the balls, hitting them with speed and power—that elusive aggressive play at its finest.

Alex attempted to emulate his style, but it fell short, the ball not going where he wanted it. If it'd been a match, he would've lost the point.

It went on like that for minutes until they exhausted all of the balls. Alex released a loud sigh of frustration and wiped his brow.

Simone moved toward him while Julian grabbed the ball hopper. "Hey, can you give us a few minutes?" she called over the net.

"No problem. I'll get these and hang out with Paul," Julian answered and started gathering up the balls on his side of the court.

When Simone reached Alex, she immediately began coaching. "Hey, so don't try to match Julian's pace, okay? Just because he hits hard doesn't mean you have to. Remember, you're a better mover than Julian, than all the aggressive players I've seen. You've got to learn to use that and your love of strategy to your advantage, got it?"

He nodded. "*Oui*. I can do that."

"Good. Now let go of trying to be something you're not. Play how you want to play and be comfortable with that."

"I suppose my anxieties are starting to bleed through into my game. I'm eager to play a tournament, but I'm nervous and afraid of letting everyone down," Alex admitted, not caring who heard him. There was nothing to be ashamed of anyway. "It goes back to the fact that I don't want to always be a wild card."

Simone shifted her stance. "I get that, but Alex, you're not a wild card like you think. I mean, you *are*."

"Well then," he said without thinking, not meaning those two words to be as double-edged and sharp as they sounded. He fought back a wince.

"Hey, guys?" Paul interjected. "I know you said you needed a minute, but come on, get on with it. The next soap is coming on right after this, and it's called 'Can Alex Hit the Ball Like a Pro Tennis Player?'" He rolled his eyes.

Alex laughed and Simone did too, but once she focused on Alex again, she stiffened. Her voice dropped low, but *maudit*, was it fierce.

"You know what, Alex? It doesn't matter what other people think. What matters is what you *know*. And somehow, a bunch of assholes who *should* have treated you like family yet didn't have convinced you that you're never going to be good enough. As long as you let them in your head, they will always win. It's time to forget the lies they've poured into you and listen to the truth, because it's finally coming from someone who gives a damn about you. If you want to be more than a wild card, then be more! Get up, get on that court, and show everyone who the hell Alex Wilde *really* is. Got it?" Her chest was heaving in and out so quickly that Alex wondered how she was getting enough air.

Her eyes were twin blue flames, her cheeks were pink from emotion and sunshine, and he smiled at her, really smiled, as she broke down each and every one of his defenses right there on the tennis court.

Mon Dieu, he loved her so much.

"Got it, Coach," he said, feeling the hope in those words spread throughout his body and fill in the missing pieces.

"Good," Simone grinned back.

"You ready?" Julian called out, breaking the moment.

Simone blinked a few times. "Yep!" she yelled before walking away.

Alex watched her go, unable to help himself. She always knew how to get to him, how to *see* him. That's one of the things that made her so good at this.

He got into position, waiting for Julian's serve. And this time, when it came over the net, Alex knew exactly what to do.

Strategizing was second nature to him, so he relaxed and played the way his body begged him to. He didn't rear back as far, opting to take a shorter swing. His strategy was to use Julian's own pace against him, which sent the ball over the net at a sharp angle, making it so Julian couldn't get to it.

Simone cheered, happiness illuminating her features, as she clapped and called out, "See, there you go!"

Paul joined in, and even Julian called out, "Good point, man."

The rest of practice went that way, with Alex having much more success than before. Simone's coaching on how to use his game properly had finally sunk in.

At the end of his time with Julian, Simone came up to him at the net first, still buzzing with excited energy. "Our three-step process is complete. You've got your feel, you've found your determination, and hell, you've got the confidence now to play the game *your* way, not someone else's way."

Alex placed his hand over his heart, hoping she knew how much those words meant to him.

Her eyes crinkled at the corners, her lips quirking as she said, "When you come back this afternoon for your two-a-day, Julian won't be here. Arlo will though, and then I'll show you the perfect thing to help bring together all of the pieces from our three-step plan, okay?"

Alex grinned.

He couldn't wait to see what she had in mind.

Chapter Twenty-Seven

SIMONE

ARLO NUDGED SIMONE'S SHOULDER AND SHOWED HER A SOCIAL MEDIA POST ON her phone, trying to give her ideas for their next move for Alex's slightly neglected social media accounts. It was hard to see in the glare of the afternoon sun on the court as they waited for part two of Alex's practice to begin.

"I think his fans will eat it up if he posts a training video like this. Don't you—holy hellhounds, who is that?" Arlo readjusted her glasses on her nose, squinting a slight fraction.

"That would be the trick up my sleeve, also known as Rhys Westwick."

"Alex's friend, right?"

"In the flesh."

Rhys ran a hand through his thick, dark hair, parted on the side, as he made his way to them. "It's nice to finally meet the woman who has helped my friend so much," Rhys said, his voice deep and rumbly, thick with a posh English accent. He extended a hand, which Simone shook.

Rhys had tennis player hands, rough with calluses like the kind she'd come to love on a certain someone else.

That word.

Love.

Simone pushed it away as Arlo instantly perked up. BBC, Masterpiece

Classic, all of that was her porn, and she was most likely dying inside at Rhys's voice. Simone gave Arlo a narrowed look, silently communicating for her to chill out before she turned back to Rhys.

"Thank you for agreeing to this. From what it sounds like, you've had a huge hand in keeping Alex from shutting everyone out," Simone said.

Rhys blushed, and she could practically hear Arlo swoon. "He's my best friend. I'd do anything for him. Including travel here to where it's bloody hot. Isn't it supposed to be autumn? Why is it still hot?"

"Because you're here," Arlo mumbled, her eyes on her phone screen.

Rhys's dark brows darted up, and Simone blew out a breath. "Rhys, this is my best friend, Arlo. Arlo, this is—"

"Rhys Westwick, I know who you are. Hello, charmed to make your acquaintance." Arlo extended her hand like she expected him to kiss it, like a duke or lord greeting a lady.

Oh, it was apparent Arlo had been binge reading historical romances and holding off on recommendations. Simone made a mental note to ask her about that later.

Rhys looked at Arlo's hand like it might bite him, his blue eyes wide, but he ended up shaking it awkwardly. Simone tried to stifle a laugh just as Alex sauntered toward them, a little extra spring in his step at seeing Rhys.

"*Mon ami!*" He dropped his bag on the court, and pulled Rhys into a big hug. It was one of the sweetest scenes Simone had ever witnessed, just the sheer happiness of it—two friends seeing each other again.

"This," Arlo whispered, turning her phone on silent and snapping a picture of the friends. "This is the Alex Wilde the world needs to get to know. Can I post this one, Coach?" She held her phone up so Simone could see the photograph.

Simone nodded. "Post it. Yeah. Of course."

Arlo diverted her attention back to the screen, her fingers flying as they typed.

"Ready to get your arse kicked?" Rhys joked, doing a silly little boxing shuffle.

Alex laughed, the sound settling over Simone like her favorite blanket. She fought the urge to close her eyes.

"Pffft. You know, the more you trash-talk, the worse you play. Might as well stop while you're ahead." Alex shuffled too, throwing a few jabs at his buddy. "*Allons y*! Let's go!" he shouted, and then they rushed the court.

Arlo shoved Simone with a pointy elbow. "Oof." Simone glared at her. "What's that for?"

"You're drooling over your tennis player with those come-hither eyes again," she whispered.

Simone blinked a few times as the guys started hitting the ball back and forth, Alex moving as if he hadn't already practiced with Julian. "I am not."

She was too. It was how she always looked at Alex if she was honest with herself.

"Oh my God," Arlo said, staring at Simone over the top of her sunglasses. "You love him. All this time, I thought it was just like or lust, but noooo. You really *love* him."

Simone frowned. "What? No."

Yes, she did. She knew it.

"I see it all over your face! Deny it all you want, but I know what I see."

Simone wasn't ready to share that piece of knowledge with anyone else because she couldn't cross that line. She and Alex knew this coaching situation was temporary, but he'd never outright said he was headed back to Calgary after everything.

Would he stay?

Oh God. Love changed everything.

After practice, Alex and Rhys stood around catching up. Arlo left about five minutes after they finished, needing to get some work done. Simone begged off as well, heading to her office to give the guys time to chat.

When Simone reached out to Rhys, she'd expressed that she wanted to talk with him privately when he arrived. Rhys was the key to cementing Alex's game, and if she could talk with him and game plan, maybe she had an even better shot at getting Alex ready for the Moselle Open.

Alex's original goal of beating Bastien didn't apply now since his stepbrother had already committed to a different tournament. However,

Simone still wanted Alex to crush all his opponents, and she hoped Bastien would see the tape.

After all, she'd seen mentions on social media regarding the nasty interview Alex's stepbrother did that very morning. She'd bet her right foot that Alex hadn't heard anything about it, not with how happy he'd been. Or maybe that was just another mask.

She sat down at her desk and pulled up the interview. She hit play on her computer screen, and the replay of Bastien's press conference began.

Alex's stepbrother was seated at the press table, his chin lifted as if he were the king presiding over his court. He ran a hand through clean-cut hair.

"Bastien, what are your thoughts about your brother getting into the Moselle Open?"

Bastien's nose wrinkled in disdain. "That's not my brother. He's my stepbrother, remember? And what? It's not like he's going to win. He doesn't win anything. Next question."

Simone clenched her fists, her nails biting her palm.

"*Ma chérie,*" Alex's throaty voice called out.

Simone blinked and snapped up her head to see him moving toward her, concern etched across his dark brow. Thankfully, she managed to turn off the video before he saw it.

"Everything okay?" His hand came to her elbow in a comforting gesture as he studied her face.

She nodded, quickly schooling her features. She wanted to say, *No. Everything's all mixed up because I'm in love with you,* but she settled for a bland, "I'm fine. How did it go?"

"It went well." He backed up slightly. "I appreciate you getting Rhys here. It means a lot. He's on his way in now, but I thought I'd stop by and thank you in person before I left."

Simone pulled a notepad out of her desk drawer, needing something to do with her hands as she spoke. "Well, of course. Anything to help."

Alex looked like he wanted to say something else but decided against it last-minute, moving to her door. "It helps a great deal. *Merci,* Simone. I'll see you." And then he slipped from the office.

A few moments later, Rhys walked in. He gestured to the door. "Would you like the door open or closed?"

"Closed, please."

Shutting the door with a quiet snick, he took the seat in front of her desk with a small, shy smile across his face.

Simone grabbed a pen, still wondering what Alex had been about to say. It looked important, but clearly it wasn't if he left without actually saying it.

"Rhys, thank you again for coming. Seriously."

He shrugged. "It's no problem. I'd do anything for Alex."

She bit down a grin. That made two of them.

"Before we get into the tennis aspect of this, I want to ask about Alex as a person, tennis aside."

Rhys sat back in his seat, clasping his hands over his stomach. "That's hard to do since Alex *is* tennis. But what do you want to know? There are some things I'll tell you and some that I'm sworn to secrecy on." His voice was playful, although his expression read that he was dead serious.

His and Alex's bond seemed unbreakable.

This felt like a game show where she could only ask one question. She needed to make this good so it didn't appear like she was prying. Her fingernails tapped a beat across her desk.

"I want him to win the Moselle Open, but I think I need to backtrack and talk about Bastien, because I'm pretty sure that's the kink in his game. Anything personal, anything to help me understand that dysfunctional family, would be useful."

Every aspect of her body burned hot with anger, just thinking about Claudette and Bastien, hell even Alex's dad, Jack. Her hands in her lap shook so much she ended up pressing them under her thighs.

Rhys sneered as he straightened. "I hate that little wanker, and I like you even more than I already did because I can see how much this bothers you. Alex is…Alex is the best sort of person, and me and my family, we're protective of him. When he told me about you, I got nervous, worried he'd get his heart broken, but I can see…" He shook his head, recalculating, not noticing that Simone practically held her breath, begging for the next words to actually tumble out of his mouth. "You're his coach, and you're ace at it. Alex's stepfamily is a piece of work, and he doesn't have anything to do with them. I'll never forget when I met him…" His eyes turned glassy as he met her stare head-on. "His bloody father forgot about him.

He did that a lot, especially during the holidays. Sometimes Jack and Claudette would leave Alex there by himself when all the other kids went home. I can still see him hunched over a poetry book with a scowl, daring anyone to get close to him."

"But *you* did," Simone pointed out.

"I did. Most people say Alex is difficult to get to know, that he has walls up. And while he does have walls as tall as Everest, if you hang in there, it's worth it." He shot her a smile that almost had her questioning if Rhys was talking about tennis anymore.

Just how much had Alex told his best friend? Oh geez. If it was anything like what she told Arlo, then it was pretty much everything.

Either way, her response was one that came from the heart, one that wasn't exactly about tennis.

"Alex is worth the wait. I'm not going anywhere."

And that was a promise.

Chapter Twenty-Eight

ALEX

ALEX STAYED AT THE TENNIS CENTER A LITTLE LATER THAN HE MEANT TO Friday night. Arlo had arranged an interview for him, and he wanted to get it over with before starting the weekend, especially with Rhys in town. The fact that Simone had reached out to his best friend meant more than she'd ever know.

Speaking of which, he was sure she was probably already gone for the day, which was for the best. He'd already realized that the two of them alone equaled too much temptation, and all he wanted was her—for everything, in every way, every day.

He heard Lula's pained voice first. "But why won't he take me? He promised me and said nothing would get in the way," she sniffled.

Alex picked up his pace heading down the hallway, drawing closer to Simone's office.

"I'm sorry, Lula. Your dad...your dad had something come up, and he said he'd take you camping another weekend."

Alex fisted his hands by his side as anger writhed in his veins. That *trou de cul* Damien had no idea what he had—his daughter still loved him regardless of his horrible ways, and all he did was disappoint her. It reminded him too much of his childhood—because, despite everything, he still loved his asshole father.

He moved faster toward Simone's door, desperate to fix things, desperate to make the Warner girls happy.

"Lula?" he asked, stopping at the open door.

Simone held her daughter against her, smoothing down her wild curls as tears tracked down her face. She wiped them quickly as Lula turned and ran to him, wrapping her arms around him so tightly an "Oof" came out of him.

"Alex," Lula sniffled.

He moved so that he knelt in front of her, taking her hands. "Lula, I have something super important to ask you, *d'accord*? I mean, okay?"

Lula turned even more serious and nodded.

"I've never been camping before, but I thought about setting up outside in my backyard, and I wondered if maybe you and your mom wanted to come and show me how it's done? I hear there are s'mores involved? And maybe a ghost story or two?"

Lula brightened, bouncing on the balls of her feet, turning to look at Simone. "Can we, Mom? Can we? Please? Please, please, please?"

Simone met his eye, and he saw everything he felt plainly written across her beautiful face, even among the remnants of the tears. She pressed a hand to her chest, her expression tender.

"Of course. Thank you, Alex."

Did she know he'd do anything for her and Lula? She had to. If she wanted the moon, he'd reach up and pluck it out of the sky for her, not caring about the consequences.

He smiled at her and Lula before looking down at his watch. "Give me about an hour and a half, and I promise it'll be ready. Simone, I'll text you my address."

And then he left because he had a mission: to let Simone know he was in love with her—and it felt like the long-term kind, the forever kind.

An iceberg shifted beneath his ribs at the realization. He knew the risks with the center, but perhaps they could be secretive about their relationship for the time being? If that's even something she was interested in, of course.

Although he planned to make his move with Simone, there was something even more important that he wanted to do. He wanted to let

Lula know she was worth it, that no matter what, he'd choose her every time.

SIMONE AND LULA ARRIVED JUST AS ALEX FINISHED SETTING UP EVERYTHING. He'd managed to rope Rhys into helping, and he was pretty impressed with what they pulled off in a short amount of time.

"Come in," Alex said as he stood back, opening the door wider. Simone and Lula stepped inside, Simone's eyes taking in everything about his rental house.

"This is a lovely home." Her eyes flicked to the bookshelf, and she headed over to it. The look she shot him sparked with heat, most likely as she remembered that night at her house. "You weren't kidding about collecting all these editions of *The Outsiders*." A smile twisted her lips.

She was killing him, and she had no idea. Alex wanted to move, to go to her, but Lula was there, and he needed to be on his best behavior...for as long as he could, at least.

"I couldn't leave them behind," he said, rubbing a hand through his hair. His suitcase had been packed with more books than clothing. "I hope I'm able to find a few more editions on my travels though. Maybe I'll get lucky in Atlanta."

The second the words left his mouth he realized how that sounded. But Simone's grin became something wicked, and she swallowed as though smothering a laugh.

"Where's the tent?" Lula asked.

It took a moment, but Simone eventually broke eye contact with Alex and turned to her daughter. "Lula, don't be rude. Remember, we're guests, and we're not staying long."

Lula appeared utterly offended. "But camping is an overnight thing, Mom, duh."

Simone arched her brow. "Don't get sassy with me, Tallulah Anne."

Alex chuckled as he pointed toward the patio at the back of the house. "I want to show you the backyard because I think you'll both be impressed with what Rhys and I came up with. There are a lot of string lights because you can never have too much. What do you think, Lula?" Alex asked as he extended his hand toward her.

She grabbed it and waved her free hand through the air. "Of course you can't. There's something magical about all these lights."

Simone chuckled under her breath and followed behind them through the house and out the sliding glass door. His backyard was surrounded by an immaculate tall, white fence, the grass within lush and green, springy beneath his feet. He wished he'd spent more time out here sooner.

Lula and Simone both drew in sharp gasps and froze, completely speechless.

Criss. Suddenly feeling self-conscious, Alex reevaluated the scene.

He'd draped sheets off the sides of a tall beach tent, a flap pulled back for entry, and inside there were rugs and more sheets and blankets, along with a ton of pillows. Lights were strung from the top and around the legs of the canopy, and he'd even placed several lanterns around the interior edge, along with bubble lights making a path to the tent itself. He'd already gotten the fire pit going, with all the makings of s'mores off to the side. It was...quite a lot.

He scratched his beard, his words sheepish. "Is it too much? Or perhaps not enough?"

Lula shook her head and hugged him again, tightly, her words soft. "It's perfect."

Mon Dieu, Alex was in danger of crying right there on the spot, especially when he looked up to see Simone with glassy eyes, a hand at her mouth. She mimicked her daughter, shaking her head, and then she hugged him too.

Lula re-situated so she could embrace both of them, and it was the first time in his entire life that he felt like he was a part of a family. The thought caused chills to pop up along his arms.

Simone nuzzled into him. "Thank you, Alex. This is...this is the most wonderful thing anyone's ever done for us," she whispered.

"I call dibs on that fluffy blanket!" Lula squealed, suddenly breaking away, running toward the tent, and diving into the blanket with a happy shriek.

Even without her standing there, Alex and Simone were still wrapped up in each other, laughing at Lula's antics. Alex brought a hand to the side of Simone's neck, gently running his thumb along her collarbone.

His voice was earnest when he spoke, making sure she understood him, that she understood the meaning lying beneath his words. "I'd do anything for you. For her."

Because tonight? Tonight he didn't want them to be coach and player. Tonight he wanted them to simply be two people who were in love with each other.

"Dance party!" Lula called from inside the tent.

"You've spoiled her now." Simone playfully bumped his shoulder as she took hold of his hand.

His head snapped up to meet her eye, his brows raised. Did she know what she was doing? A tiny dip of her chin told him everything he needed to know, that she felt the same.

Alex squeezed her hand, his lips twitching, his heart expanding so big he didn't know how it'd stay inside his chest. Hell, it could burst free and fly away—he wouldn't care as long as he had this night, this moment.

"We can't keep her waiting now, can we?" His voice was hoarse with emotion.

Lula was rearranging everything within the tent, and when they met her at the entrance, she put her hands on her hips. "You got the music, sir?"

Alex laughed as he pulled out his phone. "I have the perfect song. It's one you haven't heard of though…"

Lula cocked her head. "That's fine. As long as it's something we can all dance to."

Alex had been listening to this song on repeat as of late, each time making him think of Simone. He connected his phone to the speaker and hit play, and the opening bars of The Waterboys' "The Whole of the Moon" filtered over them.

Simone's face brightened. "I thought you'd be too young to know about this one."

He lifted a shoulder, shooting her a meaningful look. "I recognize a good thing when I see it, despite my age."

Simone pressed her lips together, trying to suppress another smile. Alex winked at her and turned to Lula, bending at the waist.

"May I have this dance?"

Lula jumped up and down. "Yes!" she squealed and put her little hand in his.

He turned to Simone with his other hand. "What about you, *mademoiselle*? We can't leave you on the sidelines now, can we?"

"Say yes, Mom!"

Lula was probably a better wingman than Rhys.

Simone took his hand, and the three of them danced around—silly and ridiculous and wild and carefree beneath the full moon and stars.

Alex memorized every aspect of that moment, careful to catalog it all so he could pull these fragments out and study them later.

Tonight, his walls had completely crumbled, and Simone's had too, and they would do what they always did when that happened—they'd meet in the middle, finding each other, finding and recognizing that solace and home the other provided.

The lyrics of the song fit how Alex felt about Simone perfectly. She saw the whole of the moon when it came to him. Everyone else always saw these pieces, never putting them together to form the real Alex Wilde. But Simone had done it, had pieced him together the first night they met.

And he had done the same with her. She was always just a CEO to everyone, but he glimpsed beneath all of that, seeing her for the amazing, incredible woman she was—on her own, as a mother, as a coach.

Bringing his attention back to the present, Alex enjoyed every moment. After they danced around his backyard until Lula was content, they made s'mores and told semi-tame ghost stories. Later, Lula crawled into the tent, laying directly in the middle, a pleased smile on her face. She patted either side of her.

"Camping isn't complete unless we all get in the tent," she said.

Simone looked at Alex, worrying her bottom lip with her teeth. "It's late. We should probably get going."

Alex shrugged and gestured to Lula, brows raising. "You heard the lady. Camping isn't complete unless we all get in the tent."

Simone turned to her daughter. "You're going to fall asleep the minute we all get in there, and then who's going to carry you to the car?"

Alex answered, "I will" at the same time Lula said, "Alex."

"I'm already being teamed up on, huh? Fine." Simone pointed at Lula. "But Alex is carrying you."

They walked to the edge of the tent, and Simone bent down, laying on a pillow beside Lula while Alex laid down on the other side.

"This is the best camping trip I've ever been on," Lula announced, her voice filled with awe as she looked up at the ceiling of the light-strung tent. She reached down and took Alex's hand in hers and then grabbed Simone's. "We're happy like a family should be," she added.

In the quiet that followed, Alex swore he could hear Simone's heart crack. His already had several fissures, and those words...they meant more than they should.

And for the longest time the three of them were quiet, until hushed little snores filled the silence. Alex turned his head to find Lula with her eyes closed, her mouth wide open. His gaze flicked to Simone, who was already watching him with a new expression on her face, one of wonder and...longing. Cautiously, she reached for Alex, taking his hand in hers. Their entwined fingers rested slightly above Lula so as not to wake her.

They shifted, both raising up on their elbows so that they could face each other.

For the first time in his life, someone had made him feel something more, made him feel as though he'd awakened from the longest slumber.

The illumination from the string lights cast Simone in a haloed glow, her lips curved into a tender smile, her eyes filled with a sweetness he didn't deserve. But maybe he did? Maybe if she could be patient with him, he could be the sort of man to love her the way she deserved, to build the sort of life for them that was them against the world. His breath stuttered at that staggering thought.

It was now or never. Could she give him a chance?

Alex brought her hand to his lips, careful to be respectful with her sleeping daughter between them. He kissed her palm and then threaded his fingers back through hers.

With a pause, he gathered his strength. "Simone, *mon Dieu*, I'm in love with you."

He was crossing their boundary, he knew.

Simone's smile grew electric, and she gently tugged their joined hands to her side. She kissed his knuckles, keeping her eyes on his.

"Oh, Alex. I love you too," she whispered.

Was it possible he'd heard her right?

"You..." He shook his head. "You love me too?"

A gentle laugh trickled from her lips, the perfect melody to this moment. "I do. It's hard not to love you, Alex Wilde."

Chapter Twenty-Nine

SIMONE

SIMONE MEANT IT. SHE'D TRIED SO HARD NOT TO FALL IN LOVE WITH THE charming man in front of her but ended up being defenseless against his beautiful soul, his giving and selfless heart, his wicked laugh, his bewitching eyes. It was everything wrapped up together that made her love the wild card that had shaken up her life in the best possible way.

Had anyone ever looked so filled with hope and elation when their love was returned? Because the way Alex looked at her right then, she wanted to frame it forever.

He still hadn't spoken. Simone kissed his hand again. "You're surprised?"

He chuckled. "I can't help but be a little shocked."

"Alex, I hope you know that you deserve all the things. It's time you recognized that, okay? You're a good man. What kind of man does this..." She gestured to the tent with her free hand. "...for a child who isn't his? I'm pretty sure you made Lula's year. You certainly brightened her day, and well, you brightened my entire life."

Tears threatened to fall with the enormity of the emotions coursing through her body. "This is...this is all a little wild, isn't it? This situation we've found ourselves in?"

"It is, but I've found I like doing wild with you, Simone."

"Same." She sighed. "It feels like I'm looking in on someone else's life. I've never been swept off my feet." She paused, knowing what she wanted to admit next, needing to share with him what a large part of her life he'd already become. "With you, I feel like I can do anything. You make me feel like nothing's out of my reach. And somehow, through all of it, you saw the real me. You helped me find her, and I like her. *A lot.*"

"So do I, *chérie.*"

They smiled at each other before turning to lay on their backs, their hands still entwined but on top of Lula's. "This is the best night ever," Simone whispered into the night, echoing Lula's earlier sentiment.

"Any night with you is," Alex responded, and they laid there looking up at the lights, filled to the brim with love and hope, falling asleep like a family.

The following day Simone woke up with her back protesting sleeping on the ground despite all the pillows and sheets and rugs. She wasn't twenty-three anymore. That was for damn sure.

Warm arms were folded around her, and when she opened her eyes, she was lying on Alex's chest, his pulse firing rapidly beneath his shirt.

"It does that whenever you're around," his sleep-husky voice greeted her.

She grinned and sat up, looking for her daughter.

Reading her mind, Alex added, "Lula is in the house inspecting my cereal collection. I may have gone overboard to impress her." He winked.

When she looked at him, she couldn't help but wonder if she'd made a mistake by not being with him sooner, regardless of all the many obstacles in front of them—the tennis center, *Damien.*

"I told you I loved you," she said, bringing her fingertips to her lips as if she could feel the words emblazoned there.

Alex shifted so that he was sitting in front of her. "You did. And I love you. So much."

To punctuate it, he gently tilted her chin up and kissed her soft and slow, asking for nothing. It was different from all their other kisses. It spoke volumes.

When they pulled apart, she swore she had heart-eyes. But what were they going to do?

She reached for his hand. "Alex?"

"What is it, *mon bonheur*?"

Simone's nose wrinkled as she traced Alex's face, rubbing his beard and then tangling her fingers in his shoulder-length hair. She couldn't grasp exactly how the term was spelled, at least phonetically. Usually, Alex corrected himself and said the English word, or she had become so accustomed to him to know the meanings of his most-used terms. That one...she didn't know.

"Say it again?"

He ran his thumb over her bottom lip. His lips quirked just slightly. But he didn't repeat it.

"If you won't say it again, then what does it mean?"

Alex shook his head with a playful smirk. "One day I will tell you. I can't divulge everything to you in one weekend." He looked outside the tent. "Now we should find Lula, *oui*?"

She nodded, although she preferred Lula to come to them. Simone never wanted to leave the confines of that tent, because outside of it was the world and worries and consequences. Inside was warm and safe and filled with their love for each other, and that was enough.

They stood up, stretching their aching bodies this way and that when Lula came marching out with a bowl of cereal in her hands...and Simone's phone to her ear.

"It's the house with the gray door. The pretty one I used to point out to you on the way to school. Okay. Fine. Bye." Lula pressed the end call button angrily and handed the phone back over to Simone.

"Um, who were you talking to, Lula? Was it Grandpa?"

Lula shook her head, looking down at her cereal with a sad sort of look on her face. "It was Dad. He made me tell him where we are, so he's coming over. I didn't want to tell him though."

Shit.

Just like that, all the fantasies and midnight declarations toppled to the ground, shattering.

Simone knew better. She figured Damien had been quiet because he'd been busy, but now...now who knew what he'd do.

Alex bent down to Lula. "Lula, you can stay out in this tent for as long as you want and eat as many bowls of cereal as you want, *d'accord*? Your mom and I are going to go inside and wait for your father."

Lula nodded, but before she went, Simone wrapped her up in a hug, talking into her hair. "Everything's going to be okay, Lula. You did nothing wrong." The tension in her daughter's shoulders eased up, and Simone pressed a kiss to her head. "Now go and enjoy that tent," she added with false cheeriness.

She didn't want to lie to Lula, but also Damien was a horrible human for guilting their daughter like he did. Her heart hurt at the mere idea of it, at seeing how sad Lula was.

Careful not to fall apart right in front of her child, Simone followed Alex inside the house, hoping for at least a minute to breathe, to gather herself, but there was none. Damien must've been at her house, which wasn't far, because an angry knock came from the door.

Alex's voice was pitched low and dangerous as he shot a deadly look at the door. "Simone, you don't have to face him right now if you don't want. I can send him away."

Simone wished it were that easy, but suddenly, her ex-husband's threats were fresh and very real.

"I...I know it's not right of me to ask, but I'd like you to stay with me while I handle this. But *I* will handle it."

She already knew there was no future for her and Alex, not after this, not after Damien finished with them, but she couldn't resist wanting to lean on him for support. She'd never really had someone to help her carry any sort of burden, and now here was Alex Wilde, wonderful and perfect, and she would have to set him free. It was either that or ruin the tennis center. Both were awful choices that made her want to double over and yell at the sky.

Alex squeezed her hand once before dropping it gently. "I'll always stay with you, Simone."

If only.

She straightened her spine, opening the door and making sure everything about her, from her expression to her body language, screamed, "Do not mess with me."

Because in truth? She was terrified that everything was about to blow up in her face like she'd been so worried about since the beginning. And yet here she'd allowed herself to fall in love with the one person she wasn't supposed to.

Damien's face was splotched red, his sunglasses—those ridiculous sunglasses—perched in his hair. He smelled like cheap perfume, and Simone scoffed at the sight of him.

"You dare come here to, what, I don't know, to lecture me, and you scare our daughter, and yet you smell like you spent all night with a cheap hooker? You blew our daughter off, Damien. You made her feel like nothing two days in a row. I don't think I can allow you to keep this up."

Damien's lips twisted into a sneer, and then he looked over her shoulder, seeing Alex.

"I'd think very carefully about what you're about to say next," Alex warned.

"It sounds like you're both threatening me. I came here to get my daughter because it's *my* weekend with her, but it seems I have other things I suddenly need to do, things to put you both in your places." A menacing laugh fell from his lips as he puffed out his chest. "And Simone, remember what I said about the spotlight? I meant *every* word of it. And now you're going to get what's coming to you. I'll be back later for Lula. You just wait." He accentuated it by lifting his phone and taking a picture, and then he rounded on his very expensive boat shoes, getting in his car in a huff. He sped off from the house loudly, tires screeching.

Once he was out of sight, Simone collapsed against Alex, feeling the weight of everything slamming down on her shoulders.

Damien had taken a picture and to outsiders it wouldn't look great— her hair fluffed about her head like a bird's nest, her second-day clothes rumpled. Alex wasn't any better. To put it not so politely, they looked like they just had a round in the bedroom.

The fallout from this could be rough for her, for Alex, for Lula, for the tennis center—for Julian, Amalie, and Paul. This wasn't about her, despite allowing herself one night where anything could be possible. Right now, she needed to do damage control, to face the consequences. She had to protect the people she loved...Alex included.

Simone allowed herself this one last moment with Alex, breathing in his scent, clutching the strength of his arms, and then she pulled away from him, both figurative and literally. She shuttered all of her walls, operating as a numb shell of herself.

"I've got to get Lula and get home. I hope you understand that I need some time?" She didn't know how else to phrase it, how else to break his heart right then, because her insides were a tangled mess.

Alex scraped a hand through his hair, looking as lost as she felt. "Of course. Time."

But she knew time wouldn't be enough.

Chapter Thirty

SIMONE

SIMONE COULDN'T STOP TAPPING HER FOOT WHILE SHE WAITED OFF TO THE SIDE of the unofficial "press room" that Arlo had created at the tennis center. Alex was filming a series of live interviews with a few different sports outlets, trying to hype up his presence at the Moselle Open.

She'd felt on edge ever since Damien's visit yesterday, his continued eerie radio silence only making it worse. Not to mention she wondered what his play would be with the photo he'd taken.

She and Alex danced around each other awkwardly, but he'd made her promise they would talk before they left the center.

This awful foreboding had settled in her bones, making everything take on a gray, worrisome sheen. How was it possible that she'd gone from having one of the best nights of her life, and admitting she loved the man of her dreams, to *this*? She held her arms over her stomach as if that would keep her pieced together.

"What's wrong?" Arlo asked, brows and mouth pinched.

Normally, Simone would've texted her best friend or Amalie immediately, but for some reason, the thought of rehashing everything yesterday made her want to cry. Now there was no way to get around it, especially since Arlo worked with them...and would most likely have to clean up whatever Damien did.

Simone took a breath and let it out slowly. "Long story short? Friday night, Damien was supposed to take Lula camping. He bailed. Alex saved the day. He and I said *I love you*."

Arlo's eyes went glassy, and she turned so she could take Simone's hands. "Oh, Sim. I know it feels like that's a bad thing, but it isn't, right? Why do you look like you just lost your best friend?"

Simone's eyes began to water as well. "Because Damien is angry now, and he threatened to make trouble for Alex and me. He even took a picture of us looking like we'd just had sex. You know how he can be. All of this terrifies me so much because I've just gotten my foot in the door, and I'll never forgive Damien if he ruins this or if he hurts Alex or the tennis center's reputation in any way. And the worst part? I know it's coming, I *feel* it, and I wonder if the whole thing could've been avoided if I hadn't gone and fallen in love."

Her best friend squeezed their joined hands. "Don't shut Alex out, Simone. I'm not only your friend, but your PR agent, so I can think about how to deal with the tennis center aspect once I see what the press is saying. And we'll take care of Damien. The most important thing is that you need to live your life. Everyone has always taken away your choices, your happiness. Don't let Damien do that now."

Rubbing her forehead, Simone felt helpless as she mumbled, "I don't know how."

"Just think about those words, let them sit. Okay?"

She nodded, although that was easier said than done.

They were quiet for a few minutes, having gone back to standing and watching Alex's interviews. Suddenly, Arlo made a sound, one Simone had heard before and only in stressful situations. It sounded like a cross between her squealing and choking. Her friend gripped her phone so tight that her knuckles were white, her face twisted up as if she tasted something sour.

"Arlo?" Dread iced every fiber of her being.

Arlo's eyes raised from the phone in an eerily slow movement. "That asshole. He did it. They screwed us over." Her face went red, and she jammed her glasses up the bridge of her nose.

Simone's stomach clenched, and she waited for Arlo to explain, even though she already knew. "Damien. It's Damien and the press, isn't it?"

Simone whispered, eyeing Alex, who wore a fake smile for the camera. It didn't reach his eyes.

Arlo lowered her phone, her black nails still gripping it tightly. "Listen, I told you we'd handle this together. I'm good at my job, okay? And this happens. Sometimes certain media outlets will screw you over, and that's just facts. Apparently, this story was worth more than the lawsuit I'm about to smack them with."

Acid coated Simone's throat. "What story, Arlo?"

She knew Arlo Phillips was the best in the business and worked her butt off for her clients, a fact the PR firm she worked for had yet to see clearly—and she knew Arlo would take care of this, but what sort of damage had already been done? The suspense was too much.

Arlo handed over her cell phone, her mouth a grim line, her eyes downcast. Simone punched in the passcode, and there it was, staring back at her.

Warner, Wilde, Love All?

The article used Simone and Alex's professional headshots at the top. She scanned the write-up, unable to stop shaking. There were phrases like "crossing a boundary" and "there's no hiding how this coach and player feel about each other." Of course, the photo Damien had taken shone as the *pièce de résistance* of the whole damn thing.

The granola bar Simone had nibbled at earlier threatened to make a reappearance once more as she scanned down to the comments section.

"Oh! Don't look at the comments," Arlo warned, but it was too late.

Simone was already torturing herself with the comments. Arlo smacked her forehead when she realized what was happening, but she quickly recovered and continued to try and wrangle the phone from Simone.

People thought she was a cougar? That was hilarious. They thought she was taking advantage of her player?

That was just the tip of the iceberg, because there were comments about Alex too, about how no one wanted to coach him, so he had to use the only thing he was good at (for those who that might be unclear, i.e., sex) to get a coach. That it didn't matter how hot his coach was or how great their relationship was, he would always be a disappointment on the court. One commenter even said, "Anyone who gets beat down like he did by his own stepbrother is a loser." Simone felt the punch in the gut with that one.

Arlo hopped around like a jittery bird, trying to grab the phone out of Simone's grasp, but Simone was taller and held it up so she could continue reading. She couldn't resist the inexplicable pull, as messed up as that was.

"For the love of God, Simone." Arlo reached a hand up toward the phone. Her next words were a grunt. "*Don't*. I'm telling you. Save yourself. Don't scroll *any* farther than you have."

And then Simone saw what her best friend meant. Her body tensed as she read the comment. Read it and reread it, felt the livid flames lick up her neck and cheeks, and she hardened her jaw. "Apparently, Simone is more like her mom than we thought. Wonder if she'll take off with Alex and leave her kid with her ex?"

Someone had taken the time to research her life. Unless…

The commenter was anonymous. But Simone knew who it was. Had no doubt in her mind, especially coupled with the picture he'd taken.

Damien.

Only he could so carefully craft the nastiest barb that would snag and tear, ripping her heart.

All her life, she'd tried to be the total opposite of her mother, a reaction that sent her into the tightly wound world she currently found herself in. The reason she slept with Alex in the first place, the reason she took this ridiculous coaching position, was to shake things up, to wake up and live her life, and now she'd only turned out to be like Katharine Warner. After all this time of trying to retreat and hide, she'd messed up in the most epic of ways, bringing negative attention to her, to Lula, to Alex, and to the tennis center.

"Shit," Arlo snarled, finally reaching high enough to snatch her phone and shove it in her back pocket, before straightening her blazer.

Simone's breathing was noisy, along with a ringing sound echoing throughout her head. She fisted the hem of her shirt for a brief moment before massaging her temples.

"This isn't happening," Simone hissed.

If it was difficult before, how would she ever be taken seriously as a coach now? How would Alex's comeback be taken seriously? Both of their reputations were scarred, ruined. Her eye twitched. Well, that was new.

"We'll fix this. *I'll* fix it. Just let's focus on right now and get Alex through this, and in the meantime, I'll figure out what we need to do."

Arlo had her hands out in front of her body, gesturing as she spoke, a tightness around her eyes that was usually never there.

Simone looked over at Alex, who smiled as he answered a question.

Her decision from the night before had been the right one—if only she'd realized it sooner. Whatever this was between her and Alex was over. Removing him from her life, her heart, would not be a neat incision. No, it would be bloody and leave raised scars that might forever ache.

But then another realization struck, one that needed to be addressed right here, right now. Simone's eyes widened at Arlo and then she spoke. "They're going to ask him about this, and he has no idea."

Unease settled in her friend's shoulders, and her face scrunched into a cringe. "I know. I've already thought about that, but if I pull him now, it'll look like we have something to hide. My bosses always say to let these things happen naturally, so we've got to let it unfurl even if I don't want to."

Simone bit the inside of her cheek, somehow managing to pull herself together and turn toward the dumpster fire that was about to be her life. It didn't take long for everything to go up in flames.

"We have a question regarding your new coach," the reporter began, sounding innocent enough. And of course, Alex wouldn't expect the shitstorm to hit so soon.

"Oh God," Simone groaned, pinching her nose. Arlo's hand came down on her bicep, squeezing slightly.

"This too shall pass. It's gonna suck right now, but it will get better," Arlo whispered.

Simone struggled to respond. Her eyes were still closed as the reporter fired off a series of questions.

"*Off-Court* magazine reported today that you two are an item and ran this photograph." The image popped up on the screen. "Is that true? It's highly uncommon in the tennis world, so of course, it's a big deal. Is that why you chose someone so unqualified, with zero experience, to be your head coach over someone with more expertise?"

Arlo sucked in a breath, while Simone gritted her teeth. The tennis world didn't have much drama, but if there *was* drama, it could be expected to be snapped up and reported on widely right away.

Alex's face turned ashen as he ran a shaky hand over his hair again and then down his neat beard. "What?" He blinked several times before color began to make an appearance on his tan cheeks. But then she saw it—something she so rarely saw in laid-back, chill Alex.

Fury.

"That's the most ridiculous question I've ever heard. I can't believe you even have the audacity to ask that. It's bullshit."

The reporter appeared to be stunned into silence, but Alex didn't care. He continued. "Simone is a phenomenal coach. She's the only reason I made it to where I'm sitting right now. I will hear no more about her."

And with that, he stood so quickly from Arlo's makeshift press table that his chair fell back, wrapping around an electrical cord, which pulled the mic down to the floor. He muttered a string of French curses before exiting the opposite side from where she and Arlo were.

This was the icing on the very fresh cake from hell.

She and Arlo needed to get to him and fast. This entire fracas made her regret ever stepping outside of her comfort zone in the first place.

After all, look where it'd gotten her.

Alex disappeared into the locker room, and Simone wasted no time following him inside, Arlo on her heels.

"Alex," Simone called out, her voice strained. He froze among the lockers, his back still to her. Thankfully, the room was empty. She couldn't do this with an audience.

Speaking of which. She turned to her best friend. "Give us a second, please?"

Arlo pointed to the door. "I'll be outside, okay?" And then she squeezed Simone's hand and slipped from the locker room.

Alex turned around slowly, an array of emotions flickering across his face—so many that she couldn't zero in on just one. Bitterness tugged at the slight lines around his eyes, anger strained his sensuous mouth, resignation hung in his arms by his side.

What was Simone supposed to say? And was this coming from Simone Warner, Alex's underqualified coach? Or Simone Warner aka Katharine Warner Jr.?

The breath she exhaled caused her shoulders to hunch forward like they might buckle from the weight. "Hey." That was the best she could offer.

She wanted to move closer, sit down, and talk with Alex instead of facing off here in the locker room, but something about this moment felt incredibly fragile.

Alex's eyes flashed, his normally warm gaze frigid. "I worried this would happen. You only wanted to stay out of the spotlight and look what I've done. I've gone and fucked everything up." He stabbed shaky fingers through his hair.

He was worried about her. God. She didn't deserve him. She loved him more than she'd ever loved a man, and she was going to have to let him go because it would be better for everyone—everyone except her, but she had other people to think about. Wasn't that the story of her life?

Her fists curled up tight enough that she could barely feel the sting of her nails digging into her palms. "We both screwed up, Alex, and now... now we've got to do what we can to fix this, which means we've got to let each other go."

This was the beginnings of heartbreak, something she'd never known, not even when she found the lipstick that wasn't hers smeared along the inside of Damien's white dress shirt, not even when she'd found him with the women on that yacht. Simone had been disappointed, embarrassed, pissed, but for all the wrong reasons. Not because she loved Damien like one should love their spouse, but because it cast them in an ugly situation in the public eye. Yeah, heartbreak was the farthest thing she felt with her ex.

But the tattered edges of her heart were starting to slowly understand the true meaning of love and loss.

Alex straightened, a fierce gleam glittering in his beautiful brown eyes. "*Calice.* I refuse to call what we feel for one another screwing up. I care for you, Simone. I probably should've let you go sooner, but I won't lie, I was selfish. I still am. I want you so much it hurts, and it pains me even more to know that by being with me, it could hurt you and Lula. I never want to do that."

Simone tried to pull in a deep breath but struggled to do so. "I'll deal with Damien. You need to focus on your game. I'll resign as your coach sooner than anticipated, obviously." She couldn't believe the words came out of her mouth. It was the last thing she wanted to do.

Alex took a step closer, his voice raspy and whisper-thin. "Simone, I've been so proud to know you, and so proud of all the chances you've taken to live the life you've always wanted. I've said it before and I'll say it again, it's not easy to start over at any point in life. So I'll ask, would you like to remain my coach? At least until after the Moselle Open? I can't make that decision for you, because I've already shown my decision-making skills are terrible." He tried to laugh, but it came out more like a croak.

Simone wanted to see this through and she would. After all, she'd come so far. Her dream was on the line, and she had to do what she could to salvage it. "If you think we can handle it until then…then of course. And afterward, we'll part ways. We always knew it would be temporary," she managed.

Alex's hand cupped her cheek, his thumb doing one quick sweep, a sad smile balancing on the edge of his lips. "*Mon bonheur*. I'll see you at practice tomorrow. *Merci* for everything." And then he pressed a kiss to her forehead and turned around, leaving the locker room without another word.

Leaving Simone to feel as though her heart had just walked out the door.

Chapter Thirty-One

ALEX

REPORTERS WERE CAMPED OUTSIDE OF THE TENNIS CENTER WHEN ALEX ARRIVED for practice the next day. Last night had been nothing short of a nightmare with the media coverage. A well-known tennis writer tore apart the Oliver Smoke Tennis Center, causing a lot of people to follow his lead. Alex's inbox had been bombarded with emails and requests for interviews and chances to "clear his name," and he was sure Simone faced the same. The mere thought made his chest hurt.

He shoved his headphones over his ears, playing his music as loud as it would go in an attempt to drown out any noise as he shouldered past all the bodies crammed at the door. Despite the music, he could still make out Simone's name as several reporters asked him questions about her. His mouth flattened into a hardened line as he made it through the entrance, shutting the door behind him, then turning the lock.

He hadn't wanted to walk away from Simone, but the guilt ate at him, gnawing away at his edges. *Merde*, this was his fault.

Paul stood in front of him in the lobby, arms crossed, looking formidable. Alex needed to apologize to the older coach for bringing all this drama to his doorstep. The press. The fucking press was outside of the tennis center. If Paul and Julian sent him packing right away, he wouldn't blame them—actually, he'd understand.

Although it would be hard to leave, knowing what he left behind.

He opened his mouth, ready to begin his apology tour. "Paul, I—"

Paul held up a hand. "I know you're upset about Simone—"

Alex's head hung at the mention of her name. "*Oui.*" He breathed through his nose. "And this." He turned around to where the reporters were trying to look through the glass and shoved his fingers through his hair. "I'm so sorry that I brought this to the center. Simone and I are—" He paused, the words bitter in his throat. "Done. So maybe that will help the damage."

Paul touched Alex's shoulder in a gesture of reassurance. "Arlo's working her magic as we speak and is managing to contain some of it." Pausing, he pulled out two pieces of Juicy Fruit from his pocket and shoved them into his mouth. "It is what it is at this point. We can't fix it. All we can do is move forward, right?"

Alex was speechless and unable to move. He hadn't expected Paul to be so laid-back about things, especially with the media having a go at the center and questioning Paul and Julian's professionalism.

With a wave toward the hall, the older man gave him a slight smile. "Come on, kid. Let's go to my office." As they walked, Paul put an arm around him, pulling him in a side hug. Alex shifted his tennis bag out of the way. "Did you know that the word of the day is *fate*?"

He raised a brow. "Um, *non.*"

The coach continued, unfazed as usual. "I know things seem rough right now, and believe me, they are. But you're here for a reason, kid. And so is she. No matter what happens next, I need you to remember that."

He could only nod, because what was there to say? He'd spent all night trying to think of ways to win Simone back, to convince her that they could weather this storm, but it still wouldn't change the things that stood in their way.

They stopped outside Paul's open office door. Rhys sat in one of the chairs, looking pissed as hell, and Julian leaned against the desk, arms crossed like Paul earlier. The mood was so ominous it was stifling.

Alex hazarded a glance at all three of the guys. "What's going on?"

Paul huffed. "You're gonna know soon enough anyway. Bastien the Bastard just announced that he's pulling out of the Paris Masters."

Alex's response was quick and sharp. "*D'accord.* And?"

Paul cut a look to Julian and then to Rhys. "*And* he's announced he's playing the Moselle Open."

The world stopped spinning. This was unheard of. Bastien was currently the number four ranked player in the world. Players ranked in the top five didn't play Moselle. Instead, they almost always chose to save themselves for the Paris Masters, because the reward was greater with higher ranking points, given that it was one of the most prestigious tennis tournaments in the world.

Bastien meant war.

Alex rubbed his chin, still disbelieving. "*Non.*"

Even that one word hadn't wanted to crawl from his throat.

Paul nodded as he tried to speak French. "*Oui.*"

Alex ran a hand through his hair, looking to Rhys. Before anyone could speak, Paul continued, "And that's why I said what I did earlier about fate. This is all fate, Alex."

Julian pushed off from the desk. "You've got us." He thumbed at everyone in the room. "But most importantly, you've got Simone. She's one hell of a coach."

Rhys stood, clapping a supportive hand on Alex's shoulder.

"I don't understand. Where is she?" Alex asked.

His friend took a step back, a wry smile twisting his lips. "Let's just say she found out before any of us. She's out on the court."

Alex moved toward the door. "I need to see her."

Paul pointed at his business partner. "You wanna take him out there?"

Julian nodded. "You bet."

"We'll be out in a minute," Rhys called behind Alex as he followed Julian into the hallway.

When they started walking, Alex knew what needed to be said. "Look, Julian, I can't tell you how sorry I am, how much I hate the position I've put your business in."

Julian stopped for a minute and cocked his head to the side, appearing thoughtful. "Do you regret it? Simone? And I don't mean as a coach."

Alex bit his lip, knowing he had to tell the truth. "*Non.* I don't regret a minute with her."

Dipping his head in understanding, Julian started walking again, Alex at his side. "Amalie and Arlo have been talking and working around the clock on damage control. It sucks, but I understand that the heart just wants what it wants. We don't fault either of you for it, and we'll figure it out as it comes. Ultimately, we just want you both to be happy." He lifted a shoulder. "But for now we focus on tennis, yeah?"

Readjusting the straps of his bag on his shoulder, Alex nodded, although a flicker of hope burned in his chest at Julian's words about happiness. "*Oui*, tennis."

Julian shot him a smirk. "You ready to do this, Wilde?"

Switching gears back to his game, Alex tried to wrap his mind around the situation. It was as if everyone knew something he didn't, which they clearly did given the Bastien situation.

"What do you mean?" he finally managed.

They went through the lobby and to the side door leading to the court and opened it. "You'll see," was Julian's ominous answer.

It was like he'd stepped foot into a tennis funhouse of riddles. But when he looked up and saw Simone on the court, everything clicked into place. She looked like a force to be reckoned with, her movements controlled and rigid as she moved about the court, setting up balloons with a printed picture on them.

As they drew closer, he saw that Bastien's face was on each of them.

Simone turned around, and he was almost certain utter heartbreak flickered across her stare before a different expression took over—one of barely restrained anger. Even then, with her ponytail askew, her eyes tight, she was stunning, and seeing her was a punch to his chest.

But he couldn't forget that Bastien was now coming after him. His personal life was a mess, and Bastien knew to capitalize on it. *Calice.*

"I'll leave you to it," Julian said before turning around and heading back inside the clubhouse.

Simone rushed toward Alex. "Let me just say this and get it out of the way. Right now, we can't think about our relationship or the tatters it lies in, got it?"

Alex blinked a few times. "Got it."

"And you know why? Because that motherfucker Bastien, that's why." She spoke those words between her teeth, hands fisted by her sides. "You're in a low moment. You've just suffered a personal setback and a ridiculous story broadcast around the tennis world, but this is a good thing."

"It is?"

"Yes. Bastien is doing this because he wants to bury you, Alex. He knows you're struggling, and he wants to finish the job. So what are you going to do about it?"

He spun around, taking in the court. "I want to win," was his honest answer. He didn't like putting his relationship with Simone aside, didn't like not addressing it right now, because he still didn't think it could just be over. But she was right. He had to focus on the Moselle Open. On Bastien. On redemption.

She walked over to one of the balloons and tugged its string down. On it was one of the most unflattering pictures of Bastien ever taken. "Good, because today's target practice..."

"I thought you didn't want me to focus on my hatred of Bastien in my game?"

Simone waved him off. "Well, I lied. Channel it into beating him, and after you do, get a new goal. But right now? *This* is the goal. You are a phoenix rising from the ashes, Alex. It doesn't matter if Bastien decides to chase you to every tournament you play. You've got to learn not to be scared and instead play determined."

He took in Simone in her adorable matching athletic gear, a scowl on her face, and he wanted her to be his more than anything. But even though she couldn't or wouldn't, at least she was still here. She was here with this intense belief in him that he was going to beat Bastien once and for all.

He threw his bag down on the bench, ripping a racket from it. "This is what we both signed up to do, isn't it? We've got to make it happen. Tell me what to do, Coach."

"You're going to serve and hit a balloon of Bastien's face every time. There are at least ten of them on this side of the court. Serve and hit one balloon, then aim for the next balloon. Basically, the name of the game today is hitting shit with his face on it."

Alex barked a laugh. "Now that I think I can do."

Just as Alex headed over to the baseline, Paul, Julian, and Rhys filtered out from the clubhouse.

"Is it sports movie montage time yet?" Paul called out.

Simone placed a hopper of balls next to Alex's feet, giving him a small smile. She turned back around to Paul, cupping her hands around her mouth. "Hell yeah, it is. We've got a tournament to win!"

The next four days they spent practicing just that. Simone was a coach on fire, developing several new drills to test Alex's strategy and focus, to get him moving, and *oui*, she still incorporated Bastien's face into a lot of them.

The press still hung around out front each day, but no one spoke to them, and Simone had placed herself and Alex on a self-imposed media ban while Arlo handled the media in their stead. He could only hope things had begun to die down online.

By their last practice before the tournament, he'd found a confidence that had never surfaced in all his years of playing.

It still wasn't enough to ease his heartbreak over Simone, but he held true to her words, not bringing it up—for now.

But once they got to Metz, it was on.

October

Chapter Thirty-Two

SIMONE

"How was school?" Simone asked, forced cheeriness in her voice as she picked Lula up in the car rider line at school.

Simone would be flying out for Metz in a few hours and wanted to see her daughter before she left. Tallulah had asked a lot of questions about Alex, about his relationship with her mom, and sadly Simone had to shut it down. She told her they could only be friends and that they were both happy with that decision, which was one of the biggest lies she'd ever told her daughter.

On top of that, she refused to discuss what happened at the press conference with anyone. Amalie, Julian, Arlo, and even Paul had tried to talk to her about it, but she'd only felt pressure in her sternum, as if she'd be sick over hurting their reputation. After apologizing, she made them agree that they wouldn't ask her anything regarding the incident until after the tournament. She could only handle one problem at a time, and the guilt from it all threatened to eat away at her each day.

Lula buckled her seat belt and turned to face her. "I've had better days, but I did what you always say, and it got better."

Simone's grip on the steering wheel tightened. Each word she spoke grated between her teeth. "Was someone mean to you?"

Lula blew out a puff of breath, pursing her lips. "They tried to be, but I told them that people only have the power we give them, and I didn't give them any, so their words couldn't hurt me." She shrugged. "They looked really confused and left me alone."

Holy hell.

Simone practically felt the color draining from her face. "What?"

Lula sat up straighter. "Yeah, it's what you always say, and it worked, so good advice, Mom."

Advice she'd never taken herself. Not once. Yet her eight-year-old daughter could. She'd spent all week training Alex in a fit of fury, all the while being heartsick over him. She repositioned her grip on the steering wheel and pulled out of the school parking lot.

"I'm proud of you, Lula Bug," she finally managed to force out, emotion making each word quiver and quake, searching for a safe place to hide.

Silence filled the car, and after Lula fiddled with the console, she smacked her palm on it, causing Simone to jump slightly.

"Mom, I think you and Alex can fix things, don't you? If you love someone, it's worth it, right?"

This kid was entirely too astute for her own good.

"You think so, huh?"

Lula tapped her chin. "I *know* so. You have to do what makes you happy sometimes, and I think fixing things with him will do that. And then I'll see him more, and we can have more camping trips. I'll share my cereal with him. Even the marshmallows." She giggled.

Simone reached for her daughter's hand, squeezing it briefly before she gripped the wheel again. "You're so smart, you know."

Her daughter rolled her eyes playfully. "I know."

Simone smiled, feeling it reach its way deep into her bones. She knew what she had to do. She had to go to war for the man she loved.

When she pulled up to Damien's house, Simone got out of the car with her daughter. Usually, she and Damien sat in their vehicles and seethed at the other person, but not this time. Well, she was going to seethe, but it was about to be up close and personal.

She walked Lula to the door, ringing the doorbell.

When Damien opened it, his forehead wrinkled, those ridiculous

sunglasses in his hair. While he was inside. Simone fought an eye roll and
bent to Lula.

"I'll miss you, you know," she said, hugging her daughter.

"I know. I'll miss you too. Will you bring me back a surprise?" Lula
asked, kissing Simone's cheek.

Simone laughed as she stood on Damien's doorstep, him standing in
the doorway like some sort of gatekeeper. "We'll see about all that. But be
good for your dad, okay? And I'll see you soon."

"Lula, honey, your mom and I need to talk for a minute. Tell her bye
and go inside, please?" Damien's tone was gentle, but Simone found
herself snapping armor into place.

He knew she was here to confront him after a week of suppressing all
her feelings.

Biting the inside of her cheek, Simone stooped to give Lula one more
hug before she disappeared inside the house. Damien was all smiles until
he shut the door behind him, stepping onto the porch.

"Running off to France, leaving your child so you can have sex with
your millionaire tennis boyfriend with the Porte des Allemands in sight.
Great mothering, Simone. Great example."

Oh, so he'd been nosy and looked up Metz. *Asshole*.

Simone took a step closer to him, confidence drawing her shoulders
back, straightening her spine. She was practically in his face. When she
spoke, her voice was low, menacing, daring Damien to cross the line again.

"Don't you ever talk to me that way again. I'm not the one who slept
with every willing person in Atlanta while *married*. If you so much as
breathe wrong in my direction, I will make sure everyone knows all the
details of how our divorce really went down. I've protected you and your
reputation all this time, for Lula's sake, and now you have the gall to
threaten me because I'm finally living my life? You can go to hell, Damien
Lennox. And I'm sure your new employer would love to hear how their
'financial advisor' is broke as a joke and living off his ex-wife's money."
His face went splotched, and she reached up and plucked his sunglasses
from his hair. "And these sunglasses? I bought them. They're mine. And I
will be revisiting the court settlement to see if I can stop paying your sorry
ass." She held the sunglasses between her fingertips, snapping them at the

nose. Damien made a sad little noise as she dropped the broken sunglasses in her purse.

"*Au revoir*, Damien, and fuck off."

Then she strode to her car, her entire body vibrating as she got inside. She didn't look back before she peeled out of his driveway, and she didn't think about him once she boarded the plane to Metz, instead thinking that maybe, just maybe, things were finally different.

She was different.

Chapter Thirty-Three

SIMONE

ALEX CAUGHT SIMONE'S EYE THROUGHOUT THE ENTIRETY OF THE EIGHT-AND-A-half-hour plane ride. He'd taken a seat beside Paul, a decision she bet he regretted. The coach's rumbling snores filled the cabin and earned him all kinds of dirty looks. Simone would've laughed at the situation, but she was too wound up.

She almost cried tears of joy when the pilot announced they were making their descent to Metz—she wasn't sure how much longer she could've endured his heated stares. Or Paul's snoring, for that matter.

"Hey, what's going on with you?"

Simone jerked her gaze from Alex, who pretended to be entranced by the in-flight magazine. Amalie poked her in the side, refusing to give up. Her sister had all but insisted they sit together, even as Julian grumbled in dissent.

"Nothing's going on," Simone said, holding Amalie's gaze. God, it was as if she saw right through to her soul. "I'm just thinking about…"

"I know what you're thinking about," Amalie said, a playful smile lifting her lips. "That French-Canadian di—"

"Stop," Simone said on a laugh. "I can't with the tennis center's reputation on the line—"

Tapping the armrest between them, Amalie skewered her with a pointed look. "See, this is why we needed to talk about this. About Alex, about *everything*. But noooo, you've been in supercoach mode and are refusing all talk non-tennis, which I get."

Simone shook her head. "There's nothing to talk about. I already messed up once and feel terrible for making you and Julian, hell, even Paul look bad."

Amalie's nose scrunched. "Oh, there's plenty to talk about. So to start, why don't you tell me how exactly you think you messed up, Sim?"

"Well, I shouldn't have been at Alex's house in the first place when Damien came over. If I hadn't, then that lovely picture wouldn't be circulating and the center wouldn't be a hot topic. I got caught up in my emotions...and of course, there's Lula to think about."

"Lula loves Alex."

"I know, but Damien might try to take her away. I don't know, I get paranoid about that."

Amalie scoffed. "Damien is a bastard who can't take care of himself. Let him try to come for our girl and we'll drag *all* of his indiscretions out for the world to see. So there, the Lula problem is fixed. Now," she added as she took Simone's hands in hers, "I want you to listen to what I'm going to say very carefully, okay?"

She nodded, although she was worried since her sister was very rarely serious.

"You can't worry about the center."

Simone opened her mouth to argue, but Amalie held up a hand, silencing her. "Listen to me. I'm an author. I deal with resolving conflict every single day. If you don't think that Arlo and I can work our way around the media, then do you even know us?" Her face split into a smile. "We will spin this relationship in a way that the center benefits. I need you to trust me on this. I'm a big girl now. Julian and I will handle taking care of the center—which I tried to tell you from the get-go." She squeezed Simone's hands, her stare leaving no room for argument. "I got you, sis. I got you."

Tears welled in Simone's eyes as she allowed those words to sink in. Hadn't that been what this journey was all about? Learning to let others in, to let them help? She didn't have to do everything on her own, to shoulder the burden alone.

"Are you sure?" she asked, her voice raspy with emotion.

Amalie's lips curled into the biggest smile. "Of course. Now when we get off this plane, you go get your man, okay?"

Her answering grin was just as big. "Okay."

Hope unfettered rose in her chest at the possibilities ahead of her.

When the plane finally landed, it seemed as though Alex made it a point to wait for her in the jet bridge. Everyone else walked aimlessly ahead, and Amalie even looked over her shoulder and winked.

Alex's face lit up when he saw her emerge, and the butterflies in her stomach multiplied.

Simone grinned back at him, her sister's words still fresh on her mind.

"Here we are in France," she said by way of greeting.

A very lame greeting, but her nerves were all over the place.

A heated stare much like the one on the plane zeroed in on her. "*Oui.* You definitely need to make the most of your trip and see all you can see."

"Perhaps you could show me around at some point during the tournament?"

Simone had been going for suave and confident, and maybe it would've went over better if she hadn't tripped over another passenger's rolling suitcase because she was too busy staring at Alex's beautiful face. It was like that moment in *2 Fast 2 Furious* when Paul Walker's character does that thing when he doesn't take his eyes off of Eva Mendes's character.

Except Eva Mendes didn't trip and nearly fall flat on her face in front of Paul Walker.

Strong arms wrapped around her, gently pulling her body up. And of course, as she straightened, she did so right up against Alex's solid form. Simone could've been on Mars for all she knew, that's how the moment felt as she stared up into his warm brown eyes.

"Easy there, *ma chérie.*" Alex's lips tilted in a crooked grin.

A shiver raced down her spine at the timbre of his voice, at his touch, his arms still enveloping her in an embrace.

"Sorry about that," Simone said, her tone and expression sheepish.

"*C'est bon.* It's okay. Although it's nice to see you catch up with me."

Her brows knitted as she shifted a little closer. "What do you mean?"

"I've already fallen, you know." He laughed and then shook his head. "That was cheesy, but I had to say it. It felt like a perfect pickup line."

Hell, everything about this moment was the perfect pickup line.

Only to be shattered by Julian's loud mouth.

"Hey, Alex! You're with me! We have to split up cabs, and I can't ride with Paul and my mom or I'll puke up everything from the plane."

Alex deflated a little but managed a chuckle. "I've been summoned, but I'll see you at dinner?"

"Of course, and maybe then I won't be so clumsy."

"Feel free to fall all you like, because I'll always be around to catch you."

And with those flirty parting words, Alex shot her a wink and headed toward Julian.

Okay, Metz was already proving to be everything Simone hoped and then some.

SIMONE PULLED HER CARDIGAN AROUND HER BODY A LITTLE TIGHTER, adjusting to the cooler October weather in Metz as she trailed behind their team. Amalie and Julian were snuggled up together, laughing. Paul and Charlotte were behind them, holding hands and smiling. Rhys and Alex walked together, in deep conversation about something. Simone and Arlo brought up the rear.

"Dinner was good, huh?" Arlo asked.

Simone nodded. She'd barely been able to taste anything thanks to her nerves. All she could think about was Alex and when they could have a moment to talk.

Up ahead in the evening sunlight, Simone spotted a dark green storefront. The sign read *La [petite] Librairie [des Jardins]*.

"A bookshop!" Simone said eagerly. Books always made her feel more settled.

Alex turned, slowly walking backward and looking incredibly sexy while doing so. "Are you going in? It says they close in an hour."

"That's not enough time," Simone joked. "But of course. I have to check it out."

Rhys slung an arm around Alex's shoulder, causing him to stop walking. Simone and Arlo paused with them. "Why don't you two go check it out and I'll..." His eyes darted to Arlo shyly. "I'll escort Ms. Phillips back to the hotel."

Arlo brightened, stepping up next to Rhys and threading an arm through his. He stilled, looking terrified. Simone had to stifle a laugh, especially when Arlo straightened, standing even taller, and purred, "Why, of course you will, Viscount."

Simone turned to Alex, brows wagging. "What do you say?"

"We should check it out. After all, I'm most at home among books," Alex admitted, leading her toward the bookshop and leaving poor Rhys to fend for himself—although he and Arlo made a very striking couple.

The bookstore was warm and cozy, wrapping Simone up in a sort of magic. Just as she hoped, she was able to relax at least just for a moment while she and Alex split up to peruse the store's offerings.

When Simone was sure Alex had made his way to the heart of the store, she managed to ask someone at the desk to help her find a vintage copy of *The Outsiders.* She remembered Alex's bookshelf, able to recall which editions sat there as if they were emblazoned in her mind forever—which most things Alex-related were.

Simone quickly paid for it and kept the package tucked under her arm, motioning to him that she'd wait outside.

Once back on the street, she released a happy sigh, realizing this was it. She was going to go after what she wanted. And not just professionally—she was already doing that by agreeing to stay on as Alex's coach. The media was going to say what they wanted either way, and her sister was right—Amalie and Arlo could handle whatever came their way, and hell, so could she. And if Damien wanted a custody battle, well, she was primed and ready to take him down.

What mattered now was Alex, and that he held her whole heart in those capable hands of his. She'd fallen for him faster than she'd ever expected, but how could she not? He was so easy to love.

A little while later, Alex emerged from the shop with his own bag, exhilaration alight on his face.

"Ready?" she asked. She had a plan.

"Actually, there's somewhere we should go."

Hmm…it appeared he had something in mind as well. Anticipation swelled in her veins as she and Alex walked along the streets of Metz, both quiet and introspective, until they arrived on the banks of the Moselle River, the Temple Neuf winking across the water. It was on an island of its own, encircled by the river with two bridges to access it. The richness of the oranges and yellows and reds of the trees surrounding it were stunning.

Alex had chosen to show her one of the most beautiful things she'd probably ever see.

"It's from a fairy tale," Simone whispered, speaking in a reverent tone, mouth slightly agape.

"*Oui*," Alex answered.

When she turned to face him, he was already looking at her, his expression so tender that Simone didn't know how she'd ever thought she could walk away from him, from the way she felt about him in the first place.

Could he see the longing in her stare? Feel it in the way she swayed closer toward him? A slight breeze blew her hair across her lips, and Alex gingerly ran the strand through his fingertips before tucking it behind her ear. After gazing at each other for a charged moment, he shifted, grabbing the bag he held beneath his arm and stretching it toward her.

Simone put the gift she'd purchased for Alex on the ground against the bottom of the overlook where they stood.

"What's this?" she asked as she took the bag from Alex.

His lips kicked up. "For you, *chérie*."

"Me?" she repeated, searching his face as her brows raised.

He nodded, his face so open and filled with hope.

Hope. She could work with that.

She lived for hope.

Slowly, she pulled a book from the bag, her eyes widening. Her other hand gently landed on Alex's wrist, and she tried not to melt into a puddle right there on the street. Her eyes began to water as she recalled the night he'd come over to watch tape at her house, the night he'd cheered her up after Damien's first series of threats. He'd studied her bookshelves, just as she'd done with his.

In her hands she held a lovely collector's edition of *Sense and Sensibility* with a stunning sage green cover and embossed artwork. One she'd wanted for so long.

"How did you know?" One tear tracked its way down her cheek, and Alex captured it with his fingertip, smoothing it away.

He dipped his head slightly so he could meet her stare as he spoke. "Because I've come to read you like my favorite book."

This man. This wonderful, precious, fantastic man.

Simone was on the verge of completely sobbing thanks to those beautiful words. They floated between them and landed on her skin like a butterfly—they spread their wings, stirring up all kinds of emotions in her chest.

"Oh, Alex, this is…this is too much," she breathed, looking down at the book that must've cost him a fortune.

He took the book from her, although the last thing she wanted to do was part with it. He set it on top of her bag from the bookshop, completely oblivious that it was for him. She wanted to open her mouth to tell him so, but this moment, this moment was important, and she was afraid to ruin it. Her pulse raced, more tears at the ready, because after so long and so many worries…could it be that Alex had come to the same realization as she since their plane landed?

With a tiny shake of his head, Alex bit down on his lip. "Nothing is ever too much for the woman I love. Tell me, Simone, can we do this? Because I want to more than anything. Of course, I worry about the reputation of the tennis center as much as you do, but I talked to Julian the other day and he said he just wanted us to be happy. I think he and Amalie understand, and Arlo's a PR machine. We can beat this. And I'd make sure Lula was protected because I adore her and don't want to lose her either." He paused, drawing in a deep breath. "It's just that I refuse to spend another day in agony of not having you near me. So will you be mine now, Simone? If you want me to wait, I will. But I'm here now, and I love you— you know that."

Simone gasped, his words settling in her chest. Amalie and Julian had given them their blessing, something that had steeled her spine in resolve. She wouldn't let Alex walk out of her life again. No, this time she was determined to let him know how much he meant to her, to Lula. The fallout from this would be dealt with by three of the toughest women in the world, herself included, so it was time for the next chapter in her life.

It was time for her to be happy.

To choose love.

To choose Alex.

Sheer relief overwhelmed her as a barely contained sob wracked itself from her body. "This is how Elinor in *Sense and Sensibility* felt, my God," she managed before Alex gathered her in his arms, one steady hand smoothing her hair as she allowed those tears of happiness to fall. "Alex, I haven't gotten the chance to tell you, but Amalie said the same as Julian." She smiled. "She actually told me that when the plane landed to go get my man."

When Alex pulled back, he tipped her chin up, looking at her with so much love and awe. "Truly?"

More happy tears streamed down her face as she nodded, her voice barely a rasp when she answered him. "Truly."

A heart stoppingly stunning smile overtook his face and kissed away each of her tears. His voice was hoarse with emotion when he spoke in between each kiss, "*Je t'aime, chérie. Toujours.* Always. Always."

Her lips split into a wide grin, and she noticed Alex's cheeks had a few tears of their own. "I love you so damn much, Alex Wilde. It's not even funny."

She wiped at her eyes, not caring that her mascara was smeared all over the back of her hand. For a minute, reality threatened to ruin everything, even as she traced the lines of Alex's face with her fingertips.

"But what about Calgary? I can't move there. I have Lula to think about, and she loves her school, and I love working at the tennis center."

Alex didn't hesitate. He cradled her face in his hands. "I'm staying in Atlanta for as long as you'll have me, *mon bonheur*. Calgary will be too cold for me these days, especially without you."

Simone resisted the urge to pinch herself. Because now, at thirty-seven, she was being swept off her feet for the first time, and it was utterly worth the wait. Everything about the man before her was worth all that they'd gone through.

With a happy sigh, she threw her arms around Alex's neck, her lips on his, *finally*. This kiss was different than any of their previous ones—it wasn't in the heat of the moment, and it wasn't tender, exactly. Instead, it was both of them pouring their hearts and souls into the movement, bleeding out all of their hurts and insecurities, swiftly stitching up the other's wounds with each dance of the tongue.

After a while she drew back, tightening her hands on his shirt, breathing in his scent, his warmth, the way he made her feel. "Tell me what *mon bonheur* means, Alex."

He kissed her forehead as he spoke. "My happiness. You're my happiness, Simone."

Swoon.

Her face hurt from smiling. "You sweet talker, you," she whispered, throwing back the words from the first night they met in what felt like a lifetime ago.

"Only with you."

Her eye caught on her book and Alex's gift beneath it. "So, I have something for you too."

Simone wavered for a split second, just because she didn't want to step out of Alex's embrace. But he'd given her the best gift he could—his heart, his words—and maybe this book could do the same, could show him she loved him just as much. She picked up the bag and handed it over.

Alex looked down at it and then back up at her. "You've already given me more than I ever expected. I want for nothing...well..." He pitched his voice lower, huskier. "I want for *something*." He cocked a brow. "But I'm not in a hurry. I want to show you how serious I am."

She laughed, unable to help it. Oh, Alex was definitely getting laid and soon. No need to wait any longer than they already had.

She tapped the bag. "Open it."

He did, and the joy on his face made the money spent completely worth it. "*Mon Dieu*, Simone!" he exclaimed, pulling the book from the bag. "This is *magnifique!*" He flipped through the pages eagerly. "I've wanted this edition for so long. Of course, leave it to you to find it. You found me after all."

"Out of all the places to hate being at a party, it had to be yours."

"*Dieu merci*, I hired an overzealous party planner, or you would've never been out there on the terrace."

Simone grinned. "True." Nerves danced in her stomach at what was about to come out of her mouth. She stood up straighter. "Maybe we should head back? Check out the view from your room?"

He nuzzled a kiss at her temple, making his way down to her lips. When he spoke, his husky words traveled over her skin. "*Oui*, it's the best view in all the city, *chérie*."

Chapter Thirty-Four

ALEX

Walking into the moonlit suite felt a little like déjà vu, except this time the barriers had fallen, the walls he'd carefully crafted around his heart had crumpled, all because of the stunning woman in front of him.

He flicked on a lamp, and Simone was immediately drawn to the balcony, just as he knew she would be. She stepped out and he followed, coming up behind her and wrapping her in his arms as they looked out into the glittering night. Temple Neuf was illuminated, the city lights all aglow and casting their brilliance on laughing passersby, yet Alex had the entire world right in front of him.

"This is a beautiful city, *non*?"

She leaned back against his chest, nodding against him, the movement tender. "I can't believe we were just down there. When I saw it earlier, I knew I had to explore it, but it's even better because I got to do it with you."

His heart thundered in his chest at those words.

"I want to do everything with you, *ma chérie*."

She turned around to face him, a soft smile a whisper of a thing on her lips. "I'm glad we can just be *us* now. That we can stop pretending."

Alex's hand went to rest on the side of her neck, his thumb doing a delicate dance along her jaw. "Oh, Simone. We will never pretend again."

Simone's eyes went glassy as she turned, not taking her stare from his as she kissed his thumb and then leaned into his palm, kissing its center. He watched her, completely captivated, the moment suspended so that it was just the two of them. She lifted his hand and placed it over her heart, not in a move that was meant to be sexy—*non*, this went deeper than that.

His own heart pounded madly, almost as if it recognized its missing half. Gently, he grasped her fingertips and brought them to his chest, connecting them. Simone let out a soft gasp, and her eyes lifted to his.

"Tonight, I want you, Simone. *All* of you." His hold on her tightened. "You are what I've been searching for, and I want to show you what no words could ever do justice. Will you let me show you?" he asked as he felt her pulse soar at his words.

"I would love that, Alex. But will you let me return the favor? To show you how so very loved you are?" She swallowed, pressing his fingertips into her shirt. "My heart feels like it's going to beat out of my chest because I've wanted this moment so much for so long. And now it's ours."

"Now it's ours," he whispered.

With her, it would always be so much more than a moment.

She was his forever.

Simone tilted her head toward the door, her eyes glittering. *Alors*, she looked beautiful. "Let's not waste it."

Who was he to deny her?

Once they moved inside Alex drew the shades, tucking them away in their own world.

He wrapped one arm around Simone's waist, pulling her closer with his hand as his other tipped her chin so that he could kiss her as deeply as he wanted, *non*, needed. He could never get close enough.

Alex took his time tasting her, enjoying the sensation of those plush lips pressed against his. Still, fire burned in his core. It blazed even brighter now that they'd bared their souls and still chose one another.

Chose the promise of a life he'd never dreamed he'd be lucky enough to have.

He didn't end the kiss as he slowly pushed her cardigan over her shoulders and down her arms. His fingers glided up her bare skin leaving goosebumps in their wake. Simone trembled before tugging on his jacket, undressing him with the same reverence as he'd done her.

They finally broke apart, their heavy panting filling the quiet of the room.

"Are you sure?" he asked in a whisper, careful not to shatter the moment.

"Yes, Alex. I'm sure," Simone breathed, her hands roaming along the front of his shirt. "I love you."

Those three words illuminated his soul, made him feel like a completely new man, drawn apart and put back together through the flames.

"*Je t'aime.*" He kissed her forehead, for she was something precious to be cherished.

She grinned at him, and then with shaky fingers, she went to the edge of his shirt to lift it.

This time when they undressed it wasn't rushed or frenzied. They didn't break eye contact as each removed another article of clothing until Alex stood in his boxers and Simone in a lacy, light purple bra and matching underwear.

Could she see how much he wanted her?

His hands flexed at his sides. "Your beauty always threatens to bring me to my knees."

Without another moment's hesitation, he lifted her in his arms and carried her to the bed, softly laying her back on the sheets, her black hair spread about her head like a halo.

How fitting.

Their lips met again, Simone's fingertips tracing a path down the side of his neck, to his collarbone, down to his navel. A shudder wracked his body at the tender caress. He leaned down to kiss her neck, reveling in the lavender and sugar scent of her.

She wove her fingers through his hair as she pulled him deeper into her embrace, and her long legs wrapped around his waist. Feeling her pressing against his erection nearly broke him right then and there. He groaned against her skin, softly biting her shoulder before he lifted her up to unclasp her bra.

Mon Dieu, she was stunning.

He palmed each of her breasts, relishing her curves, how soft she felt in his hands. She arched into his touch, her lids fluttering as his thumb and forefinger pressed down on the aching buds. He hungered at the sight of her, at the *magnifique* beauty laid out before him.

Unable to help himself, Alex dipped his head, taking one nipple into his mouth. She let out a breathy gasp as his tongue swirled around her nipple, her hips bucking against his cock. The torturous friction sent heat straight into his core.

Their underwear needed to come off.

À présent.

Hooking a finger through each strap, he pulled down the flimsy lace, leaving her bare and exposed. Alex paused, drinking in the sight of her before him.

Simone reached for his waistband, her fingers quickly working to free him of his boxers. He had to lean back to remove them, and then there was nothing between him and Simone.

Their eyes locked.

"Alex," Simone said in a whisper. She threaded her hands in his hair, bringing him to her lips, leaning back to assume their earlier position. She kissed him feverishly before smiling against his mouth. "You are everything. Can you see it? Can you feel it?"

"Oui," he panted. "I can."

His hand reached down between them, finding her wet. A deep rumble vibrated through his chest as he eased two fingers inside of her, causing her back to arch, her grip on his hair growing tighter, desperate.

"I hope you see the same when you look at me, *ma chérie.*"

And then he couldn't hold back any longer.

He took her breast into his mouth, gently biting and then licking and kissing the sting away. His fingers pumped in and out of her, and she writhed against the sheets, moaning, whimpering, begging. He sensed her nearing release, and with a curl of his fingers, she fell apart.

His name fell from her lips as she broke and shattered, her eyes fluttering while her body trembled. She repeated his name like a prayer, and he couldn't get enough. Not when it came to her.

He was bewitched.

Utterly entranced by her.

By this.

When she opened her eyes, she immediately found his stare, her chest rising and falling rapidly. "That was amazing, but Alex?"

He lifted his head a little more as he arched a brow.

She brought her hand to cup his cheek, a tiny smile on her lips. "It wasn't complete. I want you inside of me."

All of his worries and doubts took flight with her words.

"I want nothing more," he whispered.

Taking her hands, he brought them to rest above her head, his fingers threading through hers. He kissed her forehead before lining himself with her entrance, his heart thundering madly. Holding her gaze, he pushed inside of her.

Merde.

His head dropped to her neck as he groaned, his every nerve electrified.

"I'll never get enough of this, of you," he admitted before raising his head.

"Good," she whispered, breathless. "Because I won't get enough of you either."

Her legs squeezed his hips and he began to thrust, slowly at first, until she adjusted to the length of him. He pressed his lips against hers as he moved, and one of her hands broke from his grip to run up and down his back.

"Don't stop, Alex, I'm begging you," she demanded as he moved his hips faster, filling her to the hilt. Fire danced in her eyes as her piercing stare burned into him. "I love you."

"I love you," he rasped. "You were made for me." With his free hand he lifted her slightly, hitting a different angle, pushing in deeper and deeper. Instantly, her eyes fluttered and she moaned, her hips bucking against him.

"*Non.* Simone, I want you to look at me when you come. Let me see you."

Those words held a double meaning, and Simone caught on as she nodded against the pillow. Her gaze never wavered as he brought her closer and closer to the edge, and with each drive of his hips, he felt her tighten around him. He couldn't last much longer. Not when she felt this good. Not when it all felt this *right*.

"Alex, I—"

Her words died on the tip of her tongue as her lips parted. Their stares met as she cried out, her entire body tightening and curling into his.

He brought his finger to her chin, tilting her head up so that he could capture the rest of her cries with his lips. He devoured her gasps, her insecurities, *everything*.

He wrung every ounce of pleasure from her body, slowly pumping into her as she came back down from her high, her cheeks flushed and skin glistening.

When she caught her breath, Simone cupped his face, her stare earnest.

"Now look at me," she instructed, moving in tandem with him.

He lost himself in her eyes, in her body, and then he, too, fell over the edge, knowing all the while Simone would be there to catch him. As she always had since they met. As hopefully she always would.

This was not just mere sex.

This was their souls entwined with starlight and hope.

This was love.

Chapter Thirty-Five

ALEX

Alex put his arm around Simone at the table at the restaurant, tugging her closer. He'd found these little ways to touch her since Amalie had given them her blessing eight days ago. Alex's first four matches at the Moselle Open had been the easiest of his career. Maybe some could even say he was playing inspired. *Maudit*, it sure felt like it, what with Simone by his side—and not just as his coach, but as his girlfriend.

His lips curved. He couldn't help it.

"What's that smile for?" Simone leaned in and whispered.

Her blue eyes sparkled, her red lips calling to him. "I can't believe this is real," he said before he leaned down and kissed her, not caring that Julian, Amalie, Paul, Charlotte, Rhys, and Arlo sat around the table with them.

It was the night before the Moselle Open final, and Julian wanted everyone to go out as a team to celebrate.

Alex felt lighter than he ever had, like a weight had lifted. He knew he should feel worried, should feel anxious, especially since he already knew who he'd face in the final—none other than his stepbrother, Bastien Demers.

But Alex had chosen to incur one fine after another rather than speak to the press. He didn't want what happened back in Atlanta with the interview to ever happen again. The look on Simone's face—*non*. He would not allow it. The well-being of the woman he loved and their relationship were worth more than talking to the media after each match. Thankfully, Arlo was on board with the plan, even saying that his refusal was being viewed as romantic and a little edgy. But he didn't care what anyone thought anymore, as long as he had Simone and Lula in his life.

"God, I hate that guy," Arlo spat, her eyes skewering someone who was heading toward them. Alex leaned back and saw the target of his PR agent's disgust.

Bastien straightened his jacket lapels as he stopped beside Alex's seat. The perma-sneer that always graced his mouth was firmly in place. "Congratulations, Alex. I saw you made it to the final. It's just too bad your lucky run comes to an end. But that's okay. You tried."

Those last two words dripped with condescension as he patted Alex's shoulder.

Alex wasn't bothered though, especially not when Simone snuggled closer, her hand squeezing his fingers beneath the table. "I think you'll find that the story has a different ending this time. A lot has changed." Alex shrugged, taking a sip of his water.

Bastien rolled his eyes and scoffed. "Oh, please. *Nothing's* changed. You're still weak."

Alex opened his mouth, but any response died on his tongue when Julian stood up, hands on the table. "Now listen here, you little douche—"

Paul pulled on Julian's jacket sleeve. "Julian, no. This is a nice restaurant. You can't do this here."

Julian pointed to Bastien, who was pleased that he'd at least gotten a rise out of someone. "He's not going to stand there and disrespect our player though."

Charlotte went into full-on mother mode as she pointed to Julian's seat. "Julian, sit down right now."

Paul puffed out his chest. "Yeah, what your mom said."

Amalie snickered.

Simone leaned further into Alex so she could better see his stepbrother. "Bastien, the only thing weak at this table is your terrible pickup game. Maybe practice in the mirror first?" she snapped.

Alex knew she alluded to that night back in Lake Louise when Bastien had hit on her, only to have Simone scare him off. *Criss*, he loved this woman.

Bastien stood up straighter, zeroing in on Alex. "What, you have all of these people fighting for you now?" He tilted his head toward the table.

Those words bolstered Alex. *Oui*. He had a table of people who had his back these days.

He rapped his knuckles on the table before looking up at Bastien. "You know what? I do. It's more than I could ever say for you."

Alex turned, dismissing Bastien. His stepbrother hovered at the side of the table for a moment longer before storming off.

"You did good," Simone said as she kissed his cheek. "And you'll do even better than that tomorrow."

For the first time in his life, he had that same feeling. Besides, he'd already won so much. Why couldn't he get the trophy too? And to have the exquisite woman at his side help him get to this point? Even better.

Tomorrow couldn't come fast enough.

ALEX COULDN'T STAY STILL IN THE LOCKER ROOM. AT ANY MOMENT HE'D BE competing in the Moselle Open final. His nerves decided to make an appearance, but for the most part he felt more settled than he ever had before.

Paul, Julian, and Simone leaned against the lockers out of the way of his pacing.

Although Alex and Bastien's lockers were on opposite ends of the locker room, Alex heard Bastien's coach giving him a pep talk.

"Alex isn't on the same level as you. Hell, he doesn't even belong on the same court as you. It's a fluke he even made it this far." He paused. "Remember, he's just a wild card. That's all he'll ever be."

Just a wild card.

Those four words would've knocked him to his knees a few weeks ago, but not now. He'd been so hell-bent on not being a wild card that he hadn't appreciated the exquisiteness of it, of his position.

Bastien's response carried, as was most likely his intention. "I'm going to keep this match short but not sweet."

"Wow, so clever," Julian muttered under his breath with an eye roll.

Oui, Bastien was never the wittiest.

Simone popped off the locker, slamming a nearby one shut with enough ferocity that Bastien's team looked over.

She looked over at them, her voice loud and pissed off. "You know what?" she said. "Fuck those guys." She hooked a thumb at Bastien and his crew.

Alex's lips split into a grin. This woman. His *everything*. He cast a glance at Paul and Julian, and they nodded their heads in agreement.

Simone pointed at Alex. "You go out there and prove that you belong here, but don't do it for me, or Paul, or Julian, or for those assholes over there." She slung her hand toward Bastien's team. "I don't care what they say—you are Alex Wilde, The Wilde Card. The shake-up master, the beautifully unexpected. You made it here today because of what you have inside of your heart. You've earned the right to be on the court with anybody, and you know what? It won't stop after today either. Nope. After today you're going to continue to show everyone who you are. And they sure as hell won't forget it either." She threw a hand on her hip to punctuate the end of her speech. Two dots of red splotched her cheeks.

He'd never wanted her more than he did right then. Ever since they agreed to be together, they'd agreed to be professional on the court, but *merde*, he couldn't control his reaction to her. He went to her and cupped her face between his hands, kissing her with everything he had. This is what he'd been searching for all those years.

This.

Paul cleared his throat, causing Alex to pull back and smile. Simone touched her lips and grinned.

She continued, "Remember, Bastien is going to throw everything at you that he has. Don't forget how you play. You have to stay in the rallies, run everything down. Don't let him take it from you. Remember, feel your shots, be determined, and be confident. And remember most importantly..." Leaning forward, she brushed a quick kiss across his lips. "I love you."

She stepped away from him and gestured to Paul and Julian. "Guys, anything to add?"

Paul took off his hat and ran a hand over the fluff sticking up all over the place. "Well, you Warner women know how to give a speech." What had Amalie said to Julian right before his final match? Alex made a mental note to ask. "I will add that I think you chose excellent restaurants this week," Paul said as he patted his stomach for emphasis, bringing levity to a situation in a way only he could.

Julian swaggered back and forth in front of the bench, arms crossed. "I think we all know what I would like to say, so I won't even say it. I'll just keep it to myself."

Everyone waited because they knew Julian. He stopped his pacing and looked directly at Alex. "You know what? I'm gonna say it, and Paul, if you tell my mom I cussed, I'll tell her you sneak out to eat fast food."

Paul held his hands up in a surrender gesture. Satisfied, Julian shot Bastien and his crew a nasty look. "Fuck them!"

After a few rowdy agreements and fist pumps, they settled down. Simone took the moment of quiet to whisper a few more words of encouragement. "Tennis is a strange sport. You only have yourself on the court, where other sports have teammates to step in, to carry the load, to pump you up. Not in tennis. Here, it's just you. But remember, we're all out there with you. Here." Her finger touched his chest, no doubt feeling the erratic rhythm that beat beneath her touch. Alex inhaled her perfume, and it took everything he had to keep from moving. "And here." She touched his temple where his hair was pushed back by a large tie headband. "Now go out there and do the thing we all know you're capable of."

Alex pulled her in for a hug. "*Merci, mon coeur,* my heart." He kissed her hair.

"Aw, group hug time?" Paul said as he came around and hugged Alex, throwing an arm around Simone.

"Hell yeah, it is. Team Wilde!" Julian shouted as he joined in the hug.

"Team Wilde!" Alex, Simone, and Paul repeated.

Alex felt a sense of home there in that embrace, and he allowed it to rush over him, to sink and settle deep into his bones.

Then it was time for both teams to be ushered from the locker room, leaving just Alex and Bastien.

"Mr. Wilde and Mr. Demers? Come, *s'il vous plaît,*" one of the security guards beckoned.

Alex put on his headphones, not wanting to hear anything coming out of his stepbrother's mouth. He played The Waterboys' song, the one he'd danced to with Simone and Lula on what would forever be one of his favorite nights.

As the music blasted into his ears, Bastien's mouth was moving, but Alex didn't hear a single thing. The guards escorted them past life-sized photographs of all the greats lining the dimly lit hallway.

The announcer called Alex first, as was expected since he wasn't ranked as highly as Bastien. When he stepped onto the indoor court, the crowd cheered louder than he expected. He turned his music down as he waved, instantly looking for his box.

And then he smiled, knowing no matter what, he'd already won.

Chapter Thirty-Six

SIMONE

THE ARENA WAS BUZZING AT THE START OF THE MATCH, THE PULSE ONE collective heartbeat thumping madly. Simone tried to focus on the unique court—gray and blue, as she wrung her hands in and out, her breathing coming in short pants.

The press had played this match up, given what happened the last time Alex and Bastien met on the court. Thank God, Simone had made sure that Alex stayed off social media.

Bastien hadn't done the same and continued to trash-talk and allude to their previous meeting in Cincinnati and the subsequent beatdown. He was so arrogant that he reminded her of Damien, someone else she refused to think about.

She looked down on the court, taking in Alex as he strode to his bench. She knew him well enough to know that his movements were a little jittery. Why wouldn't they be?

Before he set his stuff down, he looked at their box and smiled that sweet smile of his, the one that always made butterflies come to life in her stomach.

Simone winked at him, and he returned the gesture before setting about taking out his rackets and water bottles. And then it was back to tapping her foot uncontrollably and fidgeting nonstop, just waiting for the match to begin. This was probably the worst part of being a coach, at least in her mind. This was the part where she'd have to watch everything unfold without being able to help.

Arlo grabbed her hand and squeezed it. "He's got this," she whispered.

"I know, but I just..."

"Love him. We know. Bastien's head's gotten too big with all that pride, it's gonna weigh him down when he runs. Besides, he doesn't have you as his coach. Alex does. That's the difference." She shot Simone a meaningful look before dropping her hand and returning her attention to the court.

Simone believed in Alex fully, but she just had never experienced anything like this. The nerves. The yearning. Everything was times a thousand. She hadn't felt this way back in Cincinnati. She'd felt terrible when Alex lost, but this...this was a whole different beast.

Bastien won the coin toss, electing to serve first. Of course he did. That's what most players would do.

The first set was a back-and-forth battle with Alex staying true to the game plan they had come up with. He ran down every ball, forcing Bastien into making mistakes. In the first set tiebreak, Alex got his first set point. Bastien served a laser directly at Alex, and somehow Alex managed to get out of the way and strike a deep return.

The two then started a physical crosscourt forehand rally with neither giving an inch. They both were grunting after each shot when Alex hit a strong forehand that went right past Bastien, winning the first set.

Alex pumped his fist and roared, "*Allez!*"

Simone had heard him call that out enough during the matches leading up to this one that she knew that meant, "Come on!" The entire player box erupted, Simone on her feet, clapping and shouting "*Allez!*" back to Alex.

Julian stood up, whooping, and then, well, he earned the best comment of the day by yelling down to Bastien, who was near their box, "Who's weak now, bitch?"

Simone nearly choked on her laugh. Bastien wiped his face with a towel and scowled up at them, shooting them the bird.

The crowd booed Bastien's action as it replayed on the big screen. They were already fully behind Alex, pumping him up, cheering him on. But Bastien doing that? Well, they didn't like that he couldn't keep his cool in the midst of a little heckling. Had anyone not seen Rafael Nadal get heckled at the 2021 Australian Open? The man handled it like a champ.

Simone tried to pull in a deep breath, because Alex was one set away from the biggest win of his career.

The second set was just as tense as the first, getting to another tiebreak. Damn, Bastien just would not go away no matter how well Alex was playing.

Alex started the tiebreak, serving a double fault that handed the first point to Bastien. From there he looked rattled, losing the tiebreak 7-2.

Shit. They were headed to the deciding third set. This was it. Simone knew there were other things out there aside from tennis, things that were much more important, but this win? Alex needed it. He needed to see that he deserved to be here, that he was worthy of everything he'd ever wanted.

With that thought, Simone stood up in the box. Alex had to remember that he was still in this, that it wasn't over and he just needed to hang on and keep his chin up.

She cupped her hands around her mouth and shouted, "Let's go, Alex! Believe!"

Paul echoed her, standing up as well and calling out, "Yeah, kid, you got this!" And it seemed from there every single person in the arena followed suit.

Alex could do this. After all, everyone else believed in him. It was time for him to do the same.

Chapter Thirty-Seven

ALEX

Just as the arena began chanting for Alex, Bastien decided to take an extra-long bathroom break. Bathroom breaks were common during matches, but one this long? *Non.*

The crowd did not like it one bit and booed Bastien yet again—the loudest complaints coming from his box. His lips twitched at that, especially as Julian yelled his usual obscenities.

There was a time when Alex would've been affected by such mind games as those played by his stepbrother. He would've dissected them, grown edgy, but not anymore. Alex felt strangely calmed by the situation, because he realized that the entire match he had somewhere to turn to—his family.

This was the first time in his life he had ever felt such peace and belonging.

When he looked up at his box and saw the belief on everyone's faces— Simone, Paul, Julian, Rhys, Amalie, Arlo, and Charlotte—their unwavering support gave his body a jolt. Each of them was on their feet, jumping up and down, cheering for him, pumping him up.

Family wasn't blood.

It was belief.

Those who believe in you, who love you, and accept you?

They are family.

Simone was right when she told him he needed to do this for himself, but he couldn't help wanting to win for them too.

Finally, the match resumed with Bastien serving to start the third set. Alex managed to take control of the first rally by moving his stepbrother side to side, making him work—he ended the point by hitting a blistering overhead smash.

Criss, that felt good. Alex skewered Bastien with an angry glare, followed by brushing off his shoulder in an antagonizing move. He wanted his opponent to know that he was a different player now and that he came here to win.

But the next set wasn't as easy. The two engaged in a physical third set, with each player vying for control of the match. They were tied at 5-5, with Bastien serving while down breakpoint in the game.

This was an opportunity that Alex did not need to miss. He tightened his grip on his racket, zeroing in his focus, shutting everything else out except for tennis.

Bastien served a 135-mph ball to Alex's backhand, which he returned short, allowing Bastien to put him on the run. Alex ran back and forth but didn't panic when he usually would.

Simone's coaching made him believe in his ability to remain in the tough rallies without trying to force a bad shot. That was proven thirty-eight shots into the rally when Bastien hit a strong forehand crosscourt to Alex's forehand.

Alex was ready and rushed to the ball, felt his shot as Simone taught him, and scorched the ball down the line to get the break and take the 6-5 lead in the set.

Alex turned to his box and roared, "*Allez!*" He pumped his fist into the air with a front step. He didn't waste time celebrating though, because all he had to now was win the next game.

Win the next game and the victory was his.

At the changeover, Bastien laughed at Alex, sneering. "Don't choke. Everyone is aware that you don't know how to win when it counts." Anger burned like hot lava through Alex's body. *Trou de cul.*

He tried to shake off the insult, but then he remembered that day when he found out Bastien would be playing in Metz. The day Simone had balloons with his stepbrother's face taped to them. She'd told him to channel that anger, that rage. That's what Alex needed to do.

He breathed in through his nose and refused to sit down during the break. Instead, he went to the service line and jumped up and down to keep himself motivated. It was his serve, and he wasn't going to let his past get in the way of his future.

Not with tennis.

Not with Simone.

Bastien tried stalling for even more time—managing to take the world's slowest drink of water. The crowd booed him again, but he didn't seem to mind it. Alex, on the other hand, allowed a smile to snake across his lips.

"Take your place, Bastien," the umpire warned, pointing to the baseline opposite Alex.

Bastien huffed and then jogged over to his side as Alex stepped to the line, ready to seize his destiny. On the first point Alex hit a huge serve down the middle, causing Bastien to hit the ball into the net 15-0.

Two points later, Alex arrived at 40-love and Championship Point. His heart thundered in his chest and roared in his ears, his fingers practically vibrating along the grip of his racket.

This was the moment he'd been waiting for his entire life.

Alex would show the world that he was wild in the best way, and now he had all the right cards to play.

He stepped to the line hitting the fastest serve of the entire year, a 152-mph ace out wide, and all Bastien could do was watch it go by, giving Alex the hard-fought victory.

He crumbled down onto the court, breathing a sigh of relief, quickly followed by an ocean of tears that cut across his face. He'd wanted this for so long and had never dreamed it could happen, and now…now he could see that Simone was right. Being a wild card wasn't a bad thing.

When he finally rose from his knees, his entire body lit up from the inside out. He looked to his box. Even from there, he could see tears in their eyes, pride etched across each of their faces.

He blew them a kiss and knew he needed to get to the net to shake his stepbrother's hand. Now that part he looked forward to. His lips curved even more as he stretched his hand out.

"*Alors*, looks like I'm pretty good at tennis, *non*?" he said, squeezing

Bastien's hand just a little bit.

Bastien huffed, snatching his hand back. "A fluke."

Alex shook his head. "*Non*. This is who I am. You just couldn't see it before, and neither could I."

Because sometimes you need someone else to help you clear all the mess that blocks your vision and then...then you can look in the mirror and know who you are and be proud.

Chills dotted Alex's arms at that realization as he packed up his stuff and wiped his sweaty face down with a towel. The entire time he smiled.

Everything in his life had finally clicked into place, and for the first time in a long time, he wanted to talk to the press.

The trophy presentation began, but before handing them out, the announcer had a few questions for Alex.

"Alex, will you retire the nickname 'The Wilde Card' after today's performance?" he asked.

Alex shook his head, thinking of Simone and her words. "*Non*. Never. Someone once told me that being a wild card isn't a bad thing, and today, I finally learned that's true."

The announcer translated his answer to French, and then the presenter asked, "That leads me to my next question...will Simone Warner continue to coach you after this, after you two made headlines with your relationship?"

"I want her for as long as she'll have me."

"In coaching or..."

Alex smirked, making sure to lock eyes with Simone as he answered. "Both."

Simone bit her lip as she grinned, placing a hand over her heart. He returned the gesture, hoping that woman knew how much she meant to him. He'd do his damnedest spending the rest of his life making sure she did.

The announcer, satisfied with the answers he'd gotten from Alex, pointed to the trophy. "*Mesdames et messieurs, le champion de l'Open de Moselle*, Alex Wilde! Ladies and gentlemen, Alex Wilde, Moselle Open champion!"

The crowd erupted as Alex held the trophy close to his chest, unable to believe he was actually here. That he'd finally won.

He took a string of pictures and answered a few more courtside questions from the press, giving them all the same answers he'd given the announcer.

Finally, he cleared his throat. "Pardon, but I must leave you. I'm ready to see my girlfriend. *Merci* for your time."

And without another word, he grabbed his bag and disappeared into the tunnel that led to the locker room. He didn't care if he got another fine for that. All he wanted to do was see Simone.

She was the only one in the locker room waiting for him. His pulse hammered with each step he took, drawing nearer.

He nearly dropped the trophy in his haste to get to her. He quickly set it on top of his bag, and then he gathered Simone in his arms, holding her tightly against him, her heart beating as fast as his. He swung her around, adrenaline still racing through his veins.

"We did it, Simone!"

Simone tightened her hold around his neck, her lips at his cheek. "*You* did it! I'm so proud of you!"

When Alex pulled back only slightly so he could see Simone better, tears glittered across her cheeks, twinkling in her eyes. She'd never appeared more luminous.

She clasped the sides of his face, her stare steady, her voice throaty with emotion. "I knew you would, Alex. My Wilde Card." Her lips tipped even higher.

"I like the sound of that," Alex rasped, bringing his thumb to her mouth, wanting to devour her right there in the locker room. He was pretty close to going through with it but realized everyone else from the box was gone. "Where is everyone?"

Simone gestured toward the door. "Right outside. They wanted us to have a moment first." She paused and raised a brow. "So, coach, huh?"

"I know we originally agreed that you'd coach me until we got through this tournament, but without you this doesn't exist. What do you think?"

She narrowed her eyes in thought. "I think I like that idea. I can coach you and still work at the tennis center. It sounds perfect."

Alex shot Simone a wicked smile before dipping to her lips, and in between kisses he whispered, "I look forward to taking more commands from you in the future, *chérie*."

Epilogue

SIMONE

TWO YEARS LATER

Alex's hand tightened on Simone's, and then he stopped suddenly in the hallway of his house—the one that used to be his rental.

"Wait!" He rocked back on his heels, looking incredibly boyish, and ran a shaky hand through his beard, his smile sweet. "I forgot the blindfold!" He dug it out of his pocket, holding it up like a prize. "Can I tie it on you?"

Simone quirked a brow. "A blindfold, huh? Sounds kinky. I like it."

She allowed her lips to curl slowly as she watched his eyes darken.

"We can try that out another time, *chérie*, but this is for…well, you'll see what it's for."

Simone studied him beneath his hallway lights, committing this night to her memory. She never wanted to forget the way she felt right then, that anything was possible…but she also wanted to remember the way Alex looked at her with such love in the depths of his beautiful brown eyes, the small crinkle lines that fanned out like rays of the sun. Her heart took a tumble as she smiled at him.

"All right then, let's see what you got," she said, allowing Alex to wrap a blindfold about her head and lead her through his house.

When they started dating in earnest two years ago, she'd made one request of him—she wanted time to make her own mistakes, to simply be Simone Warner. She didn't want to be anyone's wife, didn't want to live with anyone but Lula, and she wanted to make sure she learned how to do things for herself again.

He'd agreed, of course, and assured her that he wasn't going anywhere.

In the meantime, Simone had remained Alex's coach, as promised, and he'd managed to win four Grand Slams. He won the French Open, Wimbledon, and the Australian Open twice. He never won the US Open, and that was something that Julian gave him hell about. Simone also had become one of the nation's best developmental coaches, with plenty of rising stars coming to the Oliver Smoke Tennis Center to work with her, Paul, and Julian.

The sound of a door opening and then the cool air lifting Simone's hair let her know they were outside. Giddiness swooped through her stomach, trickling into her veins. Simone's fingers squeezed Alex's tighter, reveling in the strength she found there. Yeah, she had her own strength. That was never the question. It was the fact that she had his too should she ever grow tired and unable to pick herself up. Alex would always be there to wrap those hands around her wrists and pull her up and dust her off and damn, that was a heady feeling. Tears pricked her eyes at the thought.

They stopped, and then warm hands scooped up hers, bringing them to Alex's lips. He placed a tender kiss there before releasing her.

When he spoke, his voice was low and almost uncertain. "*D'accord*, here we are."

And the blindfold was off.

Simone brought her hands to her mouth, in awe at how beautifully decorated Alex's backyard was. They still had camping nights with Lula, but this…this was beyond anything she'd ever dreamed.

A gauzy white tent stood in the center, with a sign that read *The Tennis Ball Hosted by Alex Wilde*, and she stifled a laugh at that. Before the tent were row after row of string lights hanging above them. Mixed among them were a few crescent moon lights along with several stars.

Suddenly, music began to play.

"The Waterboys?" Simone's lips curved since it was still one of her favorite songs.

Alex nodded, cheeks flushed. "We danced to it the night we confessed we loved each other."

"How could I ever forget it? I smile every time I hear it."

"But what I didn't tell you that night was that I chose that particular song for us to dance to for a reason," Alex admitted.

"Oh? Aside from the fact that it's brilliant?" Simone asked playfully.

Alex grinned, taking her hand and leading her out closer to the tent, lights dancing above them. He didn't let go of her as he turned to speak. Instead, he drew her closer.

"When we met, I only saw part of what I could do, part of who I was. I was blinded by doubt and worries and being in my head too much, but you saw more than that. You saw all of me and kept me going when I couldn't get my feet off the ground. You're the reason I'm here, Simone. And..." He cradled her cheek, his thumb swiping her cheekbone. "I hope you know that I see all of you. I always have since that night at the chateau when you came outside looking like a vision in that gorgeous green dress of yours. I knew even then that you could do anything you wanted to, *chérie*."

Simone's eyes watered. "You sweet talker, you," she began, which had become their inside joke. "I hope you know that I'll always support you and believe in you and, most importantly, love you."

"And I'll strive to be deserving of you every single day of my life, but..." His smile turned roguish, eyes glinting as he bowed, her hand to his lips again. "Will you dance with me? It's *one* of my favorite things to do with you."

Her skin heated at his innuendo. Perhaps that would be after their dance. Oh, who was she kidding? Of course, it'd be after the dance.

"I'd love to. As a matter of fact, I'll dance with you anytime you ask," she grinned as she placed her hand in his, allowing him to pull her closer to him, starlight flecking across the sharp planes of his face.

One hand tightened at her waist as his other hand came up to brush the back of his knuckles across her cheek, his hand shaking as he did. She reached up and caught it, resting it against her cheek.

They didn't dance. Not yet.

"You'll dance with me in the kitchen?" he asked, his voice nearly hoarse.

"Yes."

"In the bedroom?" His eyebrows jumped.

"Always," Simone chuckled.

"On the tennis court?" A proud smile tipped Alex's lips at that.

"As Tallulah says, 'Well duh.'"

"What about down the aisle?"

She gasped as he dropped to one knee, bringing out a blue ring box and opening it.

"Simone Warner, I love you more than I ever thought I could love anyone. Being with you and being around Lula has been the greatest joy of my life. I want to wake up to you every morning and fall asleep to you each night. I want to be a stepfather to Lula because I love her so dearly. So, will you be my wife and make me the happiest man on the planet?"

"*Oui*," Simone said without hesitating. She fell onto her knees in front of him, grasping his face in her hands and kissing him. "Yes," she said as she kissed his cheeks. "Yes," she continued as she kissed his forehead. "God, yes," she added as she kissed his nose. "I want to be yours forever," she ended with as she kissed his lips.

He smiled against her mouth, and she felt his tears mix with her own. "*Oui?*"

She nodded. "*Toujours.*"

She'd been getting better with her French over the last two years.

"Always," Alex repeated as he kissed her earnestly before putting the ring on her finger. She would've said yes if he proposed with a ring pop, that's how gone she was for him.

"Now we dance to celebrate," Simone whispered.

Alex restarted the song, and they danced and kissed and danced some more beneath the moon and the stars. Simone danced horribly, and she knew it. She was offbeat because she never had any sort of rhythm to save her life, but there was beauty in the missteps because even so, she threw her head back and laughed, finally living.

Two years ago she'd started a journey—learning to love the woman who looked back at her in the mirror. Now she was approaching forty, knowing exactly who she was meant to be and who she wanted by her side.

Forever.

Thank you for reading! Did you enjoy? Please add your review because nothing helps an author more and encourages readers to take a chance on a book than a review.

Also be sure to sign up for the City Owl Press newsletter to receive notice of all book releases!

And don't miss more in the Ace of Hearts series coming soon!

Until then read more romance like ANOTHER DAY, ANOTHER PARTNER by City Owl Author, Rachel Mucha. Turn the page for a sneak peek!

Sneak Peek of Another Day, Another Partner

BY RACHEL MUCHA

Have you ever heard someone's name and immediately knew they were going to be trouble? You haven't spoken to them yet — maybe you haven't even seen them — but you can already tell, just by their name, exactly what they'll be like?

This has happened to me several times throughout my life — most notably, in the eleventh grade when Grant Hunter showed up as the new kid in school. Grant Hunter. Now that's a name. And as Mrs. Pearson told us that he would be joining our English class, I immediately knew everything I needed to know about Grant Hunter. He'd be good looking, obviously, with a name like that. His parents had to have money — Grant is a family name if I ever heard one. And good looking plus money always equals playboy. Grant Hunter, I already knew, was going to be one smooth, charming S.O.B., on a mission to sweet-talk himself into as many girls' pants as possible.

So when Grant Hunter finally entered our classroom and was directed to the empty desk beside me, I silently congratulated myself on a job well done. It was already apparent that two of my deductions had been correct. Grant Hunter was tall and lean, with a great head of dark hair and a very attractive acne-free face. He wore neatly pressed chinos and Sperry boat shoes, and as he sat down, I got a big whiff of Polo by Ralph Lauren. Definitely rich.

My third deduction, the one about him being a sweet-talking S.O.B., was confirmed a few weeks later when he charmed me out of my virginity in the backseat of his dad's BMW.

Shakespeare didn't know what he was talking about with that 'What's in a name?' speech. A name can say a lot about a person.

Just take a look at mine. Luciana Martinelli. I know, right? In my opinion, it's borderline child abuse. But, nevertheless, it tells a story. One, it tells people that my parents are too Italian for their own good, and thought that honoring their heritage was more important than giving their daughter a name that could fit on those standardized test Scantron forms — though, I will admit that my sister, Valentina, has it just as bad as me.

Two, it lets you know that I'm no pushover, since growing up with a name like that in small-town Rhode Island, which isn't known for its high Italian population, would've led to a lot of teasing — and, naturally, some toughening up.

And three, the number of syllables alone suggests that I definitely have a nickname for this atrocity, and if you call me Luciana, you're likely getting a fist to the face.

Names, man. I'm telling you.

So, anyway, I found myself having one of those moments where I jump to all sorts of conclusions about someone based on their name when I heard I was getting a new partner. And not just any partner. A partner named *Dominic Delgado*.

Seriously. I think I might've rolled my eyes, which is pretty rude to do to your police captain, but I couldn't help it.

"Drop the attitude, young lady!"

Did I mention that my captain is also my father?

"Dad, I don't need a partner," I said, pretending the eye roll was about a partner in general and not one named *Dominic Delgado*. "I work better alone."

He let out a frustrated sigh. "You need someone watching your back out there, Lulu."

I held in a wince at the childhood nickname only my family was permitted to use. For everyone else, it was Lucy. I mean, a cop named Lulu? Have you ever heard of a more ridiculous thing?

"Need I remind you about the incident with Mrs. Webber?"

"That was a fluke thing," I insisted. "Plus, my hair's almost done growing back in."

"If she hadn't had a pool, you'd be dead right now." My dad jabbed a finger at me.

This sounds weird out of context, so I'll explain. We work out of a tiny police department in Portsmouth, Rhode Island. Portsmouth is your typical little charming New England hamlet, and with a population of just around seventeen thousand, not a whole heck of a lot of crime happens. Most of the calls I go on involve drunk fishermen, domestic tiffs, or teenagers trying to shoplift a twelve-pack from the grocery store.

Being such a close-knit community, you really get to know the locals as you're cruising around every day. And Pamela Webber was one local that every cop at the Portsmouth Police Department knew quite well.

The lady is bananas. I realize there are probably kinder terms for her condition, but after what she did to me, I don't owe her any favors.

I'd gotten the call last summer. One of Pamela's neighbors complained, again, that her TV was on too loud. This might sound like a petty complaint on the neighbor's part, but I'd dealt with this exact situation before, and let me tell you — Pamela, who's practically deaf, watches her TV so loudly it'd curdle your blood if you were in the room with her. And, she left it on 24/7. Imagine living next door to that.

I'd just gone over there to kindly ask her to turn it down. That's all. It shouldn't have been a big deal.

But Pamela was in a particularly nasty — i.e., drunk — mood that day. She wouldn't turn it down and she wouldn't let me inside the house, either. I stood on her porch, my ears already screaming for relief, so I did what anyone in my position would've done. I punched a hole through the flimsy mesh of her screen door, let myself in, dove for the remote, and turned the volume the hell down.

Well, Pamela didn't like that one bit. She'd been in the kitchen cooking something, and the second the TV was shut off, she started screaming every expletive in the book at me.

"Don't make me come back here again," I yelled, already turning for the door.

Pamela must've been really fired up that day, because she came bursting out of the kitchen with a butcher's knife. A butcher's knife! I was in such a state of shock that it didn't occur to me to pull my gun on her. I mean, I never took the thing out of its holster; never had reason to. And to pull it on Pamela, Portsmouth's resident crazy drunk lady? The thought just never crossed my mind.

In the interest of full disclosure, I should mention I might've been off my game due to the one-two punch of my recent breakup and the resignation of the only partner I'd ever had.

"Why can't you just leave me alone!" Pamela screamed as she chased me around the living room with the knife. Being much younger and more agile than her, it wasn't that tough to dodge her futile jabs, but admittedly, I was nervous. She blocked the door I came in, so I darted towards the kitchen, hoping to escape out the back. I was almost home free until my foot got caught on the leg of a kitchen chair and I fell over. Pamela caught up to me and stood over me with this crazy look in her eye. I scrambled to my feet, and she backed me into a corner by the stove. The water she'd been boiling for her mac and cheese was spilling over the sides of the pot.

"Mrs. Webber! You need to drop the knife, *now*," I said in the most calm, stern voice I could muster. In an acrobatic-like move, I leaned backwards as far as I could to get maximum distance between myself and the knife, my head dangerously close to that rapidly boiling pot of water.

With my mind focused on Pamela, it took me a while to notice what had happened. But suddenly, her angry, narrowed eyes grew wide and her jaw dropped.

"You're on fire!" She lowered the knife. It took me a few more seconds for her words to register. And then I smelled it. You probably know the smell — burned-hair-on-the-flat-iron smell. That unmistakable, stale, burnt odor instantly let me know that my hair had brushed over the lit burner on the stove and caught fire. But by the time I realized this, my long ponytail had brushed against my shirt sleeve, to which the flames had quickly spread.

"You're on fire!" Pamela yelled, looking surprisingly concerned. This, I thought, was hilarious, given the fact that she'd been waving a knife at me ten seconds ago.

The intense pain on my upper arm stopped any laughter in its tracks. I started to panic, especially since it was clear that Pamela would be no help. I caught a glimpse of the pool in my peripheral vision and made a beeline for it. Which is how, a few seconds later, I found myself standing in Pamela's shallow end, soaked, with first degree burns on my shoulder and half my hair singed off.

Back at the station, my dad freaked out, though I was more concerned about my long, beautiful chestnut-brown hair going up in smoke.

Fortunately, the flames hadn't reached my scalp, so my appearance could be salvaged with a very blunt bob. Roughly one year later, my curly hair finally reached my shoulders again, which I actually preferred to my length before the incident. I'd been cursed — or blessed, depending how you look at it — with a round baby face, so the shorter hair made me look a lot more mature.

See? A silver lining.

"You're working with Dominic, Lulu," my father said. "End of story."

I sighed. It was times like this when I wondered what I was thinking, voluntarily taking a job in which my father could boss me around. I was twenty-six years old, yet Captain John Martinelli always had the ability to make me feel like little Lulu again.

"Who is this guy?" I asked. "I don't know any Delgados in town."

"Just moved here." My father glanced down at what I assumed was Dominic Delgado's personnel file on his desk. "He was a detective at Boston PD for five years."

"What's a city detective doing here?" I tilted my head. "This is a major step down. You think a guy who's solved murders and hit-and-runs is going to be happy dealing with the Mrs. Webbers of Portsmouth?"

"Maybe he wanted a change of pace, Lulu." My father massaged his temples. "That's something you can ask him while you're spending your time together."

I suppressed another groan. I know I sounded like a brat, but traditionally, partners and me just didn't mix. Greg had been grumpy, old, and by the book, and never would have approved of punching a hole through Pamela Webber's screen door. After a few months with me, he decided to retire a year early. Linda had been a skittish young woman who had no business even being a cop in the first place, which I helped her figure out pretty quickly. And Rob...

I don't want to talk about what happened with Rob.

The point is, each of my previous partners had left after being paired up with yours truly, which is why I often go long stretches working alone. I like it that way — it's just *easier*. No awkward small talk. No messy eaters getting crumbs all over my squad car.

No chance of getting my heart crushed.

I'd been hoping I was in the clear on the partner front, because it'd been almost three months since Greg hit the road — a new solo record for me. But, unfortunately, my father is just as stubborn as me. Despite all the resignations, he's never wavered on this partner thing once. And, apparently, he wasn't afraid to risk the employment status of his newest recruit to try it again. It's like he *wanted* Dominic Delgado to go running back to Boston. Then it hit me.

Of course! I'll just annoy the hell out of Dominic Delgado, like I had with everyone else, and he'd be gone in no time. Maybe then my dad-boss would finally give up on his quest to find me a permanent partner and see I was born to fly solo.

"Okay." I flashed my dad a smile. "I'll give Dominic a shot."

He eyed me suspiciously. "Really?"

I nodded. "Sure. I just hope he's not too bored around here. After a week on the job, I wouldn't be surprised if he threw in the towel and ran for the nearest city."

I'd said this in a very casual, innocent tone, but obviously, my father knows me too well to be fooled.

"I know what you're thinking, and you need to stop it right now," my father said, finger pointed at me. "You will not intentionally try to get rid of him."

My forced smile fell and I got up from my chair.

"Seriously, Lulu, don't waste your time," Dad said. "I got the impression that this guy doesn't scare easily."

Of course Dominic Delgado doesn't scare easily, I thought to myself as I exited my father's office. Someone named Dominic Delgado wouldn't be intimidated by someone like me. Dominic Delgado was probably pretty slick. Probably pretty arrogant. Definitely a fast talker. With an alliterative name like Dominic Delgado, he'd likely been blessed with the gift of gab. Great. Just what I needed. Not only a partner I didn't want, but a *chatty* one to boot.

I'd been lost in my own thoughts, wondering if I could convince Dominic Delgado that I only spoke limited English and therefore it'd be best if we didn't try to communicate, when I realized I'd forgotten to make two very important assumptions about someone named Dominic Delgado. And my omission became glaringly obvious as I walked toward my desk and saw a tall, young man standing beside it, seemingly waiting for me.

The first important assumption was, of course, that someone named Dominic Delgado would be exceedingly, incredibly hot.

And the second? He was definitely going to be trouble.

Don't stop now. Keep reading with your copy of ANOTHER DAY, ANOTHER PARTNER by City Owl Author, Rachel Mucha.

And sign up for Ashley R. King's newsletter to get all the news, giveaways, excerpts, and more!

Want even more romance? Try ANOTHER DAY, ANOTHER PARTNER by City Owl Author, Rachel Mucha, and find more from Ashley R. King at ashleyrking.weebly.com

Officer Luciana "Lulu" Martinelli prefers to work alone. Who wouldn't, after falling in love with their partner, only to have him up and leave? Unfortunately, her captain, who's also her father, is determined to pair her with someone. His latest recruit, former Boston detective Dominic Delgado, is turning out to be harder to shake than the others. Dom's as talented at his job as he is gorgeous, and the worst part is...he knows it.

Lulu can't understand why a big-city cop would want to work for a small Rhode Island police department—until he's brutally attacked after his first day on the job. Dom didn't exactly give up his old life by choice, and some pretty terrifying bad guys want him dead. Things only get stickier when Lulu's ex-boyfriend Rob resurfaces with a far-fetched explanation for leaving her, and an interesting connection to Dom.

Forced to team up with the man who shattered her heart, her dangerously charming new partner, and even her bored teenage sister home on summer break, Lulu discovers her little town isn't as crime-free as she thought — and that maybe, just maybe, having a partner to watch her back isn't the worst thing in the world.

Please sign up for the City Owl Press newsletter for chances to win special subscriber-only contests and giveaways as well as receiving information on upcoming releases and special excerpts.

All reviews are **welcome** and **appreciated**. Please consider leaving one on your favorite social media and book buying sites.

For books in the world of romance and speculative fiction that embody Innovation, Creativity, and Affordability, check out City Owl Press at www.cityowlpress.com.

Acknowledgments

First and foremost, I want to thank God for giving me a love of writing and for allowing this dream to come true. There were times when I wasn't sure it would happen, and I'm so so thankful that it did. I'm also incredibly grateful for all of the blessings He's given me in my life—my amazing husband, family, and friends, and above all, His love and grace.

This book was the hardest one I've ever written. I started it in April 2020 and between now and then, I've rewritten it four times. Yes, there were definitely times when I wanted to walk away and thought maybe writing wasn't for me, that maybe I was a fraud or imposter, but my incredible husband encouraged me daily, helping me to dig deep and not to give up. This book is a reminder that it's okay if things aren't perfect as long as you keep going. I'm beyond thankful for my family, friends, and readers who helped me get this book out FINALLY, for cheering me on and supporting me. For those of you out there who are in the same boat—keep writing and don't ever give up!

Jared, thank you for loving me the way you do—I am beyond lucky to have you in my life. It's because of you that Paul Mercado was brought into the world (lol) and thank you for creating such amazing tennis matches for our favorite tennis fellas. All of the encouraging messages and montages, for keeping me going, thank you. Thank you for reminding me why I should keep writing, why I wanted this to begin with. You are my everything and I love you more than words can ever say—thank you for giving me the greatest love story of all, for being the reason I'm able to write them. You're my favorite hero, always and forever. To our sweet cat child, Cleo, thank you for photobombing all of my Instagram pictures and for sitting next to me while I write. I love you, you precious girl.

Charissa Weaks, I am so thankful that you took a chance on me with

Painting the Lines and that I get to work with you on this series that came straight from my heart. Thank you for helping me improve as a writer and to make my stories the absolute best they can be. I've learned so much from you and appreciate you so much.

Karen Grove, I am beyond grateful for you and everything you've done to help me get to this point. I really didn't know if becoming a writer would be a pipe dream for me, but meeting you and your encouragement made me believe. I loved working with you on PTL and my Gothic and am excited about working with you again soon. Thank you for always making my stories the best they can possibly be and for being so wonderful. I appreciate you more than you know.

To Tina Moss and Yelena Casale, as well as the entire City Owl team, thank you all so much for everything you've done for me and making my dream of becoming a published author a reality. I am so proud to be a member of the Owl Squad and love working with you all. This has been one of the best experiences of my life and I am so incredibly thankful. Thank you to Rene Ostberg for your copy edits and for making sure my books are in top notch form before being published. A huge thank you to the Miblart design team for another stunning cover design—it's absolutely perfect and I love it so much!

To one of my all-time favorite authors, Natasha Boyd. Natasha, I cannot thank you enough for taking the time to read Painting the Lines and blurb it. I nearly passed out when I got your response email and fangirled for days, months, okay years now lol. *Eversea* is responsible for rekindling my love of the romance genre and I am so thankful for you on so many levels —thank you for sharing your incredible talent with the world. We are so lucky!

My mom and dad, I miss you so much and am so thankful for the too-brief time we had together. Thank you for always encouraging me to go after my dreams no matter what and for loving me. I love you both! To my second parents, Phil and TK, thank you for always being there for me and loving me like you do. I'm beyond grateful for your love and support. You've both believed in me from day one. I love y'all!

Brent King, whenever I need someone to look over a query, a synopsis, or pages, you never hesitate. I am so thankful for you and for your unending support. Thank you for always helping me and believing in me. It means so much! Love you, big bro!

Ginger, Lee, and Aaron, thank you for always being so supportive of this dream. I am so thankful for you guys and love you all! Melissa, Ryan, Tristen, thank you all for your support along this journey. I love you. A shout out to Mazie, Graham, Claire, Seth, and Sofia—I love you all!

Bonnie Ritch, I love you so much! Thank you for reading not one version of this novel but TWO! I always know that you'll tell me the truth about what works and what doesn't in these books and I can't tell you how much it means to me that you read my novels even when they're in their crappy state lol. Not only that, but most importantly, thank you for always being there and for being such an amazing friend. You are amazing and your support means the world! Some of Simone's personality comes from you because like her, you're a fighter. Keep fighting, girl.

C. D'Angelo—my TWIN! Oh, how I am so thankful to have you in my life and for our friendship. This novel has been a trip and you have encouraged me each step of the way, being my official hype girl lol. Thank you for that—it means more than you'll ever know. You're such a wonderful, brilliant, amazing friend and words can never express how much I appreciate you. I love our mantras and I'll keep saying them and believing them every day! You are such an inspiration and I am so proud of you for CRUSHING it. Thank you for being you, my dear! I love you big! Katherine Quinn—I couldn't have gotten this book finished without you! Thank you so much for all of your help and reading the different drafts and for always cracking me up—whether it's about writing or Bachelor in Paradise or villainous heroes or spice doctoring. You're an incredible, amazing, beautiful human, writer, and friend and I am so thankful for our friendship. I will send you ALL the Ben Barnes pictures as repayment for all you did for me (although I'm not sure if that's enough lol). I love you!

Christina Schad-Ramos, oh my gosh, what a joy it has been to get to know you! Thank you for being so supportive and sweet about PTL, FA, and this book! Your feedback has been invaluable and I always feel confident knowing my stories will be okay once you've read them! Thank you for that peace of mind! You are so sweet and I can't tell you how much your support means. You are amazing! Colby Bettley, AHHH omg I love you! Thank you for supporting the indie author community like you do and for being so sweet—I am so ready for you to publish more books!!! Also, thank you for beta reading this book when it was in a rough state—your feedback made such a huge difference and I appreciate you more than you know! Ashley of @owl_always_love_books, thank you so much for reading this book in such a rough state and for being so encouraging! I just adore you! I am so happy that you enjoyed the story and your feedback gave me the confidence that this was the story I wanted to tell! I love getting book recs from you and am so thankful for you and your support! You are just amazing! Muskaan Khalifa of @dirtybooksandmessyhair, thank you so much for beta reading this novel for me and for all your feedback that helped make it even better—as well as for all you've done for me! You are absolutely wonderful and amazing and I appreciate you more than you know!

Kourtney Gourley, I can't thank you enough for taking the time to beta read this novel! Your feedback helped me so much and because of that, is a stronger story now! Words aren't enough for how much I appreciate this! Thank you for being so amazing! Muskaan Khalifa, thank you SO much for always being so encouraging and for being so sweet. It means the world that you took the time to beta read this novel and give me such amazing feedback! Your collage was for PTL was the very first one ever and I remember being so shocked someone would like my book enough to make one—thank you for that. It means the world!

Lori Taylor, I am so thankful for you. You are always so sweet and encouraging and it truly means more than you'll ever know. Thank you for being you and so supportive! I love you! Erin Harvey, I am so thankful for your friendship and support throughout this whole journey—you've believed in me from day one and that means more than you know! Thank you for always being down to read a synopsis or an ARC. Thank you for everything from the bottom of my heart—you rock! Vicki Parker, thank you so much for being you! I am so glad that we get to work right next door to each other this year. You have definitely made this year easier lol. I am so grateful for our friendship and appreciate all of your support—it really does mean the world. Thank you for everything, truly. Janie Wysong, thank you for always being so encouraging and supportive of this dream of mine! It really means more than you know and is so appreciated. You are wonderful!

To all the amazing City Owl authors—I am so thankful to know you and so grateful for your support. It truly means the world! I'd also like to thank Ashley Curry, Marsha Pitchford, Laura Ezell, Christie Christensen, Michele Thompson, Pat Rios, Angela Terry, Lisa Fales, Lilly Williams, Candace Smith, Beth Merritt, Amy Mayberry, Anita Finn, Shelly Tyre, Daphne Drake, Brittany Sellers, Michelle Watson for always being so supportive about my books.

I have met so many fabulous people on Instagram and Twitter and I just have to give a shout out to you all: Naomi from @this_ginger_loves_books (thank you for loving PTL and for all of your sweet posts—you have made my day so much and I can't even begin to tell you how much I appreciate you), Kelly @andkellyreads (thank you for being so kind and hilarious and always making me smile-love youuuu), Tiffani of @tiffaniandherbooks (thank you for being so supportive and kind —I am truly so glad we met—also thank you for so many awesome book recs and for making me smile),Thuy from @tweezyreads (thank you so much for always being so sweet and supportive, for taking the time to not only read and review PTL, but for creating such stunning bookstagrams with my books—you have no idea how much I appreciate it), Rachel of @readingforamoment (thank you so much for always being so sweet and reading my ARCs—it means the world and is so appreciated! Also, thank you for all the amazing book recs!), Alison of @alisonsoverbooked (thank you so much for the amazing PTL story with Eye of the Tiger—to this day it brings me a smile and it is so appreciated), Sarah of @book.and.beagle (thank you and ALICE (!!!) for the amazing photos and review of PTL—it meant the world). To all of the other amazing bookstagrammers and bloggers out there, I love each of you and everything you've done to get me here means more than you'll know.

Thank you to Kelly Emery at Inkslinger PR. You are absolutely phenomenal and I can't thank you enough for all of your hard work in getting my books out to the world. Also, thank you for the beautiful teasers and graphics, as well and for always going above and beyond in helping me—even with those last-minute opportunities. You rock and I appreciate you so much!

A huge shoutout and thank you to Jo Webb, Kylie McDermott, and Alicia at Give Me Books PR. You are all so sweet and go above and beyond in helping get my book out to the world. Thank you for everything you do —you are all amazing!

Thank you so much to Elizabeth of Elizabeth's Pretty Little Reads. You are incredibly talented and make such stunning collages and graphics! Thank you for being so sweet and for capturing my books perfectly. I love working with you!

Thank you to Bridget and Kristen at Storygram Tours. You two are so creative and honestly made my day with your beautiful posts with my book. It was a dream come true to work with you both and I can't thank you enough for everything you've done to get my books out to the world. It means so much.

If I missed anyone, please know I am so sorry, but I appreciate all of your support more than you'll ever know.

To anyone reading this book, thank you! Sometimes I still can't believe people want to read my writing (lol), so thank you for picking up this book and taking a chance on my story. I can't tell you how much I appreciate you and your support. You're absolutely amazing and make this journey that much sweeter.

About the Author

Ashley R. King is a middle school
English teacher whose love of the
written word began when her mom
took her to the public library, letting her
check out stacks of books taller than she
was. She's the least athletic person
you'll ever meet, but that doesn't
decrease her love for her favorite sport,
tennis. She loves swoony romances and
is addicted to sweet tea. When she's not
teaching or writing happily ever afters,
she can be found snuggled up with a
book, traveling, or quoting obscure lines
from her favorite movies and tv shows.
She lives in a small town in Georgia
with her favorite person in the world—her husband, and their sweet and
chatty spoiled cat, Cleo.

ashleyrking.weebly.com

 facebook.com/ashleyrkingwrites
 twitter.com/ashleyk628
instagram.com/ashleyrkingwrites

About the Publisher

City Owl Press is a cutting edge indie publishing company, bringing the world of romance and speculative fiction to discerning readers.

Escape Your World. Get Lost in Ours!

www.cityowlpress.com

facebook.com/CityOwlPress
twitter.com/cityowlpress
instagram.com/cityowlbooks
pinterest.com/cityowlpress
tiktok.com/@cityowlpress

Made in United States
North Haven, CT
06 August 2023

40018395R00189